Corporate Social Responsibility
Challenges and Practices

Peter Dobers (ed.)

Santérus
Academic Press
Sweden

www.santerus.se

© 2010 The authors and Santérus Academic Press Sweden
ISBN 978-91-7335-012-9
Cover photo: 'Cell phones #2, Atlanta 2005, 44 x 90' from the artwork series
'Intolerable Beauty: Portraits of American Mass Consumption'. (2003–2005)
©Chris Jordan, Courtesy of Kopeikin Gallery
Cover profile: Sven Bylander
Santérus Academic Press is an imprint of
Santérus Förlag, Stockholm, Sweden
academicpress@santerus.se
www.santerus.se
Printed by BOD, Germany

Contents

1. The Many Faces of Corporate Social Responsibility

PETER DOBERS

Challenges and Practices of Corporate Social Responsibility

It is obvious that the present ways of organizing corporations, public organizations, societies, cities, and social relations are not sustainable. It is not surprising, therefore, that sustainability is generating an increased interest in business research and management practices. Major publishing houses have in recent years published large handbooks and readers that point at important themes of corporate social responsibility. In the *Oxford Handbook of Corporate Social Responsibility* for instance authors elaborate in new written chapters on the following six themes: perspectives on corporate social responsibility, critiques of corporate social responsibility, actors and drivers, managing corporate social responsibility, corporate social responsibility in global context, and future perspectives and conclusions (Crane & Matten, 2007a). The Sage Library in Business and Management present three volumes on *Corporate Social Responsibility* based on carefully edited previously published articles: volume 1 with 16 chapters on Theories and concepts of corporate social responsibility (Crane & Matten, 2007a), volume 2 with 18 chapters on Managing and implementing corporate social responsibility (Crane & Matten, 2007b), and volume 3 with 18 chapters on Corporate social responsibility in global context (Crane & Matten, 2007c). Yet another reader, the Routledge *The Corporate Social Responsibility Reader* edited by Jon Burchell, seeks to give an introduction to the many key issues and themes that emerge from the corporate social responsibility field (Burchell, 2008).

This book provides extracts from texts from different areas such as academia, corporations or NGOs. Eventually, the final illustration is the John Wiley & Son's encyclopaedia *The A to Z of Corporate Social Responsibility* edited by Wayne Visser, Dirk Matten, Manfred Pohl and Nick Tolhurst (Visser, Matten, Pohl, *et al.*, 2007). This book gives a comprehensive reference guide to concepts, codes and organizations in the field of corporate social responsibility, sustainability, business ethics and the organizations and standards in this field. Over 100 experts and creators of opinion have contributed to write about 350 relevant entries.

Of considerable importance is the greening of business. However, environmental concern is not the only factor that requires attention if sustainability is to be realized; all aspects of contemporary business and management practices have an impact on sustainability.

The broader approach to sustainability has made any organization – whether private, public, or third sector – responsible for the long-term consequences of its operations. Corporate social responsibility and corporate citizenship are expressions more clearly focused on long-term accountability, and managers, directors, and stakeholders need to be aware of these factors as commercial operations or welfare policies are organized and implemented. The globalization of markets and the global reach of many individual organizations further highlight the need to address the organizational world when discussing sustainability and responsibility.

A sustainable society with responsible organizations is dependent on the combined consequences of inter-organizational and inter-sector activities. Changes are thus required across the traditional boundaries of organizations, countries, and functional areas from large cities and globally oriented corporations to small local communities and self-sufficient family businesses in remote areas. The leadership challenge is immense, and is related to the changes required in such areas as product development, production, and distribution. However, sustainability is also based on individuals taking a firm stand. The foundation is built upon the identity, values, and moral concerns of managers, consumers, and family members playing the roles of responsible citizens and social beings.

Many companies, such as DuPont, Shell, ABB – as well as smaller organizations – are speaking publicly about responsibility and concern for sustainability. Companies are being created and business models are formulated in which sustainability is the core business idea. Products and services are being developed based on the commercial potential of sustainability targeting the so called poor people in so called developing countries (Prahalad & Hammond, 2002; Prahalad, 2006; Kandachar & Halme, 2008). Communities around the world are organizing sustainability projects. Global and regional organizations, such as United Nations, European Union, OECD and national parliaments are issuing standards, policies, rules, and regulations aimed at promoting sustainability. There are many challenges: global security is at stake; a common global political agenda is far from being agreed upon; north-south tensions have not been resolved; the balance between shareholder value and sustainability is still a tricky equation to many managers. And new, booming economies in so-called developing countries add to the pressure of economic turbulence in so called developed countries.

A growing interest in long-term corporate sustainability and a growing sense of corporate social responsibility requires new and innovative research. The Nordic Academy of Management 1st Winter Conference, March 2006 in Umeå: 'Perspectives on Corporate Responsibility and Sustainability' invited scholars to contribute to an understanding of sustainability, corporate social responsibility, and corporate citizenship; and to extend our vocabulary, empirical experiences, and theoretical approaches. The wide array of activities and challenges clearly points to the need for business research with a focus on sustainability and responsibility issues. It is a challenge to integrate these issues into the core functional areas of business. The book is based on a selection of conference papers presented at this conference mentioned above. Scholars from a wide array of areas such as accounting, organization theory, strategy, entrepreneurship, marketing, and finance came together to discuss challenges and practices of corporate social responsibility. The best papers from the conference come together nicely in four themes of this book:

- Theme 1: The Travel of Ideas of Corporate Social Responsibility
- Theme 2: Consumers and Corporate Social Responsibility
- Theme 3: Practices and Strategies for Corporate Social Responsibility
- Theme 4: Challenges for Corporate Social Responsibility

About the Themes and Chapters

Theme 1: The Travel of Ideas of Corporate Social Responsibility

In the theme of 'The travel of ideas of corporate social responsibility' I have included three chapters that relate to the notion that ideas, such as corporate social responsibility, travel the world and become part of the everyday activities of organization in many different contexts. Thereby, practitioners, consultants, representatives from civil society, and not the least academic scholars take an interest in how such ideas travel the society and the world, thereby creating 'empty spaces' (Dobers, 2004) by which ideas of corporate social responsibility or codes of conduct turn into 'an artifact, in spacing emptiness, thus constructing an empty space at the disposal of other space fillers' (Dobers and Strannegård, 2004) that can be used in many different ways, with many different intentions, and with many different results.

In *chapter 2* 'CSR Conferences as Catwalks. The Translation of an Idea' Karolina Windell focus on the very idea of 'corporate social responsibility' and how it has gained momentum since the mid 1990s. The very idea of corporations taking on responsibilities beyond profit is, of course, older than that (Carroll, 1979; Carroll, 1999) and relates back to the basic idea on the relationship between business and society. But Windell puts the explosion of interest in corporate social responsibility at the centre and shows how conferences on corporate social responsibility become arenas in which the concept is translated into different practices, activities or frameworks, and how the concept become part in the many speeches, presentations and leaflets, but also become part in informal settings such as coffee breaks, lunches and dinners. While looking at many different conferences on corporate social responsibility throughout Europe Windell shows how various types of organizations draw on different actor groups and result in 'catwalks' in which socially responsible corporations are presented and questioned, their experiences are made public and scrutinized, and their different tools are made visible or silenced. One such tool, corporate codes of ethics (sometimes referred to as corporate codes of conduct) is at the centre of *chapter 3* 'Translating Corporate Codes of Ethics' by Tommy Jensen, Johan Sandström and Sven Helin. Corporate codes of ethics have become one of the more widespread tools when managers try to turn the idea of corporate social responsibility into practical work in their own organizations. Jensen, Sandström and Helin take a critical position in this chapter when asking if corporate codes of ethics may also have contra-productive effect on moral practice when moral responsibility is set aside if it is subordinated a standardized and routinized scheme for acting in certain situations. They develop a method for studying how an idea such as corporate codes of ethics travel and thereby paying special attention to its heterogeneous materiality (Law, 1999; Law and Hassard, 1999; Law, 2004). In their chapter, Jensen, Sandström and Helin also demonstrate an increased sensitivity towards moral practice and responsibility that refrains from relying on instrumentality and anthropocentrism. In *chapter 4* 'Standardizing Sustainability. A Critical Perspective on ISO 14001 and ISO 26000' Birgitta Schwartz and Karina Tilling take on yet another translation process in which an idea of corporate social responsibility finds a form. In this chapter they focus on how the ideas of management systems in general and how particular management systems such as ISO 14001 or ISO 26000 become popular. While asking 'Why standardization of corporate social responsibility has become so attractive' they highlight possible risks with standardizing complex issues such as environmental management or corporate social responsibility. Schwartz and Tilling argue that such standardization tools have become legitimate and accepted ways of dealing with complex issues, but that this may lead to one-dimensional and simplified actions that does not challenge the organizational rationality. All three chapters make an important contribution to our understanding of how ideas and models such as corporate social responsibility, corporate codes of ethics or management systems of ISO 14001 become popular and widespread in society and among managers (Jensen, 2004; Windell, 2006; Schwartz & Tilling, 2009).

Theme 2: Consumers and Corporate Social Responsibility

As the name of corporate social responsibility signals, the corporation seems to be at the core of the concept. While this might be true on one level, we may question this on another level. Consumption, in some ways considered 'the other side of corporate production' has been identified as an important aspect of *un*sustainability (Worldwatch Institute, 2004). Consumption patterns of products and services change over time, and its relation to sustainability can be studied in terms of weak sustainable consumption and strong sustainable consumption (Fuchs & Lorek, 2005). According to this article, weak sustainable consumption on the one hand cover technological improvements that lead to increasing efficiency, single loop learning and *doing things better*, while strong sustainable consumption on the other hand include reductions in consumption levels and *doing better things*. Thus, in line with the ideas of strong sustainable consumption, I have included three chapters in this book that widen the concept of corporate social responsibility to relate to consumers, attempt to include them into the concept, or problematize the links between consumption and corporate social responsibility.

In *chapter 5* 'Corporate Citizenship and the Citizen Consumer. Introducing the CC-matrix' Johan Jansson and Jonas Nilsson argue that consumers have become an equally important stakeholder to corporations than any other stakeholders. While relating to corporate citizenship, yet another way of conceptualizing corporate social responsibility and the ways that a company can contribute to society through its core business activities, its programmes of social investments or philanthropy, Jansson and Nilsson address the conceptual gap on the role of consumers in the literature on corporate citizenship and corporate social responsibility. On the backdrop of political consumerism, they present an extended model of corporate citizenship that highlight consumers as powerful actors in society and thereby clarify the responsibilities between corporations and consumers from both their perspectives. In contrast to this conceptual chapter, Hanna Hjalmarsson, Monica Macquet and Emma Sjöström report from an empirical study in Sweden on two green labels for bananas (KRAV label and The Rainforest Alliance) in *chapter 6* 'Marketing to Consumers in Different Shades of Green. The Case of Chiquita Bananas and Rainforest Alliance'. The Swedish market for bananas is quite elaborated since it represents the world's highest consumption per capita among import countries (Lustig, 2004). Organic bananas based on the so-called KRAV label have been sold for long. KRAV develops organic standards and promote the KRAV label and is a member of the umbrella organization of IFOAM (International Federation of Organic Agriculture Movements), assembling organizations for scientists, educators, farmers and certifiers from all over the world. In 2005 the Rainforest Alliance was introduced as a new label on the Swedish market for bananas. In their study of 41 consumers buying bananas shortly after the second label was introduced, Hjalmarsson, Macquet and Sjöström illustrate brand loyalty and brand awareness, and under what conditions that corporate social responsibility can translate into consumer awareness when it comes to organic produce. In *chapter 7* 'Aesthetic Consumption. A Dilemma for Sustainable Development' Peter Dobers link consumption to population growth, economic development, design and fashion of products, architecture, interior decoration, mobility of music and cars, and tourism. In line with the previous two chapters, Dobers argues to critically examine the role of consumption, and thereby critically examine the role companies play in consumption when proclaiming promises in the name of 'corporate social responsibility'. Smart design may reduce the amount of material and energy for products and services, but when concepts such as 'sustainable design' are linked to corporate social responsibility, Dobers critically asks if design can serve sustainability or just commercialism, as expected for corporations and their market role?

Theme 3: Practices and Strategies for Corporate Social Responsibility

So far in the book we have examined how ideas such as corporate social responsibility travel in society and from different organizations to others, what role consumers may have when corporations take on responsibilities beyond profit, and how problematic abundant and fashion-centred consumption may become when considering sustainable development. In the third theme we will focus on practices and strategies for corporate social responsibility and look at both concrete cases and conceptual calls for how to study corporate practices of social responsibility (Kandachar & Halme, 2008). An understanding arises that practices and strategies for corporate social responsibility need to be understood in its full complexity.

In *chapter 8* 'Multiparadigm Inquiry into Corporate Responsibility. An ABB Corporate Aid Project Under the Global Compact Banner' Niklas Egels-Zandén and Markus Kallifatides have studied a rural electrification project in Tanzania run by the multinational corporation of ABB – Asea Brown Boveri. As an illustration of corporate social responsibility practice, this project was launched in cooperation with the World Wildlife Fund (WWF[1]) as a response to the UN Global Compact[2] and its ten principles. Egels-Zandén and Kallifatides call for research that increase our understanding of such difficult phenomena as corporate social responsibility and suggest research based on many different theoretical perspectives. This is also what they illustrate when using four different perspectives for understanding the ABB case: an officialist perspective, a pragmatic institutionalist perspective, a critical perspective and a sceptical perspective. Together, their chapter illustrate a wide and rich understanding of the ABB case of corporate social responsibility. In *chapter 9* 'The Business of Social Responsibility. Practicing and Communicating CSR' Christa Thomsen and Jakob Lauring present outcomes from case studies of two Danish companies: Novo Nordisk and Falck A/s, Region Nord. Both companies represent traditions of working ambitiously with social issues, even before the concept of 'corporate social responsibility' became widely spread. Both cases illustrate the dilemma between business arguments and social responsibility, and between ideals and practices. The chapter of Thomsen and Lauring thus shows that corporate social responsibility is an ambiguous term closely linked to the situation, and of which the participatory elements should be explored further. In *chapter 10* 'Something Good for Everyone? Investigation of Three Corporate Responsibility Approaches' Minna Halme argues for an increased attention to the *outcomes*

1   http://www.wwf.org/
2   http://www.unglobalcompact.org/

of corporate responsibility. Focus in many studies have been on the motivations of corporations to take on social responsibility, on the different ways responsibility is taken, or on which levels of corporate social responsibility a firm is at given certain actions and practices. Halme then proposes a typology that combines three dimensions upon which corporate responsibility may differ: the relationship of corporate responsibility to core business; the target of responsibility actions; and the expected benefits from responsibility practice. The action-oriented corporate responsibility typology is outlined by 1) philanthropy (emphasis on charity, sponsorship, and employee voluntarism), 2) corporate responsibility integration (emphasis on conducting existing business operations more responsibly), and 3) corporate responsibility innovation (emphasis on developing new business models for solving social and environmental problems) and the chapter explores their financial and societal outcomes.

Theme 4: Challenges for Corporate Social Responsibility

In the final section of the book I have collected chapters that map out paths and challenges for research and practice of corporate social responsibility of the future. These chapters place corporate social responsibility into new contexts and place urgent issues into the agenda for upcoming activities of such responsibility, both in research and in practice.

In *chapter 11* 'Middle-Managers Work/Non-Work Boundaries' Jean-Charles Languilaire clearly addresses the social dimensions of corporate social responsibility when talking about life domain management challenges in terms of how to deal with work / non-work boundaries. An increased demand for higher flexibility of the workforce, linked with the development of information and communication technologies that enable such flexibility, have blurred the borders between what traditionally has been understood as 'work' and 'personal life' as two distinct domains. Languilaire present illustrative narratives from four middle managers in a French context. While 'work' is understood as one life domain, 'non-work' should be nuanced and understood as based on several sub-domains such as for instance 'family', 'social life', 'personal time', and 'joint activities'. Another challenge is identified in *chapter*

12 'Matching Ethical Demands – or Not. That is the question' by Lise-Lotte Hellöre. She discusses different ways to approach the morally loaded tension between business and society. Thereby, her starting point is that corporations will never reach a full approval from society for their activities, while they still aim for balancing with changing pressures from society. Hellöre's discussion then ends in a list of conceptual clarifications and managerial implications. In *chapter 13* 'Company Strategies for Corporate Responsibility and Sustainability in an Era of Fragmented-Globalization' Nigel Roome observes that sustainable development or corporate social responsibility are contested, dynamic and emerging concepts. Thus, our ability to learn from them is limited. Roome continues in the chapter to link his discussion to globalization and how globalization waves have unfolded into unpredictable and turbulent conditions in society, stating that development cannot take place in economic terms only, that the internationalisation of business in general, and finance and trade in particular, put an increasing pressure on the world's environment, and that the globalization of culture has resulted in a cultural, religious and ethnic diversity of and in our major cities. It is therefore a paradox that company practices, managerial competencies and management education look for standardized solutions such as the many tools of corporate social responsibility that the authors have disclosed in this book, while it is also understood that locally adopted choices of how to run corporations support local complexity and global diversity, which according to Roome is a basis for resilience. Eventually, in *chapter 14* 'Epilogue: Corporate Social Responsibility. The Next Agenda?' Richard Welford, living and working in Hong Kong since early 2000s, has formulated an epilogue based on the book chapters. While important issues of corporate social responsibility are addressed in the book, Welford notes that the authors and the themes of the chapters take a somewhat Western perspective. Given the background to the book, this is naturally the case, but points to an important observation of how to engage with the huge challenges in the world, particularly in the parts of the world where the majority of the population lives (Asia for instance), associated with among others climate change, environmental degradation, loss in biodiversity, poverty alleviation, the empowerment of women, human rights and corruption.

One fundamental challenge that I see on the backdrop of this book is how the relationship between corporations and society may develop in a period of reduced commitments of welfare states throughout the world. At one level it is true that corporations may have increasing economic power in relation to that of certain nation states. At another level I would like to stress the crucial task for research to observe the conditions that by 'asking companies to take voluntary responsibilities beyond their business, we actually legitimize their increased power to decide about societal matters' which Halme so sharply noted in the introduction to her chapter.

2. CSR Conferences as Catwalks: The Translation of an Idea

KAROLINA WINDELL

Introduction

Within the last decade the issue of corporate social responsibility (CSR) has increasingly gained foothold within the European business community. Over the years, researchers, practitioners, politicians, and representatives of the civil society have been searching for clarification and definitions of corporate social responsibility (Carroll 1979, 1999; Garriga & Melé 2004), yet there is no set definition. There are varying definitions and interpretations of the content and meaning of CSR. The current debate over appropriate socially responsible business behaviour finds expression under several intertwined labels such as sustainability, corporate citizenship, business ethics, corporate philanthropy, and particularly CSR. Behind these labels we find one idea or one claim: the notion that corporations should be socially responsible. But social responsibility comes in many forms. Questions about the responsibilities that corporations should shoulder and the role they ought to play in society have fostered a public debate. Contemporary ideas about corporate social responsibility have been conceptualized under the widely used acronym, CSR. As CSR has gained momentum, the intensity of the debate over the responsibilities of business has increased dramatically. The ongoing debate includes the argument that good business practice requires not only technical efficiency and profits, but also that corporations must add value to the overall society (Margolis & Walsh 2003).

In many ways the contemporary expansion of CSR manifests a long-term debate over the relationship between business and society, one that has waxed in the past decade. Several actor groups with different agendas and geographical backgrounds have involved themselves in this debate. Nevertheless, it is difficult to outline distinctions and similarities in the views on CSR that are held by these groups or nations. Opinions about the meanings of CSR and ways of addressing CSR are ambiguous and multiple, and do not connect to any particular group of actors or geographical areas. Rather there are differences within and between groups and geographical contexts. There is no set definition of CSR, and the vague and ambiguous character of CSR has led to disputes over its definition.

One arena where actors have met in order to discuss the definition of the idea CSR is conferences. During the last ten years there have been plenty of conferences on the topic CSR. But what takes place at these conferences? What happens when individuals from different organizations meet at conferences to discuss CSR? These questions are addressed in this chapter, as we turn to CSR conferences, where CSR is translated into different practices, activities, frameworks, and issues in speeches, informal conversations, and written materials. Conferences are meeting places for people to exchange ideas but they are also sites for corporate representatives to display the corporation and its operations to an audience. This chapter describes what took place at CSR conferences around Europe in the end of 1990s and the beginning of the 21st century and analyses how CSR was constructed and translated in these settings.

Processes of Translation

Construction of ideas – such as the idea about corporate social responsibility – can be understood as processes of translation, in which ideas are circulated and take new forms. Translation is a concept that captures the process of spread, and explains how micro-level activities contribute to processes of change. It has been introduced as a concept for explaining organizational change as a consequence of the circulation of ideas, innovations, and practices. Borrowing the concept of translation from social scientists, Michel Serres, Michel Callon, and Bruno Latour; Czarniawska and Sevón

(1996) introduced translation as a concept to explain how organizational change comes about as management ideas and practices are translated into actions that may eventually be institutionalized in an organization or in larger groups of organizations. I am drawing on Czarniawska and Sevón's concept of translation by using it to understand the construction and proliferation of an idea that has travelled under the name or label of CSR.

In their two volumes on translation, Czarniawska and Sevón (1996, 2005), together with their contributors, have demonstrated that the spread of management ideas and general ideas is not the result of passive diffusion; rather it is an active process of translation, in which actors are translating these ideas to local contexts. This means that actors are translating ideas in such a manner that it fits their own organizations and needs. Translation can therefore be understood as proceeding in accordance with the context that restricts the forms of the translations (*cf.* Sahlin-Andersson 1996). The adoption of an idea among various organizations, therefore, results in variation rather than homogenization, as the idea is translated in the accordance with the varying organizational contexts (Sahlin-Andersson & Engwall 2002c). Translation means more than linguistic interpretations; it means transformation – how something is transformed through displacement. Researchers have studied how ideas are materialized and objictified into objects and into actions, and how they assume different forms in the process (Czarniawska & Sevón 1996; Czarniawska & Sevón 2005b). It has been noted that ideas that become popular and travel globally are often packaged under a label or a name, although the practices may vary (Czarniawska & Sevón 2005a; Sahlin-Andersson & Engwall 2002a; Solli *et al.* 2005).

Organizations and individuals energize ideas in translation processes by shaping and using them (Czarniawska & Sevón 1996). The concept of translation suggests that actors actively translate ideas into organizational life (Czarniawska & Sevón 1996; Rövik 1996; Sahlin-Andersson 1996), and moreover, that translation is a process by which actors may strive to fulfil their own political or economic self-interests (Campbell 2004: 84). Studies of the circulation of management ideas have primarily addressed certain actors or carriers within the business community, such as consultants, business schools, and the business press, in order to explain their flow. In these studies, it has however been argued that a broad spectrum of actors are significant carriers of management ideas (Sahlin-Andersson & Engwall 2002b; Walgenbach & Beck 2002). In studies of ideas, therefore, we need to address settings where various actors take part in order to understand how they collectively translate ideas.

In summary, although several studies have addressed the spread of ideas, only limited attention has been paid to the multitude of actors that construct these ideas, and to the role played by conflicting interest in this process. Against this backdrop, I argue that we need to examine sites where ideas are translated and developed by multiple actors. Thus including several actor groups in the analysis will teach us something about how the translation of ideas proceeds with the help of various actor groups.

Translation of Ideas Through Rhetorical Strategies

The importance of rhetoric and discourse in mobilizing new ideas, innovations, or practices have been highlighted in several studies (Mueller *et al.* 2003; Rao *et al.* 2003; Zbaracki 1998). For ideas to gain a foothold they need to be presented to their receivers in convincing ways. Organizations adopt ideas and imitate other organizations behaviour if they believe that they have something to gain from it. As Sahlin-Andersson (1996: 78) claims, 'organizations seldom have direct experiences of the organizations or practices they imitate or refer to. What they imitate are rationalizations – stories constructed by actors in the 'exemplary' organization, and their own translation of such stories'. Accordingly, widely proliferated ideas that promise success do not necessarily lead to corporate success; however, in order to become widespread they need at least to promise increased success. In a similar vein, Meyer (1996: 252) argues: 'to properly develop and travel, an idea must be organized in terms of great abstract truths, not mundane realities'.

Ideas need to be presented as simplistic and universal in order to flow and in order for the adopters to understand their relevance. For ideas about corporations to get a grip in the business community, they must be presented as rational and efficient – as contributing to corporate progress. Meyer (1996) argues, for instance, that ideas are more likely to become widespread if they are translated in accordance with the core values of the western world: *progress and justice*. This implies that ideas presented as increasing corporate/organizational outcomes are more likely to become widespread than are other ideas, and that ideas presented as contributing to justice and equality among workers, citizens, or human rights tend to flow far and wide. Hence ideas conforming to dominating norms about rationality, progress, and efficiency are more likely to be followed than are those that do not.

Rövik (2002) criticizes explanations that stress that ideas become popular either because they function or because 'their time has come'. According to Rövik, there is no evidence to support either position; instead, he emphasizes the importance of making ideas applicable to all types of organizations and presenting them in an interesting and simplified way. In addition, he sees ambiguity as a prerequisite for the proliferation of ideas. Previous studies have shown that management ideas tend to be vague, elusive, and ambiguous (Rövik 2002; Sahlin-Andersson & Engwall 2002b); attractive characteristics that makes it possible to apply the ideas to different settings and organizations.

Against this background, we can conclude that the translation of ideas involves several actor groups and implies that ideas need to be packaged and presented in a manner that makes them relevant and attractive for actors to adopt.

Participant Observations at Conferences

There is an abundance of conferences in a wide range of areas throughout the world, where ideas are discussed among the participants. Yet there are few studies examining the role of conferences for the construction and spread of ideas (see for an exception Meyer *et al.* 2005). This study drew on participant observations and document studies of CSR conferences in Europe during the five years, 2002–2006. There were numerous CSR conferences in Europe during this period, which made it impossible to address them all. To obtain a broad view of the way in which conferences contributed to the translation of CSR, I chose conferences in different European countries where different actor groups such as corporations,

governmental organizations, NGOs, consultants, researchers participated. I also chose conferences that were arranged by different
types of organizations: an industry interest organization, business networks, a university, and a standardization organization.
Examining CSR conferences with a broad representation of actors
made it possible to compare their attitudes toward CSR and their
approaches to CSR.

Participant observation requires the researcher to observe
the course of events in a particular organization or situation. A
participant observer is far more than a researcher observing; a participant observer assumes the role of a member of the organization
(Czarniawska 2004). In my case this meant that I registered at the
conferences like any other participant, and even though the organizers had been informed about the reasons for my participation, I
acted like the other conference participants. Attending conferences,
seminars, and workshops not only made it possible to observe what
took place, but also allowed me to converse with and ask questions
of the participants and organizers.

Participant observations require extensive field notes, making it
possible to recapture the events after returning from the field and
to generate rich accounts (Berg *et al.* 2002; Geertz 1973), during the
participant observations, pen and pad were my primarily assistants,
but on a few occasions I used a sound recorder and a camera. After
each observation, I transcribed or summarized my field notes in
order to rethink what I had experienced. The conferences also provided rich sources of written material on CSR: brochures, corporate
social reports, governmental reports, and advertisements of spon-
soring corporations and organizations. These documents served
as a source of information on the ways in which the organizations
perceived and worked with CSR.

The first conference I attended as a participant observer was
held under the auspices of *Svenskt Näringsliv* (The Confederation of
Swedish Enterprises); although it did not explicitly address CSR, it
was important for developing the study of CSR conferences. This
conference made me aware of the importance of conferences in the
construction of CSR and the multiplicity of actor groups that took
part in this process, and also brought me in contact with some of
these actors. Thereafter I observed another 6 conferences and studied documents from 14 more.

The Conferences

CSR conferences have mushroomed in recent years all over the world under the auspices of governmental organizations, NGOs, business networks, business interest organizations, universities, and standardization organizations. Some of them have assembled diverse actor groups; at others, only one specific group of actors has participated. Because this study seeks to explore the translation of CSR and how this process proceeds in interconnectedness among groups of actors, I sought to obtain a broad picture of CSR conferences and to capture the interaction among various actor groups. For this reason, I examined conferences that were arranged by various types of organizations in several European countries, drawing on various actor groups. In this way, I received a broad view of the conferences and could identify their similar and dissimilar features. Table 1 displays the conferences that were examined. The conferences where I conducted observations are marked in bold text.

These conferences were organized by a business interest organization *(Svenskt Näringsliv)*; two business networks (CSR Europe and CSR Sweden); a standardization organization (International Standardization Organization]; and one university (Humboldt University). Individuals representing myriad organizations participated at these conferences: corporations, business interest organizations, labour organizations, consultancies, NGOs, governmental organizations, standardization organizations, and universities.

The following part of this chapter provides a general description of the conferences: their aims, sites, and participants. Thereafter the chapter describes the main activity at the conferences – speeches – and explores how CSR was translated in these speeches.

Conference Aims

The conferences were arranged in such a way that the participants could discuss general questions about the role of the corporation in society and the general responsibilities of corporations. The conferences were also organized in order for stakeholder groups from different countries to meet, discuss, and develop the idea of CSR. One of the aims of the conferences was for participants to exchange experiences and to be inspired by each others' work with CSR. The

Table 1: Timeline of CSR conferences

2001	2002	2003	2004	2005	2006
CSR Europe Conference, Greece	CSR Europe Conference, Spain	CSR Europe Conference, Belgium	The Confederation of Swedish Enterprises: The Trust Conference		CSR Sweden: The Nordic Market Place on CSR
CSR Europe Conference, France	CSR Europe Conference, UK	CSR Europe Conference, Ireland	ISO: SR Conference		
	CSR Europe Conference, Germany	CSR Europe Conference, Portugal	Humboldt University: International Conference on CSR		
	CSR Europe Conference, Finland	CSR Europe Conference, Sweden			
	CSR Europe Conference, The Netherlands	CSR Europe Conference, Italy			
	The Confederation of Swedish Enterprises: From Defensive to Proactive	CSR Europe Conference, Switzerland			
		CSR Europe Conference, Czech Republic			

organizers also wanted to spread, mainstream, and popularize CSR by drawing attention to the idea through the conferences.

In advance of the conferences, invitations were displayed on Websites or sent to interested organizations. The conference invitations stressed the point that CSR was a business case that would lead to improved business performance. However some of the conferences calls presented the view that recent transformations in society and increasing demands from stakeholder groups had made it necessary for corporations to reflect upon their social responsibility.

In the invitation to the CSR conference arranged by the Institute of Management at Humboldt University in Berlin, in October 2004, the organizers argued that globalization had forced corporations to handle new demands in new contexts. It was also claimed that social responsibility had shifted from the state toward corporations. Based on these assumptions, the conference was aimed at contributing to a discussion among researchers, politicians, corporations, and NGOs, on the consequences to corporations and society of increased corporate social responsibility. The conference welcomed both empirical and theoretical contributions to these topics and, in particular, contributions that '[...] would inform the changes in the business community and clarify the vague meaning of CSR' (Institute of Management Humboldt University 2004).

The conference campaign arranged a few years earlier by the business-driven network, CSR Europe, was presented somewhat differently – with more positive connotations. In the brochure, *Corporate Social Responsibility – the European Business Campaign*, CSR Europe presented the conference campaign, CSR *Marathon*, in the following words.

> By integrating Corporate Social Responsibility as a core value in your business, you are not only making a significant contribution to a better society, but, just as importantly, you are recognized for doing so. And this has obvious benefits for the company. Corporate Social Responsibility can and should govern every aspect of business life. The rewards, both for the corporation and society at large, will be enormous [...] You're confronted with Corporate Social Responsibility every day, even without noticing it. It's everywhere. When your customers enter your supermarket and choose products with a good reputation. But also when your investors put money into a company with an exemplary social record. Or when you invest in the future and training of your employees, and you gain loyalty and commitment in return. In corporate terms this makes good business sense. It gives you every reason to smile. It's what the future of business is all about (CSR Europe).

The conference campaign CSR *Marathon* was part of a larger CSR campaign aiming to spread the word of CSR. The CSR campaign was arranged by CSR Europe as a response to the European Council Summit in Lisbon in 2000, at which an appeal was made to companies to take an organized approach to corporate social responsibility. *The* CSR *Marathon* was to take place from 2001 to 2004

(CSR Europe 2003c). It was to proceed in 16 countries, and a torch with a message was to be handed from conference to conference. The conference campaign was to end with the Olympic Games and reoccur every four years. However, due to the development of a new strategy within CSR Europe, the conference campaign ended in 2004 and the Olympic Games never took place (Interview Catherine Rubbens 2004).

Developing a common understanding among stakeholder groups – NGOs, trade unions, investors, consumers, corporations among others – was an explicit goal of the European Commission during this time, a goal that they sought to achieve partially through their CSR European Multistakeholder Forum. Therefore the European Commission did support the conferences arranged by CSR Europe (CSR Europe 2003a, 2003b). As stressed by the former president of the European Commission, Romano Prodi, in one of the publications on the CSR campaign published by CSR Europe in collaboration with its partner organization:

> This Campaign Report on European CSR Excellence provides a welcome bird's-eye view of the positive contributions the business community is already making in Europe. Voluntary organizations such as those involved in the European Business Campaign on CSR help to promote and deepen the involvement of businesses in socially responsible practices in Europe. The companies of this business-driven network demonstrate that companies can pursue not only profit, but also sustainable growth and social progress. Your campaign is the living proof that business companies may play a substantial part in meeting the challenge of exclusion, while at the same time, enhancing their productivity and profitability targets. Indeed, profit is not incompatible with the promotion of social justice and with finding solutions to social and labour problems (CSR Europe 2003b: 6).

Thus the conference marathon was supported by the European Commission and initiated by three organizations: CSR Europe, The Copenhagen Centre, and the International Business Leaders Forum. In collaboration with 19 national partner organizations, CSR Europe was the coordinator of the CSR *Marathon*. The objectives with the CSR *Marathon* were threefold: to bring interested people into contact with each other; to deepen awareness of CSR through training, management tools, and knowledge sharing;

and to widen the debate on social responsibility. Or as one of the members in the CSR Europe Board of Directors claimed at the CSR conference in Warsaw in 2003:

> The CSR campaign aims to bring CSR closer to you. People should learn to dialogue. They should learn to learn from each other, they should learn how to tango together. CSR is how to learn how to tango. Every company has to learn [...] it takes time to learn to not step on each others toes, it takes time to build trust (Elena Bonfiglioli Director of Community Affairs and CSR Microsoft – Member of CSR Europe Board 2003).

After the CSR Europe conference in Stockholm in April 2003, CSR Sweden was founded as a national partner organization to CSR Europe (CSR Sweden 2005). In February 2006, CSR Sweden, arranged *The Nordic market place on* CSR conference as a meeting place for corporations and their stakeholders to meet and develop new skills, strategies, and networks for CSR (CSR Sweden 2006). The conference was the continuation of *A European Roadmap for Businesses on* CSR campaign, which had been launched by CSR Europe in Brussels in 2005 (CSR Europe 2006b).

The European Roadmap aimed at energizing the European movement for corporate responsibility, to mobilize ideas about CSR, and to exchange best practices among companies (CSR Europe 2006a, 2006b). The campaign was presented as a route to achieving the European Commission's renewed Lisbon Strategy 2010, by uniting corporations to share and contribute to solutions on corporate responsibility.

A few years earlier, in order to satisfy a specific goal, the ISO arranged a conference on SR (the C was removed in order to indicate that social responsibility was for all organizations and not merely for corporations). The conference was to be a platform for delegations from national standard institutes with ISO membership and for other interested actor groups to present their views on the launch of a social responsibility standard. The aim of that conference had been to mainstream CSR by developing common knowledge and reaching consensus on the meaning of CSR. As the Deputy Secretary General of ISO expressed in one of the welcoming speeches at the conference:

SR is not new, but it has received attention from all stakeholders during the last years. SR is to become mainstream. ISO needs to engage in
consensus building around SR and that is what we are going to do hear
during these two days (Kevin McKinely Deputy Secretary General ISO
2004).

The feedback from stakeholders was supposed to form 'the platform for decision making' by the Technical Management Board
of ISO, which had the task of deciding whether or not ISO should
launch a social responsibility standard. There was a pre-conference
to the ISO conference, which aimed at informing representatives of
developing countries on the CSR debate in the industrial countries
and preparing the delegations to take a stand at the ISO conference.
At the end of the second conference day of the main conference, a
vote took place in order to determine which stakeholder groups
were in favour of and which were against the ISO SR standard.
The voting demonstrated that a consensus had been reached, and
it was argued that a guidance document should be launched to
'help to popularize and spread SR' (Kernaghan Webb AG Member
2004). A few days after the conference, the technical Management
Board announced that ISO was to continue its work in the area of
CSR (ISO 2004) . The guidance document would seek to develop
CSR for corporations and organizations of difference sizes and in
different cultures and to develop a common terminology for CSR.
Moreover it was agreed that the guidance document should be a
complement to the existing CSR instrument, and it was announced
that ISO would stay out of government-regulated areas.

Altogether the conferences were aimed at addressing questions
about the social responsibility of business. The organizers emphasized that the role of business in society had changed and that
corporations should respond to this change. By organizing conferences, they wanted to present a venue for discussions about the role
and social responsibilities of business in society. The conferences
explicitly addressed CSR and were aimed at developing a common
understanding and common methods for turning CSR into corporate practices (with the exception of the ISO conference 2004 that
primarily aimed to debate whether or not ISO should launch a social
responsibility standard).

Conference Sites

The conferences were similar in structure and organization in terms of participants, keynote speakers, conference speeches, and topics of the conference tracks. Other common elements were long coffee breaks and lunches; receptions and banquets in exciting locales; and VIPs such as presidents or members of royal families, who brought their blessings to the conferences.

The conference sites were conference centres, hotels, and government and university auditoriums. The conferences were sponsored by several corporations, and their brands were displayed all over the venue. The exception was the ISO conference, which did not have corporate sponsors, and corporations and other organizations had to be satisfied with handing out reports or comments about their views on a social responsibility standard.

As the participants arrived at the conference centres, they were guided to the registration arena, where they were given a name tag and a paper bag containing conference programs, participants' lists, information brochures from large corporations and organizations, information about the presentations of invited guests, and sometimes even a tourist guide and a map of the city centre.

In the centre of the conference location, there was usually a large coffee table where hot and cold beverages and fruit and sandwiches were served. In a circle around the coffee table, there were often a number of booths or 'market stalls', where representatives from corporations and organizations handed out brochures, made computer presentations, and answered questions about their work with CSR issues. The written material that was dispersed by organizational representatives in these booths or market stalls could be of widely differing types: corporate social reports, advertisements, descriptions of standards and frameworks, the organizations policy documents or newspaper articles. The organizations that were represented at these market stalls were often large multinational corporations, although smaller national corporations or international organizations such as the World Bank were sometimes represented as well. The participants gathered piles of documents during the coffee breaks and lunches and stopped to converse and exchange business cards with other participants who were standing at the same market stalls.

The conferences served as an ideal place for making contact with new people, establishing connections, and finding customers or service providers. The conferences were organized in a manner that contributed to networking and mingling. Several extended coffee breaks were scheduled during the conference days, and participants gathered in small groups around the coffee table, conversing and exchanging business cards. Instead of tables with chairs, small round tables were placed at the conferences site, around which the participants could only stand; in some situations only a few tables were available. For this reason, people were constantly circulating in order to find some one to talk to and a table to rest against.

The conferences were always opened and concluded with some form of reception or dinner party. Just as during the lunches and coffee breaks, there were either small tables around which participants could stand, or there were tables with open seating, allowing participants to choose their dinner partner. Participants tended to use this time to find out more about each others' backgrounds and experiences in the CSR area.

In several respects, the CSR conferences were a site for individuals interested in CSR to meet, establish contacts, and exchange experiences. The participants represented different organizations and could engage in conversations with individuals with similar and dissimilar backgrounds and experiences.

Conference Participants

The number of participants at these conferences ranged between 200 and 400. They represented organizations from the private, public, and civil sectors. Participation tended to be similar at all the conferences, so here the participants at the ISO conferences are being used as an illustrative example of participants at the CSR conferences.

In order to register for the ISO conference, participants were required to identify the type of organization they represented, making it possible to demonstrate the exact dispersion of the represented organizations. The ISO conference, hosted by the Swedish Standards Institute (SIS), drew 355 participants from 66 countries. Although there was a broad representation of countries at the other conferences, the ISO conference had an extraordinary represen-

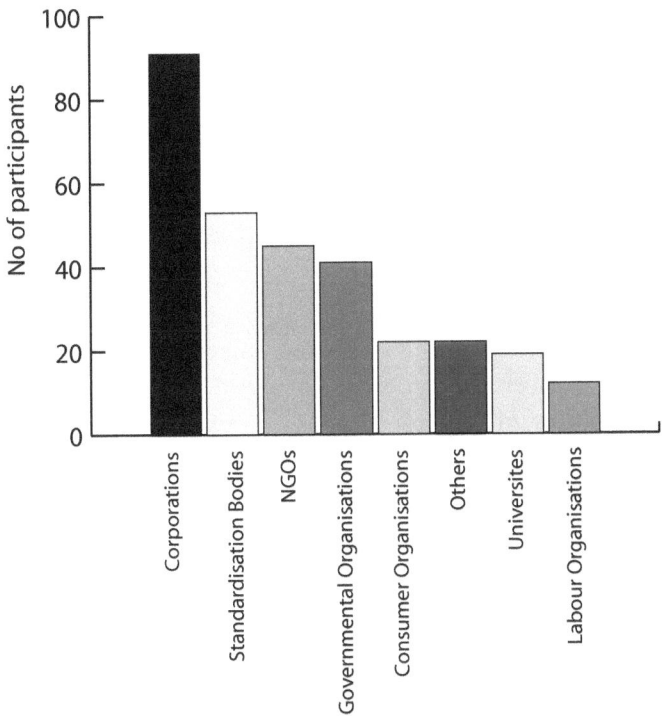

Figure 1: Categories of participants at ISO SR conference, 2004

tation of nations. As displayed in Figure 1, the participants mainly represented corporations, NGOs, standardization-, governmental-, consumer-, academic-, and labour organizations.

As Figure 1 demonstrates, the number of corporate representatives is considerably higher that the number of representatives from other actor groups – which was consistent with all the other conferences studied. Behind the label 'corporations', we also find representatives of consultancies that were incorporated. At the ISO conference, the number of standardization bodies was relatively high compared to other conferences. Moreover the number of representatives from universities or other educational programs was relatively low in comparison to the conference arranged by the Humboldt University a year later. Journalists, researchers, and representatives of the ISO boards are placed in the 'others' category.

A group of participants or representatives of the same organizations seemed to be travelling from conference to conference, as they could be seen and heard at a number of European conferences in the period 2001–2006. These persons were representing a non-profit organization, a business network, or a larger corporation, and they were often keynote speakers at the conferences. Some of these persons were also involved in the European Commission's CSR EMS Forum that was launched in 2002: Viscount Étienne Davignon, Chairman of the Advisory Board CSR Europe, for example.

During the conferences I conversed with participants, asking them their reasons for attending the conferences, and receiving a variety of answers, depending on the organization that the participant represented. Consultants, for example, claimed that they wanted to learn more about CSR and find new customers. Representatives from NGOs claimed that they wanted to make contact with corporations, in order to collaborate with them or in order to convince them to use their CSR frameworks. The corporate representatives argued that they had little knowledge and understanding of what CSR actually meant, and wanted to learn more; or they stated that they had understood that CSR was an area that every corporation must address in the future. The conferences, they suggested, were one way of obtaining a good overview of CSR area and meeting experts that could help them develop their CSR work. Yet other corporate representatives declared that they were advanced in the area of CSR and that they had been working with CSR issues or sustainability issues for a long time, and that they participated at the conferences in order to present their CSR work to the other participants.

Conference Talks

Conferences are sites devoted to talk – people conversing with each other in order to build relationships, make contacts, and share information. These talks can be of different kinds – small talk, conversations to build new business relationships, or even debates. And conferences also feature a particularly important type of talk: the formal and well prepared speeches. Even though the participants spent a great deal of time talking to each other during coffee breaks and at dinner receptions, plenty of their time was spent listening to keynote speakers talking about their CSR work. In fact, the main activity at these conferences was the performance of conference speeches. This section explores the keynote addresses, which displayed various forms of CSR and CSR work. Through them, CSR was translated into oral and visual presentations, as the speakers described their work and showed PowerPoint slides to strengthen their arguments.[1]

Ambiguous Headings

Before I describe the character of the conference speeches, it is necessary to discuss the conference headings. In advance of each conference the organizers drew up a conference program; they were similar in composition, and divided each conference day into sessions. Each conference track – plenary session or workshop – was given a heading in advance, splitting CSR into topics that related to a variety of corporate issues. Most of the sessions proceeded sequentially, but there were also parallel sessions. In such cases some participants moved between sessions in order to listen to specific speakers. The headings of the sessions demonstrated different understandings of CSR, and CSR was connected to various sub-topics through these headings. Figure 2 shows a program from one conference that demonstrates this.

As the headings in the conference programs demonstrated, the plenary sessions and the workshops covered a diversity of topics that were related to business life in general. Yet it was possible to discern 20 main topics that reoccurred in most of the conference programs.

These conference topics can be understood to represent four categories of headings (see Table 3). These categories related CSR to business operations and to the role of business in society. The first category – *corporate management* – included headings that drew on the topic in various ways, relating CSR to such diverse topics as the recruitment of new employees and health and safety issues at the workplace. Several other conference tracks discussed supply chain

---

1 The quotes that are reproduced in the following sections were derived primarily from my conference notes; but on some occasions they are reprints from speeches or transcribed from audio recordings.

RESPONSIBLE BUSINESS - A NEW STRATEGY FOR DEVELOPMENT.

Innovative business management in CEE Region

6 – 7 October 2003, Warsaw, Poland Within the framework of the European Business Campaign for CSR 2005.

Under the auspices of Minister Barbara Labuda, Secretary of State, Presidential Chancellery

PROGRAM OF THE CONFERENCE

DAY 1, October 6, 2003

Up to 12:15 Check in

12:30 **CHAIRMEN'S OPENING ADDRESS**
Przemek Pohrybieniuk – Responsible Business Forum
Prof. Witold M. Orlowski – Head of the economic advisors to the President of Poland
OPENING SESSION
Barbara Labuda, Secretary of State, President'ial Chancellery
James Warren Evans, Sector Manager, ESSD, World Bank
Jerzy Hausner, Minister of Economy, Labour and Social Affairs, Poland*

13:15 **BUILDING PARTNERSHIPS FOR PROMOTING CSR**
Moderator: Paul Mitchell, Chief, Development Communications Division, World Bank
Leo Johnson, Strategic Consultant Market Development Group, International Financial Corporation
Adrian Hodges, Managing Director, International Business Leaders Forum
Ellen Kallinowsky, Head Learning Forum, UN Global Compact
Visnja Jelic-Mueck – Croatian Business Council for Sustainable Development
Janusz Górski, President, Spedpol

14:45 Coffee and networking break

15:30 Panel discussions
1. HOW TO CREATE A POSITIVE CLIMATE FOR CSR
Moderator: Robert W. Crown, World Bank
Dominique Be, European Commission – *Public Sector Roles in Strengthening CSR*
Henryka Bochniarz, President Polish Confederation of Private Employers – *Private Sector Perspective*
Maxim Behar, Chairman, Bulgarian Business Leaders Forum – *Practical examples*

2. CSR CHALLENGES – IMPORTANCE OF CO-OPERATION BETWEEN SECTORS
Moderator: Boleslaw Rok, Responsible Business Forum
Piotr Mazurkiewicz, DevComm-SDO, World Bank – *Introduction to CSR and Multi-stakeholder Dialogue*
Michael Warner, ODI – *Building Partnerships for Sustainable Development*
Sanjay Gandhi, UNDP – Public-Private Partnerships – *Case Studies from the region*
Mateusz Żelewski, Steering Committee UN Global Compact/Johnson&Johnson, Poland

3. CSR IN CEE – BEST PRACTICES
Moderator: Andrzej Brzozowski, Sustainability Controller, ABB
PKN Orlen, the City of Plock, UNDP – *Cross-sectoral partnership project*
Kirka Kikov, CEO, Umicor, Bulgaria – *CSR component in the firm's development strategy*
Susan Simpson, Director, International Business Leaders Forum – *Regional perspective*

17:30 Coffee and networking break

18:00 **EUROPEAN CSR FRAMEWORK – CHALLENGES FOR CEE COUNTRIES**
Keynote speakers: Aleksander Kwaśniewski *, President of Poland

Panel discussion: *What's the meaning of responsible business in Central Europe?*
Moderator: prof. Witold M. Orlowski, Head of the economic advisors to the President of Poland
Viscount Etienne Davignon, President Board of Advisors, CSR Europe
Matthias Kleinert, Senior Vice President, DaimlerChrysler AG
Jerzy Gruhn, President, Novo Nordisk

19:00 Banquet and CSR recognition ceremony

Figure 2: Conference program from 'Responsible business', 6–7 October, 2003 in Warsaw.

management, and how corporations could control their production in developing countries in order to minimize the risks of employing child labour.

Table 3: Four categories of conference headings

Corporate Management	Development of CSR into corporate practices	Corporate relationships to the environment	Corporate relationships with the local and global society
Recruitment. Health and safety. Supply chain. Control of production. Marketing. Charity and donation.	Implementing, reporting, and evaluating corporate social responsibility	Impact on the environment. Contribution to reducing environmental damages	Human rights issues. Local community involvement

The second category – *development of* CSR *into corporate practices* – included conference tracks that debated how CSR could be implemented in corporations, how corporations should report on their social responsibility practices, and how these activities could be evaluated from a financial performance perspective and in relation to other corporations.

The third and fourth categories – *corporate relationships to the environment and society* – addressed the influence of corporations on nature and human beings, and their responsibility for improving the conditions of the environment and human lives. These categories included discussions on the appropriate actions of corporations in following the UN Declarations of Human Rights.

A variety of topics was discussed in relation to CSR at the conferences. Several keynote speakers recognized the multitude of topics that were debated under the CSR label, and claimed to be confused about the meaning of CSR. Confusion over the content and practice of CSR was also addressed in the conference speeches. Extensive parts of the conferences were allotted to discussions about the definitions of CSR, as illustrated by the following quote:

> We need to focus on different aspects of SR issues. But what is SR? One definition is that it is voluntary SR initiatives in addition to the compliance to law. A definition is needed (Lars Flink ISO 2004).

The keynote speakers did not only explicitly address the definition of CSR in their speeches; they also presented a diversity of frameworks, guidelines, standards, and codes of conducts that were attempts to materialize CSR. There were displays of frameworks and guidelines originally developed by the Global Compact; the International Chamber of Commerce policy, Corporate Citizenship/Business in Society; the OECD guidelines for multinational corporations; the ILO conventions; the UN Declaration of Human Rights; the Global Reporting Initiative (GRI); AccountAbility management tools; and SA 8000; among others. And their speeches provided reasons for using those particular frameworks.

The ISO SR conference was, in a sense, a response to the multitude of frameworks that had been circulating in the business environment over recent years. ISO representatives argued that there was a problem with too many CSR initiatives, and that ISO must launch a new standard to make it easier for corporations to handle the demands of corporate social responsibility. But the ISO conference was, of course, also arranged in order for different stakeholders to meet and discuss the wisdom of ISO continuing its development of a social responsibility standard: ISO 26000.

> There are 100 initiatives and many of them constrain our market. If ISO gets involved and gets all the initiatives together we think that it is better to have one standard then 100 (Fabio Tobón TMB for DC 2004).

The explicit aim of the ISO conference was that the participants should reach a consensus concerning ISO's involvement in CSR. And, as noted above, the conference did end with such a consensus: that ISO should proceed with their work on the social responsibility standard. This was not the only conference at which keynote speakers stressed the importance of reaching a consensus, or at least elucidating the meaning of CSR. At the CSR conference arranged by CSR Europe in Warsaw, in 2003, Polish Secretary of the State, Barbara Labuda, illustrated the disunity in CSR in a dramatic way. Before she left the rostrum she asked the audience to stand up, close their eyes, and turn toward the north. A quiet giggling spread in the auditorium as the participants realized that they did not know how to turn north. As the participants opened their eyes, they saw that they were faced in every possible direction, which allowed the Secretary of the State to conclude by saying: 'Today we see CSR differently. We must therefore reach consensus regarding its meaning, so that we can face the same direction' (Barbara Labuda The Secretary of the State 2003).

Conference speakers expressed their confusion over the meaning and content of CSR, and claimed that the idea needed to be elucidated. In advance of the conferences, however, the organizers had developed conference tracks to highlight certain aspects of CSR and to create an interface with other particular topics, thereby defining the content of CSR by the very programs they printed. CSR was related to different parts of corporate management, developments of CSR into corporate practices, and the role of business in relation to the environment and society. However the formation of CSR continued in the conference speeches, in which speakers presented their views on CSR and their work with CSR. Hence by listening to and observing the speakers, the audience was served with a variety of interpretations of CSR. For this reason, the next section closely examines the conference speeches.

Conference Speeches

The conference speeches were central elements at the conferences. They were organized in similar ways, partly as large plenary sessions in which the keynote speakers presented their ideas, thoughts, and work with CSR; partly as small workshops in which the keynote speaker debated with members of the audience on a specific topic.

The keynote speakers were often representatives from corporations, although they held different positions in their companies. Several of them were CEOs; there were also corporate board members, communication managers, and marketing managers. Some keynote speakers held titles like 'Director of Public Affairs' or 'Director of CSR'. Representatives from governmental organizations, academia, consultancies, and NGOs were also regular keynote speakers.

The stated aim of the conferences was that the participants should join in discussion, share information, and exchange best practices. As stressed in the conference call to the CSR conference in Warsaw, in April 2003.

The main objective of the conference is to present and examine trends in corporate social responsible business practices in Poland and other

Central and Easter European Countries and to share the best practices
from companies, government and civil society organizations that support
and implement the CSR concept in their activities (CSR Europe 2003a).

The speakers expressed their views of what CSR was and what it
was not, and presented their CSR work, practices, or frameworks to
the audience. The keynote speakers used their time to present their
own interpretations of CSR and images of the socially responsible
corporation. The speakers not only expressed their perspectives on
CSR, but their speeches often reflected their views on the role of the
corporation in society. For this reason the speeches often revealed
either conflicting or shared notions about CSR.

As described previously, the conferences were organized both as
plenary sessions and as workshops. The plenary sessions took place
in large auditoriums; whereas the workshops were set in smaller
conference rooms. During the plenary session, a moderator called
the keynote speakers to the podium one by one. Before each speech,
the moderator elicited responses to a few personal questions from
the keynote speaker. After that short introduction, the keynote
speaker gave a speech, usually with the help of a PowerPoint
presentation, and the audience responded with applause. Three
speeches were usually held, one after another, followed by the three
speakers sitting at the podium to engage in a panel discussion.
The moderator posed questions to the speaker, and the audience
also had the chance to ask questions – an opportunity that several
participants took advantage of. During the plenary sessions, the
auditorium was filled with participants listening and taking notes.
Participants also engaged in conversations with each other and
moved in and out of the auditorium in order to make phone calls,
refill their coffee cups, or talk with other participants.

As the keynote speakers entered the rostrum to present their
work with CSR, the audiences were faced with a multitude of corporate CSR practices and served with myriad CSR frameworks that
had been developed by NGOs, consultants, or by the corporations
themselves. The keynote speakers displayed their interpretations of
and aspirations for CSR. In this way, diverse activities that could be
labeled as CSR were presented to the audience.

The speech by James Warren Evans, Sector Manager, ESSD,
the World Bank, at the CSR conference in Warsaw, April 2003,

provides a good example of CSR being turned into concrete activities. On behalf of the organization he represented, Warren Evans reminded the audience that the World Bank is not a corporation with a profit-maximizing goal. The World Bank's stakeholders wanted them to help eradicate poverty and it had responded by starting to assume social responsibility. He then presented and exemplified the CSR work at the World Bank, which was as varied as using fair trade coffee, constructing low-energy buildings, and providing toilet paper to shelters for homeless.

Another example from the same conference, illustrating the variety of practices that was presented as ways of turning CSR into a concrete form, was the speech given by Elena Bonfiglioli, Director of Community Affairs & CSR at Microsoft. Elena Bonfiglioli emphasized the importance of creating credibility in the eyes of one's stakeholders, and described how Microsoft had donated computers to a PC lab for pupils. Bonfiglioli stressed that the business community and society need to be united, and concluded with the following words: '[...] Doing the right thing is doing the right thing for business' (Elena Bonfiglioli Director of Community Affairs and CSR Microsoft – Member of CSR Europe Board 2003).

A prominent element in the conference speeches was the use of 'good examples' or the demonstration of best practices that illustrated how corporations ought to work with CSR. The keynote speakers often took the opportunity to present their organizations as socially responsible or demonstrate the frameworks and standards that they believed would create fruitful CSR practices. The following quotes made by corporate representatives from Siemens and Phillip Morris in their keynote speeches exemplify this perspective.

> We embrace corporate responsibility to advance society. Our ideas, technologies and activities help create a better world. We are committed to universal values, good corporate citizenship and a healthy environment. Integrity guides our conduct toward our employees, business partners and stakeholders (Rosa Riera Siemens AG 2004).

> There is one strong clear message; we do not want children to smoke, this is what we are committed to. Our employees, shareholders, regulators, adult smokers and society as a whole expect us to do so. We do not run a successful business by ignoring societal expectations. So yes, smoke pre-

vention is to Philip Morris a business interest and it is one of the highest
priorities that we have (Dettmar Delbos Philip Morris GmbH Germany
2004).

In their speeches the speakers often described their understanding
of CSR and how they sought to develop it into a practice. Speakers
representing consultants or sometimes NGOs presented tools and
frameworks that would facilitated the implementation of CSR
in corporations. These speakers not only displayed their own
frameworks of how to deal with CSR, but they also contextualized CSR by illustrating how CSR was part of shifting ideas about
corporations. The speakers argued that expectations about what
corporations should contribute to society had changed over time.
In particular, this meant that new groups of actors were mobilizing
new demands, stressing the view that corporations should do more
than maximize their profits to their shareholders.

An example of this type of argument could be seen in the speech
held by Leo Johnson, Strategic Consultant Market Development
Group, International Financial Corporation (2003). Johnson
started his speech at the CSR conference in Warsaw, October 2003,
by showing the audience a picture of a man who he claimed had
first changed the world and, thereafter, had been defeated. The
man on the picture was Milton Friedman. Leo Johnson asked the
audience if they could quote Milton Friedman and the audience
mumbled the correct answer: 'the business of business is business'.
Then Johnson asked rhetorically if Friedman's way was the right
way, whereupon he showed PowerPoint slides of corporations that
had behaved irresponsibly in recent years and had become posters
in the media. Subsequently, Leo Johnson described how stakeholders scrutinizing corporations had become a strong and influential
force on corporate reputations. Johnson concluded the speech with
the following advice: '[...] deliver what you say you are going to
deliver and ask what the stakeholders want'.

Other consultants, as well as NGO representatives, more explicitly presented their frameworks of CSR, whereby they often
stressed the importance of not neglecting CSR, and recalled the
latest corporate scandals. Their presentations often included slides
with pictures and logotypes of corporations that had been accused
for misbehaving and acting irresponsibly. Several presentations

also included slides with flow charts and detailed descriptions on how to proceed with a CSR strategy. Speeches described changing conditions in the business community, in particular, highlighting such increasing demands of stakeholders as the scrutinizing of NGOs, and accentuating the point that CSR provided corporations with 'a license to operate'. The speakers often used visual rhetoric to demonstrate the changing conditions for businesses in society. In particular, the keynote speakers used visual rhetoric – exciting photos, illustrations, pictures in their slides – to emphasize that the globalization, the increase in NGOs, and consumer demands had made it impossible not to address CSR.

General societal problems were linked to CSR through the speeches, and it was stressed that corporations could contribute to solving these problems by increasing their social responsibility – helping to reduce world poverty and improve the environment by being socially responsible. Yet CSR was presented as an idea from which corporations, rather than the general society, could benefit. The conference names and the headings of the conference tracks often contained words with such positive connotations as 'Competing for a sustainable future' or 'CSR: A smilestone in future business', indicating that CSR was an opportunity rather than an obstacle to business. To benefit from CSR, it was argued, CSR needed to be defined, mainstreamed, and developed into useful management tools. The keynote speakers even expressed the position that CSR was an imperative for the corporations' pursuit of profits. The following two examples are from CSR Europe's CSR conference in Warsaw in 2003.

> To succeed in today's competitive market CSR is important [...]. CSR is a voluntary must and it is not just for big business but also for SMEs (Anna Diamantopoulou European Commissioner for Employment and Social Affairs 2003).

> Business is into CSR because of the self interest in business. The price to pay for not being seen as a good citizen is too high (Viscount Étienne Davignon President Board of Advisors CSR Europe 2003).

The question of whether or not corporations should assume any social responsibility was seldom mentioned at these conferences, although critics did raise their voices on occasion. At *The Trust*

Conference, arranged by the Confederation of Swedish Enterprises in Sweden, in April 2004, for instance, David Henderson, former OECD Chief Economist and author to the book, *Misguided Virtue – False Notions of Corporate Social Responsibility*, made the following statement.

> I am the black sheep. Business should act responsibly, but that should not mean that it incorporates the doctrine of CSR. CSR is leading in the wrong direction. How do corporations contribute to society? By economic progress. There is no need to apologize for capitalism, nor for profit-oriented business enterprises. They have long been, and still remain, forces for economic progress. This primary role of business has not changed. It remains the same in the 21st century as it was in the 20th century, or for that matter in the 19th. The idea that a new era has recently dawned, in which the purpose and mission of business have to be redefined in the name of "Corporate Social Responsibility" (CSR), is false (David Henderson 2003).

Such critical statements were rare at the conference. Different opinions about the responsibility of corporations were expressed, but they seldom lead to hot-tempered debates.

The speakers called attention to certain corporate behaviour as being social responsible, and highlighted particular practices as being CSR practices. By listening to the keynote speakers, the audience received various pictures of the meaning of CSR for corporate practices. The audience was also served with different frameworks that could be used in order to implement or report social responsibility. CSR was primarily addressed as a business case that corporations must attend to in order to handle increasing stakeholder demands. However even though most of the keynote speakers highlighted the view that CSR was a corporate imperative, they did not always share the same view on definition, implementation, and regulation of CSR. On the contrary, the participants often had dissimilar understandings of what CSR meant and what it implied for corporations in particular and society in general.

Conflicting Views

The outspoken aim of the conferences was to discuss the role of business in society, to develop CSR practices, and come closer to a common definition. Views of the scope of social responsibility were often dissimilar. The conference speeches were filled with calls and suggestions for the appropriate behaviour of corporations, and conflicting views of the role of corporations expressed. The argument either emphasized that corporations should primarily attend to the shareholders' interests or to the interests of the overall stakeholders. However the predominant opinion was that corporations must attend to the interests of their stakeholders in order to secure the interests of the shareholders. It was thereby stressed that neglecting the demands of stakeholders would lead to bad publicity, which in turn would affect the shareholders. The keynote speakers emphasized that corporations should contribute to a better society and better business through the use of CSR.

> Responsible business is solution for problems, which are essential for the business and for the society and for the business in society (Elena Bonfiglioli Director of Community Affairs and CSR Microsoft – Member of CSR Europe Board 2003).

Despite disagreements about the scope of CSR and whose interests were paramount, the correlation between CSR and profitability was highlighted at the conferences. CSR was presented as an issue that would either increase profitability or hinder the loss of profitability. This quote from the director of CSR at BAE systems, speaking at the conference at the Humboldt University in 2004, captures these ideas.

> At BAE systems we would contest that there is, or needs to be, a trade-off between the business focus and CSR. Instead we would argue that the two need to be aligned in order to meet stakeholder and business needs. Furthermore, unless CSR is truly aligned with the business focus, then it will not have the credibility to be recognized and integral aspect of the business performance (Deborah Allen Director Corporate Social responsibility BAE Systems 2004).

Concerns were often expressed during the conference that it was possible to interpret CSR in too many ways, which would turn the idea into empty words. The keynote speakers emphasized their view that CSR needed to be regulated, either through the development of voluntary rules or through coercive regulation. In fact the pros and cons of this position became a recurrent question at these conferences. Keynote speakers argued that one precise definition or even a standard had to be developed for CSR, or it would be impossible to evaluate and measure CSR. Concern was expressed that CSR would become a marketing gig without serious intentions if it were not regulated. This view is illustrated in the following quote from a representative of Greenpeace at the CSR conference, Humboldt University, Berlin, 2004.

> Corporate Social Responsibility and Issue management are basically decent-sounding terms. But to be meaningful, these terms have to be acted on and not remain empty words. In most cases, however, CSR and Issue management are used as a front or a whitewash (Hamadan Fouad Director Communication Greenpeace in Germany 2004).

Several keynote speakers argued that for CSR to become more than mere 'window dressing', some kind of a regulative framework was a necessity. At the same conference at Humboldt University in 2004, the Deputy Head of the Unit European Commission Employment and Social Affairs underlined the importance of finding one common framework.

> Regulation is necessary to define a CSR reference framework, i.e. the scope of communication tools, their terminology, methodology, and required skills. The CSR reference framework should built on existing EU and international principles agreed instruments such as the ILO and the OECD guidelines for multinationals using them as benchmarks (Dominique Bé Deputy Head of Unit European Commission Employment and Social Affairs 2004).

Not all conference speakers agreed, however; they stressed that CSR had to remain a flexible concept that could be adjusted to different context and different industries, and that coercive regulations were therefore impossible. The primary argument was that self-regulation was the best way to promote CSR, and it was claimed that voluntary action would develop CSR further than laws ever would. Laws would only turn CSR into a minimum standard; whereas a self-regulation through best practice and benchmarking would develop CSR in a more successful way and make corporations even more socially responsible. Therefore CSR should be 'mainstreamed' into business on a voluntary basis through self-regulation, in an interaction among corporations, professionals, governments, and diverse stakeholders. It was therefore stressed that corporations should be guided by well established international and European business principles and conventions such as the Universal Declarations of Human Rights, EU Charter of Fundamental Rights, ILO Declaration on Fundamental Principles and Rights at Work, and the OECD Guidelines frameworks. Additional regulations were not needed, the argument continued; they would merely hinder the development of CSR. As stressed in the report distributed at the *The Nordic Marketplace for* CSR conference arranged by CSR Sweden in Stockholm, 2006:

> [a]t this stage, any regulatory frameworks would jeopardize the innovation and learning process required to achieve necessary consistency and credibility (CSR Europe 2006b).

At this conference one of the members of the advisory board of CSR Europe, Viscount Étienne Davignon, declared that the 'threat of coercive regulation' no longer existed, because CSR Europe had joined in an alliance with the European Commission in order to develop CSR on voluntary basis. Thus the risk for coercive regulation had disappeared.

> When there are conflicting interests, governments tend to regulate; but we have convinced the European Commission that it is not possible. And that CSR should be promoted by best practice. If they were to regulate, it would only be possible to regulate on minimum obligations, and then the corporations would not have a motive to do more (Viscount Étienne Davignon Chairman of the Advisory Board CSR Europe 2006).

Because the CSR conferences that took place between 2001 and 2006 addressed similar questions and themes, it is difficult to distinguish any development or changes in the CSR debate. Definitions of CSR as well as regulation, with its conflicting views, were recurring topics. The ISO conference in 2004 was organized to discuss the launch of a voluntary standard for social responsibility by 2006, and regulation was the primary theme. Representatives from other organizations were participating in order to promote their frameworks and to oppose the development of a single

standard. Nevertheless, a negative attitude toward coercive regulation seemed to be emerging. The last conference studied was held
in February 2006, and more outspokenly addressed questions of
coercive and voluntary regulations; certain forms of voluntary
regulations were seen as the appropriate regulation.

Over the years it was explicitly argued that CSR should be
developed through self-regulations rather than by coercive rules.
Self-regulation implied that corporations should seek to develop
a social responsibility through best practice and benchmarking.
However concerns were also expressed that CSR would merely
become empty words without regulation, and for this reason several organizational representatives participated at the conferences
in order to mobilize their frameworks and voluntary rules of CSR.
At the same time acceptance that a common definition of CSR
lacked were gained.

Concluding Remarks – Catwalks and Talks

At the conferences diverging notions about what corporate social
responsibility actually meant in theory and in practice were
expressed. The participants did however agree that CSR was an
issue worth while paying attention to. The conferences drew attention to CSR and constituted an arena for different participants to
meet in order to discuss the issue of corporate social responsibility.
The conferences functioned as 'fashion catwalks', in which forms
of the socially responsible corporation were both presented and
questioned. Organizational representatives at the conferences
displayed their interpretations and views of CSR in their speeches,
in which they advocated their practices, work, and frameworks of
CSR. Conference participants presented their work with CSR and
gave voice to their own interpretation of the socially responsible
corporation, calling attention to certain corporate behaviour as
being responsible and highlighting particular practices as being
CSR practices. In this way notions and images of a 'responsible corporation' were shaped and reinforced, as were acceptable corporate
CSR strategies. At stake was the very definition of CSR, and judg-
ments of appropriate and inappropriate CSR practices were passed.

In this sense CSR was constructed in a translation process in which actors presented their individual interpretations of CSR to each other at the conferences. The translation process set off already by the formulation of the conference program and continued during the conference speeches when actors were forming CSR by describing their preferred way of working with CSR. And the translation was carried on during coffee breaks, lunches, and dinners when the participants discussed and judged the presentations carried out during the conferences speeches. Hence it was during these 'catwalks' as well as informal talks that notions about the social responsible corporation were constructed. However one common definition was not agreed upon, but a common notion about what were legitimate CSR practices and what were not and what a social responsible corporation was and what was not, was established.

In these processes of translation the rhetoric played a central role. Both oral and visual rhetoric were used on the 'catwalks' – conference speeches – in order to convince the audience about the importance of CSR and about the supremacy of particular interpretations of CSR. In order to fit into different organizations, ideas must take various forms, and the ideas need to be presented and packaged in a way that renders them crucial for organizational attention. In the speeches CSR was presented as an imperative for corporations to pay attention to as it was related to corporate profitability. In other words, CSR was translated into an idea that constituted a business case rather than an obstacle for businesses. CSR was not about restricting and regulating corporate behaviour it was about new business opportunities.

The new-institutional argument implies that ideas travel far and wide if they are translated in accordance with the local and institutional context (Campbell 2004; Czarniawska & Joerges 1996), if they are universally applicable, and if they are presented in accordance with dominating values in the institutional environment (Meyer 1996; Rövik 1996). In the corporate world, this means that ideas need to be presented as rational means in order to reach increased corporate profitability and success. Presenting CSR in this manner made it legitimate for corporations to allocate resources to CSR activities. It is therefore apt to argue that CSR were constructed into a new management idea that was rhetorically connected to corporate profitability. The dominant arguments were that corporations should take a social responsibility either to hinder the loss of profits to increase their profits.

Although different groups of actors participated at the conference, and although the conferences aimed to be 'multi-stakeholder forums', a majority of the participants represented corporations. The predominance of corporations demonstrates the fact that the business community, along with other organizational groups, played an important role in mobilizing CSR. Corporate representatives could listen to others, while taking advantage of the opportunity of presenting their corporation as socially responsible; and thereby setting the agenda for the interpretation of CSR. One reason for the form that CSR took – as a management idea connecting social issues to corporate profit – was the dominance of corporate representatives at the conferences.

Although a variety of views on CSR were brought forward in the conference speeches and frustration was expressed over the ambiguous forms of CSR, there were few debates. The conferences were an important venue for the participants to meet and establish contacts with new customers and partners. In this respect, conferences were neither the site for hot-tempered debates and conflicts nor a place to find the anti-CSR faction. Thus participants were networking rather than involving themselves in intensive debates. During the speeches, underlying, and conflicting assumptions about the role of the corporation in society were put forward. On the one hand, corporations were described as an important force that needed to contribute to a better society by solving societal problems; on the other hand, it was proposed that corporations should increase their profits and attend to their shareholders. However in several respects, CSR was constructed into an idea that matched both these perspectives. By serving noble causes and investing in CSR activities, it was argued that corporations would not only contribute to a better society, but become more profitable in the long run.

The consensus was that no common definition of CSR had yet been developed, which suggests that discussion does not always lead to clarification. In this respect, the translation of ideas does not necessary imply that the idea is translated into a precise and common definition; rather vagueness is maintained. This makes it possible for the idea to spread, to develop, and to flourish into different contexts. Because CSR lacked a set definition, it could be translated into various corporate practices, frameworks, management tools, and meanings, which fit with different interests and organizational and geographical contexts.

On the basis of this study I also imply that translations do not proceed in isolation or is carried out by one actor group rather translations involve plenty actors. Translation is a collective process that involves interaction among various actors – various actors take part and jointly decide which translations are appropriate and not. For this reason, translation should not only be studied from one actor group but rather it should focus on how different actor groups influence and are influenced by each other when carrying an idea into new settings. I propose that we need to address translation as an active process in which ideas are constructed, transformed, and circulated; but I also argue that researchers and organizational theorists need to attend to the interplay among several actor groups and to the contesting views that may arise in these collective processes.

3. Translating Corporate Codes of Ethics[1]

TOMMY JENSEN, JOHAN SANDSTRÖM AND SVEN HELIN

Introduction

This chapter is about the study and understanding of corporate codes of ethics (CCES). According to Schwartz (2001: 248), such a code could be defined as a 'written, distinct and formal document which consists of moral standards used to guide employees or corporate behaviour' and these objects have become one of the more widespread tools that companies rely upon in their corporate responsibility work (Kaptein, 2004). The CCE is, however, not a recent fad in the business community (Graves, 1924), but it seems that corporate scandals, such as the ones with Enron and Parmalat, constitute the main driver for rejuvenated interests in such codes.

Companies' work with CCES also attracts the attention of management and organization scholars, and the golden question seems to be whether or not these codes are effective. That is, how does the implementation of, and work with, a CCE influence the ethical behaviour of employees and managers? Do these actors, as a result of this work, develop a better moral practice or is the code only a rhetorical device? Effects along these lines have also been encountered in earlier research. Some studies, under different circumstances, identify positive effects on moral practice (cf. Kaptein & Wempe, 1998; Stohs & Brannick, 1999; Boo & Koh, 2001) whereas others rather see the code as playing a mere symbolic

---

1   A rough draft was presented at the Nordic Academy of Management's winter conference in Umeå, Sweden, 16–18 March 2006, and an early full paper was presented at the European Business Ethics Network's annual conference in Vienna, Austria, 21–23 September 2006.

role (Adams, Tashchian & Shore, 2001), or mere window-dressing (McKendall, DeMarr & Jones-Rikkers, 2002), constituting an important symbolic artefact (Stevens, 2004). In sum, though, this research is inconclusive regarding the effect on moral practice (Schwartz, 2001; 2004). The answer seems to be: it depends.

In this chapter, however, we would like to emphasize a third alternative: the implementation of a CCE can have a contra-productive effect on moral practice. This would be caused by the code a priori determining solutions to moral dilemmas and thereby numbing, or unburdening, the employee or manager's moral responsibility. This alternative (the contra-productive argument) is to a large extent absent from previous empirical research on CCEs. In our view, this makes CCE-research narrow in its approach to the relations between working with the code and moral practice. Through the approach developed in this chapter we attempt to fill this gap. We aim to put forward the possibility that CCEs, maybe more often than we think, might be morally contra-productive. At its simplest, this effect can be depicted as follows: The moral question 'should I do this?', phrased by potentially responsible humans in organizations, is at risk of being locked up and locked in through the manifested routine suggesting to individuals to look for answers in the statutes of the code ('what does the code say?'). But, moral responsibility is not possible to fixate as such. It is spontaneous as it reaches out trying to fulfil moral calls from others. When calculated, routinized and subordinated to something else, moral responsibility is set aside (Bauman, 1989; 2003; Levinas, 1969). Organization members acting on this spontaneous call are thus at risk of being punished for not turning to the code and for not applying the, by necessity, highly simplified ethical statutes to the complex moral dilemma.

A question here is of course why most previous studies have not taken on this alternative. One reason, we believe, has to do with research methodology. Turning our attention to previous research in the field then, we also find that studies directed to the understanding of how these codes work as transformational objects and how they, in practice, influence moral practice, are lacking. This echoes findings from other scholars as well (Nicholson, 1994; Stevens, 1994; Cassell, Johnson & Smith, 1997; Adams *et al.*, 2001; Schwartz, 2001; Dillard & Yuthas, 2002). The bulk of empirical CCE-research has rather been focused on analyses of content (what's in the code) and whether they lead to more ethical behaviour (is the code effective). Studies that do try to take on a transformational focus (*cf.* Montoya & Richard, 1994; Kaptein & Wempe, 1998; Somers, 2001; Wood & Callaghan, 2003; Schwartz, 2004; Snell & Herndon, 2004, Helin & Sandström, 2008) still prove insufficient, however, since codes are assumed to be 'dead' missiles that when shot into the organization may, or may not, 'hit' human beings (Helin & Sandström, 2007). This might also be why earlier CCE-research dodges the question of moral practice and moral responsibility. Alas, the code is not really granted such a capability.

So, we see part of the problem lying in the ways previous research has been approached. In the chapter, we also place research methodology up front and continue with a focus on moral practice. Our first aim is therefore to outline a methodological approach in which the 'travel' of the CCE is made the focus of the research and in which the code is granted a capability to influence human world-views and strategies for addressing and solving moral dilemmas. For this we draw our inspiration from writings in Actor-Network Theory (ANT), especially its 'and after' (see Callon, 1998, 1999; Law, 2004; Law & Mol, 2002). Hence, with forthcoming theoretical concepts, the CCE becomes an intermediary in a *heterogeneous materiality*, travelling due to a wide range of *translations*, and with a capacity for *bending moral space* (see also Jensen, Sandström & Helin, 2009).

Our second aim follows from the first, placing emphasis on developing a sensitivity towards moral practice and responsibility that does not rely upon anthropocentrism, calculability and instrumentality; one that also alerts us to the possibility that a CCE could have a morally contra-productive influence on organization members' moral practice. For this we draw our inspiration from moral philosophers, such as Jonas (1984) and Levinas (1969), and writers explicitly addressing the issue of morality in organizations (*cf.* Bauman, 1989; McMahon, 1995; Jones, 2003; Roberts, 2003; ten Bos, 2003).

The chapter is structured according to these two aims. We begin with the methodological approach, which we set up against three benchmark studies. We then proceed with a discussion on moral practice and responsibility, ending our chapter with a discussion on some of the implications of our approach to the study of CCES in action.

Corporate Codes of Ethics in a Heterogeneous Materiality – a Methodological Approach

Approaching ANT, one issue in particular, which is central to our framework, is how *ontology* is approached. Lee and Hassard (1999: 393) write that 'contemporary research strategy takes recourse increasingly to trajectories that are empirically relativist and ontologically realist (*cf.* sociological triangulation). In contrast, for us, the research strategies of ANT largely invert this position'. Callon and Latour (1981: 286) also suggest that an actor is: 'Any element which bends space around itself, makes other elements dependent upon itself, and translates their will into a language of its own'. These capabilities are, in organization studies, normally considered the property of human beings, but our position here is that following ANT does *not* mean that scallops (Callon, 1986), Pasteur's microbes (Latour, 1988), a spreadsheet (Law, 2002), or a CCE, have the ontological status of a human actor.

From ANT we learn rather that the first mistake is to impose our categories prior to action. Human and nonhuman, following Law, 'are treated as effects or outcomes, rather than explanatory resources' (2004: 157). It is thus only after the network has been assembled, or performed, that we can say something about the role and significance of different elements (Callon, 1991). The social still has priority here, but no longer are social courses of action exclusively the properties of humans only: 'we are sociotechnical animals, and each human interaction is sociotechnical. We are never limited to social ties. We are never faced only with objects.' (Latour, 1999b: 214). The CCE is here our scallop, microbe and spreadsheet, and as such, it might perhaps be able to bend space, make others dependent and translate wills. We write 'maybe', as we do not know, not in advance.

There are a lot of suggestions on what the (philosophically) intricate word ontology might mean in this case. Suffice it to say here that it has less to do with the philosophical efforts of understanding reality – to identify and describe basic categories and entities – than conceptions of reality as such (i.e. worldviews). What is of importance is, thus, that humans reflect upon being and that humans have (different) views of the world. This does not, however, imply that solely humans have the capability needed to mould, change and construct other elements. It merely stresses that humans, unlike nonhumans, have intentions with what they do. They have moral concern, imagination and a subconscious, making it possible for us to speak of an ontological realm of agency exclusively the property of humans. To put it bluntly, humans are the only living things that reflect upon and try to change 'being' (other living things just are). Recent developments in ANT (and 'its after') also seem to have become softer in that an ontological difference between humans and nonhumans has emerged (Jensen, 2004).

So, again, our position is humans-only in the ontological realm, but what about epistemology? Epistemology (or theory of knowledge) is here understood as the means of production to attain knowledge, as well as a process. There are a lot of different theories of knowledge and each one contains truth, objectivity, justification, etc. Thus epistemologies, like our worldviews, are socially constructed. We hold that our worldviews and theories of knowledge of the world are socially constructed, but the world is still real. If ontology concerns worldviews then epistemology might mean strategies for making sure that a certain kind of knowledge prevails. Both are subject to power-battles, but only epistemology can consist of humans and nonhumans. Sharing epistemological space with nonhumans is an empirically realist and epistemologically relativist position in which humans and nonhumans have, at least potentially, similar capabilities. Both are essential to the construct of epistemological possibilities (the construction of different strategies of, and different routes to, knowledge). In such a way 'things-that-go-to-work' are organized and moulded by humans with worldviews and intentions, at the same time as nonhumans cause network-effects (Callon & Law, 1997; Law, 1999, 2002) that configure human epistemology and ontology (Callon, 1999). Put differently: nonhumans map out the world which humans perceive and act upon.

Zooming in to the main focus, in this view of heterogeneous materiality, nonhumans have the epistemological capability to:

(i) draw things together by reducing, compressing and ordering worlds; (ii) re-present and amplify different 'thing-ish' versions of worlds (in double plural since multiple versions exist), including abstractions and concretions, subjects and objects, languages and symbols (Jensen, 2004; 2006).

To summarize the argument so far, we state that CCEs are not only rhetorical devices, or carriers of information, but that they have the capability to construct and organize the very things (humans and nonhumans) that they describe (*cf.* Callon, 1998). A CCE could thus construct and organize individuals' moral practice, which could lead both to the betterment of moral practices but also to the numbing, or unloading of moral responsibility. It does so by changing the way individuals perceive (ontology) and act upon the world (what epistemologically constructed strategy and route is appropriate, best, believable, true, justified, etc.). Viewed as such, CCEs can no longer be understood as a human trajectory only. Ethics, or business ethics, is no longer an anthropocentric ethics.

In the next section, we take a closer look at translation processes, in which CCEs 'go to work' as important epistemological elements via their capability of potentially bending moral space.

Translation Processes

The translation process of a CCE, following Jensen (2004), could be depicted as follows: For something to travel, human or nonhuman, it *has to be simplified* (Callon & Latour, 1981; Latour, 1986). When something travels it does so because it has, temporarily, made things a little bit less complicated. As the translation process continues, however, simplifications pile up, resulting in complexity. Despite the fact that each of the simplifications still make things less complicated, the complexity arises out of the numerous associations between different simplifications. Complexity is thus not used here in its ordinary meaning, that something is of a complex nature, but rather that something (an event, a situation, a result etc.) is characterized by *things not adding up*, that escape logic and order (Law & Mol, 2002). A third ingredient in this version of the translation processes is blurring. Blurring, slightly reminiscent of Baudrillard's (1994) simulacra, the world of hyper reality, not only indicates that something is changed when translated, but that *something is also lost in translation.* What is lost is the original of what is translated (in our case the CCE, but the CCE in turn contains numerous lost aspects of reality).

Moreover, what is lost is also found. Humans continuously translate pasts, presents and futures, and through this process they find and lose different parts, building up sediments of translations (Latour, 1999b). This in turn means that multiple versions of the world circulate (Mol, 1999). One aspect of this translation process is, though, that simplification, complexity and blurring do not occur as a fixed sequential process, or as a regular order of things. It is not a matter of first simplification, then complexity and then blurring. On the contrary, these processes do not always add up themselves: appearing simultaneously they are more like disordered cascades and in themselves multiple orders and multiple realities. Simplification, complexity and blurring do not plough a single route, a single order; consequently there is no regular processual rhythm to learn from and follow repeatedly (Jensen, 2004).

So, when nonhumans and humans are translated they travel, but they travel handcuffed, blindfolded and gagged – they are black-boxed. According to Callon and Latour (1981: 284–285), such a 'box contains that which no longer needs to be reconsidered, those things whose contents have become a matter of indifference. The more elements one can place in black boxes – modes of thoughts, habits, forces and objects – the broader the construction one can raise.' As more and more black boxes are closed, the actor-network expands to gigantic proportions. Epistemologically (now referring to our possibility to have an account, or knowledge, of the phenomena in question), large actor-networks are no more complex to study and understand than small ones because they are of the same size and shape. The micro-macro division does not exist in a heterogeneous materiality – actor-networks only have shorter or longer orbits (Callon & Latour, 1981; Latour, 1987; Latour, 1999a).

What also surfaces is power. When humans struggle for power they strive for the right to define and diagnose problems, suggest treatments, and allocate the task of fixing the problems. Through these translating activities, when humans translate humans and nonhumans (but are also translated by humans and nonhumans), actors connect and disconnect to each other (Latour, 1986). Power is therefore crucial in order to understand the translating process, but how is it to be defined in a heterogeneous materiality? Power is almost never something that only can be possessed (e.g. status and hierarchical position); it has to be exerted. What also emerges is a shift from senders to translating receivers and that what makes elements circulate and grow in actor-networks also depends on the actions of others (Callon, 1986; Latour, 1986).

Furthermore, bearing in mind that raising constructions is a human affair only, we argue that when humans and nonhumans travel they grow because they are subordinated to human actors successful at exercising power. Those humans who cannot are ontologically mute and epistemologically hijacked intermediaries (who might have a different worldview, but are forced to act in specific ways) through which translations may be drawn together (reducing, compressing and ordering), re-presented and amplified. An individual facing this situation has a hard time changing the actor-network's constellation and strategies. In this sense, humans, epistemologically speaking, can be less powerful than nonhumans. Nevertheless, individuals without the necessary power today can be emperors of tomorrow. Actor-networks are instable constructions (*cf.* Greener, 2006), or in other words, 'it takes *effort* to sustain stable networks of relations' (Law & Singleton, 2005: 337, italics in original).

Filling the Methodological Gap

Equipped with the conceptual framework elaborated upon here, we would expect to encounter numerous translations of the CCE, all of which are travelling, but with shorter and longer orbits. Given that we can never expect homogeneity (one translation, a regular process), this framework calls for a case study methodology that takes on mobility in both time, as stated in 'blurring' above, and space (Czarniawska, 2004; Law, 1994; 2004; Latour, 1987; 1999b). In other words, follow the code.

Methodologically, a heterogeneous materiality demands *spatial* openness simply because we can never know a priori which human and nonhuman actors that are translated. For case studies, which traditionally means focusing on an organization, the heterogeneous material voyage is by no means limited to traditional organizational boundaries, whether they are formal or informal.

Important to follow on the translation voyage of the CCEs could, for example, be ethical theory, the authors behind the code, other ethical codes, financial calculations, audits, procedures, routines, employers, leaders, customers, competitors, lawyers, norms, elements of nature, and more.

A heterogeneous materiality demands openness in *time* as well. As we saw earlier the past, present and future are translated over and over again, and thus give rise to circulation, 'here and now', of multiple pasts, presents and futures. This implies that not only do we have to take into account different versions of the past, present and future, as they are translated here and now, but we also have to travel in time. As we methodologically talk about a process we are always in a becoming present, always here and now strictly speaking, but we have to follow yesterday's interferences between humans and nonhumans to understand today's (which, again, demand spatial openness too).

Another open and fluid matter, intertwined with time and space, is between those who have enough power to raise successful constructions, and those who have not. When following the CCE, we can (and should) expect shifts between centre and periphery. Central actors today, despite their spatial homestead, are always at risk of becoming tomorrow's peripheral actors, because some other actor increase in size at another actor's expense (and the same pattern can be located historically too). A version of a CCE is made central during one month of implementation and then maybe made peripheral until next year's signing of the code. If the CCE travels to a union representative, some of the blue-collars on the factory floor, or to the law firm engaged by the company in question, the researcher has to consider following these actors, however peripheral they might seem to be, since they might become powerful translators of the CCE. Furthermore, actors that resist translation attempts, and are successful at that (that is, they are raising competitive actor-networks) are also empirically interesting (Greener, 2006). How do they manage to grow; what strategies do they use?

Summing up so far, we understand translations as processes in which humans try to assemble humans and nonhumans into an actor-network (a black box). A process which demands investigation in 'all the negotiations, intrigues, calculations, acts of persuasion and violence, thanks to which an actor or force takes, or causes to be conferred on itself, authority to speak or act on behalf of another actor of force' (Callon & Latour, 1981: 279; *cf.* Callon, 1986). As we travel alongside the human-nonhuman interferences, we can thus expect that some humans do have the necessary power to translate, while others have not. We can expect that some things have the necessary capability to cause network effects, while others have not. Sometimes the CCE becomes centre (black-boxing); sometimes it does not – it is signed and done, placed in the periphery, losing its epistemological capability (black-boxed). But again, this is not possible to settle a priori.

By outlining the travel of CCEs in a heterogeneous materiality and the translation process therein, we have begun to sketch the outlines of an alternative methodological approach to the study of CCEs. To make a case-study, we now realize, might mean travelling to distant spaces and times, far away, and not obvious, from what was a priori anticipated (Law & Singleton, 2005). Below we set our emerging methodological approach up against three benchmark studies on ethical codes, and we do this predominantly to set the stage for our second aim.

A Heterogeneous Material Critique of Earlier Benchmark Studies

There are examples of scholars conceptually approaching this 'black box' of business ethics research. In the following, we review three studies that from different theoretical perspectives serve to increase our sensitivity to what is actually taking place in the process of implementing and working with a CCE. As we see it, they are among the few scientific articles attempting to link the knowledge gap identified earlier in this chapter. Our benchmarks are: Nicholson (1994), Cassell, Johnson and Smith (1997), and Dillard and Yuthas (2002).

From an institutional theory perspective, Nicholson (1994) develops a framework for analysing ethical functioning, which relates to how organizations identify CCEs and deal with ethical issues. Goals or interests are here acted out via (i) expressive forms, (ii) voluntary actions and (iii) instituted forms. In other words, codes are expressed in different elements. Actors (individuals or groups) express values and beliefs in everyday discourse by talking or writing in documents, i.e. expressive forms. In day-to-day action, such as when dealing with customers or developing new products, actors are also taking voluntary action and action always consists, Nicholson (1994: 587) argues, of a 'moral reasoning surrounding behaviour and its constraints, and the sources of moral authority to which appeal or attribution is made'. Organizational charts, responsibility rules, procedures and (formal) codes of ethics are then examples of instituted forms. These elements are all closely related, but not necessarily congruent. Describing business ethics as such, as three interrelated elements of organizational rules, facilitates the analysis of business ethics not just as a static code system followed or not followed by the actors; it allows for a dynamic analysis. Formal as well as informal rules, Nicholson argues, may guide action but may also be loosely coupled to action and values. Hence, new formal rules, such as CCEs, may constrain action and subsequently change norms in the organization.

Cassell *et al.* (1997) have a similar approach to Nicholson, arguing for studies of '*how* the actual process of design and implementation is undertaken and experienced by those involved' (pp. 1077–1078, italics in original). To understand how codes work in organizations, the authors also argue that the organizational context cannot be separated out. Codes are developed and communicated in a specific organizational setting, which has impact on the intention behind the codes as well as on the codes' actual effect in terms of individual behaviour and organizational practice. In their contextualist model, Cassell *et al.* (1997: 1088–1089) argue for the usefulness of focusing on the 'interactions between a number of different inter-related individual, group and organizational factors that impact upon ethical behaviour', where organizational factors also include the process of designing and implementing the code. By bringing not just organizational factors, but also a psychological (cognitive) focus into their model, they seem to extend Nicholson's framework: CCEs are in the organizational context seen as formal control mechanisms and as 'vehicles for bringing ethical norms' (1994: 1081). Codes are in that sense structure-like vehicles that might carry norms into the organization.

In a third conceptual idea for studying CCEs, Dillard and Yuthas (2002) argue for a structuration perspective approach (see Giddens, 1984). A cognitive perspective has its limitations, the authors declare, and structural forces have for some time been ignored in the study of business ethics. A structuration perspective on business ethics instead means how to find out 'how social norms and values are constituted, and reconstituted as and within, ongoing social structures by engaged social agents' (Dillard & Yuthas, 2002: 53). Ethical decision-making is not carried out in a vacuum, but is the result of historical structures and power struggles, as well as of human agency. Structures guide the way human beings act and are to been seen as memory traces shared in a community. CCEs are in the structuration perspective not structures, i.e. not memory traces, but ethical artefacts that may have an impact on action if the actors find them meaningful, legitimating, or powerful in terms of control over resources. CCEs may, in this approach, change structures if the actors consider the codes in their day-to-day action. CCEs are thus artefacts that may (or may not) give meaning to the active structures in the organization.

As we see it, all three of these conceptual ideas are creditable since they challenge what might be considered mainstream CCE-research. They extend the focus from the codes and the specific position of the receiver of the code, as the context in terms of control systems, social structures, history and action, is taken into consideration. Codes as formal control tools are also understood as related to action, but this is still not taken for granted. The studies and their frameworks, at least to a certain extent, take into consideration that action may be loosely coupled to the codes in the organization.

However, they may all be criticized from the heterogeneous materiality perspective elaborated on here. For example, Cassell *et al's* implicit use of a contingency theory perspective may be criticized for being too deterministic and Nicholson's framework for not considering events and processes outside the formal organization. Taken together these two studies seem to concentrate on the initial force – the sender. In their framework, what is in need of explanation is what accelerates or slows down the diffusion process. Humans and nonhumans are therefore only considered as passive receivers that do not change what is diffused, hence the assumption of homogeneity and that ideas, routines, management principles, blueprints, etc. are copied rather than changed (*cf.* Latour, 1986). Dillard and Yuthas do, however, try to balance the deterministic dilemma between structure and agency, between the initial force and the receiver, and to open up the organizational boundaries. They argue that structuration theory 'aids in understanding [the] dynamic nature of ethical norms [...] and how agents operate in unpredictable ways that can support or undermine organizational norms.' (p. 61). But, even if structuration theory allows for a change of both structures and human agencies, the structural forces are always outside and above action (on a macro level). Mysteriously, it seems, structures shape human and organizational conduct, and equally mysteriously human touch changes structures (cf. Latour, 1999a & b).

When it comes to the code itself, all three studies pay attention to the nature of the code in more or less the same way (albeit still based on different theoretical underpinnings). For Cassell *et al.*, codes are vehicles for bringing ethical norms; for Nicholson, codes are instituted forms; and, for Dillard and Yuthas, they are ethical artefacts. Codes are understood and treated as more or less passive artefacts that people in the organization, due to different rationales and reasons, pay attention to, or not. To put it more bluntly, codes are 'dead' missiles shot into the organization and they may, or may not, 'hit' the human beings in the organization. The object (the code) is left to its objectivity. The CCE is held as something neutral; a passive voice or a blueprint upon which organizational change is performed. The code, although not in a human sense, is not 'alive'.

A Heterogeneous Materiality and Morality – Filling the Moral Gap

So the CCE is not dead, but surely not entirely alive either. What we have explored so far are some of the potential methodological implications that a heterogeneous materiality might bring to the study of CCEs. Relying upon the ideas in our framework we now turn to the role of the CCE in enhancing, or securing, a moral standard in organizations and to what actually can happen with moral practice if we stay tuned to the assumption that CCEs are vehicles for bringing ethical norms (Cassell *et al.*, 1997), instituted forms (Nicholson, 1994), or ethical artefacts (Dillard & Yuthas, 2002). That is, if we stay attuned to the idea that codes are basically neutral and passive artefacts.

Albeit not always the main purpose of implementing a CCE, representatives of organizations often claim that a code, as indicated by the earlier quotation of Schwartz (2001), is meant to reduce moral ambiguity by guiding humans in their daily encounters with moral dilemmas. Hence, in this view, implementing a code is not just a show-off, a case of plain window-dressing, or a matter of simply gaining legitimacy. To some extent this can be expected from CCEs, but our main argument is that moral practice cannot be fully understood in this way. Even worse, it might result in the promotion of something that could actually prove morally contra-productive.

A basic assumption, and this includes the three frameworks reviewed earlier, is that a CCE is something that needs to be decoded and understood in a similar way in the organization. Thus codes are assumed to communicate clear messages that reasonable rational humans can transform into ethical thinking and action. Ethical thinking and action are thus considered something that is possible to *calculate*. When moral problems do occur, in this view, they do so either because individuals ignore the codes or because of errors in the institutional, contextual or structural frameworks. Human misconduct can be corrected through different forms of punishment or education. Often, organization members have signed the code and acknowledged that they have read, understood and accepted the instructions outlined in the code. Errors can be corrected through better organizational coordination and routines.

Extending the discussion from these assumptions, in view of our moral framework, humans' capability to act morally, to start off with, is non-calculable. If we calculate, we think first of ourselves and not primarily of the Other's moral demand, which is an uncon-ditional duty (Levinas, 1969). Therefore we cannot easily speak of moral responsibility, which is altruistic in nature, in organiza-tions (employee-employer relations, employee-employee relations, employee-customer relations, business-to-business relations and so on) – a setting in which returns are expected (Bauman, 1989, 2002; Jones, 2003; Roberts, 2003). To understand moral behaviour we need to separate calculative intentions from emotions as emotion is the initial source that triggers the will to act on behalf of the Other (Jonas, 1984). Evidently, to understand moral practice we need to keep these together, but we need to be sensitive to this collabora-tive nexus since calculability easily blocks our emotions (Bauman, 1989; 1993; 1995; Levinas, 1969).

Furthermore, every moral situation is radically unique, and thus genuinely uncertain. The Other's face, in Levinas' (1969) terms, is always radically different and thus not readily communicated from a faceless distance, for instance through e-mails, written codes on the intranet or in an organizational memo. Psychological and physical moral distance can not be over-won by technology (Bauman, 2002; Jonas, 1984). Moral responsibility needs closeness to the Other's face and this directly contradicts an assumption that passive artefacts such as a CCE, when shot into an organization, can actually function as a moral compass and dampen uncertainty. In this sense, ethical commandments – 'if this happens, then you should do this' – have, by necessity, to beforehand determine numerous different moral dilemmas. In other words, ethical commandments generalize moral practice first by reducing what is to be counted as a moral dilemma and then by standardizing possible responses. Different situations, humans and nonhumans, times and spaces, are all a priori decided through the codes. Dillard and Yuthas (2002: 61), in their concluding remarks, also reflect along similar lines, arguing that '[t]he attempt to present ethical decision making through rationalizing formal structures has had the effect of obstructing self reflection and allows the abdication of personal responsibility for the consequences of one's actions.'

This brings us back to the anthropocentric view prevailing in CCE research. The objectified belief that the CCEs are neutral and passive renders other misconceptions to the moral realm of practice: it holds moral practice as something that only belongs to humans. In the view of our emerging approach, this is not so. To feel and have moral responsibility is quite rightly a human concern, and the anthropocentric view has in this sense got it right, but as Latour puts it: 'Of course, the moral law is in our hearts, but also in our apparatuses' (2002: 253) and therefore 'morality is from the beginning inscribed *in the things* which, thanks to it, oblige us to oblige them' (2002: 258, italics in original). Thus CCEs oblige us humans to oblige them.

Once more the human and nonhuman worlds coincide and not even the moral realm escapes nonhumans' epistemological capability (assisting in smashing the dream of clear communication, calculability and a priori generalization, and the assumption of 'dead' objects). Thus, we speak of a heterogeneous *moral* materiality and by doing this we emphasize that scientific communities, different forms of bureaucratic coordinating mechanisms (hierarchies and divisions of labour), capitalistic and state-owned corporations, and technologies amongst many other possible examples, all are collectives of humans and nonhumans that construct and visualize moral possibilities on how to think and act. More precisely, an organization is a heterogeneous material fabric that constructs numerous different moral possibilities.

What we suggest here is that the study of CCEs might benefit from viewing morality as a collective matter, but not in the usual anthropocentric manner, as in the majority of ethical theories (Jonas, 1984) and the theoretical underpinnings in the three frameworks reviewed earlier. Instead we address collectives in which humans and nonhumans have the capability to alter things, albeit in the former we include ontology and epistemology, whereas in the latter only epistemology. It is crucial that both can influence the moral state of affairs. This should, however, not be confused with moral responsibility. Organizations are remarkably often portrayed as acting for the moral good or bad, but this is not only a convenient rhetorical and pedagogical tool used to simplify complex matters (the CCE plays a role in this, of course). This is also a common ontological merger between nonhumans and humans.

McMahon (1995) has convincingly showed the impossibilities of equating the moral status of organizations with that of individuals and we take a similar stance. Organizations are capable of action just because humans individually and collectively (together with nonhumans) produce these events (McMahon, 1995). In producing these events individuals have to decide, if the collective's ends fit the individual's moral judgment. Thus moral concern is an individual duty: I am morally responsible for the Other (Levinas, 1969) and the actions I have performed. Through organizations we might explain our and other's immoral behaviour, but despite how hard we try to provide rational and logic explanations, we can never escape our individual moral duty and responsibility for the Other. Morality cannot be judged by these criteria at all (Bauman, 1989).

What we try to pinpoint here is that there is no valid relationship between organizations' moral products (outcomes of goods and bads) and individual moral responsibility and duty. The latter cannot be excused on behalf of the former. In practical terms this 'means that however much a human being may resent being left alone /.../ to his or her own counsel and responsibility, it is precisely that loneliness that contains a hope of a morally impregnated togetherness. Hope; not certainty.' (Bauman, 2003: 93). CCEs can therefore be accused of functioning as a neutral managerial technology, delivering alibis, or moral step-ins (Jones, 2003; Roberts, 2003; ten Bos, 2003). We would like to add to this critique that all of this may be perfectly legal in the strict juridical sense of the word, but from the moral standpoint outlined here, collectives of humans 'cannot be used as a shield by the members of the organizations, a license to adopt certain ends, or certain means of achieving them' (McMahon, 1995: 551).

Returning to the common but unfortunate ontological merger between nonhumans and humans, what could be said about individual moral responsibility vis-à-vis collectives of humans applies to nonhumans as well. Blaming nonhumans, such as organizations or CCEs is an immoral and lame excuse. Consequently, we can never think of organizations as moral elements in themselves; individuals are morally responsible, not nonhumans. At the end of the day we can aim at understanding the nonhumans' role and function in moral hazards, but never should it be possible to wash away moral guilt by blaming the nonhuman part in this heterogeneous collective materiality.

Despite all the good intentions to better individuals and organizations moral conduct with the help of CCEs, we argue that assumptions (and performance of) clear communication and calculability, a priori generalization and the anthropocentric views on ethics can prove to be morally contra-productive. The framework presented here puts forward that this can even be quite common, witnessing the accelerating travel of CCEs among different kinds of organizations and the belief in ethical codes as moral compasses. What we need are other moral accounts and methodological studies of how multiple translations of CCEs flourish in moral practice. However, we will never master the heterogeneous material world of humans, nature, animals, technologies, organizational forms, CCEs, cultures, moralities (Latour, 2002; Jonas, 1984), but we have every possibility to act morally, given that through the alternative framework sketched in this chapter, we might have gained (dare we say) a better knowledge of the foundation of morality and the contra-productive potential of CCEs.

As Bauman (2003: 92) points out, morality does not serve any purpose; it is a prereflexive spontaneity and an innately prompted manifestation of humanity, of life itself. Trying to do good and avoid bad, that is, making moral choices between good and evil, is thus in this sense always radically uncertain (and an individual responsibility too). We need, however, to expose our selves to the risk of making morally wrong choices to refrain from 'craven impulses to run for cover that authoritative commands obligingly provide' and to keep our moral sensitivity and our 'boldness to accept responsibility' (Bauman, 2003: 93). Indeed, uncertainty is not a threat to morality, on the contrary *'uncertainty is the home ground of the moral person and the only soil out of which morality can spring shoots and flourish.'* (Bauman, 2003: 93, italics in original).

Conclusions

In the chapter, we had two aims. The first was to outline an alternative methodological approach to the study of CCEs, in which the code itself is granted an epistemological capability to influence moral practice and in which the processes in which the code goes to work are made the key concern of the research. Framing both these aspects we developed an approach holding *the CCEs as travelling in a heterogeneous materiality.* This approach laid the ground for our second aim, in which we outlined a view on morality that resulted in *a departure from anthropocentric ethics* and in fostering a greater sensitivity to the possibility that a CCE could have a *morally contra-productive influence* on organization members' moral practice.

By doing so, we have extended earlier frameworks in the field from rather objectified, passive and neutral views of the code, to an approach in which the scholar has to be open to the idea that the code has the potential, or epistemological capability of playing a more active part in the networks assembled. It is our contention that empirical studies based on the emerging approach outlined here might result in more full descriptions of how these processes take shape in practice and thereby also help shape more realistic expectations about the work with CCEs.

4. Standardizing Sustainability: A Critical Perspective on ISO 14001 and ISO 26000

BIRGITTA SCHWARTZ AND KARINA TILLING

"P - h - a - r - m - a - c - y", Pippi spells out, "Isn't that where you buy medusin?"
"Yes, that's where you buy *medicine*", Annika answers.
"Wow, then I have to go and buy some immediately", Pippi says.
"But, you're not ill, are you?" Tommy asks.
"What you aren't, you can become", says Pippi. "Every year people get sick and die because they don't buy medusin in time. That, I will not risk".
(Lindgren, 1946/1992;29, our translation)

Introduction

Bearing in mind the above quotation from Pippi Longstocking, the same logic can be found underlying the international standard for environmental management, ISO 14001. That is, it manages environmental impact according to a standard by adhering to environmental legislation, handling possible environmental risks related to organizational activities, and establishing goals and routines in order to improve environmental performance in a proactive way.

The creation of standards for management systems, for example, ISO 9000 standards for quality and ISO 14000 for the environment, has become common in today's organizations, including both companies and public sector organizations. In total, over 100,000 organizations in almost 140 countries have implemented and certified an ISO 14001 system (ISO World, 2007).[1] Accordingly,

---

1   The entire ISO 9000 and 14000 series for quality and environmental management have now been implemented by some 887,770 organizations in 161 countries.

approximately 3,700 organizations are registered to follow the alike European Union regulation for environmental management, EMAS (European Commission, 2007). According to the ISO 14001 standard, any organization can have their environmental management system audited and, after approval by a third party audit, it can be certified.[2] The implementation of environmental management systems (EMSs) has been popular among organizations, as the implementation of standards for organizational social responsibility, as ISO 26000,[3] now under development, will likely be as well.

In 1999, then UN Secretary General Kofi Annan, in an address to the World Economic Forum, asked business leaders to join an international initiative on environmental and social principles, the Global Compact (UN, Global Compact, 2007). This initiative has prompted responses from academia, focusing on how to make corporations more 'civil' (e.g., Zadek, 2001). Critical views have been articulated by researchers, who argue that social and environmental sustainability today gets measured and presented in glossy reports, unfortunately guided by financial reporting traditions and aims (Norman and McDonald, 2004). As much as academia should help foster more sustainable development by formulating tools, models, and techniques, in this chapter we argue for a need for critical analysis of the widely used model, recognized as a key feature of organizational sustainability, namely, standardized environmental management systems. Here we focus on the concept of EMSs, highlighting the possible risks associated with standardizing complex issues. We will perform our analysis in light of ongoing work with ISO 26000 and the operationalization of the Global Compact and similar social accounting initiatives that aim to standardize corporate social responsibility (CSR). Two research questions then can be formulated: (1) Why is the standardization of CSR so attractive? and (2) What happens when the complex and contested issues of environmental and social responsibility are standardized?

2   Japan has taken an ISO 14001 lead having obtained almost 16700 certificates, followed by the UK, China, Spain, Germany, Italy, the USA, and Sweden.
3   Note that ISO 26000 is not a management *system* standard like ISO 14001, yet a standard for defining the scope of social responsible organizational management.

On the method

Our study examines the standardization trend, citing examples from the research literature and the PhD research of one of the authors, Karina Tilling (Tilling, 2008), focusing on the environmental management project implemented by Swedish government agencies. These sources focus on the experiences and consequences of standardization as such and of environmental management standardization in particular. These findings are significant, as a counterpoint to expectations regarding the ISO 26000 standard. Empirical examples showing how other ethics standards, such as codes of conduct, work are drawn from the research literature and NGO reports.

Ongoing efforts to develop the ISO 26000 standard for social responsibility, as well as the involved actors' expectations, are discussed here with reference to a seminar in Stockholm (May 2005) that the authors attended. This seminar could be described as an ISO 26000 'world in miniature', from a Swedish perspective, involving representatives of various CSR stakeholder groups. Represented at the seminar were a financial investor (Banco), large corporations (e.g., Volvo), the Swedish labour organization LO, and NGOs (e.g., ECPAT and the Fair Trade Center). The ISO Technical Committee, TK 478, developing the ISO 26000 standard and the Foreign Ministry of Sweden were the organizers of this ISO 26000 seminar. We use narratives from the representatives attending the seminar to discern the various stakeholders' positions regarding ISO 26000 in section companies and NGOs approve for standardizing sustainability.

In February 2007, we observed yet another public seminar on the ISO 26000 process, held after a recent international meeting in Sydney in January 2007. This seminar was arranged by the Swedish Foreign Ministry and the Swedish Standards Institute, SIS. As well, two representatives of a participating NGO, the Fair Trade Center, were interviewed by the authors to investigate their expectations of the ISO 26000 standard and their experiences of CSR work.

Other official documents from the Swedish government, ISO, the UN, etc., dealing with social responsibility and environmental management have also been used. This means that the underlying rationales of the ISO 14001 and ISO 26000 processes have become the focus of our study, in terms of the arguments invoked by involved actors. Before discussing these ISO standards in further detail, however, let us start with a theoretical review of standardization and the popularity of management models.

Standardization of sustainable development as a modern phenomenon in global society

Why is standardization so attractive when it comes to organizational management? In whose interest is increasing standardization and the implementation of standards? The creation and implementation of rules in society could be understood from the perspective of organizations being embedded in society, making them appear to be more influenced by their environment than by internal management (Brunsson & Jacobsson, 2000). Standardization as a modern rule-setting phenomenon is highlighted by Brunsson and Jacobsson (2000), who argue that standardization is the new mode regulation in organizations and society at large.

Globalization is also identified as an important factor driving the popularity of standardization, dissolving, or at least challenging, local norms and traditions. 'Standardization is done at a distance in time and space from the people and the situations concerned', Brunsson (2000: 26) notes. At the same time, societies and cultures worldwide are arguably becoming more uniform, which in turn is regarded as a driving force of standardization in the first place (Brunsson, 2000).

The concept of sustainable development (SD) in relation to organizational management as discussed here could also be related to Czarniawska and Joerges' (1996) discussion of global ideas that travel to other places by being 'translated' into objects. That is, viewing SD as a set of ideas objectified via ISO 14001 and ISO 26000 standards. Sevón (1996) explains the 'translation' of an idea as the adaptation of an idea by an adopting organization so as to fit the organization's own prerequisites. Looking at the ISO model of SD (i.e., ISO 14001 and ISO 26000), we could say that it is based on SD ideas translated into an object – according to ISO, a productive and effective model for companies that feel the need to deal with SD issues and with their impact on environmental and social issues via their business activities. The travel of the ISO model among organizations and companies is also supported by the model's legitimacy (Schwartz & Tilling, 2009), as we will discuss later on. As Czarniawska and Sevón (2005) point out, however, this travel is guided by fashion, in that people imitate desires or beliefs that appear attractive at a given time and place, which leads them to translate ideas, objects, and practices for their own use.

A trend, such as the standardization of CSR management, quite reasonably needs to have stakeholders or carriers if it is to be a trend in the first place. Sahlin-Andersson and Engwall (2002) take an interest in the role of carriers in the spread of management knowledge. Significant carriers identified are business schools producing managers, global enterprises producing standardized management, management consultancies transferring management knowledge to organizations, and media companies producing business news, all four of which influence management practice.

Carriers, such as ISO, could also convert management knowledge to a product that provides competitive advantages to firms and makes managerial practices more portable (Suddaby & Greenwood, 2001). A knowledge producer seeks to extend the life cycle of its knowledge products by extending their scope of application, seeing them as 'product platforms' that can be used with minor modification in new markets (Gilmore & Pine, 1997, cited in Suddaby and Greenwood, 2001).

Summing up the theoretical overview in relation to the first research question, SD practice is arguably an item on the organizational agenda that makes organizations tend to act alike, by applying standardized concepts in order to make complex issues manageable in legitimate ways.

Perspectives on consequences of standardized sustainable development management

Brunsson and Jacobsson (2000) discuss the likelihood that formal standards could be expected to spread more easily than norm or practices developed, over time, by social processes and that often require special social conditions to emerge in the first place. Along the same lines, Rövik argues that modern management concepts could be viewed as commodities, characterized by user-friendly, easily communicable content that assures effective output in relation to total implementation costs (Rövik 2002). The easy adoption of a standardized concept might also bear the risk or consequence of inhibiting innovation, freezing development in a fixed form that might be difficult to change (Brunsson & Jacobsson 2000). Following a standard imposed from outside the organization could even prevent organizations from making their own decisions regarding necessary actions (Brunsson 2000).

Making sustainable development issues a focus of standardized management systems, to be treated as management issues rather than contested issues of radical change, has been criticized before. As early as 1997, when ISO 14001 was new, Richardsson and Welford (1997) argued that environmental strategies often existed outside the core business activities of organizations; they related this phenomenon to the development of ISO 14001, which did not embody any actual rethinking or change in business logic. Instead, ISO 14001, developed by the business world itself, might actually be reinforcing business as usual (Richardsson & Welford 1997). Following a standard like ISO 14001 or adopting the upcoming ISO 26000 can, according to this perspective, be viewed as the act of organizations seeking legitimacy. This search for legitimacy might also lead to a focus on simply having 'the right procedures and produc[ing] the right documents, rather than [on] ... actually doing something differently' (Jacobsson 2000: 45).

Furusten explains organizational attraction to standardized management models such as ISO 9001 for quality (related to the upcoming ISO 26000) in terms of organizations sticking to 'a discourse on general models for what should be' (Furusten 2000). The aim of a management standard, such as ISO 9001 on quality, 'is to indicate what is best for all concerned ... rather than taking an interest in actual practice' (Furusten 2000: 84). From another related perspective, the standardization of environmental management can be considered in view of its disregard of contemporary organizational research findings, for example, trusting greatly in formal structure and top-down management (Moxen & Strachan 2000).

Empirically, that organizations seek legitimacy by implementing standards is supported by a study of Swedish companies implementing environmental management systems, one conclusion being that it is fully possible to implement an environmental management system, and even have it certified, without actually improving significantly in environmental performance (Ammenberg 2003). Developing a greater focus on organizational sustainability management techniques rather than on actual outcomes in terms of more responsible performance also influences how sustainability issues will be interpreted. That is, the environmental management techniques, including accounting and auditing, come to influence the actual issues they aim to manage, normalizing environmental issues in existing management discourse (Power 1997, Tilling 2008, Schwartz & Tilling 2009). Signs of inadequacies in a standardized environmental management tool, such as ISO 14001, could also be interpreted by the tool's advocates as simply indicating implementation problems, rather than indicating that the wrong tool is being used; this could in turn lead to lack of rethinking and innovation outside of the frame of the standard (Tilling 2006). Summing up, while the standardization of management techniques need not impose radical change, it could still satisfy a need for legitimate action.

The sustainability concept opens up for the social issue

Corporate interest in sustainable development, as stated at the beginning of the chapter, first concentrated on its environmental aspects. In recent years interest in social issues has increased, and the concept of CSR has been increasingly emphasized. In 2000, the UN started its work on the Global Compact, an international initiative to bring companies together with UN agencies, labour, and civil society to advance universal social and environmental principles. The Global Compact code of conduct is based on principles derived from the Universal Declaration of Human Rights, the International Labour Organization, the Rio Declaration on Environment and Development, and the United Nations Convention Against Corruption. The ten principles of the code are presented in the Appendix.

Through the power of collective action, the Global Compact seeks to advance responsible corporate citizenship so that business can be part of the solution to the problems arising from globalization. In this way, the private sector – in partnership with other social actors – can help realize the vision of former UN Secretary General Kofi Annan: a more sustainable and inclusive global economy. Today, hundreds of companies from all regions of the world, together with international labour and civil society organizations, are engaged in the Global Compact.

Codes of conduct: are they a tool for change?

The experience of companies that have worked with ethics codes for several years indicates that it is not easy to change the conditions of labour in the developing countries where many suppliers are situated. One example presented in Ethical Corporation Magazine (2004) is Levi Strauss ('Levi's'), which started to apply an ethics code of conduct to its suppliers back in 1991. By 1996, the company had begun developing tools for factory social auditing to be used worldwide. After some time, however, Levi's realized that this model had inherent flaws. The cost of Levi's annual non-financial audit is USD 3.5 million a year, and it has proven to be ineffective when using traditional methods to check factory compliance with Levi's code of conduct. Levi's are now more interested in the dialogue models pioneered by some trade unions as a part of the solution, and stresses that workers, NGOs, other companies, unions, and governments need to participate.[4] The company notes that it is important to the process that brands give up some control to workers and to enlightened supplier factories, and that there is a need to collaborate with suppliers and stakeholder groups on these new approaches to raising standards in supply chain standards (Ethical Corporation Magazine, 2004). From this example we can see that to gain legitimacy and effectiveness regarding social issues, Levi's chose another way than the audit way, which they found ineffective.

---

4   Levi's is now trying a participatory approach, with pilot projects and initial trials of a new worker dialogue-based system to improve factory conditions. In a pilot project, Levi's with one of the suppliers jointly decided that meetings with workers were needed, so they could hear worker concerns and give them greater representation before factory management. In view of the number of workers (500), they began holding monthly meetings between management, the workers' elected representatives, and 50 randomly selected workers.

The problems with ethics codes and auditing systems are also discussed in a report the consulting company Acona made for Insight Investment. The report found that current supply chain management practices and the drive for ever-greater efficiency put pressure on suppliers and their factories, essentially forcing them to contravene ethics standards in order to meet buyer requirements. The need for flexibility – responding quickly to changes in demand from customers – can lead to high levels of compulsory overtime (discouraged by most ethical trading codes). Seasonality – the demand for certain products year round and the need for high volumes at peak times – can increase the demand for contract and temporary employment. Constant price pressure can translate into pressure for suppliers to reduce wages below levels defined by legislation or by the buying companies' own ethics codes. The report concludes that some companies may be inadvertently pursuing a buying strategy that creates tension, or in some cases directly conflicts, with their commitment to ethical sourcing. Such pressures, often exerted on suppliers needlessly, are the result of bad buying practices, such as inefficiencies, indecision, poorly designed incentives, and a lack of trusting business relationships (Insight Investment Management Ltd and Acona Ltd, 2004). This could also be explained by decoupling (Meyer & Rowan, 1977; Weick, 1976; Brunsson, 2002), where the buying company's organizational structure and demands on suppliers relate to different divisions, such as an ethics/sustainability division and a purchasing division. This decoupling helps the company meet the demands of other actors and avoids public embarrassment, while keeping production activities running smoothly.

It is not only buying companies that decouple their activities but also suppliers. A study of the toy industry (Egels-Zandén, 2007) found that Chinese suppliers had consciously developed methods for deceiving the organizations that monitor their activities to determine whether they are fulfilling the demands of buying companies. The formal systems being monitored were decoupled from the suppliers' actual operations. This led to the detection of several areas of non-compliance with the ethics codes; in practice, however, there were multiple areas of non-compliance. Examples of how to deceive monitoring organizations include instructing employees on what to say, paying compensation for 'correct' answers given by employees, forging salary lists, forging time cards, hiding part of the workforce, and forging employee contracts. The study found that the buying companies, i.e. retailers, were surprised when this deception was pointed out to them; they seemed unaware of their suppliers' lack of compliance with their codes of conduct (Egels-Zandén 2007).

In the report 'Cheap, fast and submissive', Bjurling demonstrates that today Chinese workers in the toy industry do not understand the applicable ethics codes or their legal rights. The Hong Kong organization Christian Industrial Committee, which cooperates with the Fair Trade Center, states that Swedish companies must see to it that the workers know their rights, otherwise it is difficult to improve their situations (Bjurling 2004). The CSR approach has also faced the criticism that its underlying assumptions are false, since voluntary reporting does not improve performance, voluntary codes and management systems do not actually change corporate behaviour, the consumer does not drive change, and the investment industry cannot provide the strongest incentives for CSR (Doane 2005). Even if these voluntary codes do not seem to achieve their goals in terms of actual improvements, interest in standardizing SD management still remains. In the next section we will discuss the increasing interest in standardizing SD practice, experience with ISO 14001, and expectations for the new standard, ISO 26000.

Environmental and social responsibility in a Sustainable Development Context

The most-cited definition or vision of sustainable development is that of the UN World Commission on Environment and Development (WCED), which focuses on meeting the needs of present and future generations: 'Humanity has the ability to make development sustainable – to ensure that it meets the needs of the present without compromising the ability of future generations to meet their own needs (WCED 1987: 8).' Stating the importance of viewing SD as a process, the WCED continues: 'Yet in the end, sustainable development is not a fixed state of harmony, but rather a process of change in which the exploitation of resources, the direction of investments, the orientation of technological development, and institutional change are made consistent with future as well as present needs (WCED 1987: 9).' SD is often related to its three supporting pillars, namely, economic, social, and ecological sustainability. One answer to the sustainable development challenge in business has accordingly been more transparent reporting of activities as they impinge on these three pillars. The 'triple bottom line' (3BL) has gained acceptance, which entails that companies also report social and ecological figures, guided by the tradition of financial reporting. ISO claims that the ISO 14000 series contributes to the 3BL in both its economic and ecological aspects, since resources will be used more effectively, reducing environmental impact. With the new ISO 26000 standard, the third leg of the 3BL, the social one, will be in place. Soon, all three dimensions of 3BL will be covered by standards.

The development of standards for environmental and social responsibility

Internal control systems regarding environmental impact were formulated in the 1970s and 1980s. In 1988, the International Chamber of Commerce agreed on guidelines for environmental auditing. In relation to the UN Conference on Environment and Development in 1992, the international business community and the World Business Council for Sustainable Development initiated efforts to standardize EMSs, efforts embodied in the ISO 14000 series. This initiative aimed to find internationally anchored forms for environmental efforts in companies, increasing the business community's environmental credibility (SEPA, 2003). In 1996, the first edition of ISO 14001 was issued, standardizing environmental management.

The popularity of ISO 14001 and EMAS, as well as being due to a desire for more effective environmental efforts, could also be explained by organizations wanting to legitimize current activities as environmentally responsible. When analyzing the 2004 report of the Swedish Environmental Protection Agency (SEPA) evaluating the EMS project in 240 government agencies, the confidence in the EMS model as such is obvious. Evaluation of these agencies'

EMS project, aiming to integrate the environmental aspects of their activities, indicates that the best results were achieved for activities having substantial direct environmental effects, that is, construction, energy use, and copying on paper. The indirect aspects situation, however, is less favourable: 'Few agencies address indirect environmental aspects, such as the effects of their regulations and grant decisions, in the framework of their EMS' (SEPA 2004: 12). Only some ten percent of the agencies report that the EMS has affected their approach to areas such as provision of information, training, and advice, and even fewer report progress in decisions regarding permits, grants, R&D, and international activities (SEPA 2004). SEPA states that 'ISO 14001 offers poor support for handling indirect environmental aspects, whether it be a matter of the impacts of companies' products or those of agencies' decisions (SEPA 2004: 15).' Still, the conclusion of SEPA is that this is a project that deserves to be continued, even if the indirect environmental impacts of government agencies have not yet been successfully or genuinely ameliorated by EMS efforts after up to seven years time. As suggested in the study by Tilling (2006), it would be reasonable to interpret Swedish government decisions concerning this project as having been made in imitation of how companies manage environmental issues; in other words, the public sector is interested in using EMS for legitimizing purposes. Seen in this light, the most important thing becomes implementing the now institutionalized EMS model as a *sign* of environmental integration and credibility, not the environmental effects as such. In Pippi Longstocking's words, quoted in the introduction, the legitimate EMS models become the 'medusin'.

Standardizing of CSR by ISO 26000

In 2002, discussion started regarding development of a new ISO standard for social responsibility, and in 2004, ISO started developing the standard. ISO considered that organizations wanting to create CSR credit internally and for their stakeholders could demonstrate their engagement in society with the help of an ISO CSR standard. Standard development work is being led by two member organizations representing Sweden and Brazil.

The new ISO 26000 standard aims to help companies and organizations organize and manage their social responsibility, to help improve people's working and living conditions, and to create better opportunities for comparisons between different organizations working with social responsibility (SIS 2005). ISO 26000 aims to provide guidelines for organizational social responsibility; the guidelines will be voluntary and not intended for third-party certification (Foreign Ministry of Sweden and SIS, Seminar, 2007).

According to the new work item proposal, the ISO 26000 standard should (ISO, 2008):

- assist organizations in addressing their social responsibilities while respecting cultural, societal, environmental and legal differences and economic development conditions;
- provide practical guidance related to operationalizing social responsibility, identifying and engaging with stakeholders, and enhancing credibility of reports and claims made about social responsibility;
- emphasize performance results and improvement;
- increase confidence and satisfaction in organizations among their customers and other stakeholders;
- be consistent with and not in conflict with existing documents, international treaties and conventions and existing ISO standards;
- not be intended to reduce government's authority to address the social responsibility of organizations;
- promote common terminology in the social responsibility field; and broaden awareness of social responsibility.

The above list of ISO 26000 aims is rather ambitious, covering awareness, practical guidance, creation of common CSR terminology, and performance improvements in a standardized form.

Companies and NGOs approve for standardizing sustainability

A Swedish initiative in the context of CSR standardization was arranged in Stockholm for 24 May 2005. The Foreign Ministry of Sweden and TK 478 arranged a seminar about their work on the new ISO 26000 standard. At this seminar, several organizations involved in this work were represented and they presented their views on the upcoming standard. One common opinion was that it was important that organizations use only one CSR standard; today several standards apply to ethics issues, making it difficult for suppliers to compare ethics performance. The upcoming ISO standard is seen as the most attractive, due to ISO's good reputation stemming from positive experiences with the ISO 14001 environmental standard and the ISO 9000 quality standard. As the representative of the investment bank Banco said, 'ISO has a history and is a well-known standard; other standards are not so well known and are difficult to understand' (Foreign Ministry of Sweden and TK 478 , Seminar, 2005).

A representative of AB Volvo, arguing along the same lines in favour of ISO CSR standardization, said that a common CSR standard would be useful and that ISO is well known and creates organizational credibility (Foreign Ministry of Sweden and TK 478, Seminar, 2005). Volvo has a long tradition of cooperating with governments and authorities in Sweden and is often involved in projects initiated by the public sector (Schwartz 1997, 2006/2009). Volvo is also an actor in the ISO 26000 project, allowing it to influence the development of the standard and giving it direct access to the secretariat. Another Volvo representative, from Volvo Car Corporation, is vice chair of the standardization work globally. This representative claimed that multinational companies must work with social issues regarding their trade marks, due to media exposure of companies that mishandle these issues.

At the seminar, the organizational desire to define what CSR was all about was clearly articulated by various stakeholders who expressed their core expectations regarding the new ISO 26000 standard. They saw this standard as the outcome of what could be said to constitute the 'demand side' of management concepts defining legitimate CSR action. Companies currently have different definitions of CSR, and the Volvo Car Corporation representative said, 'Here the ISO 26000 does a great job which I have been missing' (Foreign Ministry of Sweden and TK 478, Seminar, 2005, our translation). Another expectation is that the standard could simplify contact with Volvo's stakeholders. Volvo currently receive many questionnaires from different organizations regarding social issues; it hopes that ISO 26000 can be used for communication with all stakeholders, which in turn can save

Volvo time in these contacts, the Volvo representative argued.

Consumer organizations requested that ISO should work on a standard for social responsibility (SR). NGOs seem to be content with the standardization of SR as such, although they would all like their perspectives to be included in it. Even they regard ISO as trustworthy; for example, the representative of ECPAT said that an ISO standard would confer legitimacy in the eyes of all sectors of society (Foreign Ministry of Sweden and TK 478, Seminar, 2005).

From the interview with Bjurling and Lindholm (2005), representatives of the Swedish NGO Fair Trade Center (FTC), it was stated that the work on developing ISO 26000 for social responsibility is positive, in the sense that making social behaviour measurable, which will allowing accounting, will make it possible to follow up on the policies set by companies. Today it is difficult to follow up on company implementation of their ethics codes because the results are retained internally and not published in any official documents. However, standardization such as ISO 26000 will not guarantee that companies will help workers improve their working conditions. The risk of standardizing performance on social issues is that the focus will be on the standardization process itself and not on how to improve working conditions at suppliers in developing countries (Interview, Bjurling and Lindholm, 2005). The report entitled 'Cheap, fast and submissive' stated that some of the investigated companies that had not devised formal ethics codes actually had better working conditions for their employees (Bjurling, 2004).

The International Labour Organization (ILO) is also involved in ISO 26000 development. The ILO negotiated with ISO regarding the content of the standard, and has come to an agreement regarding acceptable working conditions, although the negotiation process with ISO was sometimes hard. A representative of the Swedish labour organization LO said at the ISO 26000 seminar that the ILO is the only international organization that has the legitimacy to set standards for social and labour issues, and that ISO acknowledges the ILO as the only representative organization internationally recognized to make recommendations as to legislative standards for social and labour issues (Foreign Ministry of Sweden and TK 478, Seminar, 2005). Labour organizations are of the opinion that it is impossible to certify organizations according to ISO 26000 because there are already a great many collective agreement processes involving organizations and companies; moreover, these agreements differ between countries. Social responsibility is also seen by the ILO as a public responsibility that includes social and political processes; this makes standardization efforts regarding social responsibility different from other standards that relate solely to technical processes. For these reasons, the ILO argued that the ISO 26000 standard should be a guidance standard only. Others attending the seminar commented that a certification process would threaten the ILO's strong role today and the efforts of labour organizations.

According to our interpretation, the seminar centred on an agenda of legitimacy. Legitimacy was spoken of from different perspectives, the most common one concerning finding a legitimate way to deal with today's contested corporate social responsibility issues in a way that can be defined as 'right'. Assuming that gaining legitimacy is the underlying agenda for those actors who back the development of ISO 26000, we will now turn to the questionable consequences of standardizing social and environmental responsibility.

A critical approach to the standardization of CSR

Management systems, like ISO 14001 and the upcoming ISO 26000, can be criticized on the same basis as is used to justify their existence in the first place; that is, making complex issues, such as environmental impact and social responsibility, manageable. Underlying our analysis is the doubting question of whether environmental and social SD could be addressed in more progressive ways, by accepting the political nature of the issues and acknowledging the complexity of the reality involved in the relationship between environmental and social impact and organizational action.

Why is standardization of CSR so attractive?

> "I would like to buy four litres of 'medusin'", Pippi asks the pharmacist.
> "What sort of medicine", the pharmacist answers impatiently.
> "It would be best if it helped against disease", Pippi says.
> "What sort of disease?", the pharmacist replies.
> "Well, I think I will have one that is for whooping-cough, chafed feet, stomach pain, rubella, and if you have poked a pea up your nose and such. It would also be good if you could polish furniture with it. A really proper 'medusin' it should be". (Lindgren, 1946/1992; 30, our translation)

Standardizing methods, for example, the standardization of environmental management and social responsibility guidelines, as done in ISO 14001 and ISO 26000, can be compared with Pippi Longstocking's 'medusin', helping you regardless of the problem, or more specifically, for all possible purposes. ISO labels the ISO 9000 (for quality) and 14000 (for the environment) standards as 'generic management system standards', meaning that 'the same standards can be applied to any organization, large or small, whatever its product – including whether its 'product' is actually a service – in any sector of activity, and whether it is a business enterprise, a public administration, or a government department' (ISO, 2007a). These standards are applied in order to satisfy customers, comply with regulations, and meet environmental objectives (ISO, 2007a). ISO states that 'to be really efficient and effective, the organization can manage its way of doing things by systemizing it' (ISO, 2007b). As expressed by the Volvo representative at the earlier mentioned seminar on ISO 26000, there is an organizational desire today to define CSR and find one appropriate approach, because of its complexity and many interpretations. This point was also made by ISO, as referred to above, which espouses the benefits of generic management systems.

The ISO standards could collectively be viewed as an example of a product platform of established knowledge products, which, with minor modifications, constantly enters into new markets (Gilmore & Pine 1997; Suddaby & Greenwood 2001). That is, ISO 26000 could be seen as a knowledge product, or commodity (Rövik 2002), developed out of a known and legitimate platform of related management standards, such as ISO 9001 and 14001 for quality and the environment, respectively.

The interacting supply and demand sides of CSR *standardization*

Standard setters, such as ISO, and management consultants are here seen as comprising the supply side of CSR management standardization. The standard setters need adopters and the management consultants, or gurus,[5] need buyers, giving both parties strong incentives to develop a new management standard for the 'emerging management market' of social and environmental responsibility.

Figure 1 depicts our analysis in a simple market model, consisting of the interacting supply and demand sides involved in CSR standardization, both sides being motivated driving forces behind the development of a generic standard. The demand side, i.e. the standard consumers, consists of organizations in search of a legitimate model to help them act in line with societal CSR demands. The translation of sustainable development ideas, whether they concern social or environmental responsibility, by ISO into the manageable ISO model could be interpreted as answering companies' desires to handle these complex issues in line with their beliefs (Czarniawska & Sevón, 2005).

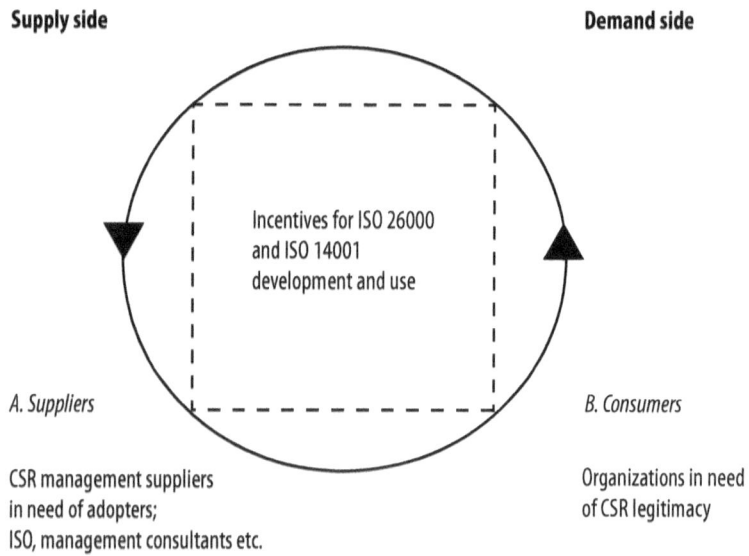

Figure 1. A sustainability management market model consisting of supply and demand sides, both of which support ISO 14001 *and* ISO 26000 *development and use.*

5   To use the expression of Brunsson and Jacobsson, 2000, p. 6.

At the same time, however, it could also be argued that ISO is stepping into the UN's shoes in developing a global standard for organizational social and environmental responsibility, since ISO is using the UN's SD concept for its own purpose

What happens with the complex and contested issues of environmental and social responsibility when standardized?

Here, sustainable development is seen as a set of politically contested issues, challenging power relationships and economic structures in society. In that sense, SD could be described as a case where power relationships are genuinely both present and at stake. We highlight the perspective of legitimacy in relation to the popularity of standardized EMSs and the development of the standard for social responsibility. In doing so, we argue that these 'answers' are natural in relation to the questions asked, that is, asking for a legitimate way of handling complex and demanding environmental and social issues. In particular, we would like to focus on what one can and cannot say and do, that is, the appropriateness and legitimacy aspects of possible interpretations of environmental and social performance as now being institutionalized in a generic management systems approach. As we see it, standardized management systems, as generic as they may seem, come with specific assumptions that are more or less expressed but not addressed or problematized. At the same time as the management systems approach is becoming institutionalized, context-specific, culture-specific, political, and power issues are being shunted out of the centre of attention. It is reasonable to argue that social and environmental issues become depoliticized as they become generic and manageable by standards. Here we see a risk, rarely discussed, concerning what management systems for sustainable development actually accomplish in the interests of sustainability, if one defines sustainable development as a complex of inter-organizational, societal, and politically contested issues challenging the structures of today's society. We would like to stress the need today to ask and analyse *what doesn't fit* into the generic management systems for environmental and social issues, for example, by problematizing the concept of sustainable development.

ISO states that the ISO 14000 series is concerned with 'environmental management', meaning what an organization does to 'minimize harmful effects on the environment caused by its activities, and to achieve continual improvement of its environmental performance' (ISO 2007c). Could a different mode of asking questions regarding SD make room for other answers than those the standardized management systems offer? Today, a central question seems to be how business can minimize its negative impacts on society and the environment, logically leading to the development of voluntary management approaches, such as CSR initiatives (Doane 2005).

Problematizing the CSR standardization decontextualization

It could be argued that standardization of management processes is based on the idea of decontextualization, that is, creating distance from the activities concerned. In this case, the decontextualization by standardization concerns matters of social responsibility, which could be argued to have an inherently contextualized definition. 'How can we be sure that standardizers find the best solutions for everyone?', Brunsson and Jacobsson (2000:16) rhetorically ask. Brunsson and Jacobsson (2000) are referring to the likelihood that formal standards could be expected to spread more easily than a norm or a practice developed, over time, by social processes and that also often require special conditions to emerge in the first place. The easy adoption of a decontextualized standardized concept also comes with the risk of inhibiting innovation, freezing development in a fixed form that might be difficult to change (Brunsson & Jacobsson, 2000).

We argue that the questions asked limit, or define, the choice of possible answers. If we ask for more environmentally or socially friendly ways of doing 'business as usual', ISO 14001 or ISO 26000 become suitable tools. If we instead ask what roles companies and public organizations should play in steering society towards a more sustainable course of development, the answers would be more pluralistic and complex than those offered by decontextualized standards.

Implementing standardized management systems seems to be a process of placing the system itself in focus, as a legitimizing symbol of responsible organizational action. Operating on a systems level, sometimes constructed with auditing in mind, makes abstraction from complex environments possible, using management systems. Accounting serves to make visible a world of action and ability to control. (Power 1997) 'The verifiable assertion, and hence the audit process, can be shifted away from the complexities of natural environment impacts to the working of the management system.' (Power 1997: 86) At the same time, the actual performance or doing is not questioned; in fact, evidence of practices not working could be overlooked since the auditing itself is in focus. Relevant to this are the experiences referred to earlier, namely, deficient application of CSR codes by companies paying lip service rather than actually changing things for the better. This could in turn be interpreted within the theoretical frame of decoupling, whereby hypocrisy is the logical consequence of an organization's conflicting agendas (e.g. social responsibility versus profit), which include striving for legitimacy by becoming a 'civil' corporation (Meyer & Rowan 1977; Brunsson 2002). Against this background, ISO 26000 can come to serve merely as a decoupling tool rather than as a reforming force promoting social responsibility. It could also be argued, given that legitimacy is a driving force, that ISO seeks the participation of NGOs and labour organizations in the consensus-based standardizing process for legitimizing purposes. At the same time, these organizations and their interests get 'hijacked'[6] when standardized. The FTC, however, said that even though they are positive regarding the focus on their issues, they will leave the cooperation if not satisfied with the results (Interview, Bjurling & Lindholm 2005).

Analyzing the standardization of environmental and social issues from a different angle, the standards also addresses somewhat special questions related to SD. The management systems address and, accordingly, respond to questions of improving individual organizational performance *in* the existing systems context. That is, standardizing guidelines for building an internal system for the purpose of improving organizational routines and activities, while otherwise accepting business as usual

---

6   To use the expression of Richardsson and Welford (1997), interpreting environmental management.

6. Conclusions

Why are management systems for environmental and social issues so attractive, then? Ending in the same spirit as we began, returning once again to the world of Pippi Longstocking, we argue that the 'medusin' solution to complex social and environmental issues will be contested and further researched as practice unfolds. The interpretation here is that the ISO 14001 and the upcoming ISO 26000 standards are accepted and legitimizing ways of dealing with complex issues. The demand, or consumer side, could also be said to be interacting with the desire of the supply side of SD standardization, which comprises ISO and consultants selling management and implementation services.

So, what happens to sustainability issues when they are standardized? The standardized systems do not necessarily challenge business as usual, since in them environmental and social improvements are limited to the existing systems context, which is based on organizational rationality and a widespread popular management discourse. At the same time, something happens with the interpretation of what environmental and social issues *are*, beyond or parallel to the management activities themselves. Since the interest in sustainable development issues and CSR practices is increasing among organizations, the issues themselves seem to be regarded as of importance. The risk, though, with standardizing these complex issues is that they will become one-dimensional and oversimplified for the sake of taking some action – any action – to reverse environmental degradation and improve social conditions for employees. From a critical perspective, this 'one system fits all organizations and purposes' approach can be questioned, not only for its assumptions as to organizational rationality, but also for being 'slippery' and, more importantly, for shifting attention to a symbol away from actual results.

Appendix

GLOBAL COMPACT, CODES OF CONDUCT:

Human Rights

Principle 1   Businesses should support and respect the protection of international human rights within their
sphere of influence; and

Principle 2   make sure they are not complicit in human rights
abuses.

Labour

Principle 3   Businesses should uphold the freedom of association and the effective recognition of the right to collective bargaining;

Principle 4   the elimination of all forms of forced and compulsory labour;

Principle 5   the effective abolition of child labour; and

Principle 6   the elimination of discrimination in respect of
employment and occupation.

Environment

Principle 7   Businesses should support a precautionary approach
to environmental challenges;

Principle 8   undertake initiatives to promote greater environmental responsibility; and

Principle 9   encourage the development and diffusion of environmentally friendly technologies.

Anti-Corruption

Principle 10   Businesses should work against corruption in all its
forms, including extortion and bribery.

(UN, 2007, Global compact, Internet.)

5. Corporate Citizenship and the Citizen Consumer: Introducing the CC-matrix

JOHAN JANSSON AND JONAS NILSSON

Introduction

The last few decades have been marked by an increasing awareness and concern regarding the environment and the sustainability[1] of western consumption-focused lifestyles (Berry & McEachern, 2005; Dobers & Strannegård, 2005; Lampe & Gazda, 1995; Worldwatch Institute, 2003). Today, issues such as the use of nonrenewable sources of energy, global warming, and waste management are ever present topics. The significance of sustainability issues is becoming evident in different context and arenas, as people seem to care about sustainability as citizens, as activists, and as consumers. *Citizens* are showing interest as voters as so called green parties have been elected to represent citizens in many European countries. Interest has also fuelled movements as *pressure groups* such as Greenpeace has become more accepted in the debate on sustainability. Moreover, people are expressing this interest in sustainability as *consumers* (e.g. Gardyn, 2003; Harrison, 2005; e.g. Micheletti, 2004). Consumer concern is evident considering the recycling behaviour and the sales growth of environmentally labelled products. The amount and reach of products that have environmental labels have increased and there is evidence that some segments of consumers now prefer ecological or fair-trade labelled products when available in the market (Auger *et al.*, 2003; Creyer & Ross Jr, 1997; Roberts, 1995). In this market, concern and activities regarding sustainability has become a natural

---

1   Sustainability refers to the long-term maintenance of systems according to environmental, economic, and social considerations (Crane & Matten, 2004: 24)

part of life in the 21st century for people in the roles as citizens, as activists, and as consumers.

Given this development it is not surprising that the corporate world has responded. Nowadays, most multinational corporations claim to assume some form of responsibility for the environment, for their employees' and for their consumers (Sen & Bhattacharya, 2001). Environmental reports and impact analyses have become a natural part of most companies' annual reports (Adams & Zutshi, 2005; Hockerts & Moir, 2004; Hummels & Timmer, 2004). Even companies that are known for having a poor previous record with regards to sustainability now take responsibility for environmental and social aspects of their business operations. An example of this is Shell, that was involved in the highly publicized Brent Spar incident, and now provides environmental and social reports emphasizing their environmental performance (Wheeler *et al.*, 2002). In this way, it is not rare that companies spend millions on sustainability programs. Companies like Ben & Jerry's and the Body Shop even use social conscience as successful marketing strategies. Ben & Jerry's make efforts to use sustainable packaging, work for social and economic justice, and have partnered with organizations like Greenpeace to educate consumers of environmental hazards. The Body Shop have incorporated social values into their product line for many years and keep making widely publicized social campaigns (Mirvis & Googins, 2006).

Thus, there is little doubt that the recent years have brought changes to the corporate sector with regards to sustainability and responsibility issues. Corporations' today claim to assume responsibility with regards to environmental, economic, and social issues, usually considered to be outside of their traditional focus of profit maximization. A multitude of concepts have been used to describe this phenomenon, such as corporate social responsibility (csr), business ethics (be), and corporate social performance. One of the latest additions to this terminology is corporate citizenship (cc), which has grown to become one of the more popular concepts to describe the social responsibility initiatives practiced by corporations. Corporations that use cc principles in their terminology and communication include dhl, Pfizer, Motorola among many others. Examples of cc statements made by these companies are listed in Table 1 below.

Table 1: *The use of* CC *in practice (emphasis added)*	
COMPANY	STATEMENT
DHL (www.dhl.com)	'We believe commitment to good **corporate citizenship** is a fundamental part of achieving sustained value creation for both society and our company, and thus to ensuring the future of the work that we do... We also believe, in line with our values, that we have a **responsibility** to be a positive force in society by harnessing our core competencies in logistics and transportation to achieve social as well as commercial goals, where relevant ... At DHL, we believe that it is as important to be a **citizen** as much as we are a corporation.'
Pfizer (www.pfizer.com)	'**Citizenship** defines our role in local and global communities and how we strive to conduct business **responsibly** in a changing world... Being a good corporate citizen includes listening to, understanding, and responding to our stakeholders about their needs regarding Pfizer's policies and operations. Stakeholders are people or groups who affect, or are affected by, Pfizer's business activities.'
Motorola (www.motorola.com)	'As a global **corporate citizen**, Motorola creates products and technologies that benefit society by making things smarter and life better for people around the world. We are dedicated to operating ethically, protecting the environment and supporting the communities in which we do business.'

As displayed in the table, different companies define their CC initiatives in somewhat different ways. A more general definition is put forth by the World Economic Forum (2003) as they define CC:

> Corporate citizenship is the contribution a company makes to society and the environment through its core business activities, its social investment and philanthropy programmes, and its engagement in public policy.

Although the definition of CC presented by the World Economic Forum is accepted in some circles, a general definition of CC is difficult to find as different academics, researchers, and practitioners hold different opinions of what CC entails. In this way, some researchers largely equate CC with such concepts as CSR and BE (Carroll, 1998; Carroll, 1979). However, CC could also be argued to be different from the other concepts because of its strong emphasis on *citizenship* (Matten *et al.*, 2003). The focus on citizenship is an important distinction from the other concepts, since it refers to the political nature of the firm. In this respect, citizenship is often used to highlight the natural place of the firm in society with rights and responsibilities like that of other citizens.

Some research, however, takes this aspect of corporate citizenship further. As corporate influence could be argued to have increased at the expense of governments and private citizens, some researchers argue that the corporation plays a part in administering citizenship rights to individuals (Matten & Crane, 2005). The foundation of this perspective revolves around the argument that corporations have grown increasingly large and powerful. In doing this, the corporation is taking over some of the functions that we traditionally associate with the state, such as responsibility for worker pensions, community development programs, and support to the education system (Crane *et al.*, 2004). Thus, because of the shift in power relations among actors in the marketplace, corporations are becoming more important for citizen welfare.

This chapter is about the role that consumers play in a situation when corporations are becoming increasingly powerful and important for sustainable development. As previous research within CC could be said to be oriented mostly towards conceptual research from a one sided organizational or management theory perspective (e.g. Moon *et al.*, 2005), we attempt to focus on the role of the consumer in this context of increasing corporate influence. With a foundation in the literature on CC (e.g. Matten & Crane 2005; Matten *et al.*, 2003; Crane *et al.*, 2004) and political consumerism (Micheletti, 2004; Micheletti *et al.*, 2003), we argue that the consumer and the corporations have created a new market based arena where consumers and corporations meet. In this context, the consumer could be argued to have power as an economic voter, influencing corporations with actions in the marketplace. With these two theoretical disciplines in place, we focus our attention on what is required for sustainable development in the context of more powerful corporations in relation to governments. As a consequence of the important role of both corporations and consumers, we argue that sustainable development is more likely to be achieved if a joint responsibility for sustainability is taken by both consumers and corporations.

The purpose of this chapter is thus to address the gap on the role of the *consumer* in the cc-literature. By using the extended definition of cc and the emerging field of political consumerism we shed light on the nature of consumer influence and responsibilities in cc. We argue for the inclusion of the consumer into the theoretical field of cc as a more comprehensive way of addressing cc in particular and corporate responsibility in general.

We start by discussing corporate responsibility and the concepts of csr and cc. We arrive at the extended definition of cc as the most promising for including the consumer into the responsibility discussion. Second, we review the role of the consumer by focusing on the emerging area of political consumerism and the concept of citizen consumers. In the last section, we bring these two areas together, in what we term the cc-matrix, to highlight the responsibilities of corporations and citizens for a sustainable future.

From Corporate Social Responsibility to Extended Corporate Citizenship

Ever since the corporation was formed there has been debate on its responsibilities. Mostly these debates have been carried out from a legislative perspective focusing on what the corporations are responsible for, who they are responsible to and also what their purposes are, or should be. After the great depression in the 1930:s, citizens tried to get governments around the world to restrict corporate power, since it was a general belief that much of the problems caused in the great depression was a direct effect of corporations not taking their responsibilities seriously towards society as a whole (Bakan, 2004). This movement succeeded to some degree since Roosevelt in 1934 created the New Deal, which was a package of regulatory reforms designed to restore economic health by, among other things, harnessing the powers and freedoms of corporations. As retribution to this restriction and as a means to win back trust from the general public, large corporations themselves started to emphasize their social responsibilities and how they were better suited than large governments to care for the citizens (Bakan, 2004; Giddens, 2002). Gerard Swope, then president of General Electric, expressed a common attitude among big-business leaders when he in 1934 stated:

> organized industry should take the lead, recognizing its responsibility
> to its employees, to the public, and to its shareholders rather than that
> democratic society should act through its government
> (cited in Bakan, 2004: 19)

In spite of north American corporations already in the 1930:s promoting images of themselves as caring and socially responsible they saw their powers more restricted for many decades following the New Deal. It was not until the mid 1980:s when technology, new laws and more liberal ideologies started to reverse this trend. One reason behind this reverse is thought to be the inabilities of governments to deal with the oil crisis in the 1970:s which led to a more negative attitude in the general public towards governments (Roberts, 2005). Neoliberalism was embraced which meant that policies of deregulation and privatization were adopted by many governments (Bakan, 2004). This development together with technological innovations in transportation and communications has made large corporations multinational as they have thereby become close to as powerful as some national governments are today. This globalization of power also means (or should mean) a globalization of responsibilities and it has become the subject of many debates.

Although slow to start, when the academic debate on corporate responsibility gained momentum in the late 1970:s and early 1980:s it quickly became a growing research area with several new academic annual conferences and journals seeing the daylight. The most common concept discussed in relation to corporate responsibility is CSR. It is only in the last few years that this term has been questioned and a new concept, CC, has been introduced. In order to discuss CC it is termed important to start by first defining what the differences are between the two concepts and then by looking at how the CC literature and research relates to the consumer.

Corporate Social Responsibility

Probably the most cited conceptualization of CSR is the four-stage model developed by Carroll (1979). CSR is in this model viewed as a multi-layered concept, which can be divided into four parts: economic, legal, ethical, and philanthropic responsibilities. The economic responsibilities of a corporation are required by society in the form that companies have owners (or shareholders) who require return on investments and also employees that are dependent on the company for wages. Moreover the corporation has customers that depend on the economic value of the goods and services that it produces. The legal responsibilities are also required by society and demands that the company abides by the law. Thirdly the corporation has ethical responsibilities to do what is right, just and fair even when there is no actual law stating that they should do so. Therefore, Carroll argues that ethical corporate responsibilities are expected by society. Finally the philanthropic responsibilities of the corporation are desired by society and include actions to improve conditions for the society in which it is active. It is the two latter responsibilities that are at the heart of CSR since they define the corporation away from just mere compliance to economic and legal regulations and laws.

Carroll (1991) describes these four responsibilities as layers in a pyramid, so that real social responsibility requires the meeting of all four levels after each other. From these responsibilities comes the definition:

> Corporate social responsibility encompasses the economic, legal, ethical, and philanthropic expectations placed on organizations by society at a given point in time. (Carroll & Buchholtz, 2000: 35)

According to Carroll (1979), companies can respond to societal pressures by simply reacting, by being defensive, by accommodating and accepting responsibility, or by being proactive and thereby working to identify and meeting the social pressure before it damages the company. Many companies that have become involved in so called scandals are shifting their strategies from reaction and defence into proaction. A vivid example of this is what Shell did a few years after the Brent Spar incident in 1995. They launched a highly publicized campaign with the purpose of washing away the bad rumours and promoting a new more socially acceptable image. (Mirvis, 2000).

This proactive strategy of proclaiming responsibility can easily be mixed up with other marketing claims made by companies today, a fact often pointed out by critics. Perhaps this is one of the reasons why the concept of CSR is slowly giving away to another concept called corporate citizenship (CC).

Corporate Citizenship

The term corporate citizenship emerged mainly during the mid 1990s. Since then it has gained popularity, both from the practitioner side and from the academic ditto (Altman & Vidaver-Cohen, 2000). A joint statement by the World Economic Forum in 2002 on 'Global Corporate Citizenship-The Leadership Challenge for CEOs and boards' seem to have fuelled the interest further. Another proof of the popularity of the concept is the birth (2001) of a new journal: Journal of Corporate Citizenship. Why then has CC as a concept become so fashionable? Is it just a relaunch of the old CSR-concept in new clothes, or does it actually contain something new which warrants a new terminology?

Crane and Matten (2004) argue that there are several possible reasons why CC has become popular both in the business world and also recently in academia. According to them, the business community were never completely happy with the language surrounding business ethics and CSR since these concepts imply something that is opposed to, or even patronizing of, the way corporations do business. Similarly CSR can be viewed as something that businesses should do additional to their 'normal' activities and not something representing what they are. Since corporations in general terms are sceptical towards more regulations from government, CSR in part was seen as just an extra burden that would not contribute to the efficiency or profits of the firm. Further on, most of the terms dealing with corporation's role in society have been introduced by academics, making it difficult for the business world to accept the terminology and the foundational premises of these concepts. In contrast CC as a concept was not only coined by practitioners, it also bears a meaning that corporations have a justified place in society similar to other citizens, thus not mentioning what the corporation should do, but merely what the corporation is. This equates the corporation with other citizens and implies that a corporation has the same, or similar, rights and responsibilities as other groups and that it is intimately interlinked and dependant on other parts of society. From this understanding of citizenship, corporations have in large part set their own agenda and have started to fill the concept of being 'good' corporate citizens with content. From this the second question then arises which is how CC differs or furthers the notion from CSR. Depending on perspective CC can be viewed as both less, equivalent or more than CSR.

The Limited and Equivalent Views of CC

Ever since the debate on CC gained momentum in academic circles a concern has been the lack of a proper definition. The CC conceptualization needs to add something new to the CSR debate or introduce a new perspective in order to merit its existence. Otherwise there is a risk of just furthering the confusion with new terminology instead of clarifying it. Recently a noteworthy attempt has been made to clear up some of the differences between CSR and CC.

Matten and Crane (2005) address this issue as they argue that there are three different perspectives on CC in the current theoretical debate. The two first ones, the limited view of CC and the equivalent view, do not add anything new to the conceptualization and thereby understanding of corporate responsibility in society. The limited view of CC essentially equates CC with corporate philanthropy (see for example Carroll, 1991) and in this perspective CC is viewed as a basically economic approach of long-term profit maximization as a result of progressive self-interest. The equivalent view of CC which can be said to equate CC with CSR (for example Maignan & Ferrell, 2001) can be thought of as a rebranding or a relaunch of old ideas based on the CSR literature. Thus these two views do not add anything new besides a new terminology.

Apart from the problem of confusing the concepts with one another there is also a risk that CC is only treated metaphorically, i.e. that corporations *can be viewed* as citizens and thereby should take responsibility. However several calls have been made recently to go beyond the metaphor in order to analyse the changing role of corporations in society today from a new perspective. It is not until we go from the metaphorical sense of CC to actually discuss what CC means that we come in contact with the notion of the extended view of CC that Matten and Crane (2005) introduce.

The Extended View

The extended view of CC, which draws heavily on political science in its reference to citizenship, uses the citizen as a starting point instead of the corporation. Matten and Crane (2005) argue that in order to understand corporate citizenship there is a need to first focus on citizenship from its 'original' political theory perspective. Although there are several ways of looking at citizenship the most common one is the liberal view where citizenship is defined as a set of individual rights (Faulks, 2000). Furthermore the extended view draws heavily on Marshall's (1964) categorization of citizenship into three aspects of citizen entitlement: social, civil, and political rights. The social rights provide the individual with the freedom to participate in society and are therefore also called positive rights. The civil rights provide freedom from abuses and interference from for example the government and are often called negative rights since they protect the individual. The political rights include the rights for the individual to take part in the process of forming collective attitudes and wills in society. The main actor for all these rights is the government, which guarantees these rights for individual citizens.

When using the conceptualization of the citizen above it is hard to directly translate this framework to the corporation. In order to view the corporation as a citizen it is perhaps most fruitful to compare it to the government. For example Wood and Logsdon (2001) argue that businesses are powerful public actors that have an obligation in society to respect the 'original' individual citizen's rights. In the light of the last few decades' neoliberal wave in the industrialized world, often referred to as 'Reaganomics' or 'Thatcherism', it can be argued that multinational corporations are gaining power on account of public governments, especially in countries with less developed regulatory systems (Matten et al., 2003).

A similar argument can be made based on the decline in voting numbers across the industrialized world (voter apathy) and the sometimes radical individualism amongst citizens (Micheletti,

2002). If corporations are gaining power in comparison to normal citizens (voters/consumers) it would mean that the regulating system (governments) are using its legislative and other powers to tip the scales towards the corporations rather than the citizens.

Table 2: Three views of corporate citizenship (Crane & Matten, 2004: 64)

	LIMITED VIEW	EQUIVALENT VIEW	EXTENDED VIEW
Initiation	Voluntary	Partly voluntary, partly obligatory	Partly voluntary, partly imposed
Focus	Philanthropy, focused on projects, limited scope	All areas of CSR	Citizenship: social, political, and civil rights
Role of the company	Active, strategic focus	Rather passive, living up to demands of society	Active political; stepping in for government failure
Main stakeholder group	Local communities, employees	Broad range of stakeholders; society in general	Broad range of stakeholders; society in general
Role of self-interest	Dominant	Tolerant, but not the primary motivation	Mixture of self-interest and responsible attitude towards society
View of capitalism	Endorsing; social engagement is part of the business interest	Critical; threatening to neoclassical views of capitalism	Accepting; though using CC as a disguise for corporate power
Motivation	Economic	Ethical and legal	Economic and political
Moral grounding	No particular; 'tit for tat' appeals to economic rationality	Liberal or socialist orientation, strong reference to ethical reasoning and grounding	Grounding is not moral, but comes from changes in the political arena

It is in this context of development that corporations are coming into power and increasingly taking over the functions regarding protection, facilitation and enabling of citizen rights. This shift in favour of the corporation brings with it increased power over individual citizens, but it also means an increase in the responsibilities of the corporation. A responsibility that is much more emphasized in the extended view of cc than it is in the concept of csr (See Table 2). Thus Matten and Crane (2005: 173) define cc in this extended form as: '*Corporate citizenship describes the role of the corporation in administering citizenship rights for individuals.*'

The social, civil and political citizen rights are administered by different corporations in different ways depending on what the governments are letting corporations do. For example, corporations in countries where governments do not provide health care provide their own workers with access to the company medical centres. Corporations have also been known to influence governments to restrict civil rights of individual citizens in order to provide safe access to natural resources. Finally in the area of political rights, individual citizens can be viewed not only as voters in a democratic system but also as voters on different corporations by boycotting or purchasing products from the actors on the market. Crane and Matten (2004) thus argue that the corporation in regards to social rights takes on a providing role, in regards to civil rights, assumes an enabling role, and when it comes to political rights the corporation assumes a channelling role.

In this extended conceptualization of cc it is more apparent that corporate citizenship might be the result of a voluntary, self-interest driven corporate initiative, or of a reaction to public pressures. Crane and Matten (2004) go on to argue that in this view cc is essentially a descriptive conceptualization of what happens, or could happen, rather than a normative conceptualization of what should happen when the power-scales are tipped towards the corporation.

The extended view of cc has contributed to the view of responsibility of corporations in that it defines a clearer framework for analysing responsibilities. However, one of the problems with this conceptualization is however that it to some extent views individual citizens and consumers as passive, as it primarily focuses on the corporate role in the citizenship debate. The extended view of cc does not include a framework for how pressure can be put on corporations to take responsibility for citizenship rights, when governments fail to do so.

This issue is problematic as a power shift in favour of corporations do not only affect the relationship between the government and the corporations. It also affects the individual citizens in society. Very little attention in the cc debate has been on this changing relationship between corporations and the individual citizens. In order to discuss this relationship we argue that more input is needed from the consumer side of the equation. Therefore we now start looking at citizenship from this side.

The Consumer and Corporate Citizenship

Consumers and consumption is a key element of our economic system as this largely drives economic development. We argue that corporate citizenship, in its extended form, highlights the role of consumers as powerful actors in society. As governments' power to regulate and control businesses has decreased, corporations, NGOs, and consumers are increasingly setting the agenda for the future. In this section, the role of the consumer is addressed.

The Increasing Role of Consumerism

We live in a society which is marked by the influence of consumption. Sometimes described as a consumer culture, the age we live in is fundamentally affected by consumption as a way for people to make sense of the world. As consumers in most western countries have their lower tier physical needs already satisfied we increasingly strive to satisfy the higher order needs, such as self-actualization, through consumption (Harrison et al., 2005b). In this sense, we increasingly think of ourselves in market-terms. When we shop for clothes we spend time and energy in keeping up with fashion and trends. By doing this, we do not shop for clothes just to keep warm, but to satisfy higher order needs. Thus, shopping is much more than just buying physical objects that meet our basic needs (Princen et al., 2002). Goods are also entities of meaning that consumers use in order to understand and interpret the social realm of the world we live in. On this topic McCracken (1988: xi) argues.

> The consumer goods on which the consumer lavishes time, attention, and income are charged with cultural meaning... They [consumers] use the meaning of consumer goods to express cultural categories and principles, cultivate ideas, create and sustain life-styles, construct notions of the self, and create (and survive) social change.

Thus, consumption has moved from satisfying basic physical needs to be used to interpret the world, express our identity, and construct notions of ourselves. In the context of CC, it could be argued that social responsibility could constitute a key component in consumer efforts to develop an identity in the marketplace. Thus, consumer value does not have to occur for selfish reasons, but can arise from social responsibility and ethics (Holbrook, 1999). By consuming certain things in the marketplace, consumers can buy and support the ideals of social responsibility. Higher order needs can be satisfied by shopping for products with an eco-, fair trade- or socially responsible label. In this way, consumers can feel good about supporting social and ethical goals through their shopping behaviour.

The Base for Influence: Consumer Economic Votes

As we have established consumption as something more than merely a process to satisfy physical needs, we now focus on what role the consumer has in the extended definition of CC. As mentioned above, the extended view of CC draws from a shift in power from governments to market-based actors, mainly large corporations. In essence, this shift has reduced the influence of the political arena since governments today have difficulties solving threats and problems facing its citizens. As the political arena has lost certain influence, the power has shifted to the arena of the marketplace. However, instead of consisting of governments and citizens, this market-based arena consist of consumers and corporations. In this sense, consumers can in some respect be likened to citizens that vote on political parties as they choose what company to support (Dickinson & Carsky, 2005). Thus, consumers could be argued to be economic voters.

The marketplace today is filled with options for the socially minded consumer (Jordan *et al.*, 2004). Environmental, social, and ethical labels now exist on many products from everything from low involvement products like milk and coffee to high involvement services like mutual funds (Berry & McEachern, 2005). Even certain cars in Sweden are now termed as environmentally friendly (Bil Sweden, 2006). By choosing these products, consumers could be argued to use their influence as economic voters. Consumers choose to vote for companies that fulfil certain socially responsible criteria just as well as they choose to not vote (boycott) for other companies that are perceived as not to live up to social expectations. Several examples of this exist including how consumers now choose more locally produced food to support the local community (e.g. Cowe & Williams, 2001). Moreover, companies like Nestlé and Shell have experienced boycotts because of their perceived questionable activities (Clouder & Harrison, 2005).

Theoretical View: Political Consumerism

Little attention has been paid to the theory of consumption as voting (e.g. Shaw *et al.*, 2006). However, a continuing rise in the consideration of social responsibility among consumers and producers suggests its rehabilitation and further exploration would be worthwhile. Recently, many areas of literature have addressed the consumer in the role as an economic voter. These areas include political consumerism (e.g. Micheletti, 2003; e.g. Micheletti *et al.*, 2004), ethical consumerism (e.g. Harrison *et al.*, 2005a), and green consumerism (Peattie, 1995). All these theoretical areas recognize the role of the consumer in the marketplace albeit in somewhat different ways, as green consumerism highlight consumption for environmental aims while ethical consumerism highlights the ethical aspects of consumer behaviour. However, the theoretical viewpoint that has the most in common with CC is political consumerism as both concepts highlight the presence of an arena for citizen influence outside the traditional political sphere, something that is not a central theme of the other two theoretical frameworks. Thus, by using political consumerism as a theoretical point of departure for addressing the consumer as an economic voter it is possible to highlight the important role of the consumer responsibility for sustainable development within the context of the extended view of CC.

Political consumerism is largely the concern of scholars within political science. In terms of consumer influence as an economic voter, a key concept in the political consumerism literature is that of the citizen consumer (Micheletti, 2003). The term could be interpreted as to highlight the importance of the dual role of 'ordinary' people today. It largely refers to the notion that people can have power for change in both the market based and the traditional arenas of influence. In these different arenas citizen-consumers have the power to influence in different ways. In the traditional arena, the citizen votes, while the market based arena is influenced by consumer power by choosing to shop certain products or to avoid other products. Moreover, the term could also be used as a way to describe a responsibility-taking consumer. Citizen consumers know of their power in the market based arena and use it in a similar way as they do on election day. Micheletti (2003: 16) expands on this notion:

> When they [consumers] shop smartly they combine their role as consumers and citizens and have the potential to act as exuberant citizen consumers with the power of agents to develop new content, forms, and coalitions to solve the problems of risk society and global injustices. Their actions that combine the public role of citizens with the private role of consumers can be seen as having agency because they can help unfold new structures of operations and build new institutions to tackle global problems.

Thus, citizen consumers can be seen as having power in the market and agency for influencing society through their consumer behaviour. Therefore, we argue, the consumer has an important role in the overall governing structure. Consumers can (and have to) influence the political process by exercising their power as agents of change and this can be done by influencing the corporations.

The New Role of the Consumer

In recent years, the consumer has received a more central role in the discussion on sustainability. The area of political consumerism calls for an altered view of the consumer altogether. In the literature, consumers are increasingly taking a more important role as citizen power is decreasing and corporations are taking over some of the traditional roles of the government. The new arena is the market with a focus on the interplay between corporations, consumers, and NGOs. As governments increasingly find it difficult to address 21st century social problems, the market based arena will increasingly become more important. Hertz (2003) comments on the new role of the consumer:

> While politicians are allowing corporations increasingly free rein, and
> while traditional voting is seen to be increasingly ineffective as a means
> to political expression, shopping has been imbued with a new political
> significance. It is the most effective weapon in the armory of ordinary cit-
> izens, enabling people to press for some degree of accountability in gov-
> ernments, international organizations, and multinational corporations.
> (Hertz, 2003: 135)

One key effect of this change in power is that responsibility for
societal issues is placed upon the consumer. The consumer, who is
used to being treated as a selfish economic man are now to a higher
extent responsible for the welfare of others. As the consumers are
responsible for evaluating products and incorporating concern for
social responsibility it is important that consumers step up and
accept this responsibility in their shopping behaviour.

However, consumers taking responsibility for social, ethical,
and environmental issues is something that is still to happen on a
larger scale. Although there are educated and involved consumers,
there is a large segment of consumers that do not incorporate these
issues in their shopping behaviour (Roberts, 1995). Issues that have
to be overcome for consumers to buy socially labelled goods on a
wider scale include credibility, confusion, and cynicism (Mendleson
& Polonsky, 1995). That is, consumers often perceive shortfalls in
quality of environmentally labelled goods and there is a belief that
the labelling may just be a way of selling a product without really
doing something good for social, ethical, or environmental issues
(Crane, 2000). This is reflected in a recent American poll where
26% of non green consumers said that environmentally friendly
products were too expensive, while 12% said that the quality was
not as good as regular products (Gardyn, 2003). This fact brings
forth an important dimension of sustainability in an overall societal
perspective. Consumers have the option of choosing whether to
support sustainability or not. There are no laws or rules that require
the consumer to assume responsibility in their shopping behaviour.
Instead this has to be done in a voluntary manner. This has major
consequences as if consumers choose not to assume responsibility,
the new market based arena will not be likely to function towards
sustainable development. Thus, in terms of sustainable development, it is of importance that consumers assume responsibility and
demand accountability for the market based arena to function.

In reference to the extended view of CC, political consumerism highlights the same societal phenomenon, the change in power-relations between governments and corporations. However, while political consumerism does so from the consumer perspective, CC largely emphasizes the corporate perspective. That is, the difference between the extended view of CC and political consumerism lie largely in their emphasis. Therefore, the inclusion of the citizen consumer into CC should be a natural extension of both areas of literature. In the next section we put forth a matrix as how this inclusion of the consumer in the CC terminology could be seen conceptually.

Towards a Sustainable Future

It is our view that sustainability requires the involvement of multiple actors to be meaningful in reality. So far we have argued that the one-sided focus on corporations in the CC debate has its limits both from theoretical and empirical points of view. By explicitly introducing the consumer into the theoretical field of CC there is potential to understand how corporations and consumers jointly are responsible for a sustainable future. In this way we can combine corporate citizenship with the citizen consumer to get away from the largely one-sided view of sustainability as a corporate responsibility. Here we take the first step and highlight the importance of consumer responsibility in combination with corporate responsibility.

The CC-Matrix

In addressing the joint responsibility between corporations and consumers we put forth the CC-matrix (see Figure 1). CC in this respect is the abbreviation for both corporate citizenship and citizen consumers. The matrix has potential of clarifying the responsibilities between corporations and consumers when some power is being transferred from governments and citizens to corporations and consumers. By using the CC-matrix, issues concerning social, civil and political rights can be discussed from both an individual citizen perspective and from a corporate perspective.

The CC-matrix is a combination of responsibility for sustainable development from both consumers' and corporations' viewpoints. The issue that is highlighted in the CC-matrix is that under the new market based conditions; both these main actors have important roles in sustainability. On the horizontal axis in the CC-matrix is the CC-concept as developed in the extended view. The amount or determination of a corporation's CC activities in relation to other stakeholders can be categorized as higher or lower. A corporation with a low level of CC activities would be a firm that either expresses little consideration for CC activities or one that express consideration but do not actually manage its resources and relationships in a long-term sustainable manner. In this way, this category of companies do not assume responsibility for stakeholders or the surrounding environment from a sustainability perspective. A corporation with a high level of CC activities, on the other hand, would be a firm that accepts its role in society and conducts business in a way that considers and balances interests from all stakeholders in a long-term sustainable manner.

On the vertical axis the consumers' responsibility is illustrated. Consumer responsibility in the market based arena involves the original citizenship rights in the form of social, civil and political rights. Due to voter apathy and the increasing focus in society on materialistic values and thereto connected activities such as shopping, the most prominent change here is that the political rights of consumers can be upheld by citizens when they are acting as consumers. By using these rights, citizen consumers are viewed as economic voters by shopping products and services from responsible companies as well as boycotting products and services from irresponsible companies. Consumers can in this sense take a higher level of responsibility for sustainability by using their power as economic voters in the marketplace. However, consumers can also choose to take little or no responsibility for sustainable development in the market both as consumers and as individual voters. They can then be said to achieve a lower level of citizen consumer responsibility. Combining the two sides in the matrix produces a conceptual framework of possibilities for a sustainable future with regard to responsibility-taking by the two actors. Here, the traditional focus in the CC literature, that the corporation is the only actor to influence sustainability is challenged. Instead, by accounting for

The CC-matrix		Corporate citizenship and responsibility taking	
		High level of corporate citizenship responsibility	Low level of corporate citizenship responsibility
Citizen consumer and responsibility taking	High level of citizen consumer responsibility	Joint responsibility for sustainability ← - - - - - -	Consumer driven initiative for sustainability
	Low level of citizen consumer responsibility	Corporate driven initiative for sustainability - - - - - - →	No responsibility for sustainability

Figure 1: The CC-matrix

consumer responsibility in addition to corporate responsibility, a more comprehensive picture is painted of the possibilities of a sustainable future.

In a very fundamental manner, the CC-matrix brings up three issues regarding sustainable development. The first issue of the matrix is that there is a *joint* responsibility for sustainability. Despite the focus of previous (largely management based) literature on normative frameworks for corporations, one sided attempts of sustainability is likely to fail. Instead, many different actors have to be involved in developing sustainability. This matrix incorporates two, arguably important actors, that represent one part of sustainability. This does not mean that other primary actors such as governments and international organizations such as UN, are not important for sustainability, they merely fall outside of the model as it focuses on the relationship between corporations and consumers exclusively.

The second point brought out from the CC-matrix, as displayed by the arrows between the boxes, is that there are *continuous flows of pressure* and influence between the different actors. In the market based arena, no actor stands alone without any pressure from others. On the other hand, the actors also have power to influence other actors. This process of continuous pressure flows between actors, either in a positive (sustainable) or negative (unsustainable) direction and will be discussed further below.

The third point of the cc-matrix is that it highlights a dynamic view of sustainability in that it *does not assume equilibrium* of any powers or responsibilities. The extent of social, civil and political rights of both corporations and citizens are constantly being redefined depending on other stakeholders and on the market arena on which the pressure occurs. There is no set optimal goal in the matrix. For instance if a new sustainable energy source is discovered and commercialized the pressure will move what is considered sustainable into the future. New discoveries and technologies are thus constantly shaping the notion of possible sustainable practice at each instance in time. In reality a perfect balance between the stakeholders will be rare, as new and changing problems to assume responsibility for, will occur. Having outlined the three fundamental issues regarding the matrix, the specifics of the cc-matrix is discussed below.

Joint Responsibility – Greater Possibility of Sustainable Development

The box on the top left hand side in the cc-matrix represent an outcome where both consumers and corporations assume high levels of responsibility with regards to sustainable development. In essence this means that consumers are actively using their power as economic voters in their every-day activities. It also means that corporations accept and work actively with cc programs that, viewed in a cc perspective, play a role in administering social, civil and political rights for citizens.

As both actors in the matrix take on high levels of responsibility, the market based arena works in favour of sustainable development. Several examples can be found where corporations and consumers have used the market based arena for achieving a higher degree of sustainability, based on the knowledge at that time. In Sweden, an example of this include the fact that 45 % of all cleaning products sold are eco-labelled (Konsumentverket, 2002). As the negative effects of cleaning products became known, corporations started introducing products that limited harmful effects on the environment. Consumers currently seem to be embracing this opportunity to make a difference by choosing eco-labelled products to a high extent.

Consumer Driven Initiative for Sustainability
– Sustainable Development in Jeopardy

The box on the top right represents an outcome where only one of the actors, consumers, assume responsibility for sustainable development. In these cases, sustainability will primarily be driven by consumer citizens alone. This consumer driven initiative for sustainability is likely to arise when consumers perceive sustainability related problems that can not be addressed in their role as citizens alone. Thus, consumers have to address these issues in their role as economic voters. This initiative involves shopping goods and services from responsible companies and boycotting irresponsible companies that are not taking their responsibilities for a sustainable future. However, if responsibility for sustainability is not taken by corporations, the consumers may have limited opportunity to do this. If there are no sustainable goods and services to purchase, the consumer will have difficulty using their influence on corporations directly. Thus, sustainable development in this box is in *jeopardy*, leaning either way.

A well known example of consumer driven initiative for sustainability occurred when Shell wanted to sink the oil platform Brent Spar in the North Sea in 1995. Activist groups opposed the sinking of the platform in favour of towing the platform to land and dismantling it, and consequently started campaigning against Shell in the media and by occupying the platform. Consumers responded to the activist call by boycotting Shell gas stations. For some Shell gas stations in mainland Europe, this resulted in a 50% decrease in profits for the months of the boycott (Zyglidopoulos, 2002) In essence, Shell has been argued to have misjudged the sensibility of their customers (Mirvis, 2000). Although it is debated on what option regarding the dismantling of the platform was the best for the environment, this example is a fitting example on how sustainability could be lead by consumers as opposed to corporations. Shells president commented on this issue:

... In essence, we were somewhat slow in understanding that environmentalist groups, consumer groups, and so on were tending to acquire authority. Meanwhile those groups we were used to dealing with [e.g., governments and industry organizations] were tending to lose authority.

(Herkstroter, Shell's president in 1995 after the Brent Spar scandal, cited in Hertz, 2003: 131–132)

Corporate Driven Initiative for Sustainability
– Sustainable Development in Jeopardy

A corporate driven initiative for sustainability is likely to arise when corporations perceive benefits to acting in a sustainable manner. As corporations now, to a larger extent could be argued to find themselves in a role of being part in administering citizenship rights, these benefits can occur when corporate privileges are threatened. Different actors in society, such as consumers, NGOs and governments, will at some point demand sustainability. A corporate driven initiative towards sustainability could thus be a defensive act in protecting the role of corporations in society. However, a corporate driven initiative towards sustainability is unlikely to lead to true sustainability if consumers do not take their role as economic voters as well. Should consumers not bring benefits to the sustainable companies by purchasing goods and services, it is likely that the market based arena will not provide sufficient incentives for corporations. Therefore, sustainable development in this box could be argued to be in *jeopardy*, also.

One notable example of a corporation trying to take its' responsibility is Volkswagen that in 1993 introduced the Golf Ecomatic car on the German market. The car was designed to switch off the engine automatically when it was not in use, for example at traffic lights, and then switch it on again as a gear was used. A decrease of about 20–25 % in fuel consumption was achieved by this technology and it thus won several environmental awards. The poor driving behaviour of the car and a hefty price tag failed to attract buyers (only 3 000 vehicles were sold) although the advantages were said to outweigh the disadvantages with the car (Beise & Rennings, 2005). This can be viewed as an example of a corporation taking responsibility, but where customers do not assume theirs.

No responsibility for Sustainability – Little or no Possibility of Sustainable Development

The box on the lower right represents a scenario when neither of the actors take responsibility for sustainable development. Here, the market based arena is not functioning well. There is no interest among consumers to use their economic votes to achieve sustainable development. Moreover, there is no interest for corporations to use their extended influence to act in the way of influencing sustainability, at least not in a positive way. This results in the market based arena to work against sustainability. Thus, in this box, there is little or no possibility of a sustainable future.

Current examples from this field include the travel and aviation industry. Although the emissions of greenhouse gases from air travel is only 3 % of total greenhouse gas emissions it is the contributor that grows at the fastest rate. Since the 1960s passenger traffic has increased by approximately 9 % every year (IPCC, 1999). Largely this increase comes from the introduction of many more short flights and a fierce competition in the airline industry that drives the customer prices down. Consumers are not showing any signs of using other modes of transportation even though the awareness of the environmental problems of the airline industry is growing (Ekstrand, 2006). This is a situation where neither actor shows any interest in sustainable development. Therefore, the market based arena is not working towards long-term sustainability.

The Flows and Interaction Among the Actors

Having outlined the possible outcomes that comes from the market based arena, the focus now moves to the second major implication of the CC-matrix, the pressure and influence that the different actors have on each other. In the CC-matrix, these flows of pressure and influence are outlined by the arrows between the boxes.

There are two major flows that are highlighted in the CC-matrix. Both of these focus on the important role of the consumer in the market based arena towards sustainable development. It should be noted however that these are not the only flows of pressure and influence between different actors with regards to sustainability. Instead, these should be seen as examples of how these flows can function.

The first important pressure point lies between the consumer driven initiative for sustainability and the joint responsibility for sustainability boxes. Here, there is pressure from consumers and consumer organizations to change corporate behaviour towards a more sustainable approach. It is in this box where consumer power is needed the most and economic votes play a crucial role in managing sustainability. In this respect, boycotts and consumer activism is also an important tool for consumers to use. By using these pressure and influence points, there is a tendency for the corporation to answer to the pressure and implement a better sustainability strategy. Thus, the consumer can, by using their power in the market based arena, influence corporations toward taking more responsibility for sustainability. The example of Shell and Brent Spar highlights this pressure that consumers can put on corporations. Nowadays, Shell has one of the more comprehensive social responsibility programs, arguably because of the consumer pressure that the company has been exposed to.

The other arrow highlights what happens when the situation is reversed and the consumers show little interest to use the market for political means while corporations do implement programs for sustainability. In this case of corporate driven sustainability, there is little pressure on the companies to invest in sustainability programs. As consumers do not reward or punish corporations, the focus will be on other aspects of the product or service. Since sustainability programs cost money in the short term, there will thus be a tendency for companies to move towards the bottom right corner.

Put together, these two arrows show the importance of the consumer in taking responsibility within the framework of corporate citizenship. The consumers work as a driver and a guarantee that the sustainability programs that the corporations put forth will be achievable.

Conclusions

In this chapter we have outlined a conceptual model in which we describe the consumer inclusion into the CC debate. We think of this model as being the first step towards actively incorporating important stakeholders into CC. Since consumers are finding themselves in a new role in society we argue that consumers is the most important group among the stakeholders. We have intentionally left out governments, NGOs, and employees, to focus specifically on consumers. Furthermore, we make no claim that we are painting a complete picture as we recognize the influence of the other actors and stakeholders to the company.

There is a pressing need for future research within CC in general and with regards to the consumer influence on sustainability in particular. With regards to CC there is a need to further develop the extended view through empirical and theoretical studies. Furthermore, there is a need to look at other stakeholders and their influence on the extended view of CC. As consumers are only one of many possible stakeholders that influence corporate sustainability, there is a need to focus on other actors such as governments, employees, and NGOs. An important issue is also the interaction between these actors and corporations in forming and implementing CC initiatives.

With regard to the more specific theories addressed in this chapter, there is a need to focus on empirical data. CC in general is characterized by a lack of empirical studies. Instead, the field has been largely theory driven. In this case, there is a need to focus on consumers and their influence on CC in the corporate world. We argue that a good way of doing this is to start with the consumer side in the conceptual model. At least two issues are important to address. First, there is a need to address external effects of consumer responsibility taking. When and how do consumers actually influence corporations? Second, there is a need to look at consumer internal motivations for taking responsibility for sustainability. Why do some consumers assume responsibility while others do not? By researching these issues the area of CC can be expanded and become more empirically grounded. This research would then have the potential to further a more sustainable future for corporations and consumers.

6. Marketing to Consumers in Different Shades of Green: The Case of Chiquita Bananas/ Rainforest Alliance

HANNA HJALMARSON, MONICA MACQUET
AND EMMA SJÖSTRÖM

Introduction

In the autumn of 2005, fruit company Chiquita ran a national TV advertising campaign in Sweden to inform consumers about its certification by Rainforest Alliance,[1] an American non-profit organization working for the conservation of tropical forests. The certification indicated that Chiquita has taken measures to reduce the negative environmental impact from banana cultivation and harvesting. The TV advertisement showed animated frogs, which is the symbol of Rainforest Alliance, jumping among big and bright yellow, flawless bananas. This nature-oriented advert indicated that Chiquita bananas were environmentally friendly, and handled under responsible working conditions. Everyone did not agree with this, however. The Rainforest Alliance certification does not fulfil the EU requirements for organic cultivation. Hence, Chiquita's marketing campaign could mislead the consumers, and consumers could mistake the Rainforest Alliance certified Chiquita bananas for organic bananas. In line with this argument, the Swedish Society for Nature Conservation; (SSNC[2]), filed a complaint to the Consumer Ombudsman, part of the Swedish Consumer Agency.

At this time, there were two green labels for bananas on the market: The KRAV label issued by SSNC, which is a certification

---

1   www.rainforestalliance.com
2   http://www.naturskyddsforeningen.se/in-english/About-us/

for organic cultivation, and the Rainforest Alliance label. In other words, there were two labels, but in different shades of green.

What about the consumers then, do they also come in different shades of green? This question led us to seize the moment and collect some data from consumers in a grocery store, after the marketing campaign by Chiquita was launched.

Through a number of semi-structured interviews, we got insights into how consumers make purchase decisions when it comes to bananas, including whether they prefer KRAV-labelled organic bananas, Chiquita's Rainforest Alliance certified bananas, or another brand of banana, and why. Interviews were complemented by a questionnaire study, with the purpose to examine how consumers perceived Chiquita's campaign and if it influenced their choice of banana brand.

Our data collection enabled us to study advertising effects in a real life context, right after purchase, and moreover to get qualitative insights into consumer perceptions of a 'green' marketing campaign. We were also able to study if and how advertising effects vary with the level of environmental awareness and ad scepticism among consumers. In a wider perspective, this study thus contributes to increased knowledge about how consumers relate to potential ecological and ethical consequences when they make purchases. We are able to answer questions such as whether consumers are aware of such consequences, and whether green consumers are as sceptical to ads as previous studies indicate.

The chapter is organized as follows: First, we give brief overview of the banana market. Then a theoretical and empirical background on green marketing and green consumers follows. This background is also used to substantiate our expectations of consumers' perceptions. After this, we describe our method in further detail. We then present the results from the study, which are thereafter discussed, followed by our conclusions. The chapter ends with implications and suggestions on future research.

The Banana Market

Banana production is an area where conventional production methods have been questioned and where over time more environmentally friendly alternatives have been introduced. The conventional methods of growing bananas involve replacing the natural diversity of the rainforest by a monoculture, with harmful consequences to ecological systems. The conventional plantations also require large amounts of pesticides. Moreover, the employment conditions of plantation workers are typically considered to be poor, as they are for example often exposed to dangerous chemicals (interview with SSNC, February 2006) and have to carry heavy banana stocks across long distances, often resulting in chronic back problems (oral presentation by SSNC, spring 2005).

The negative consequences on working conditions, human health problems, and ecosystems got a breakthrough in the media in the mid-1990s, and gave banana brands, such as Chiquita, bad publicity. This was a reason for Chiquita to start working with Rainforest Alliance, to help them clean up their 'spotty' reputation.

Despite the fact that bananas cannot grow in Sweden, it has the highest banana consumption in the world per capita among import countries (Lustig 2004). Organic bananas have now been on the market for several years. If a product is to be labeled as organic in Sweden it has to be produced according to the EU legislation of organic production, and are certified by the Swedish association KRAV. KRAV is a member of IFOAM – International Federation of Organic Agriculture Movements, an umbrella organization for organic production worldwide (KRAV, 2006). According to KRAV standards, organic products are produced without the use of pesticides, fertilizers or GMOs (Genetically Modified Organisms), and certain standards for animal welfare apply such as having access to the outdoors. The farms are controlled once a year, making sure that they live up to the rules (KRAV, 2006).

At the time of this study, the banana brands available on the Swedish market were Chiquita, Dole, Baninis, Del Monte, and Fyffes. These bananas could potentially also carry the KRAV label, if they fulfil KRAVs requirements for organic production. Bananas can also carry the Fairtrade label, which certifies that certain social, economic and environmental standards have been met during production. In Sweden Fairtrade bananas tend to also be organic (i.e. would carry both the Fairtrade and KRAV labels).

Marketing Green Products

The threat of exhausting the world's natural resources, such as the rainforest, has by now been a recurrent theme in the public debate for more than three decades (Conolly & Prothero 2003; Zinkhan & Carlson 1995). An increasing number of corporations are finding a shift towards sustainable production methods is desirable both from an ethical point-of-view and with regard to long-term profitability (Doane 2005).

In many countries, Sweden included, there are now groups of informed consumers who prefer organic products due to either environmental, health, or animal welfare concerns, thus making green the offering of green products a potential competitive advantage. In the late 1980s and early 1990s, several labels signalling environmentally friendly production were introduced on the Swedish fast moving consumer goods market. Due to public concern about national environmental problems at the time, such as the use of chloride in paper production, along with increasing environmental demands, SSNC began cooperating with businesses in the labelling of Bra Miljöval,[3] which means 'good environmental choice'. Soon, other, similar labels such as Svanen[4] and KRAV followed suite (Boström 2001). These so called eco-labels have potential advantages both to businesses and consumers. From a company perspective, the eco-label legitimates its products and production methods and moreover serves as a competitive advantage to reach the green consumer. From the consumer perspective, the label serves to reduce uncertainty with regard to whether the product really is environmentally friendly, and thus guides his or her decision process when choosing between products (Rahbek Pedersen & Neergaard 2006).

According to market research, a large majority of consumers think that there are already too many eco-labels and that it is difficult to keep track of what they all mean (Rahbek Pedersen & Neergaard 2006). According to SSNC, consumers are generally able to handle no more than three eco-labels (interview with SSNC, February 2006).

The idea behind green marketing is the practice of a sustainable development, defined by the Brundtland Commission in 1987 as:

3   http://www.snf.se/bmv/english-more.cfm, 2007-04-06.
4   http://www.svanen.nu/Eng/about/, 2007-04-06.

'development that meets the needs of the present without compromising the ability of future generations to meet their own needs',
(WCED 1987, p. 43) and involving the coordination of the social,
economical, and ecological dimensions of society. The definition
of sustainable development has been criticized for being vague and
imprecise (Daly & Cobb 1994; Starik & Rands 1995), though the
vagueness has also been praised for making a consensus easier to
achieve (Reisch 1998). The fact that it is considered more important to agree than to know what is agreed upon broadens the scope
of green marketing, as even small changes reducing the environmental impact become marketable.

At the same time, products carrying an environmental label
are often seen as profitable. This is both due to the fact that some
consumers are willing to pay a higher price for environmentally
labelled products, and that green consumers are a growing segment
on the market.

However, marketing communication of eco-labels is often
scarce due to the limited resources of label-issuing environmental
organizations such as SSNC (interview with SSNC, February 2006).
According to previous research, there are a number of factors that
contribute to the success of marketing of green products: In order
to increase the sales of environmentally friendly fast moving consumer goods, marketing activities, including public relations such
as events, press, TV documentaries, etc., must inform consumers
about the relation between their own consumption patterns with
regard to individual, green products and their environmental
effects, rather than encourage a focus on price and quality aspects
(Solér 2001). But this is not enough. The additional costs of green
purchases must also be minimized. It has been argued that almost
all consumers are actually green, that is, if having the choice
between two equal alternatives where the only difference is that
one is more environmentally friendly, the great majority states that
they would pick the greener (Kardash 1974). Thus, changing consumer behaviour into more sustainable patterns should be fairly
easy when the environmentally friendly alternative is just as good,
available on the store shelf, and sold at a comparable price to other
options. When there are visible differences, differences in taste or
availability, and when the environmentally friendly alternative is
more expensive, purchase habits will be more difficult to change,

because this involves a sacrifice of money, efforts and pleasure for the consumer (Ekström & Forsberg 1999). It is important that the business infrastructure allows widely available and affordable green alternatives in order not to make the green purchase unnecessarily complicated or expensive.

The Chiquita/Rainforest Alliance Campaign

Today, there is a trend toward the highlighting of ethical and environmentally friendly practices in many companies' marketing, because CSR – Corporate Social Responsibility – schemes generally offer good PR (Doane 2005). Consequently, Chiquita has, as previously mentioned marketed the certification of its bananas by the non-profit organization Rainforest Alliance in order to inform about the company's environment-friendly production methods.

This type of marketing does not always mean that the company has changed its practices very much (Doane 2005), something that consumers consequently may be prone to suspect. Rainforest Alliance's strategy is to urge large actors to become somewhat more environmentally friendly in their production, rather than to require full organic production to be certified (interview with SSNC, February 2006). While this may be a more cost-efficient approach than a full-on organic certification in accordance with EU standards would require and hence attract more businesses to adhere to the standard, it also implicates marketing risks: The fact that Chiquita bananas do not fulfil the requirements to be sold under the well-established organic KRAV label may cause consumers to be sceptic towards the Rainforest Alliance certification and/ or think that it is a 'greenwashing' ploy on the part of Chiquita. Alternatively, consumers may begin to doubt the value of KRAV. The more competing green labels, the more difficult it becomes to keep track of what they mean and the differences between them.

Expectations About the Campaign's Effects

The above discussion brings us to some expectations about consumers' reactions to the Chiquita campaign. Ideally, a good ad or commercial ought to have positive influences on the chain of advertising effects; from conscious awareness through recognition or recall, ad and brand attitude, brand purchase intention, and eventually, purchase (Rossiter & Percy 1987). This has been found in several laboratory studies, though it has almost never been tested in the field (Obermiller & Spangenberg 1998). Nevertheless, our first expectation is that awareness of the Chiquita/Rainforest Alliance campaign has a positive influence on the attitudes to, and purchase of the Chiquita brand. Also, awareness of advertising ought to provide consumers with knowledge about the Rainforest Alliance certification label.

However, due to the complexities in this particular case, both when it comes to consumers' environmental friendliness and their potential knowledge about the differences between the KRAV and Rainforest Alliance labels, the results may not be in line with what we expect.

Green Consumers: Who Wants 'Green' Bananas?

Even though many Swedes are concerned about environmental problems and have positive attitudes to green consumption, the sales of environmentally friendly fast moving consumer goods remain low (Solér 2001), as in the rest of Europe (Reisch 1998). Even so, self-proclaimed ethical consumers ranked groceries as highly linked to environmental, human rights, and animal rights issues (Wheale & Hinton, 2007).

A large 1998 survey of Swedish consumers showed that less than 15 percent regularly purchased organic milk, meat, potatoes, or bread. The top purchase criteria for these products were taste, durability, and nutrition, whereas ecology was the least important criterion. Ecology was also more commonly associated with health than with the environment. Organic products were perceived as being more expensive than conventional alternatives, which was also the main reason for not choosing them (Magnusson *et al.* 2001).

Another study of Swedish consumers showed that the top purchase criteria for all food products were taste, quality and health. Environmental consequences on the other hand ranked in seventh place among eight candidates. When correlating these criteria with the purchase of organic foods, the correlation with health was higher than the correlation with environmental consequences, again indicating that health is a more salient reason for organic purchases than is the environment (Grankvist & Biel 2001).

In a study of CSR, it was found that other important considerations when making choices between alternative food brands are
that they come with a complete list of ingredients, are labelled with
country of origin, that the company keeps its promises, and takes
responsibility for its products. However, that they are organic or
environmentally friendly was less important to the purchase decision. Nevertheless, in order to convey the image of social responsibility, the company must also provide good working conditions and
proper animal care. Perhaps single purchases and overall corporate
image are separate entities in the minds of consumers (Stadeus *et
al.* 2004). The single purchase is governed by habit and automatic-
ity, that is, doing without thinking (e.g. Nordfält 2005). Then,
the environmental consequences may not readily come to mind
or are rationalized as unimportant in such small scale. That is, the
production process and its side effects are not considered a product
or brand attribute when making choices in the store.

Even so, there are groups of consumers who view their consumption choices as politically and/or environmentally significant
(Connolly & Prothero 2003; Rahbek Pedersen & Neergaard
2006). They believe that their accumulated purchases can influence world politics, as they perceive multinational businesses as
important political actors. Thus, they are less concerned with
price and other costs (Micheletti, Follesdal, & Stolle 2003). In
part thanks to the ease of information flow through new elec-
tronic media, consumers are becoming increasingly aware of
poor practices by companies or countries and sometimes chose to
boycott some goods for political reasons. For example, businesses
with certain countries of origin, such as French fries in the US
during the war against terrorism, French wines after the tests of
nuclear weapons in Polynesia, and South African wines during the
times of apartheid. Well-known examples of company boycotts
are Shell after sinking their oil rig Brent Spar in the North Sea
1996, and the accusations against Nike for using child workers in
their sweatshops (Doane 2005).

These examples point to an awareness of the relationships
between humans and nature, as well as to power relations within
human societies, business and politics. Many people believe that
the choice of what to buy is an easy way to state an opinion and
that a massive boycott may be a more effective road to change

than an often bureaucratic political decision process or business self-regulation.

Green consumers have been estimated to have the following characteristics (Peattie 1992): They are inconsistent in what products, and on what occasions they choose a green product. They are confused about what products that can be considered as green. Further, green consumers cut through existing market segments, and women tend to be greener. If consumers have children they become more aware of, and have a larger interest in environmental problems. The green consumers are also estimated to become more sophisticated, and gather more information and become more cynical towards green claims (i bid). They also perceive social and environmental issues to be more important than brand names (Wheale & Hinton 2007).

A problem when marketing to green consumers is that many of them dislike and/or are sceptical to marketing and marketers (Shrum, McCarthy & Lowry 1995; Straughan & Roberts 1999; Zinkhan & Carlson 1995). For example, Jonsson (2004) found that Swedish consumers adhering to the lifestyle of sufficiency or voluntary simplicity, that is, those preferring a simple life to material surplus for various reasons, had a common disregard for market capitalism and consumer culture. On the other hand, a study of Irish consumers indicated that many actually simultaneously bought an image of themselves as environmentally aware when consuming responsibly (Connolly & Prothero 2003). That is, the environmental friendly choice was to an extent symbolic and status-related in conveying them as 'better persons'. This indicates that many green consumers are perhaps still being influenced by the marketing and consumer culture rationale and are thus possible to reach with conventional marketing methods.

Expectations About the Green Consumers

Our expectations related to this are that consumers that are more environmentally conscious are more sceptic to advertising in general and are thus less likely to be positively influenced by the Chiquita/Rainforest Alliance campaign. There could also be differences between consumers in various 'shades' of green.

Methodology of the Study

Autumn 2005, the authors noticed the Chiquita/Rainforest Alliance campaign running frequently on Swedish TV. As mentioned, SSNC criticized the campaign for making consumers believe that the certification of Chiquita bananas by the non-profit organization Rainforest Alliance indicated that the Chiquita bananas were organic. Thus, this study was undertaken in order to examine consumer perceptions of this issue. At the same time, we also took the opportunity to study the chain of advertising effects in a real world, store setting. This was an excellent opportunity, since most consumer studies are measurements of attitudes and intentions, and not related directly to a purchase as in this study.

It can be noted that three banana brands were available in the store at the time. Chiquita's Rainforest Alliance-certified bananas and no-brand KRAV-labelled bananas were sold side by side in the fruit department at a similar price; Chiquita at 1,99 Euro/kilo, no-brand KRAV at 2,10 Euro/kilo. Moreover, Baninis; smaller Dole bananas in a plastic bag, were sold next to the check-out counters at 1,05 Euro/bag.

Interviews With Banana Consumers

Shortly after the end of the TV campaign, in December 2005, 41 consumers who had just purchased bananas were approached outside the check-out counters of a local supermarket in central Stockholm.[5]

We purposely approached all consumers that we saw buying bananas, and most of them agreed to participate in our study. The interviews were semi-structured and began with questions about how come they had purchased bananas today, if they had thought about the brand and if so why, if they had noticed the TV commercial and if so how they perceived it. Some consumers also agreed to be filmed. Notes were taken by hand for all interviews.

The Questionnaire

After the interview the participants were handed a brief question-naire including questions about ad attitude, brand attitude, eco-logical awareness, and ad scepticism.

5   Konsum on Sveavägen.

The questionnaire included three indexes measured on 5-point semantic differential scales:

- Ad attitude: bad-good, dislike-like, not informative-informative, not trustworthy-trustworthy, ugly-cute, not convincing-convincing.[6]

- Brand attitude: bad-good, dislike-like, poor quality-good quality, not trustworthy-trustworthy, not environmentally friendly-environmentally friendly, not ecological-ecological.[7]

- Awareness and attitudes toward the brand Rainforest Alliance: good-bad, like-dislike.[8]

Then there were a number of 5-point Likert type scale statements:

- Brand purchase intentions (with regard to the next banana purchase, as the participants had just made a banana purchase): 'Next time I purchase bananas, I (1) want, (2) intend, and (3) am likely to purchase Chiquita bananas; and (4) probably purchase another brand, namely _____".[9]

- Ecological awareness (adapted from Antil and Bennett's (1979) Socially Responsible Consumption Behaviour (SCRB) scale): 'Consumers in general think too little about the environment when making purchases', 'People worry too much about damages on the rainforest caused by our consumption' (reversed), 'I would gladly donate one week's pay to an environmental organization which I trusted', 'People should urge family and friends not to use products with negative environmental consequences', 'I would gladly pay more for ecological goods', and 'There is no major difference between ecological goods and other goods' (reversed).[10]

- Ad scepticism (from Obermiller and Spangenberg's (1998) Scepticism to Advertising Scale): 'I believe advertising is in general informative', 'Most of all advertising is truthful', 'Advertising is a trustworthy source of product information', 'I feel I have been accurately informed after viewing most advertising', and 'Most advertising provides consumers with essential information'.[11]

---

6   Cronbach's alpha was .89.
7   Cronbach's alpha was .88.
8   Cronbach's alpha was .91.
9   Cronbach's alpha was .90.
10 Cronbach's alpha was only .54 (though even if it would be slightly higher if the reversed items were removed (as is often the case), as it would still not exceed .60, we keep the summed measure as it is).
11 Cronbach's alpha was .89.

Results: Perceptions of Different Shades of Green

The results can be interpreted as if both consumers and bananas come in different shades of green.

It can be argued that consumers ought to be both behaviourally and attitudinally 'loyal' to green products in order to be regarded as dark green. However, they need not be loyal to green production for 'green' reasons. In the case of bananas, they might for example prefer KRAV bananas because they taste better or are healthier, not because of their sustainable cultivation. But either way, they exclusively buy organic bananas and will not consider other alternatives. Light green consumers are either behaviourally or attitudinally loyal to green products. In the banana case, they may buy organic bananas if they are available and reasonably priced. Yellow banana consumers do not care about brand or consider other aspects than green production more important, for example colour and price.

When it comes to bananas, KRAV bananas can be considered the dark green choice, Chiquita the light green alternative. Other, non-certified banana brands, hence non-green, can be called yellow.

Below, we describe some of our findings with regard to our expectations when it comes to different shades of green, both from the interviews and from the survey. If we detected what banana the consumers actually bought, or they told us so, we give this information in brackets, for example [Chiquita], after the quotes.

The Campaign's Influence on Purchase

The first expectation was that awareness of Chiquita's campaign would have a positive impact on consumers' attitude to the Chiquita brand and knowledge of its certification by Rainforest Alliance. It was moreover argued that the complexities in this particular case would complicate the matter.

As it turned out, consumers who recognized the campaign often related to the frog, and sometimes also to the rainforest.

Yeah, the frogs are cute, something about the rainforest, right?
(two young women buying for work)

Some of the consumers did mistake the Chiquita bananas for organic, just as ssnc feared. In this sample of 41 consumers, three took the Chiquita bananas for organic bananas.

> Yes, something far-fetched, with frogs. It should mean that the bananas were organic. [Chiquita]
> *(older man who eats bananas with ice-cream for dessert)*

> The commercial was for Chiquita, some kind of frogs that live in the rainforest. The message was that they're protecting the rainforest. That's good. The frogs are symbols of some brand, but I don't remember what it's called. I think it means that the bananas are organic [KRAV]
> *(daughter, about 10 years old, the family always have bananas at home)*

> I think they're organic, isn't that what the commercial is for?
> *(woman in her 20s, buying bananas for a friend because she took hers)*

Of the sample, 18 consumers, 44%, had noticed the commercial and consequently, 23 consumers, 56%, had not. Almost all; 17 people, 94%, of the consumers who had seen the commercial remembered the brand name Chiquita.[12]

However, only two remembered seeing another brand or label, Rainforest Alliance, and none of them remembered its full name. Hence, it seems like the label with the Rainforest Alliance certification, and the campaign did not result in consumers actively connecting Chiquita with the labelling, and it indicates that the awareness of Rainforest Alliance remains fairly anonymous on the Swedish consumer market. However, there was no difference in the attitude towards Rainforest Alliance, who most said they had not heard of. This is perhaps not surprising, given that it is an American organization.

The impact of having recognized the commercial was tested with mean comparisons with independent sample t-tests.[13] Those who had recognized the commercial had a significantly more positive attitude towards the Chiquita brand.[14] With regard to brand purchase intentions, there may have been a higher propensity to buy

---

12 $\chi^2 = 29.9$ (1), p = .000.
13 Since the variables had a normal distribution even though the samples were small of consumers who had or had not recognized it.
14 mean 3.62 compared to 3.11, $t = 1.917$ (39), $p = .010$.

Chiquita bananas among those who had seen the commercial,[15] though not significant in this sample. Moreover, regression analyses showed no significant relation between ad and brand attitude, though there was a significant relation between brand attitude and brand purchase intention of Chiquita bananas.[16]

Finally, a chi-square test showed that significantly more consumers than expected had actually purchased Chiquita bananas after having seen the commercial.[17]

Thus, it seems like campaign awareness had some effects both on brand attitudes and actual purchase.

Next, we are going to take a look at some quotes from consumers in different shades of green.

Dark Green Consumers

As previously described, dark green consumers exclusively buy organic bananas and will not consider other alternatives. In the interviews, many of the consumers were quite specific that they wanted KRAV bananas. As previous studies have indicated (Granqvist & Biel 2001), it was not necessarily because of the concern for the environmental impact from production, but rather for taste or health reasons:

> I buy KRAV bananas both for the taste and because they are organic. Quality is the determining aspect. [KRAV]
> (middle-aged woman buying bananas to eat, 'what else?')

> They taste better, it is a better production. [KRAV]
> (young woman buying bananas because they are healthy)

> I usually buy KRAV. They are somewhat more expensive, but they actually taste better. That's why I buy KRAV. [KRAV]
> (middle-aged woman buying bananas to eat)

> They taste better and are healthier because they do not use pesticides. [KRAV]
> (woman, who very often buy bananas)

---

15   mean 3.06 vs. 2.52, n. s.
16   $R^2 = .234$, p = .001, $b = .616$, $p = .001$.
17   8 compared to 0, $\chi^2 = 9.85(2)$, p = .007.

One interesting finding was also that there was no difference between men and women in the way that they related to environmental aspects in their purchase decisions. Not only a number of women, but also several men between 20–40 years old considered ecosystem and working condition influences when making purchase decisions, and they were often well informed on this issue.

Light Green Consumers

We described the light green consumers as being either behaviourally or attitudinally loyal to green produce, and may buy organic bananas if they are available and reasonably priced. An interesting finding was also that many consumers went shopping for someone else, which has already been seen in previous interview quotes. This person or these persons sometimes also determined their brand choice, which could both influence the consumers to choose organic bananas or to choose something else:

> My girlfriend complains that Chiquita are real crooks, so I shouldn't buy that brand, they destroy the rainforests and blablabla ... Thus, I buy KRAV labelled bananas. [KRAV]
> *(man in his 30s, buying bananas for his office)*

> I usually buy KRAV, but now they didn't look good, they were brown and spotty – those at home won't eat them. [Chiquita]
> *(middle-aged man buying bananas because they are tasty)*

> I want to buy organic, but now there were no KRAV bananas, so I took these Rainforest Alliance instead. [Chiquita]
> *(middle-aged woman who likes to eat bananas but complains that they hardly taste like bananas anymore)*

As noted, some interviewees were uncertain whether Chiquita bananas are organic or not. Those who thought they were not organic often judged from the colour and size rather than from the absence of a KRAV label:

> I don't think the Chiquita bananas are organic. The KRAV bananas come from Ecuador or something and they are smaller. The Chiquita bananas are large. KRAV bananas are smaller and taste better.
> *(middle-aged woman buying bananas to eat)*

> You can see if they're organic on the spots. KRAV bananas
> are spottier, so I don't think Chiquita bananas are organic.
> *(young man buying bananas for a snack)*

'Yellow' Consumers – Ignorant to Environmental Impact

Yellow banana consumers, as we describe them, do not care about brand or consider other aspects than green production more important, for example colour and price. Those consumers were not aware of and did not care if there were different banana brands on the market:

> No, I take what they've got. They've only got one kind, I thought.
> *(middle-aged woman buying bananas to eat with sour milk for a snack)*
>
> I don't think they were branded. [KRAV]
> *(young postman buying bananas because they are healthy)*

Many of the consumers considered other aspects more important than brand:

> I always choose yellow, ripe bananas
> *(middle-aged mother buying bananas for her kids)*
>
> I always take the cheapest
> *(younger mother buying bananas for her kids to take on an outing)*
>
> Brand? Colour and size are more important.
> I don't care if it is KRAV or not.
> *(older woman who buys bananas for breakfast every Friday)*
>
> I usually buy Baninis because they are next to the check-out counter
> *(young woman buying bananas for a healthy and tasty snack)*

Some of the interviewed consumers did however not give production issues much thought, as evidenced by the following quotes:

> Can bananas be organic? Isn't it all the same thing?
> *(older woman buying bananas for breakfast)*
>
> We don't buy anything that grows in the rainforest, do we? Only koala bears live in the rainforest, feeding on eucalyptus and such ...
> *(older woman making purchases for her sister)*

Even though the quote above may be an extreme example, it could be an expression of the way nature is perceived by some consumers. In film documentaries, nature is often shown as untouched, completely lacking interaction with human beings (George Monbiot, in the documentary 'The Planet'). It is presented as separate and not influenced by humans, and not influencing humans. If this image is accepted, it can be hard for consumers to relate to the ecosystem-impact of their purchase.

The not so ad-sceptical Environmentalists

The next expectation was that ecological awareness would be positively related to ad scepticism, that is, that the ecologically aware consumer is also more sceptical to advertising. A correlation analysis of this sample however shows that the consumers with a higher score on environmental awareness were no more sceptical towards advertising than the others.[18] In fact, the two constructs do not seem to be related at all in this study.

In order to examine the expectation that ecologically aware consumers were less likely to have noticed and be positively influenced by the Chiquita/Rainforest Alliance campaign, we first divided the sample according to their level of ecological awareness. Because the majority of participants had a positive attitude to ecological values,[19] it was decided to let those with a mean less or equal to the scale mid-value 3 constitute the less ecologically aware group, whereas those with a mean above 3 were counted as more ecologically aware. Still, the distribution was very skewed, with only 7 respondents in the less ecological group and 34 counting as more ecologically aware. Chi-square tests showed that there were no differences in the attention of and attitude to the ad between more or less ecologically aware consumers. However, independent samples t-tests showed that the more ecologically aware consumers had a significantly less positive attitude to the Chiquita brand,[20] and that even though not significant their brand purchase intentions were lower.[21] However, there were no

18 $r = .-043$, n. s.
19 sample mean = 3.79.
20 mean 3.28 vs. 3.81, $t = 1.972$ (14), $p = .069$.
21 mean 2.70 vs. 3.38.

differences in actual brand purchase, according to a chi-square test.

For the examination of the expectation that consumers more sceptic to advertising would be less likely to have noticed and be positively influenced by the Chiquita/Rainforest Alliance campaign, we divided the sample according to the same principle as above,[22] ending up with 8 respondents as less sceptic and 33 as more sceptic. Here, a significant difference was again found for brand attitudes, with more sceptical consumers being less positive towards the Chiquita brand.[23] Though not significantly, they also had a lower brand purchase intention.[24] Interestingly, the more sceptical consumers also were significantly less prone to have actually purchased Chiquita bananas.[25]

Some consumers spontaneously added that they hadn't seen the commercial because they intentionally avoid TV commercials:

> No, I don't watch during the commercial breaks, they're so bothersome.
> *(middle-aged mother buying bananas for her daughter who eats them slanted in sour milk for breakfast)*

One consumer even had a personal strategy to make sure that she did not watch any commercial on TV.

> I haven't seen any commercials because when there is a commercial break, I turn off the TV and leave the room.
> *(woman in her 60s, buying bananas to eat)*

The Counter-Campaign Strikes Back

Some of the consumers had noticed the complaint against Chiquita by SSNC, and a few consumers specifically avoided Chiquita bananas. SSNC did not only complain to the Consumer Ombudsman, but also wrote about this issue on its homepage, in mail-news and in the magazine that is distributed to its 570 000 members.

22   the higher the scale mean, the less sceptic to advertising, sample mean 2.41.
23   mean 3.23 vs. 3.95, $t = -2.986$ (20), $p = .007$
24   mean 2.72 vs. 3.21
25   $\chi^2 = 5.18$ (2), $p = .075$

Even though they did not explicitly mention that they were aware of the SSNCs information on the difference between organic and Rainforest Certified bananas, some interviewees took a sceptical stance towards Chiquita.

> Yes, the frog. The message is that they are supposed to be environmentally friendly. But then I read that they hadn't done very much. I suspect they are not organic.
> *(man in his 30s, buying bananas for his office)*

> I don't care what brand, but I avoid Chiquita due to poor working conditions. That's more important than the environment to me.
> *(young man buying bananas for a snack)*

Sometimes the reluctance and boycott against Chiquita depended on someone in the social network who influenced the purchase. The previously quoted man, who told us that his girlfriend says that Chiquita are real crooks, is an example. Thus, both the Chiquita and SSNC campaigns appear to have had some effect, but in different ways: At the same time as the Chiquita campaign seems to have positively influenced customers who did not relate their purchase to ecosystem impacts and working conditions, the counter campaign by SSNC led environmentally aware consumers to have an unfavourable image of Chiquita.

Discussion – from Yellow to Light Green

To sum up the results, it seems like awareness of the Chiquita/ Rainforest Alliance campaign in terms of ad recall and recognition was associated with higher brand attitudes towards the Chiquita brand, but had no influence on the knowledge of or attitudes towards Rainforest Alliance. This was perhaps because Rainforest Alliance is an American organization and as such, previously unknown to most Swedish consumers.

Moreover, awareness of the campaign was associated with having actually purchased Chiquita bananas, and perhaps, though not significantly in this sample, with future brand purchase intentions. It thus seems like the campaign had some effects, even though it should be noted that less than half of the banana purchasers that participated in our study had even noticed it. Alternatively, it may be that consumers who already had a positive attitude to the Chiquita brand were more receptive to the commercial.

According to the interviews, you would not think that the campaign had any influence at all, since most consumers claimed that brand was unimportant and other factors, such as colour, size and taste, were more important. This highlights the importance of using indirect measures such as surveys, rather than only direct questions, in order to gauge the influence of advertising, which is probably often unconscious. On the other hand, the semi-structured interviews with consumers gave interesting information about the consumers purchase decisions. Hence, the two methods, questionnaire and interviews, are complementary and can fruitfully be combined.

The previous findings of an association between ecological awareness and scepticism to advertising (Shrum, McCarthy & Lowry 1995; Straughan & Roberts 1999; Zinkhan & Carlson 1995) could not be replicated in this study. The spread of the variables was actually quite small,[26] which may be a partial explanation. If almost all consumers are environmentally friendly and sceptic to advertising, the lack of variation will cause a low correlation.

Another finding that was not confirmed in this study was that women should care more about ecosystem and working condition impact than men (Peattie 1992). There were actually just as many men who considered those issues related to the purchase. It might be that the perception of women as more environmentally friendly is based on measurement of attitudes instead of explaining the actual purchase, as in this study.

As the ecological awareness was not related to purchase, it can also be superficial and due more to social desirability than actual concern. As been stated before, attitudes and stated intentions are not automatically transformed into action, since the purchase intentions of environmental purchase are fairly high at the same time as the actual purchase of those products is rather small (Solér 2001). This considerable difference between stated purchase intention of green products and the low rates of consumers who in

26   s = .75 vs. 76.

reality buy those products has been called the halo effect (Webb & Mohr 1998), and is a true hindrance towards an extended green market. It was the yellow consumers, those ignorant towards ecosystem impact, who bought the light green bananas, Chiquita, even though one consumer saw Rainforest Alliance as the second best alternative.

However, it was found that the dark green consumers, as well as the consumers more sceptical to advertising, had a more negative attitude towards the Chiquita brand. The consumers more sceptical to advertising moreover had a lower, actual purchase frequency of Chiquita bananas.

The interviews also indicated that some consumers explicitly avoid Chiquita and that even though there were varied opinions on whether the campaign implied that Chiquita bananas were now more environmentally friendly, many consumers preferred the organic option KRAV. Counter campaigns by CSOs – Civil Society Organizations – can have a severe impact on consumer perceptions of a product. As noted about green consumers, they are getting more sophisticated and are sceptical towards green claims (Peattie 1992).

Even though most consumers support environmental values as long as it does not imply any extra costs, the green consumers, who purchase KRAV bananas are fewer, and even so, the light green consumers would not buy them if they really were green, in the sense of unripe. That is, they often put price, appearance or taste before ethical concerns. This is supported in previous research, where green consumption is still rather rare in comparison with other consumption styles (Autio 2004; Cooperative Bank 2004; Roper ASW 2002; Solér 2001; Magnusson et al. 2001; Grankvist & Biel 2001). Whether consumption is rational, economical, or hedonistic, it generally shares the basic rationale of value for money on the individual level, with no regard for environmental consequences or producers' working conditions, at least not at the point of purchase. Working conditions are by most consumers ignored as are potential concern of negative ecosystem impact. Many consumers do not reflect on the effects of their consumption on the environment or on other peoples' lives, and perhaps, neither do they want to know.

An example of a product, where this seems to be the case, is bananas according to this study.

Bananas, as most everyday food products, are a low involvement category to most consumers, that is, there are neither social nor economic risks associated with the individual banana purchase. The potential environmental risks are seemingly far away, not least geographically. This means that ad processing is likely to be peripheral (Petty & Cacioppo 1986) explaining why several respondents were uncertain about the campaign's message. There was also a long time delay between the extensive critique about unacceptable working conditions and severe negative ecosystem impact, and the launch of the Rainforest Alliance certification. Nevertheless, it seems like the sheer awareness of the campaign, regardless of the degree of thorough elaboration, had some positive effects for the Chiquita brand, as brand attitudes, actual purchase, and perhaps future purchase intentions as well were higher among those who had paid attention to the marketing campaign. So even if Chiquita tried to inform consumers about the connection between their purchase and ecosystem impact, as suggested by Solér (2001), the consumers purchasing the Chiquita bananas did not seem to be aware of this connection.

SSNC argues that there is a risk that the introduction of the Rainforest Alliance certification erodes the meaning of the KRAV label and makes sustainable production less valid as a sales argument. For example, within SSNC, not even organic production methods are said to be sustainable, as sustainable production is an ideal that has not yet been reached, whereas Rainforest Alliance is marketed as a label signalling sustainable production in the US, with no objections. Moreover, in the coffee industry, Gevalia, the major coffee brand in Sweden, is, at the time of writing, about to market its organic coffee with both the KRAV label and the Rainforest Alliance label, further confusing the meaning of the two labels (interview with SSNC, February 2006). Perhaps in part due to the fuzzy definition of sustainable development (Daly & Cobb 1994; Starik & Rands 1995), some people in our study seem to believe that Chiquita bananas are now organic even though they are not KRAV labelled. Additionally, Chiquita bananas are perhaps in general larger and less spotty than KRAV bananas, although we noticed no apparent differences, which might cause consumers to believe that they can now buy flawless bananas that are still organic.

Whereas bananas, as mentioned, today are a low involvement category to most consumers, for the environmentally aware, the involvement level might be higher, as they have knowledge of the environmental risks associated with conventional banana growing. To them, the production process has become an important product attribute, an actual part of the product. In order to encourage more environmental friendly consumption, other consumers might need to be reminded of the long-term, harmful effects to the global environment from their own, accumulated consumption. This is not evident, or perhaps blocked-out, in everyday purchasing. Previous research shows that so called perceived consumer effectiveness, that is, the belief that individual purchases may have environmental or social impact was the main predictor of environmentally conscious consumer behaviour. This provides an alternative and less misanthropic explanation to the lack of actual eco-label purchases despite an outspoken environmental concern than sheer cost considerations. Perhaps it is not only because the less environmentally friendly alternative is often cheaper that it is chosen, but also because the consumer perceives that his/her purchase has no impact anyway. Thus, it is recommended that marketing explicitly and clearly shows how individual purchases have actual impact on environmental or social concerns (Roberts 1995; Straughan & Roberts 1999). The TV commercial informed consumers that 'we, Chiquita, care about the rainforest'. Perhaps it would have benefited from more explicitly pointing out how the consumer cares about the rainforest by purchasing Chiquita bananas. Moreover, in order to communicate such information, a cute frog in a TV commercial is perhaps not the best method, as such a strategy is more low involvement/transformational than high involvement/informational (see Rossiter & Percy 1987). Instead, print advertising with written information might be better. As it turns out, Chiquita has also produced brochures with such information, available in stores. Though, judging from the results of this study, they have not caught consumers' attention.

Conclusions – Different Shades of Green

Our findings in this study of perceptions of bananas confirm that consumers come in different shades of green, here termed light and dark green. The dark greens however, buy organic bananas for different reasons. It could just as much be for health or taste reasons, as environmental concerns. Hence, green consumers seem to be a heterogeneous group and not a collection of people in a well defined segment. The dark greens, that is, the consumers buying organic bananas on a regular basis are aware of the meaning of organic production, and rely strictly on the KRAV label. The consumers who mistook the Rainforest Alliance brand for organic did not belong to this category of consumers, and were not primarily interested in organic bananas.

Hence, for the dark green consumers, the Rainforest Alliance label does not seem to be a threat to the Swedish organic label KRAV. For the light green consumers, there might be a risk of misunderstandings, but they will at least buy light green bananas. For the yellow consumers, finally, advertising the Chiquita/Rainforest Alliance connection may cause them to make a light green choice, whether or not they are aware of its ecosystem consequences.

The organization Rainforest Alliance is a fairly anonymous player on the Swedish market, and therefore the label does not communicate any values or inherent qualities, at least not yet. The campaign by Chiquita tried to combine the Chiquita brand with the rainforest and the frog. This message did reach the consumers who recalled having seen the campaign, and a larger part of the consumers having seen the campaign bought Chiquita bananas. Our conclusion is that, Chiquita strengthened their relationship with its present consumers through the campaign, and in that sense they might have avoided loosing customers to another banana brand or to the organic banana market. In other words, the campaign resulted in a message that communicated 'Our bananas might not be dark green, but at least light green'.

Implications

Companies with global strategies must be aware of, and will have to react on local variations in demands from consumers, and civil society organizations' judgement of what a responsible product is. The Chiquita bananas are in some countries sold as 'sustainable bananas', a name that would likely lead to a complaint on the

Swedish market. Chiquita's campaign led to a counter-campaign of the well established civil society organization SSNC in Sweden, and that campaign also had an impact on the consumers' preferences.

If Chiquita is really making an effort to produce in a more environmentally friendly manner, they should probably try to fulfil the requirements of organic cultivation for all of their bananas. However, changing from one production system to another can be a fairly long step, and in a free market economy the consumers' choice of products sends messages to the producers and brand owners.

The study also shows that many purchase decisions depend on one product as complementary to other products and in relation to people in the consumer's personal network, both for whom the purchase is made, for example children, and other people's perceptions of the purchase in the personal network. This differs from surveys on attitudes towards a product only relating to the consumers own preferences. Because the interviews where made, and the questionnaire filled in, right after the purchase of the product, the consumers relate to the actual setting in which the purchase was made. This more complex picture of the purchase decision means that marketing to green consumers must be more perceptive to the different shades of green, instead of relying on fairly simple ideas about individual green consumers' purchase attitudes.

Future Research

Our study suggests that more research is needed on what consumers in different countries really mean by 'environmental friendly' and 'sustainable' production. Does it imply that absolutely no poisonous substances are used or is it enough to follow established rules and regulations? And how do consumers interpret different environmental labels, such as KRAV and Rainforest Alliance? It is possible that the meaning of Rainforest Alliance and the differences between KRAV and Rainforest Alliance will become clearer with time, as more products or brands are certified. But it is also possible that there will be increased confusion on the different shades of green.

7. Aesthetic Consumption. A Dilemma for Sustainable Development and Corporate Social Responsibility?

PETER DOBERS

Introduction

In 2005, I had an article with Lars Strannegård in *Business Strategy and the Environment*: In that article, we explored design, lifestyles and sustainability and concluded with the notion that aesthetic consumption in a world of material abundance is highly problematic and might pose a dilemma for sustainable development and corporate social responsibility (Dobers & Strannegård, 2005).

In this chapter I want to explore this notion even further. It has a two-folded aim: First, I bring in some insights of Hans Rosling, a professor in public health science, that our world has indeed become a better place today, than it was in 1962, pretty much thanks to the fact that the population explosion has *not* taken place as anticipated back in the 1970s (Meadows, Meadows, Randers *et al.*, 1972). My point by bringing up his illustrations is that we will see many more persons to be able to consume beyond needs and follow their desires and sometimes addictions. Second, I bring in the notion of design, aesthetics and style and link that to sustainability. And by bringing them together, we have an interesting situation for us to study more in depth, especially out of the perspective of corporate social responsibility.

Population Growth and the
Illustrations of Hans Rosling

Hans Rosling was appointed professor in 1997 in international public health science at the Karolinska Institute in Stockholm and is currently active at the Department of Public Health Sciences. Although his research concerns the links between poverty and health in rural Africa, he has become well-known beyond the academic contexts through his presentations debunking taken-for-granted myths about the developing world in the 'south and east', which is no longer worlds apart from the economic power and lifestyles issues of the developed countries in the 'north and west'. Most of these countries of the so called developing world show similar trajectories toward health and material wealth as the countries in Europe or North America for instance; moreover, many countries move twice as fast as countries in the north and west have had.

When I first heard Rosling presenting his thoughts I had my perspectives shifted and my research writing have somewhat changed due to his presentations. It is not only his observations of economic and social trends based on large databases that are impressing, but his way of presenting them. He has been responsible for developing a software free to use for all that presents data such as average length of life, infant mortality rate, number of child birth per woman and the economic growth in most dynamic and interesting ways, as opposed to the static slides we all have come to know.

The non-profit organization of Gapminder[1] has developed the Trendalyzer software that has been supported by SIDA, the Swedish International Development Cooperation Agency with about 15 million SEK enabling SIDA to use Gapminder software to illustrate how far the world has come in achieving the Millennium Goals. This cooperation ended in March 2007 when Trendalyzer was sold to Google,[2] making it available to millions around the world.[3] Rosling has co-founded *Médecines sans Frontiers* in Sweden and has become a member of the International Reference Group of the Swedish Academy of Science.

1   http://www.gapminder.org
2   http://googleblog.blogspot.com/2007/03/world-in-motion.html [Accessed on
    April 13, 2008]
3   http://tools.google.com/gapminder/

Trendalyzer and Rosling's presentations visualize solid statistics in exceptional ways including many data from United Nations and the World Health Organization. The software turns development statistics into coloured and moving bubbles and flowing charts that make complicated global trends comprehensive and somewhat playful. An excellent tool in research. Having Google take over the software, Rosling's vision of having public statistics free, searchable and understandable has been realized that has also won him many prizes, both internationally and nationally.

One of his claims in his lectures is that the main problem to an evidence-based view of the international health situation is the division of countries into developing and developed countries (or under-developed and industrialized countries). Instead, we should move beyond the rhetoric of a duality and leave illustrations of countries as belonging to one of two groups behind in favour of a health view in which many countries can be found on a continuum within a wide disparity of previously developing or developed countries. Rosling thus promotes an evidence-based view on international or global health instead of relying on the colonial concepts of 'we' and 'them' and finds it somewhat surprising that basic facts about the world health remains unknown to large audiences (Rosling, Lindstrand, Bergström, *et al.*, 2006).

The bubble map of figure 1 below shows the world in 1962 according to two dimensions of all countries. The *lying axis* shows the dimension of child deaths before the age of five years in per cent that is a signifier of economic development of having the money to afford soap and the most basic hygienic products on an individual level and a basic health care of infants and young children on a societal level. The *standing axis* shows the dimension of the fertility rate of how many children per woman are born that is a signifier of human development and equality between men and women.[4] Each bubble is a country and the size of the bubble corresponds to

4   In his talks Rosling often uses quite colourful languages and he illustrates these dimensions by using two rooms available to most people living in material wealthy regions of the world: the bathroom and the bedroom. While economic development is illustrated by having soap and clean water in the bathroom he illustrates the human development and equality by pointing to the bedroom while stating that 'if women had a say about what was going on in the bedrooms in 1962, then would not so many children be born, least to say 'produced' since women took care of family and the children'.

the size of population in each country. The colour of the bubbles corresponds to continents: Africa: turquoise. America: green. Arab States: orange. Asia: red. Europe: blue (see also figure 2 below). The largest bubbles in the middle of the top row represent China and India with family sizes of six to eight children and a child death rate of more than 20 per cent before the age of five years.

The industrialized countries were at that time down to the left: A woman had less than four children and the children death rate before the age of five was less than ten per cent. The developing countries were up to the right: A woman had more than five children and the children death rate before the age of five was well above ten per cent. The question Rosling then asks is: 'Have things become better in developing countries since 1962? – Has the world become a better place?'

In 2003 we have a completely different world! Just look at the difference between figure 1 and figure 2: In 2003 China had less than two children per woman. Some countries in Europe had about one child per woman, and still a few die before the age of five. The *explosion* of population that was so much anticipated in late 1960s (Meadows, Meadows, Randers *et al.*, 1972) has not taken place. According to the Rosling's numbers, the population is still growing, but at a much smaller rate than only two generations ago such as in the 1960's (Rosling, Lindstrand, Bergström *et al.*, 2006).

Population Growth and Economic Development

According to the numbers of Rosling most countries in Asia, Latin America and the Arab world today have small families and child mortality is low. Many developing countries of the 1960s have become industrialized countries in the 2000s. Today they export bicycles, TV-sets, clothes and shoes and consume the way as we are. My point of bringing up some statistics from early 2000 is that the economic development that lies behind the child mortality rate enables many people in the formerly developing countries to consume in the same way as people have in the so called industrialized countries. It is often said that 'An average Chinese family consumes a fraction of what an average American family consumes'. How true this may be, it is also interesting

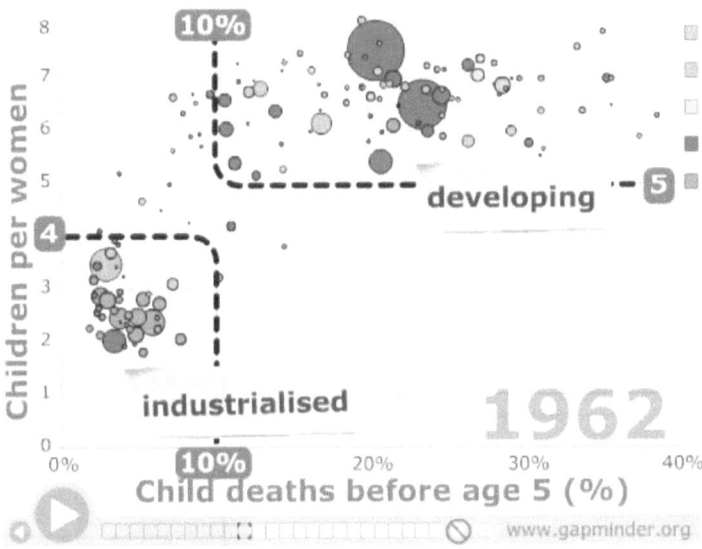

Figure 1: Hans Roslings bubble map showing world health data from 1962.
© Gapminder. Used with kind Permission from Gapminder
(www.gapminder.org).

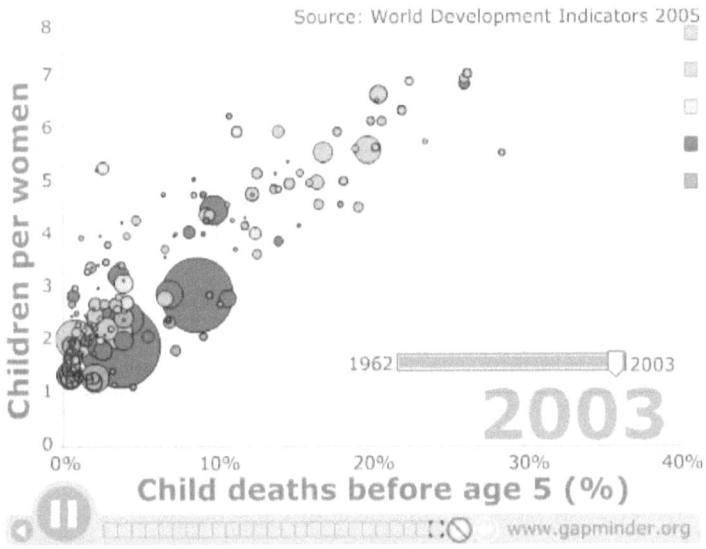

Figure 2: Hans Rosling's bubble map showing world health data from 2003.
© Gapminder. Used with kind Permission from Gapminder
(www.gapminder.org).

to ask 'Which consumer group will grow faster?' Let us look at
some statistics from Matthew Bentley, a former UN Environment
Programme consultant in France as quoted in the introduction to
the 2004 State of the World Report by the Worldwatch Institute
(Gardner, Assadourian & Sarin, 2004).

Table 1: Share of world private consumption expenditure and share of world population by region, 2000 (Gardner, Assadourian & Sarin, 2004)

REGION	SHARE OF WORLD PRIVATE CONSUMPTION EXPENDITURES (%)	SHARE OF WORLD POPULATION (%)
United States and Canada	31.5	5.2
Western Europe	28.7	6.4
East Asia and Pacific	21.4	32.9
Latin America and the Caribbean	6.7	8.5
Easter Europe and Central Asia	3.3	7.9
South Asia	2.0	22.4
Australia and New Zealand	1.4	4.1
Middle East and North Africa	1.4	4.1
Sub-Saharan Africa	1.2	10.9

Private consumption expenditures have four doubled since 1960
that is the amount spent on goods and services at the household
level that topped $20 trillion in 2000, up from $4.8 trillion in
1960 (in 1995 US dollars). Some of this fourfold increase occurred
because of population growth, but much of it was due to advancing
prosperity in many parts of the globe, just as the Rosling figures
have illustrated. These overall numbers show enormous disparities in spending; the twelve per cent of the world living in North
America and Western Europe account for 60 per cent of global
private consumer spending, while the one third living in South Asia
and sub-Saharan Africa account for only 3.2 per cent. What these
numbers do not show however is that great inequalities within each
region exist. The wealth and consumer spending in East Asia and

the Pacific for instance is to a high degree distributed to a minority of their population.

COUNTRY	PEOPLE IN THE CONSUMER CLASS 2002 (MILLION)	SHARE OF POPULATION (%)
Table 2: The 'global consumer class'. Absolute number of people in the consumer class and share of population in different countries by 2002 (Gardner, Assadourian & Sarin, 2004)		
United States of America	242.5	84
China	239.8	19
India	121.9	12
Japan	120.7	95
Germany	76.3	92
Russian Federation	61.3	43
Brazil	57.8	33
France	53.1	89
Italy	52.8	91
United Kingdom	50.4	86

Furthermore, Matthew Bentley has described the existence of a what he calls the 'global consumer class' (Bentley, 2003). This class is characterized by people having incomes over $7,000 of purchasing power parity (an income measure adjusted for the buying power in local currency). Although the 'global consumer class' itself ranges widely in levels of wealth, its members are typical users of televisions, telephones, and the Internet, along with the culture, ideas and life styles of for instance leisure, travel, cars and fast food that they transmit including all the implicit sustainability problems that go along.

This 'global consumer class' totals some 1.7 billion people—about a quarter of the world population. In the table 2 above we see a few large countries, their 'global consumer class' in absolute numbers and in per cent share of population. Not surprisingly, countries like USA, Japan and the larger European countries top the list in terms of a large share of the population belonging to the 'global consumer class'.

More interesting is that almost half of the 'global consumer class' lives in developing nations, with China and India alone claiming more than 20 per cent of the global total. And most interesting is that the growth of the 'global consumer class' will take place in these countries, where the share of people in the 'global consumer class', of the total population, is still very low (19 and 12 per cent). The current numbers would look much different since the economic growth in these two countries have been unparalleled in the beginning of the 2000's and the 'global consumer class' in China has certainly left their equivalent in USA far behind. In fact, the combined 'global consumer class' in China and India of more than 360 million people (probably 400 million at the beginning of 2010s) is larger than this class in all of Western Europe (although the average Chinese or Indian member of course consumes substantially less than the average European).

The growing 'global consumer class' shares our consumption habits in a material sense. But what I want to illustrate further below is that design, fashion and aesthetics play an increasingly important role in our societies in general and for the 'global consumer class' in particular.

Design and Fashion of Products

Some products are designed in ways that many people recognize them as designed; when looking at highly designed furniture for instance, you could hear someone say, 'Wow. This lamp is cool! It has some really hot lines'. Those are typical remarks for things being designed. That is how we hear about design in everyday life, journals and TV shows. Thereby, good design is a product that someone thinks is beautiful, cool or hot. Design is something that *looks* styled. It has to do with the outside, with the external appearance. According to Wikipedia,

> Design, usually considered in the context of applied arts, engineering, architecture, and other creative endeavours, is used both as a noun and a verb. As a verb, 'to design' refers to the process of originating and developing a plan for a product, structure, system, or component. As a noun, 'a design' is used for either the final (solution) plan (e.g. proposal,

drawing, model, description) or the result of implementing that plan (e.g. object produced, result of the process).[5]

This description shows that design is a result of that someone has thought, planned, and has intended to do something. Such a definition helps create consent on one level, but it hides the fact that design has many perspectives to it, many meaningful threads that weave an interesting network of perspectives. And all these perspectives help explain why the interest in design has increased so much lately. For instance, design can be related to a product when thinking of a chair, a car or a wine glass. Design can be related IKEA in flat packages from production to point of purchase or even to your home destination. Design can also be related to ecology and technology when thinking of different types of cars that have more or less an environmental impact. There are many more perspectives of course, but I would like to point to the relation of expressivity and identity when considering design.

These should not be underestimated. Design is in many aspects a matter of people wanting to express themselves, both as a designer and as a consumer. When thinking of the many brands surrounding our social lives, design has become an important identity marker. Now. Aesthetic ideals and design have always been formed by a cultural elite: In the 18th century there was a chain of translations from the Royalty, aristocracy, the high nobility, and then to the rest of the people. And that is just as it is today: the well-informed design-interested people in media and art industries lead the way before the uninterested mass consumers, the mass market. Mass markets of today are saturated markets and thus subject to fierce competition. Products are equal to each other in a technical sense, and often industrial production has been able to cut large costs through increased work specialization, mechanizing, mass production. As an example, it is said that in 1986 it took 100 hours to assemble a Saab car compared to the 30 hours to assemble a Saab car twenty years later and 20 hours to assemble a Toyota car.

It seems as if the most cost cutting lies behind, and that car makers need to charge their offer with other values that increase brand value and sales revenues instead, such as with emotion, ethics,

---

5   As retrieved on August 22, 2008 at http://en.wikipedia.org/wiki/Design.

aesthetics and epic (Strannegård & Salzer-Mörling, 2004): a) *emotions* that products or companies evoke such as Porsche or Alessi; b) *ethics* that actions and communications of values that companies stand for such as The Body Shop or Paul Newman; c) *aesthetics* and an aesthetic experience on behalf of the consumer that a certain company or product evokes such as Apple, iPods, iPhones or iPads and d) *epic* and a story of the company that can be offered that strengthens the consciousness of sustainability aware consumers such as Patagonia or Ben & Jerry's.

Ethics, emotions, aesthetics and epic are illustrations of how design can contribute to upgrade an offer of products with similar functions, but different design to them. For industry, businesses focus more and more on revenues, because the cost side is not enough to create profit. The large margins can be created with ethics, epic, emotion and aesthetics. And design is the tool by which these offers differ from the mass.

One illustration of how design and branding can increase revenues is that of toilet brushes. Alessi has once said: 'People have an enormous need for art and poetry that industry does not yet understand.' The toilet brushes of this producer are made of happy coloured plastics with fun forms and thus differ widely from the most simple toilet brushes in white plastic that can be found at IKEA for instance. The price also differs hugely: at IKEA you can buy VIREN, their cheapest toilet brush, for only 8 SEK, while you pay more than 600 SEK for the designed version from Alessi.

Design and Fashion of Architecture and Interior Decoration

In this context of design and aesthetic consumption it is further interesting to see how architecture and design melt together in the land of consumption. I showed a slide of an Issey Miyake shop in New York, designed by Toshiko Mori, professor in architecture at Harvard. This example illustrates an interesting web of connected brands like i) clothes designed by Issey Miyake, ii) shop decoration signed by Toshiko Mori, and iii) the academic chair signed by Harvard School of Business. This co-branding process is commented by a colleague of Mori at Harvard, professor Rem

Koolhaas, whose idea is that shopping and commercial interest are the driving forces of design (Koolhaas, Chung, Inaba *et al.*, 2001b; Koolhaas, Chung, Inaba *et al.*, 2001a; Koolhaas, Hommert & Kubo, 2001). Shopping has infiltrated, colonized and in many ways replaced public life. City centres, suburbs, streets, airports, hospitals, schools and the Internet are formed by shopping. Shopping is not an activity in the city, but it is the essence of the city. Shopping is not enabled by the city, but it is the core of constructing the city.

Koolhaas observes that there are two things that have reformed commercial life in the last century. First, we have a designed climate. Flaneurs and consumers are willing to stroll in attractive, weather protected and well tempered indoor environments. If you are not protected against heat or cold, against rain or sun, then you are much less inclined to be out for a stroll. So, shops and malls have to be designed to protect consumers from all of the above to make them shop in the stores. But this is no new venture. Bazaars and arcades have been around for far longer than our contemporary shopping malls. During the 1930s, indoor air became an asset, and air conditioning is the first thing that revolutionized shopping, according to Koolhaas. Ads appeared that showed: 'Manufactured Weather brings within four walls the weather that nature makes on those rare, perfect days that poets sing about' or 'Bad air is bad business'. Air conditioning enabled the success of shopping malls. By air conditioning, buildings could get a depth otherwise not possible. The store premises no longer had to be close to windows. Second, and the next thing after air conditioning, according to Koolhaas, having big impact on how public space is designed, is the escalator. The escalator enables smooth motions that lifts do not. There is no impatient waiting in front of full lifts, no locked-in experiences in stalled lifts, but a smooth motion in fancy escalators next to nicely exposed products. And the business logic is simple. 'Increased motion means increased revenues'. Different floors of commercial temples could be linked together and people can move up and down with no physical strain.

If air conditioning has enabled depth, then escalators have enabled shopping space to grow vertically. Both have extended shopping into a more three-dimensional space. Both have made shopping less painful, and have enabled the mobility of people for increased consumption. Thus, we are increasingly brought up to become consumers, brought up as consumers and brought up to view ourselves as consumers.

Design and Fashion of Mobility

This point is also illustrated by the first north European art exhibition on tourism, named 'Tourist Class' during the fall of 2005 at Malmö Art Museum. Pieces from twelve artists were on exhibition for two months to comment on the 'art' to attract tourists to picturesque local bars, exotic places recommended in guide books from all over the world. One installation was the 10 minute film 'Less expensive earth' by Mounir Fatmi that is about tourists in crowded pools in Tanger while the population only has water for about 2–3 hours daily. In the film, a boy looks into the tourist centres and says: 'When I grow up, I want to be a tourist'. In this case, becoming a tourist is yet another way of consuming, a way of perhaps over consuming. Given this enlightening comment from the arts world, one may ask: Has our identity as a consumer become more important than our identity as a citizen? We often hear; buying fair trade labelled goods, environmentally produced vegetables, fruit and meat etc. is just as important as, or more important than, voting in general elections.

Mobility has for long been a desired aspect of life. Being a tourist most often means being mobile and travelling to new places and new impressions. If we cannot travel away from our everyday lives, we can surround ourselves with many gadgets of mobility instead. I want to present two other examples besides tourism. The first example relates to music and about bringing music to places where people want to be, which is of course nothing new. In modern times of the 1950s, there were big boxes for bringing along your portable LP player. In the 1970s you had the early hip-hoppers that brought along their ghetto blasters (physical). In the 1980s you spelled mobility in the name of Walkman. In the 1990s it was the mobile CD player. And in our times it is the iPods and other mp3-players, and of course iPhone telephones, that enable us to bring along our complete music and photo collections (and movie collection with iPads?) (And the concept of 'Walkman' has made a comeback in SonyEricsson cell phones.) The function of bringing music along is simple, but add some smart design, it becomes cult, the aesthetic consumption of iPods has become an iconographic signifier of our times, and thus has become an important and integrated aspect of our identities.

Yet another example of co-branding, as we have seen with the store of Miyake, designed by Mori, whose chair was at Harvard, is the co-branding of iPod and Tunebuckle. iPod you cannot have missed to hear of. Tunebuckle[6] you have probably not heard of. A smart entrepreneur came up with the idea to sell a product with distinct connection to *the* product of young people today: the iPod, and in this case, the iPod Nano of 2006. The Tunebuckle was designed to hold an iPod Nano lying in a metal pocket integrated in the belt buckle. I ask myself what happens with all those belts once the iPod Nano is redesigned in shape and form (which it has every year three times since the Tunebuckle was launched, and the buckle has not been redesigned accordingly ...). Another example from the clothes industry is that Levi's in the fall of 2006 started selling a pair of jeans where iPods of different models could fit into a special pocket. It seems that consumption in industrialized countries is increasingly based on our *desires* as social beings rather than on our *needs* as physical beings.

The second example of mobility that I would like to present is the growing market of so called environmental cars in general, and the hybrid models powered by gas and electricity of Toyota Prius and Toyota Lexus in particular. These cars have become increasingly popular in and around Stockholm due to the Stockholm Trial in 2005 and 2006 and the congestion tax system currently employed in Stockholm, by which a tax is imposed on Swedish registered vehicles that enter and exit the Stockholm city zone during weekdays between 6.30 a.m. and 6.29 p.m. The current system was foregone by the Stockholm trials:

The Stockholm trials 22 August 2005 – 31 July 2006
On 2 June 2003, the Stockholm City Council adopted a majority proposal to conduct a trial implementation of congestion charging. The formal decision on implementation was made through the Riksdag (Swedish Parliament) issuing The Congestion Tax Act (2004:629) on 17 June 2004.

6   http://www.tunebuckle.com/

The trials started on 22 August 2005 with extended public transport. On 3 January 2006 the trial implementation of a congestion tax started. The trials were concluded by 31 July 2006. They have been evaluated continuously from a number of different perspectives. This evaluation was summarized in a report in early summer 2006.[7]

The primary objectives of the trials were to reduce congestion, increase accessibility and improve the environment. The purpose of the (full-scale) trials is to test whether the efficiency of the traffic system can be enhanced by congestion charges. 'Environmental' cars do not pay congestion charges and are in many examples not charged with parking fees etc. According to BIL Sweden[8], the market share of environmental cars has jumped to 37,9 % of the total market for September 2008, and 32,1 % of the total market for the first nine months of 2008. I am not an economist, but this explosion of interest in 'environmental' cars goes far beyond the group of people being most devoted to sustainability (Jansson, Marell & Nordlund, 2009). This is because of the interplay of two, if not many more, driving forces: 1) Traditional forces like economic means of control make a difference, it seems obvious. 2) But we need to accept a new understanding that environmental cars have become cool and hip among people, that design and fashion play a role in what cars we drive as well, and then not only in terms of more horse powers for instance.

Reflections for Research Agendas

Despite the previous examples of this chapter that deals with marketing designed products and how fashion helps influencing how we consume products and that we consume at all, this quote by the design guru Bruce Mau helps us to understand that design is much more philosophical than you may imagine at first:

7   http://www.stockholmsforsoket.se/templates/page.aspx?id=183 as retrieved on 070115.

8   http://www.bilsweden.se. According to their web page, ' BIL Sweden was formed in 1941 and represents manufacturers and importers of cars, trucks and buses. Together our members represent 99% of all new registrations in Sweden. BIL Sweden is dealing with matters relating to automotive safety, automobile taxes, environmental protection, distribution, trade policy, traffic policy and Swedish and international regulations. ' http://www.bilsweden.se/web/In_English.aspx as retrieved 081006.

... life doesn't simply happen to us, we produce it. That's what style is. It's producing life (...) Style may be presented as theory, serendipity, or happenstance. But fundamentally style is a decision about how we will live. Style is not superficial. It is a philosophical project of the deepest order. (Mau, 2000) page 27

Very interesting that lavatory brushes can be sold for so much more than the IKEA version, and buyers do not feel fooled at all. At some point I can understand it. At some other point I just do not understand it, because corporate social responsibility is also about bringing quality and reliable products at fair prices to customers. I want to end this chapter with four research agendas for better understanding corporate social responsibility and sustainable development, or even more importantly to point out; why we have an unsustainable situation in the first place.

First, *aesthetic consumption has become more important for sustainability than production.* We ought to critically examine the role of consumption, and thereby critically examine the role companies play in consumption when proclaiming promises for a sustainable development. Corporate sustainability may be used by many people, but it may still remain misunderstood since the corporation is the wrong unit of analysis when interested in sustainable development because the latter takes place in society to which companies just as any other actor contribute through corporate social responsibility for instance. When reflecting of the increasing market share of hybrid cars for instance, we can ask ourselves if design can serve sustainability or just commercialism, as expected for corporations and their market role?

Second, *'everyday life' has become more important studying than products.* It may be fruitful to rely on 'everyday life' in the Gergenian sense (Gergen, 1991; Gergen, 1994) that our lives and identities are constructed around all the relations we surround ourselves with (social including technological), thus becomes important also in a sustainability context, which means that it does matter what restaurants we dine at, what hotels we spend our nights, or how and whereto we travel if at all. It is what we do in our everyday lives, and the way we live our lives, that is crucial for understanding sustainable development, rather than focusing on products and the point of purchase (Zukin, 2004).

Third, it seems that *understanding desire, bad habits and addiction of people* and how corporations exploit these has become more pressing to focus on in our studies of an unsustainable development. We should focus on the unhealth of 'shopping addictions' to understand another side of business ethics and current consumers.

Fourth, *understanding tourism is yet another important area for sustainability-related research.* Tourism is not only the worlds biggest industry according to the World Tourism Organization, it seems to be the worlds fastest growing industry as well, which leads to that hardly any place is spared from the commercial powers of tourism and the economic rhetoric of growth. Thus, to study the performative role of guide books and guided tours and its consequences on society, organizations and individuals could very well be an important study in sustainability and corporate social responsibility (Adolfsson, Dobers & Jonasson, 2009).

And I am a bit worried, that most companies are more willing to exploit our addictions, rather than to explore our needs, or to contribute to sustainability by innovation and business models for the base of the pyramid (Prahalad & Hammond, 2002; Prahalad, 2006; Kandachar & Halme, 2008). It becomes crucial to understand the mechanisms behind *aesthetic consumption.* If aesthetic consumption promotes a lifelong identity project, then we will have a problem. Our basic social needs are about to be seen and valued as we are, and not consume per se. In what ways does corporate social responsibility have to do with this? If we think aesthetic consumption is bad, who is responsible for that? What is the difference to other demands put on companies? Governments? Consumers?

8. Multiparadigm Inquiry into Corporate Responsibility: An ABB Corporate Aid Project under the Global Compact Banner

NIKLAS EGELS-ZANDÉN AND MARKUS KALLIFATIDES

Introduction

Corporate responsibility practices are multifaceted and complex phenomena. Some researchers interpret them as indications of a corporate shift from a shareholder to a stakeholder perspective (e.g. Halme, 1995; Stormer, 2003; Soppe, 2004); others as a new type of expression of a business as usual under corporate hijacked labels of 'sustainable development' and 'Corporate Social Responsibility' (CSR) (e.g. Fergus & Rowney, 2005a, 2005b). Similar complexity characterises the link between corporate responsibility and successful financial performance with some researchers claiming them to be incompatible and others claiming that corporate responsibility is a prerequisite for long-term financial performance (e.g. Griffin & Mahon, 1997; Margolis & Walsh, 2003). Furthermore, there seems to be little consensus on what comprises 'Corporate Social Responsibility', 'Corporate Citizenship' or 'Sustainable Development' in either academia (e.g. Preston & Post, 1975; Sum & Hills, 1998; van Marrewijk, 2003; Matten & Crane, 2005), or practice among corporations, NGO's and unions (e.g. Egels-Zandén & Hyllman, 2006; Shanahan & Khagram, 2006).

Given that corporate responsibility practices can be character-ised as multifaceted and even paradoxical phenomena, they are difficult to understand and explain from a single scientific paradigm (cf. Lewis & Grimes, 1999; Lewis & Kelemen, 2002). Therefore, and in sharp contrast to a Kuhn (1970) inspired view that the fittest scientific paradigm will survive in corporate responsibility research, we argue that a multiparadigm approach is more fruitful when analysing corporate responsibility practices (*cf.* Welford, 1998). Despite this, there are few studies into corporate responsibility that adopt a multiparadigm inquiry. Two of the most systematic of these studies, Welford (1998) and Dobers *et al.* (2001), conducted what Lewis and Grimes (1999) label 'multiparadigm reviews', i.e. they identified divides and gaps in existing corporate responsibility research by categorising previous research through paradigm lenses (mainly those lenses developed by Burrell & Morgan (1979)). Both studies concluded their reviews with an identified lack of research from a 'radical humanist' paradigm (more specifically Welford (1998) stressed the importance of critical theory, which he located on the boarder line between the 'radical humanist' and the 'radical structuralist' paradigm). While valuable for identifying biases in current research and sensitising researchers regarding the potential impact of paradigmatic choices, these review studies only start to explore the potential of multiparadigm inquiry. Importantly, they fall short of illustrating the practical effects of adopting differing paradigms. As Brocklesby (1997) and Lewis & Kelemen (2002) argue, multiparadigm *reviews* serve well as a starting point for multiparadigm inquiry, but needs to be followed by multiparadigm *research*, i.e. research that uses paradigm lenses to collect and ana-lyse data (Lewis and Grimes, 1999). This has yet to be done in the corporate responsibility literature, leaving the multiparadigmatic inquiry in its infancy in this strain of research.

To address this lack in previous corporate responsibility research and further develop multiparadigm inquiries, we present a multi-paradigm research study of a rural electrification project in Tan-zania run by Swedish-Swiss multinational corporation Asea Brown Boveri (ABB). The project was launched, in partnership with the World Wildlife Fund (WWF), as a response to the UN Global Compact and is in this chapter treated as an example of corporate responsibility practices. We analyse this project based on four paradigmatically different theoretical perspectives: i) an official-ist, ii) a pragmatic institutionalist, iii) a critical, and iv) a scepti-cal perspective. In addition to contributing to the research into corporate responsibility, the study also contributes to research into multiparadigm inquiry. Since the publishing of Allison's (1971) and Hassard's (1991, 1993) influential studies, there have been constant calls for more multiparadigm research (e.g. Bolman & Deal, 1984; Morgan, 1986; Lewis & Grimes, 1999; Lewis & Kelemen, 2002). Despite this, there are still few such studies in organization theory (notable exceptions include Gioia *et al.* (1989), Bradshaw-Camball & Murray (1991), Lee (1991), Martin (1992), and Rhodes (2000)). This study addresses this gap by moving beyond the realms of multiparadigm reviews (e.g. Smircich, 1983; Morgan 1986; Alvesson, 1987; Grint, 1991; Reed, 1996) and theoretical discussions of multiparadigm inquiry (e.g. Gioia & Pitre, 1990; Das, 1993; Schultz & Hatch, 1996; Lewis & Grimes, 1999; Lewis & Kelemen, 2002), into the realm of practical multiparadigm research.

In the next sections, we first discuss the here studied topic: corporate responsibility. We then present the four theoretical perspectives used in our analysis and show their linkages to different social science paradigms. Following this, we outline the method of the study and present the case of ABB in Tanzania. This case description that, per necessity, already is imprinted with our (theoretical and other) preconceptions, will nevertheless in the following be treated as a text upon which alternative readings from each of the four theoretical perspectives are possible (*cf.* Rhodes, 2000). The chapter then concludes with a discussion of the similarities in and differences between these four readings of corporate responsibility practices, and the potential for multiparadigm research into corporate responsibility.

Corporate responsibility

What corporate responsibility (or related concepts) comprises is subject of both academic and practitioner debate (e.g. Carroll, 1999; van Marrewijk, 2003; Matten & Crane, 2005; Egels-Zandén & Hyllman, 2006; Shanahan & Khagram, 2006). Despite this debate, most observers would agree that there has been a surge in both academic research and practitioner initiatives into 'corporate responsibility' (e.g., Waddock *et al.*, 2002; Shanahan & Khagram, 2006). For example, corporations increasingly produce corporate responsibility reports, adopt codes of conduct, and partner with non-governmental organizations (e.g., Sethi, 1999; Guillén *et al.*, 2002; Nijhof *et al.*, 2003; Arya & Salk, 2006).

The launch of the UN initiative the UN Global Compact in 1999 can be seen as an important milestone in the CSR movement.[1] The Compact drew together previous corporate responsibility initiatives into a concrete ten principle program under the influential UN banner. With over 2,500 companies having signed the UN Global Compact, it seems to be the currently most well recognized CSR standard (e.g., Banuri & Spanger-Siegfried, 2001; Petersmann, 2002; Cavanagh, 2004; Fussler, 2004; Hsieh, 2004; Kuper, 2004; Williams, 2004). The launch of the Compact, in 1999, was also of symbolic importance, since, as Thérien and Pouliot (2006: 55) note, it marked 'a major turn in development thinking. After decades of hostile relations, the UN and business now acknowledge their common interest in the promotion of sustainable development' (*cf.* Kuper, 2004; Williams, 2004; Jenkins, 2005). The principles of the UN Global Compact are:

> *Principle 1:* Businesses should support and respect the protection of internationally proclaimed human rights; and
>
> *Principle 2:* make sure that they are not complicit in human rights abuses.
>
> *Principle 3:* Businesses should uphold the freedom of association and the effective recognition of the right to collective bargaining;
>
> *Principle 4:* the elimination of all forms of forced and compulsory labor;
>
> *Principle 5:* the effective abolition of child labor; and
>
> *Principle 6:* the elimination of discrimination in respect of employment and occupation.
>
> *Principle 7:* Businesses should support a precautionary approach to environmental challenges;
>
> *Principle 8:* undertake initiatives to promote greater environmental responsibility; and
>
> *Principle 9:* encourage the development and diffusion of environmentally friendly technologies.
>
> *Principle 10:* Businesses should work against all forms of corruption, including extortion and bribery.

---

1   We here use the concept 'movement' in much the same way as in Thörn (2006), meaning that movements contain movements within movements as well as conflicts between actors within a specific movement.

The ABB project studied in this chapter is a part of the CSR movement in three different regards. First, it was presented by ABB as a CSR project, serving as an operationalisation of ABB's more general CSR commitment (including codes of conduct, donations, and sustainability reports). Second, it was a response to the UN Global Compact, and, third, it was a part of a recent aspect of the CSR movement – the so-called 'bottom of the economic pyramid' movement (e.g., London & Hart, 2004; Prahalad 2006). The main idea in the bottom of the pyramid movement is that by selling products to the poorest four billion individuals of the world, sustainable development will simultaneously be achieved.

Four theoretical perspectives

The purpose of this chapter is to move beyond multiparadigm *reviews* of corporate responsibility into the realm of multiparadigm *research*. Lewis and Grimes (1999) and Lewis and Kelemen (2002) distinguish between two main types of multiparadigm *research* studies. First, studies could be based on analyses of a similar issue from multiple theoretical perspectives (e.g. Allison, 1971). Second, studies could be based analyses of a different issue for each perspective (e.g. Hassard, 1991). The choice between these alternatives is related to the researchers' position in what has been known as the 'paradigm wars' (e.g. Jackson & Carter, 1993). Burrell and Morgan (1979), in similarity to Kuhn (1970), claimed that their four identified social science paradigms were incommensurable. While this position has enjoyed support from some researchers (e.g. Jackson & Carter, 1991, 1993), others have opted for a more liberal view of the possibility to combine different paradigms (e.g. Reed, 1985; Willmott, 1993; Weaver & Gioia, 1994; Schultz & Hatch, 1996). In this 'war', we sympathise with the latter position, and, hence, embrace a stance that allows for multiple theoretical perspectives to meaningfully be applied and compared regarding a similar issue. As Schultz and Hatch (1996) clarify, this does *not* mean that we necessarily accept an integrationist view of paradigms. Rather, it only means that we believe paradigm interplay to be fruitful by way of contrast.

When this discussion of paradigm wars is linked to the second choice in multiparadigm research, i.e. that of multiple theoretical perspectives on a single issue versus multiple issues, a relationship emerges. Proponents of paradigm incommensurability generally analyse multiple issues, since they perceive that no relevant comparisons are possible between diverging theoretical perspectives on the same issue. On the other hand, proponents of paradigm interplay generally analyse a single issue in order to increase the understanding of how different theoretical paradigms inform the analysis. As explained above, we support the latter view and will, in accordance with this line of previous research (e.g. Allison, 1971; Bradshaw-Camball & Murray, 1991; Lee, 1991), therefore analyse a single issue, i.e. corporate responsibility practice, from multiple theoretical perspectives.

In multiparadigm inquiries, the choice of theoretical perspectives is central. Similarly to the bulk of previous multiparadigm inquiries in general and into corporate responsibility (e.g., Welford, 1998; Dobers *et al.*, 2001), we structure our choice of theoretical perspectives based on Burell and Morgan's (1979) classification of social science paradigms. These authors identified four distinctly different paradigms in social science research: the functionalist, the interpretative, the radical humanist, and the radical structuralist paradigm. These four paradigms are separated by their positions in two social science debates: the subject-object debate and the consensus-conflict debate. To provide a holistic theoretical framework for the analysis, we have chosen one theoretical perspective from each of the four paradigms. Evidently, there are multiple theoretical perspectives to choose from in each paradigm, so our choice is just one of many possible ones. The rationale for our choices is that we have selected perspectives that we perceive as influential in organizational studies.

The first of our four perspectives is the *officialist* perspective that belongs to the functionalist corner of Burrell and Morgan's (1979) matrix (objectivity and consensus). The second perspective is the *pragmatic institutionalist* perspective that belongs to the interpretative paradigm (subjectivist and consensus). The third perspective is the *critical* perspective that with its focus on power relations belongs to the conflict part of the matrix but that balances between the 'objective' and 'subjective' extremes (*cf.* Welford, 1998). Hence, the critical perspective balances between the radical humanist and radical structuralist paradigm. Finally, the *sceptical* perspective belongs to the radical humanist paradigm (subjectivist and conflict). In sum, the chosen perspectives mirror Burell and Morgan (1979) four paradigms with the partial lack of a perspective from the radical structuralist paradigm. This is due to the replacement of such a perspective with a critical theory perspective – a perspective that have been identified as missing in previous research into corporate responsibility (Welford, 1998).

An officialist perspective

An officialist perspective, intimately tied to the globalisation of liberalism (free trade, pro-growth, formal democracy) (Hovden & Keene, 2002), begins with a modernist assumption that western and other citizens of the world are becoming more informed, more knowledgeable, and are reasonable and good-hearted people who put pressure on their governments, and corporations, to 'do the right things' (e.g. Giddens, 1990, 1991; Castells, 1996; Boli & Thomas, 1999). They may act as members of NGO's, as voters, as consumers, as employees, and/or as investors – but they do act. Together with the existence of free and critical media this creates tremendous pressure on corporations and governments to behave in accordance with the norms set up (*cf.* van Tulder & Kolk, 2001; Waddock, 2002; Roberts, 2003; Frenkel & Kim, 2004; Åhlström & Egels-Zandén, 2006).

Corporations also try to respond to these pressures by interpreting them through the 'business as usual' lens, i.e. what can be labelled strategic change within 'strategic exchange' (*cf.* Watson, 1994; Hart & Milstein, 2002). The slogan is that corporations can 'do well by doing good' (*cf.* Rowley & Berman, 2000). Hence, with stakeholders' demands of what comprise 'desirable' corporate actions changing (*cf.* Freeman, 1984; Donaldson & Preston, 1995; Waddock, 2002), corporations respond by altering their behaviour. However, these adjustment processes are difficult, and researchers within the officialist perspective take particular interest in managerial 'irrationalities' in the form of not realising the demands of their time. Such analysis is then often followed by normative advice regarding how to more 'successfully' manage corporations.

The bulk of previous research into corporate responsibility falls within the officialist perspective (*cf.* Welford, 1998). This is, for example, illustrated by the focus on analyses of official documents (such as annual reports and press releases), responses to surveys (both the researchers' and practitioners' surveys such as that eventually resulting in the KLD database ranking often used in corporate responsibility research), and/or interviews with CSR and other corporate managers. The assumption is that these official statements mirror, although potentially imperfectly, actual corporate intentions and practices, and that if discrepancies between 'talk' and 'practice' are identified advice is given regarding how to overcome these 'implementation problems'.

A pragmatic institutionalist perspective

The officialist's notion that 'talk' mirrors 'practice' and that stakeholder pressure sparks corporate practice, is questioned in a (neo)institutional perspective. With foundational texts in Meyer and Rowan's (1977) and DiMaggio and Powell's (1983) rereading of Max Weber, a veritable flow of research in organizational sociology and organization theory has followed both in general (e.g., Scott, 1987; DiMaggio & Powell, 1991; Johansson, 2002; Campbell, 2004), and in relation to corporate responsibility (e.g. Hoffman, 1999, 2001; Hoffman & Ventresca, 2002; Campbell, 2007; Marquis *et al.*, 2007). The underlying assumption of the institutionalist perspective is that legitimate social action is by necessity different from rational action; social action demands a subscription to publicly accepted normative frameworks (institutions) whereas rational action can be achieved in a myriad of, sometimes inexplicable and not seldom illegitimate or dubious, means. Organizations, taken as the prime 'object' of study, are understood as applying decoupling as a highly functional technique for survival. Hence, 'talk' is not assumed to mirror 'practice'. Rather, the opposite is argued for – the purpose of much talk is to *not* mirror practice as to allow for both legitimate (talk of) social actions and effective (practice) actions to be undertaken. Similarly, stakeholder pressure is argued to lead to alterations in 'talk', leaving few traces in corporate 'practice'. The interest of the researcher from this institutionalist perspective becomes looking for signs of rationalised myths of organizational life, covering for other, and perhaps more varied, organizational realities, and/or for actually trickling through to everyday practices. John Meyer (of later dates than 1977) is primarily associated with this kind of idea of eventual trickledown of ideas, rather than perpetual decoupling (e.g. Campbell, 2004).

If this general institutionalist perspective is linked to pragmatism, a pragmatic institutionalist perspective emerges (e.g. Czarniawska, 1993; Czarniawska & Sevón, 1996). In addition to critiquing the officialist position that 'talk' mirrors 'practice', the pragmatic institutionalist also question the notion that decoupling is problematic – a point that traditional (neo)institutionalists have been unclear about. Following the pragmatist spirit, the focus in pragmatic institutionalism is that organising should produce desirable and functional results – regardless of how this is achieved. Several pragmatic institutionalists note that decoupling may be a promising way to achieve such desirable results (e.g. Brunsson & Olsen, 1989; Mosse, 2005). Hence, rather than *de*coupling being problematic, pragmatic institutionalists often argue that it is couplings that are problematic and, consequently, should be minimised.

A critical perspective

The critical perspective is doubtful, to say the least, of both the officialist and pragmatic institutionalist perspectives lack of power analysis. The officialist perspective is, from a critical perspective, perceived as naïve in assuming that outcomes are decided by the principle of rationality and effectiveness. Likewise, the institutional perspective is perceived as naïve in lacking a power perspective (*cf.* DiMaggio & Powell, 1991; Blomquist, 1996; Beckert, 1999; Maguire *et al*, 2004), leading to a too extensive focus on *how* ideas travel rather than *what* ideas that travel. Regarding *what* ideas that travel, a critical perspective particularly focuses on analysing the spread of what is perceived as the epiphany of Western civilisation – the Enlightenment ideas (e.g. Horkheimer & Adorno, 1944/1997).

Spurred by the work of Horkheimer and Adorno, a critical perspective would frame CSR issues as a continuance of the process of Enlightenment – summarised in its implicit credo – out with the gods *and* the qualities. Enlightenment opposes religion (superstition), believes in Science as reason's finest accomplishment, but its

Progress is systematically tied to an expulsion of certain qualities of human existence. In the work of Habermas (1981/1984), this is expressed *inter alia* as the colonization of the 'life world' by the 'systems world'. Another useful concept 'antagonism' is provided by Laclau and Mouffe (1985). Antagonism comprise the idea that social life is perpetually marked by struggle over meaning and over resources between collectives, i.e. it is an updated Marxism emphasising that collectives do not necessarily equal (economic) classes. By combining Habermas (1981/1984) and Laclau and Mouffe (1985), it is possible to ask the question: whose life world is colonized by whose systems world? Hence, a critical perspective would expect to find a potential colonization project luring beneath the CSR and UN Global Compact labels with some actors – notably those inspired by Western, individualistic, scientific, secularised and liberal values – forcing their systems world on the life world of other actors. The remedy for such colonization resides, according to a critical perspective, in more adequate human communication (Habermas 1981/1984).

To date, little research into CSR has been done from a critical perspective (Welford, 1998). However, intimately related issues, such as international relations in general, and global corporate activities in particular, are clearly the subject of an immense critical literature (e.g. Korten, 1995; Perlas, 1999; Hovden & Keene, 2002; Quarles van Ufford & Giri, 2003), and informed debate is growing on environmental management as discursive practice (e.g. Prasad & Elmes, 2005; Newton, 2005). When applying the critical perspective to organizational analysis in this chapter, we take cues from, for example, Clegg (1975), Alvesson & Willmott (1992) and Deetz (1995).

Sceptical perspective

The sceptical perspective is related to the critical perspective with its focus on power relations. However, while the critical perspective expresses hope of potential remedy through rational dialogue, the sceptic perspective is less hopeful representing a pessimistic version of a critical perspective (e.g., Foucault, 1975). Dominating ideas, more seldom than not promulgated in the form of scientific discourse are seen to permeate human relationships, giving rise to conceptions of knowledge, including self-knowledge, in turn constituting power relations. Centres and peripheries are created and recreated by and through these discursive formations, constantly privileging the observing, monitoring, censoring centre at the expense of the peripheries. Attempts at rational dialogue are suspected to give rise to more intrusive 'technologies of government', perhaps 'well-intended' but still, in essence, mechanisms for power and its reproduction.

CSR-research guided by a sceptical approach is hard to come across. Surely, this would have to be related to CSR as a discursive expression coming from the centre, from the towers of power in western economies and their prime organizational loci: states and large multinational corporations. In the same vein as when Michel Foucault suspected the penal system to work first and foremost productively by constantly producing criminality and criminals – in the service of dominating interests – CSR could indeed be conceptualised as technologies of government producing something in the service of dominating interests. In this case, the stated purpose – expanding markets for multinational corporations – would be a prime suspect when formulating what that purpose would be. The idea that the processes involved would be turned into something unequivocally 'positive' to the peripheries would be regarded with great scepticism (e.g. Ferguson, 1997, Young, 2002). The ambition of the sceptic is to promote *resistance*, always related to the particularities in time and space.

Method

Multiparadigm research studies into a single issue tend to utilise a qualitative case research method, and collect material mainly from interviews, observations and written sources (e.g. Allison, 1971; Bradshaw-Camball & Murray, 1991; Rhodes, 2000). Comparable with previous multiparadigm research studies, this chapter builds on material from an explorative study of an ABB rural electrification project in the village of Ngarambe in Tanzania (Egels, 2005; Egels-Zandén & Kallifatides, 2006). Material was collected through written documentation (e.g. web-pages, e-mail communication among the involved actors, policies, budgets, time schedules and contracts), direct observation, and interviews. In total, thirty-four representatives from ABB and its different types of business stakeholders (e.g. Ericsson and Tetra Pak), non-governmental stakeholders (e.g. United Nations Development Program (UNDP), the World Bank, the World Wildlife Fund (WWF) and unions), governmental stakeholders (e.g. the Swedish International Development Cooperation Agency (SIDA) and Tanzanian government agencies), and village stakeholders were interviewed. The key representatives involved in the studied project in Tanzania were interviewed two to five times during the study. The focus of the interviews was on discussing the Ngarambe project in general and particularly instances of conflict between the actors involved. The material for the study was collected on three different geographic levels: an international, a Tanzanian and a village level. Since there were limited written sources available at the village level, material was here mainly collected by means of observations and interviews. In comparison, written information was more heavily used at the international level.

Following the collection, the material was then coded and analysed as to construct a chronological representation of the project encompassing the events that the involved actors either perceived as central or controversial in the project. This representation of the project was then sent to several of the interviewed key actors involved in the project to validate the description of the project. All the respondents' suggested changes were then incorporated into the final version of the description of the project. Despite the fact that this description of the project, per necessity, is imprinted with our theoretical and other preconceptions, we then treated it as a text upon which alternative readings from each of the four above described theoretical perspectives were possible (*cf.* Rhodes, 2000).

Bringing Electricity to Ngarambe

Initiating Access to Electricity

In a form reminiscent of traditional 'aid',[2] incumbent CEO of ABB, Göran Lindahl, launched its project Access to Electricity in a direct and well announced response to the Global Compact at the Johannesburg summit in 2002. This launch was preceded by an ABB attempt to find a partner for its newly developed ambition to create a rural electrification project. Initially, in the beginning of 2002, ABB approached Swedish donor agency SIDA (Swedish International Development Cooperation Agency) for such a partnership in connection with SIDA's large scale project around Lake Victoria in Tanzania. ABB found SIDA difficult to persuade into this partnership; the latter claimed to have difficulties seeing what ABB would be able to contribute. While SIDA had been involved in rural electrification in Tanzania for some years with other commercial, and non-commercial, partners, ABB, at that time, had little experience in small scale rural electrification projects (of approximately 20–200 houses). As discussions with SIDA shored, ABB decided to approach the World Wildlife Foundation (WWF) instead.

At the time, a collaboration with WWF was already in place and ABB corporate headquarter had provided a three year budget for this collaboration. Top managers at ABB came up with the idea to direct some of the existing funds to a project related to rural electrification in Tanzania. The preference of sub-Sahara Africa was related to the low level of rural electrification in this region. Of the 1.6 billion people 'lacking' access to electricity around the globe, 500 million live in sub-Sahara Africa, making it perhaps the world's region most 'in need' of electricity (IEA 2002). The preference for Tanzania was, in turn, related to a hope of partnering with SIDA somewhere down the road.

WWF embraced this idea and a budget plan was created for the rural electrification project. The size of the project was limited by both the total budget for the ABB-WWF collaboration and by the fact that several projects were already running when this particular

2   The international donor community has largely moved from the format of aid projects to programs and other kinds of structural support within what is known as the World Bank Good Governance Agenda (e.g. Abrahamsen, 2004; Mosse, 2005).

idea was raised. As it turned out, a previous joint project was ending in 2002, leaving some financial space for a new project in 2003. It was agreed upon by the manager of corporate partnerships at wwf International and the senior vice president of sustainability affairs and the project manager of Access to Electricity at abb to allocate these funds to rural electrification.

wwf International at this stage took on responsibility to identify a suitable Tanzanian village for a pilot project. The goal was to find a village that was experiencing a positive spiral both in terms of conservation of wildlife and economic development. wwf Tanzania (wwf tz) recommended the small and remote village of Ngarambe located just outside the Selous Game Reserve. After having chosen Ngarambe as a pilot project, abb, to repeat, launched its project Access to Electricity at the World Summit in Johannesburg in the summer of 2002.

Background on Ngarambe village and Selous Game Reserve

The village Ngarambe is located just outside the north east part of the Selous Game Reserve. This game reserve is one of the most important areas for the elephant and rhino populations in Africa. Selous Game Reserve in total covers an area larger than the size in Switzerland. In 1976, the game reserve contained around 110 000 elephants. This number was, mainly due to heavy poaching, reduced to 50 000 in 1986 and 30 000 in 1989. At this time, the Tanzanian government decided to take action to increase the protection of wildlife by, for example, increasing police and army efforts to monitor illegal hunting, steeply increasing the penalties for poaching, and illegalizing all trade in ivory products.

In order to assist the Tanzanian government, wwf got involved in the wildlife conservation of Selous Game Reserve in mid 90s (the number of wildlife has stabilized since then and is now increasing steadily). After a couple of years, the wwf in 1997 started to involve the villages around the game reserve in the conservation. These villagers had often been forced by the Tanzanian government to move out of the game reserve, when it was created (as no humans were allowed to live in the reserve). Additionally, the villagers were not allowed to hunt any of the animals neither inside nor outside the reserve. The wildlife, consequently, provided little, if any, commercial value to the villagers. Furthermore, the wildlife regularly destroyed the villagers' crops to the extent that wildlife was seen as producing a negative result for the villagers. It was in this setting that WWF TZ started to work with the villages surrounding the reserve in an effort to find a way for wildlife to be valuable to the villages and consequently reducing the risk of them getting involved in illegal hunting of wildlife.

A controversial power source

After the choice of Ngarambe for the pilot project, ABB and WWF turned to the issue of power source. Since ABB sold its power generation division some years ago, the Access to Electricity project could in theory choose whatever power source judged to be suitable. This issue was initially handed over to ABB TZ and WWF TZ in order for these organizations to provide alternatives. Initially, mainly wind power, solar cells, water, grid-extension and diesel were considered. Given the lack of water sources and existing electricity-grids, these options were ruled out quickly. Wind power was, in turn, considered too unreliable and incapable of producing the full amount of electricity needed for the village. This left solar cells and diesel as options. While recognizing that diesel was environmentally unsustainable, ABB TZ and WWF TZ suggested it as the only viable alternative given the project's limited budget. ABB TZ and WWF TZ also recognized that diesel was probably the most commonly used power source in small scale electrification in Tanzania and, in addition, ABB TZ had extensive experience in designing electrification systems based on diesel. The international manager of Access to Electricity and particularly the project manager at WWF International were, though, dissatisfied with this solution. Eventually, ABB allowed WWF to make the final decision on power source, given the budget restraint.

The stakes increased as departments at WWF International, particularly related to CO_2 emissions, started to internally criticize the potential use of diesel claiming that such a project would damage WWF's credibility and send the wrong symbolic signals in terms of how rural electrification should be carried out in the future. The WWF project manager had in essence three choices: endorse diesel, abandon the project or renegotiate the project budget to widen the range of viable options. Knowing that ABB was in the aftermath of its financial crises, the manager found a budget increase highly unlikely. He decided, after lengthy discussions with WWF TZ, to prefer proceeding with diesel to terminating the project. However, he insisted on utilizing the most environmentally friendly diesel engine on the market (equipped with all the additional environmentally friendly features that the producer could offer) and on having a feasibility study done in a second phase of the project concerning wind power as back up. The Access to Electricity manager agreed to divert funds from the budget to accommodate these suggestions. The choice of diesel has since then been questioned by several stakeholders on the international level, a few on the Tanzanian level, and rarely any on the village level.

Disagreement about the desirability of electricity

On the international level, ABB's stakeholders seem to view the provision of rural electrification as highly desirable. The UN WEHAB initiative, for example, identifies energy, and thus also electricity, as one out of five priority fields together with water, health, agricultural productivity and biodiversity. Similar claims could be found in the World Energy Council's recent report on the future of African energy (WEC 2003) and in the International Energy Agency's reports (e.g. IEA 2002). The conducted interviews with stakeholders at the national Tanzanian level indicated that this picture also holds for this level. The World Bank in collaboration with donor agencies, for example Swedish SIDA, is now also up-scaling its activities to ensure that such rural electrification takes place. This is materialized in Rural Electrification Funds (REF), which have been created, or are in the process of being created, in for example Tanzania, Uganda and Senegal. These funds will centralize and coordinate most international funding activities and provide subsidies for parts of the initial investment (but not the operation) of rural electricity systems.

In Ngarambe there was initial scepticism, with some villagers not wanting electricity to their houses. Partly, this seemed related to ignorance of the benefits of electricity. Partly it also seemed related to a mistrust of companies in general and in this case ABB. Additionally, some villagers' beliefs stood in sharp contrast to the provision of electricity. This was particularly evident with the village's traditional medicine man, who to this day, has not allowed any ABB employee to set foot in his house and let alone install electricity. As the project proceeded, most villagers, though, seem to have become positive of having electricity.

Cables below ground

To keep costs down, ABB TZ initially envisioned monitoring the distribution cables between the engine and the houses above ground. WWF TZ, however, rejected this solution with reference to the fact that the elephants, often showing in and around Ngarambe, might topple the poles and get electrocuted. This was seen as particularly problematic to WWF TZ, since conservation of wildlife was the reason for it presence in Ngarambe. ABB accepted this position and decided to incur the additional cost of placing cables below ground. It was agreed on by ABB, WWF and the village government that villagers should dig the trenches necessary.

Two weeks later when it came to digging the trenches the villagers, though, refused to do this without some financial reimbursement. The argument made was that the recent drought had rendered a shortage of food and that digging the trenches would both divert valuable time away from farming and demand a lot of energy. The villagers that were not getting electricity to their individual houses were particularly resistant to helping. At this time, the only project members in the village were two ABB technicians assigned to install the distribution cables. With few relationships with the villagers and hardly any to the village government, the technicians were unable to persuade the villagers to change their minds. Furthermore, digging trenches was a labour intensive task, so the technicians could not do it themselves. This left them with three alternatives: do nothing and delay the project, give the villagers whatever money they had, or contact WWF TZ or ABB TZ. The only possible way to contact WWF or ABB was through a radio in a WWF camp eight kilometres away. With no car in the village, the technicians started walking to this camp on a road surrounded by head-high vegetation in an area with a fairly dense population of lions, rhinos and elephants. Upon spotting some lions down the road, the technicians decided to turn back. After this experience they were very reluctant to walk between the village and the camp, which in effect left them cut of from the rest of the world. In order to finish the tasks they were hired for by ABB, the technicians decided to take money out of their own pockets and unofficially pay some villagers to help them dig the trenches.

After about two weeks, the WWF project manager arrived at Ngarambe and got word of the resistance to digging the trenches. He called to a meeting with both the village government and a group of younger villagers and claimed that if the villagers did not live up to the initial agreement concerning the trenches, WWF would no longer be able to support the electrification project. Eventually it was decided that the villagers getting electricity should provide the trenches to their individual houses, that the school children were to dig the trenches to the teachers' houses and the school, and that the villagers jointly should dig the trenches to the rest of the public houses. This agreement was honoured to most part, but upon the WWF manager leaving the village the technicians on some occasions found it necessary to unofficially pay those digging.

This need to provide financial compensation to villagers for tasks originally agreed on by the village government that the villagers should perform occurred in several other occasions as well for the project manager of ABB TZ and the ABB technicians. In most of these cases this was not reported to either ABB International or to WWF TZ. Technicians used their own 'pocket-money', and they did not seem to consider this particularly problematic. Rather it was seen as a fact of life in Tanzanian society and a part of the way things were done.

Since the cost of installing distribution cables was a function of the distance between the generator and the houses, ABB TZ wanted to prioritize the electrification of houses near the generator to maximise the number of houses receiving electricity within the project budget limits. However, influential villagers living far from the generator protested, and argued that provision of electricity should be based on village status rather than proximity to the generator. Despite these protests, ABB TZ decided to provide electricity to those houses close to the generator, leaving some traditionally influential villagers without access to electricity.

Training village technicians

Since the villagers were supposed to take over the operation of the electricity system, ABB agreed to provide necessary training for two villagers. These were initially assigned by the village government, who claimed them to be the most skilled for the jobs. After two weeks of training, however, the ABB team was not pleased with their performance. This was partly due to their level of technical know-how, but also to their working routines. For example, complaints were raised that one of the villagers, a devote Muslim, without notice left for prayers five times a day. The team felt that in an emergency he would choose going to the mosque over repairing the electricity system potentially putting the electricity system and other villagers in danger.

The ABB TZ project manager decided to take the issue to the village government and request that additional individuals were to receive training. After some discussions, ABB received permission to train four additional, both assigned and volunteering, villagers. When training these, it became evident that the two initially assigned villagers had been selected for tribal and family reasons. One of the new trainees (referred to as the 'handy-man'), performed very well and the ABB team wanted to promote him to head village technician. This caused a serious controversy with many villagers.

Due to his religious belief and origin in tribes outside the village, the handy-man had previously been denied to marry a woman from the village and had also been denied citizenship status in the village. The latter was vital as only citizens of the village are allowed to own land in and around the village. In terms of marriage, he was originally accused of having HIV, but even after having provided a negative HIV test he was still denied to marry within the village. Hence, the handy-man did not have a prominent position in the village at the time of the electrification project.

The ABB team, though, argued that the handy-man's technical know-how was essential for the long term functioning of the system and that it was in the interest of the villagers to appoint him for securing their electricity. Additionally, the team argued that tribe, religion and know-who should not be decisive factors in recruitments. Eventually the handy man was appointed head technician and is now more respected, trusted and accepted in the village and has also been granted permanent citizenship.

The future of Ngarambe and Access to Electricity

ABB seems to have adopted a similar 'business model' in Ngarambe as the one proposed by the Rural Electrification Funds, i.e. that the villagers themselves should finance the long-term running and maintenance of the electricity system (for in depth description see below). This financing is probably the biggest challenge for the village. While diesel was an attractive power source thanks to its low initial investment cost, the running costs associated with it are high. It also seems that the villagers are yet to realize the actual cost of operating the system, shown in the fact that the current price for diesel is set about five times too low for covering the actual costs. ABB currently provides the diesel for the village in order to allow them to build a financial buffer for the long-term survival of the system. After a year or two the villagers, however, most likely will need to find the money to operate the equipment as ABB and WWF willingness to pay shores.

To collect payments from villagers, a village board was established. ABB and WWF emphasised the necessity of including women in this board. Traditionally, women have had little influence on public decision making in Ngarambe, and several villagers also argued that this village board, like others, should only be open to men. After negotiating with the villagers, however, ABB and WWF managed to allow women to join the board, set up to collect payments.

It is also unclear if ABB has developed a business model in which the villagers can financially support the running and maintenance themselves. Finding such a business model seems necessary for ABB when it tries to scale up its Access to Electricity project in Tanzania, Senegal and Uganda in partnership with WWF as well as other commercial and non-commercial organizations. In all of these countries, ABB hopes to receive subsidies from the newly founded REF's and plan to only enter projects based on a commercial, rather than philanthropic, logic.

In order to receive subsidies the REFs place three different demands on the firms. First, the firms are demanded to comply with the World Bank guidelines in terms of sustainability. It is currently, though, unclear how strictly this will be monitored. In fact, several of the individuals interviewed expected monitoring to be fairly limited, since many of these rural areas are extensively difficult to get to and consequently also difficult and expensive for outside organizations to monitor. Second, the REFs only provide subsidies for part of the initial investment and not for the long term running of the electrification system. This means that the villages themselves have to find ways to financially cover the cost of running and repairing the system. Finally, the REFs prioritize rural electrification projects based on either how much initial investment it requires or the tariff the firm propose to charge the villagers for the use of the system (given that the projects live up to the first and second criteria). Hence, the focus seems to be on keeping costs down if a firm is to receive subsidies from the REFS. It is currently not only questionable if ABB has found a business model that lives up to the second prerequisite, but also questionable if it is able to keep costs down in order to compete for the subsidies. Regarding to the first aspect of compliance, ABB seem to comply with the demands in practice, even though its local representatives at ABB TZ seem to have little, if any, knowledge of what comprise 'human rights', the UN Global Compact or related criteria. Rather, they describe their actions as based on the ABB 'culture', something that ABB international finds satisfactory although greater knowledge about the how to connect the current practice to international criteria is seen as a corporate aim in the future.

Summary

The focus of the conducted study was to describe the central decisions and arisen conflicts related to the electrification project. Table 1 is a summary of the story so far.

Table 1 – Conflict issues in ABB's electrification project in Ngarambe

CONFLICT ISSUE	ABB	INTER-NATIONAL STAKE-HOLDERS	TANZA-NIAN STAKE-HOLDERS	VILLAGE STAKE-HOLDERS	CONFLICT OUTCOME
Part-ners and financing	a) SIDA financing b) WWF collaboration financing	a) SIDA uninterested b) WWF interested			WWF collaboration financing
Power source	Low initial investment, i.e. bias to-wards diesel	Renewable sources	Slight pref-erence for renewable sources	Indifference between sources	Diesel and fea-sibility study of wind
Generation equipment	Unclear	Environmen-tally friendly (WWF)	Unclear	No extra equipment	Environmen-tally friendly
Provi-sion of electricity	Highly desir-able	Highly desir-able	Highly desirable	Disagree-ment among villagers	Installed elec-trical system
Ratio-nale for prioritizing villagers for electricity	Financial ca-pability and proximity to engine	Financial capability	Financial capability and need of electricity	Status and position in village	Financial capability and proximity to engine
Distribu-tion cables	Above ground	Unclear	Below ground (WWF TZ)	Below ground	Below ground
Digging trenches	No unofficial payments to villagers	No unofficial payments	No unofficial payments (WWF TZ)	Unofficial payments	Some unoffi-cial payments
Village technicians	Know-how	Know-how	Know-how	'Know-*who*'	Know-how
Board for collection of pay-ments	Men and women both represented	Men and women both represented	Mainly men repre-sented	Only men represented	Men and women both represented
Operation financing	No subsidies for opera-tions	No subsidies for opera-tions	No sub-sidies for operations	Subsidies for opera-tions	No subsidies for operations

Readings from multiple perspectives

An officialist reading: progress and impediments

In an officialist reading of the case, ABB is seen as a giant on its back, coming out of recent history of scandals, poor financial results, and turmoil. In turn, the UN Global Compact is seen as a golden opportunity for ABB to make an attempt at worldwide publicity of a very different kind. Thanks to ABB's vast technological know-how and global presence, it is well positioned to undertake rural electrification projects and to do so in response to the UN Global Compact. Furthermore, subsidies could potentially be received by the Rural Electrification Funds, leading to future rural electrification projects being short-term profitable as well as viable in terms of public relations.

The Ngarambe case is, from an officialist perspective, a success with almost every stakeholder being satisfied and an electricity grid being installed in Ngarambe. Traditional culture (comprising, for example, the medicine man, pre-eminence of tribal relations, and a backward gender regime) has also been challenged thanks to the project. Hence, the project evokes hope of positive spirals of both economic and political development (democratic organising being spurred on by the project). As a bonus, all this is likely beneficial for the elephants and rhinos in the area.

As the officialist would expect, everything does not, in an initial project like this one, turn out to be perfect. The choice of diesel over solar power is obviously not the best possible path to the future. Here, future projects might be able to do better, since technology is always evolving and eventually solar or other renewable technologies will become competitive. In this spirit, ABB is currently analysing the possibility to use wind power as, at least, a backup power source in both Ngarambe and its future projects. In the meantime, development will take place in Ngarambe, hopefully enhancing social conditions even for ecological issues to come to the fore of local decision-making.

Overall, the Ngarambe case illustrates that it is possible to do business even in sub-Sahara Africa, taking due notice of, for example, London and Hart's (2004), Hart's (2005) and Prahalad's (2006) advice of establishing connection with various stakeholders with local knowledge and with local villagers in order to act culturally sensitive and cautiously. Importantly, ABB, and the other organizations involved, will be able to learn from the project. In fact, there has already been a decision in ABB to set up a human rights checklist to secure that human rights to an even greater extent are respected in future rural electrification projects, acknowledging that these kinds of projects take place in conditions where transgressions are not unlikely to occur (although there were only limited instances of such problems in the Ngarambe project in the form of some unofficial payments and potential child labour). A reason for the need of a human rights checklist is that awareness is nonexistent among locally employed ABB employees of issues such as the Global Compact and CSR. This will be subject to reform in the future, through, for example, the introduction of the checklist. Hence, in accordance with the recommendations from an officialist perspective, ABB tries to increase the couplings between 'talk'/'policy' and 'practice' by more explicitly coupling the CSR discourse and project practice on a local level.

An institutionalist reading: paradoxical processes

From a pragmatic institutionalist perspective, CSR and the UN Global Compact are fashionable ideas in contemporary managerial discourse emanating after a period of well publicised attention in the West to financial, ecological and social corporate scandals. Since organizations like ABB are dependent upon legitimacy, they must adhere to the UN Global Compact principles to be perceived as serious players in the global community (Meyer and Rowan, 1977). Standing outside Global Compact would, from such an institutionalist perspective, soon become problematic for ABB, to say nothing of questioning, or explicitly deviating, from these principles.

As an institutionalist would expect, demands in terms of both measurable effectiveness (such as return on capital) and demands from local stakeholders (such as the traditional medicine man) often stand in conflict with the rationalised myth of 'CSR' and the UN Global Compact (e.g. Meyer & Rowan, 1977; Brunsson, 1989). On an overall level, ABB handles this tension between different demands and rationalised myths by presenting its Ngarambe project as a collaborative cross-sectoral partnership of 'development aid' (the anathema of traditional business, supposedly about profits) in CSR focused contexts, and as profitable 'business' in other more finance focused contexts. The trick is, of course, for ABB to present a case for harmony among the demands put on the organizations: we can do good and do well, at the same time, especially in the long run.

On a practical level, on Tanzanian soil, some principles turn out to be possible to follow, while others must be sidestepped. The clear instance of decoupling 'talk' (ABB's and the UN Global Compact policy on environmental sustainability) from 'practice' (actual choice of power source) is striking in this respect. While Tanzania should be unusually well suited as a case for solar power, the very technology that spurs the global environmentalist move-ment is chosen, and that in turn, is eventually accepted by all parties involved. Arguably, this is possible since the project can be presented as a case of adherence to some other highly rationalised myths, such as 'development through electrification' spiced with acculturation in Western meritocracy, gender equality, wildlife conservation, and local democracy. The issue of power source can also be dealt with through a promise of future improvements. Furthermore, one could certainly argue that the project comes up against other principles of the Global Compact besides the promo-tion of environmentally friendly technology. Child labour could be seen here (European and U.S. school children could certainly not be counted on to dig trenches up to their teachers' houses), and the general practice of unofficial payments to those who demand it could be seen to promote patterns of corruption.

However, these decoupling details remain at the Tanzanian level, through filtering of such information by ABB TZ and WWF TZ in their communication with ABB International and WWF International, and, in turn, filtering by ABB International and WWF International in discussions with international stakeholders (such as, for example, UN agencies, the World Bank, SIDA, Western NGOs, and media). Hence, the project's organising of informa-tion flows allowed for decoupling between 'talk' and 'practice', and made such decouplings difficult to monitor. This decoupling made Access to Electricity's international stakeholders perceive the project's performance to be in line with the UN Global Compact principles, while simultaneously, at least partly, meeting local stakeholders' demands. While the officialists, and ABB, perceive this decoupling as problematic, pragmatist institutionalists, on the contrary, perceive it as beneficial for the project. For there to be an electricity system in Ngarambe both local and international stake-holders need to be satisfied, so decoupling is necessary for meeting both international stakeholders' demands ('talk' of non-corruption and no child labour), and local stakeholders' demands ('practice' of unofficial payments and children digging trenches). Pragmatic institutionalists would even argue that some of the project's tight couplings caused unnecessary friction in the project. For example, time and energy was wasted on convincing the village government to include women in the financial committee, and ABB's initial resistance to providing unofficial payments rendered delays in the project and put their representatives in potential jeopardy. Consequently, pragmatic institutionalists would, in sharp contrast to officialists, argue that the project succeeded *despite* couplings of 'talk' and 'practice', and that couplings should be minimised, not maximised as the officialists would argue, in future projects.

A critical reading: unfinished business

A critical reading would first point to the partial adequacy of the officialist, rather than the insitutionalist, reading. ABB did, at least in most part, what it said it did. There is an electricity system in Ngarambe, and in general the Global Compact principles were followed. However, a critical perspective would host suspicion that what is done, is done in the wrong way – without adequate moral consciousness – and has bad consequences for those least deserving of them (i.e. the Ngarambe villagers). From a critical perspec-tive, the electrification of Ngarambe is a textbook example of Enlightenment. It is a colonization of the Ngarambe villagers' life world by a Western systems world. The idea that electricity is good is a given. The idea that the systems world (ABB, SIDA, WWF, and the government of Tanzania) has a right to meddle in the affairs in Ngarambe is also beyond questioning. The entire process is marked by a logic of expediency (Mannheim, 1936; Jackall, 1988), the mark of Western rationality. Gods and goddesses will be challenged (as in the demise of the medicine man in Ngarambe), and qualities will tend to be put to the side (for example, by adding a bit of corruption). From a critical perspective, A BB's involvement in the process has nothing to do with authentic wishes to do 'good' business, just good PR. Settling for second best, several other organizations play along in this on all points besides when the power source was in question. Despite the promising sign of true quarrels over this issue within several organizations (i.e. signs of rational human communication (Habermas, 1981/1984)), expedient action, rather than informed decision, prevailed. Short-term budgets were allowed to direct and delimit action, rather than going for the best possible solution. Hence, it is a classic example of 'goal displacement' in the service of the strong (ABB), to the detriment of the weak (the environment and its spokespersons).

The type of instrumentalist attitude shown in the ABB case to the world in general, and to people (in Ngarambe) in particular, is the mark of Western reason, in its amputated form, the one critical theory exposes and is opposed to. Here, a golden opportunity was foregone to involve resource poor people in rural Africa in a project for the future. The villagers were invited into the process well after all major decisions had been made. Local resistance was dealt with in the spirit of getting the job done rather than convincing all parties concerned through rational communication. The principles and overall aims of the project were never an issue, not even for the local Tanzanian representatives of ABB. Hence, the project entailed little of the type of dialogical nature that the critical perspective finds essential for avoidance of colonization of life worlds and, thus, genuinely successful projects.

However, while the village of Ngarambe is being enlightened with local tradition left in a weaker position, the programme of Enlightenment remains intact. Never do ABB discuss with its international stakeholders that the project's instances of non-compliance with the UN Global Compact principles indicate that there is something wrong with the principles themselves. At least, this is not done in discussions with its influential stakeholders capable of influencing the Global Compact and similar standards. Consequently, the principles of the Enlightenment remain unchallenged by ABB's Ngarambe project, while changes in the direction of these Enlightenment principles occur locally in Ngarambe.

A critical perspective would highlight this uneven distribution of changes and argue that we have witnessed an effort at world-wide *progress* through, among other actors, a Western MNC, translated into a business project, implying to a large extent a transport of a set of taken-for granted ideas and practices from Västerås, Zürich and New York to Ngarambe sparking changes on that very local level. In a well-known pattern of patrimonial bureaucracy (Jackall, 1988), credit for the success of electrification gets pushed up to global levels, and the muddling details remain at the local, and far away level. In other terms: change is achieved in Ngarambe, but not necessarily only in the manner desired for. This comes about because of a lack of organizational change on the global level. Western corporations remain permeated by technocratic consciousness (Alvesson, 1983), and, indeed that is our tradition, the one we seem remarkably unable and unwilling to cast off.

In that tradition, assuming all to be the Same, the very real Other(s) are not asked what they think, want, need, wish, dream and hope for. And, then again, the principle of asking the Other is not included in the principles of the UN Global Compact. Hence, what comes across as the main issues (what 'to do' in Ngarambe in general – and 'why', and highly important issues such as the choice of power source) are determined before ever including the villagers themselves. The decision parameter is the principle of expedient action. 'Here is a budget, what can we do with that' instead of 'what budget do we need in order to do something really good' and 'if we don't get it, we might just as well abstain from doing things at all'. From a critical perspective, ABB as an organization has sadly shown little willingness to promote conscious reflection geared towards authentic involvement in the issues at hand.

A sceptical reading: a project in need of local resistance

Access to electricity is formulated as something beneficial to actors close to power. So is the Ngarambe project. All this could be interpreted as a not-so-disguised expression of the interest of Capital in accumulation with increased levels of production and consumption needing to be created to sustain growth of capital. This is overtly attested to in the officialist descriptions as well. The only difference is that what in the officialist perspective is something mutually beneficial, is in the sceptical perspective something mutually malevolent, reinforcing consumerist materialism, ecological distress and white supremacism ('we' can teach 'them' how to 'develop'). From where comes the right to meddle in others' affairs across the globe, thrashing traditional family patterns, cultural practices and levels of relative autonomy vis-à-vis the surrounding world? From where comes the right to enclose, rank and normalise all others in a globally managed space?

The rational discussions that might look like perfecting the Ngarambe project from a critical perspective would entail even more intrusive normalising measures, including the training of special normalising personnel, spreading the Western gospel with quite a bit of 'cultural sensitivity'. Again, this very much sounds like the officialist reading of the case. We would here in particular point to the well known organizationally routine promise of future embetterment which consists of intensified set-ups of internal guidelines for normalising activities, i.e., setting up personal communication with 'locals', trying to understand their mores, and act accordingly. All this in close cooperation between a commercial enterprise (ABB), a not for profit organization (WWF), and the Tanzanian government. The Western gaze homes in on its subjects, thus constituting them.

What differs between an officialist and a sceptical reading is the overall value attributed to these prospects. A sceptic is not convinced of the superiority of western life-forms and technology. The question of ecological sustainability might perhaps be seen as the strongest case for the sceptic; what spreads through this particular project, as it actually happened, was diesel technology – a part of the enormous problem of global warming.

Inconsistent understandings of corporate responsibility

If we compare the four readings of the case, we find that they yield highly differing results. Table 2 summarises the main points of each reading.

Table 2.

PERSPECTIVE	MAIN CONCLUSION	PROJECT EVALUATION	RECOMMENDATIONS
1. Officialist	An attempt to do good	*Success*	Stronger couplings between 'talk' and 'practice'
2. Pragmatic institutionalist	Both coupling and decoupling of 'talk' and 'practice'	*Success*	Weaker couplings between 'talk' and 'practice'
3. Critical	Enlightenment project	*Failure*	Rational communication with locals and other stakeholders
4. Sceptical	Enlightenment project	*Failure*	Abandon project or mini-mise communication

As can be seen in Table 2, there are both similarities in and differences between the four readings. First, for the officialist and
the pragmatic institutionalist reading CSR represent a significant
change in the business environment that pressures firms to alter
their talk and/or practice. The studied ABB project is in these
readings interpreted as a novel phenomenon spurred by external
changes. In contrast, the critical and the sceptical readings present
CSR as more of the same – as a continuation of Western actors'
Enlightenment and colonial projects. The ABB project is but yet
another manifestation in our belief in science, expedient action,
and rationality. Second, the officialist and the pragmatic institutionalist readings focus on something being done. The officialist
does this based on the assumption that CSR practices are desirable
per se, while the pragmatic institutionalist pays limited attention to
the content of CSR practice. In terms of the ABB case, both readings
concur that something has happened – most notably a working
electricity system in Ngarambe. In contrast, the critical and the
sceptical readings focus on *what* is being done rather than *if* something is being done. They pose the question of what is the content
of CSR practices and are displeased with the provided answer (at

least in the analysed ABB case). Combined these aspects make the officialist and the pragmatic institutionalist readings conclude that the ABB project is a 'success' and that CSR projects are desirable (at least if they resemble the ABB case). In sharp contrast, the critical and sceptical perspective readings conclude that the ABB project is a 'failure' and that CSR projects are undesirable (at least if they resemble the ABB case).

These discrepancies between perspectives even regarding the fundamental question of whether the analysed project is a 'success' or 'failure' seems to be related to the inclusion of power relations in the analysis. When emphasis is on the consensus part in Burrell and Morgan's (1979) matrix (as with the officialist and pragmatic institutionalist), CSR projects are seen as desirable. However, when emphasis is on the conflict part in Burrell and Morgan's (1979) matrix (as with the critical and sceptical readings), CSR projects are seen as undesirable. This divide illustrates a central blind spot in the CSR field, since CSR practices are almost exclusively presented as desirable. Hence, the bulk of previous CSR research can arguably be said to be based on a win-win logic (cf. Shanahan & Khagram, 2006), ignoring alternative win-lose interpretations of CSR practices.

Even if we leave this larger divide between perspectives emphasising consensus or conflict, interesting differences remain. First, the officialist reading coins the ABB project a 'success' despite *decoupling* tendencies, i.e. despite instances of discrepancies of talk and practice, while the pragmatic institutionalist reading coins the project a 'success' despite *coupling* tendencies. The difference between these readings is clearly illustrated in that the provided recommendations for future CSR projects are diametrically different. The officialist argues for tighter couplings, i.e. an abandoning of organized hypocrisy, encouraging ABB's current attempts to introduce human right checklists and educate local project managers to influence them to more stringently implement the ABB and UN Global Compact policies. The pragmatic institutionalist, on the other hand, argues that such development will have detrimental effects, since organized hypocrisy is the only fruitful way to adhere to the posed inconsistent local and international stakeholder demands. In turn, such perceived adherence is essential if CSR projects are to achieve results (in the ABB case an electricity system), making pragmatic institutionalists recommend more decouplings rather than less in future projects. Second, the critical and sceptical readings also disagree on recommendations for future projects. While the critical reading recommends rational communication as a remedy for the Enlightenment tendencies, the sceptical reading is highly critical of such 'solution'. For the sceptic, Enlightenment is the problem, to be resisted and subverted, however futile it might be. Consequently, the sceptical perspective finds hope in local resistance and abandonment of CSR projects, while the critical perspective finds hope in rational communication.

Multiparadigm research into corporate responsibility

The above identified differences between the four readings illustrate that analyses of corporate responsibility practices from a single scientific paradigm will be constrained and limited. As Rhodes (2000) and Law (1994) argue, each reading of text, i.e. each analysis from a certain theoretical perspective, simultaneously allows the researcher to see certain aspects while suppressing others. For example, the ABB project is a 'success' from two perspectives, but a 'failure' from two others. Hence, each reading tells an academic story that also conceals alternative stories. The identified differences between understandings of corporate responsibility in the here conducted study indicate that it is central to adopt and develop a multiparadigm approach for a richer understanding of the complexity of corporate responsibility practice. At least, it illustrates that researchers within this research field need to be cautious when interpreting the 'findings' of their studies. This is particularly so, since previous research into corporate responsibility has been fairly homogeneous in terms of deriving theoretical perspectives from paradigms that downplay the role of power relations (cf. Welford, 1998). Hence, since the corporate responsibility research field is not characterised by a multiparadigm approach as a whole, individual researchers need to be even more cautious when interpreting their 'findings' and making recommendations for future CSR projects.

While a multiparadigm approach provides us with a richer understanding of corporate responsibility practices, this is not to imply that the 'true' nature of these practices can be exposed. On the contrary, our different readings of the studied case illustrate that it hardly makes sense to discuss a 'correct' or 'true' reading of CSR practices, since each reading is dependent on the theoretical perspective put to use (*cf.* Rhodes, 2000; Lewis & Kelemen, 2002). There are dozens of other, equally viable, theoretical perspectives that could have been used in this and future studies, likely leading to dozens of alternative readings of CSR practices. As Pondy and Boje (1980:84) notice, researchers tend to shift the function of 'theory' after having conducted multiparadigm research from that of 'truth proving' to 'insight seeking'. Applied to research into corporate responsibility practice, we would be sceptic of research claiming, explicitly or implicitly, to unveil the truth of corporate responsibility practices, and instead opt for research aimed at increasing our understanding of these complex phenomena using multiple theoretical perspectives.

Concluding discussion

In this chapter, we have argued that a multiparadigm research approach is fruitful when studying corporate responsibility. We have also argued, although implicitly, that such research is valuable for influencing both the academic world and the world outside academia, and that the writing, publishing and reading of this book is of value. Our focus has been inward looking, acting *as if* corporate responsibility and academic research into corporate responsibility matters. To conclude this chapter, we want to shortly criticise this approach using a fifth theoretical perspective – a cynical one.

Cynics have been around for some time (Cutler, 2005), and their spirit is available for those willing to adopt it. A cynical perspective is difficult to place in Burrell and Morgan's (1979) matrix, since it rather hovers over the matrix than fits inside it. As Gibson Burrell (1997) noted, cynics rant and 'piss in public' in the spirit of 'I'm no J. Derrida but still ...'. Cynics would laugh, for instance, at our petty belief that corporate responsibility practice and research matter. As long as the rich countries have export subsidies and import restrictions, use WTO and IMF for their purposes etc., CSR is an abbreviation for *corporate asocial response-inability*. There are fundamental problems in the world such as violence, illiteracy, illness, poverty, and non-functioning 'democracies' (e.g., Gill, 2002), and nothing a corporation like ABB or the CSR movement will do can ever fix this. If governments, NGOs, and corporations *really* cared, CSR would not be the solution, no matter how pompous and serious we parade as being. Global democratic politics would *perhaps* fix it. Similarly, if the authors of this chapter and the others in this book *really* cared, we would not sit in our offices writing rarely read texts about unimportant corporate practices. We would simply leave our offices with a 'fuck you' echoing from our lips, trying to make a difference rather than publishing glossy books. Real change would be premised of us all not only parading as human beings, rather than, to use Diogenes' favourite analogy, dogs.

9. The Business of Social Responsibility: Practicing and Communicating CSR

JAKOB LAURING AND CHRISTA THOMSEN

Introduction

It is often argued that there is a link between social responsibility and competitive advantages (Thomas 1990; Ross & Schneider 1992; Porter & Linde 1995; Waddock & Smith 2000; Porter & Kramer 2003). In this context, the optimization of productivity, the attraction and retention of qualified personnel, as well as motivation and improvement of the working environment have been mentioned as examples of positive outcomes of social responsibility policies. Social responsibility, though, should not be practiced solely for philanthropic reasons. It has been claimed for instance, that social responsibility can increase competitiveness by improving the internal and external image of a company, and by creating a sense of security and belonging for all types of employees. On the one hand, it might be argued that social responsibility has become an acknowledged business parameter. On the other hand it could also be argued, that public discourse of responsibility towards weaker minorities is gaining ground in private enterprises.

Many private organizations have developed an interest in corporate ethics and value-based leadership, and to a greater extent than previously they have employed non-traditional financial aspects of organizational life, such as working environment, knowledge, competencies, ethics and social responsibility in business strategies and policies (Thyssen 2003; Thyssen 2004). While it was traditionally stated that 'the business of business is business', it can now be added that the introduction of public discourses to private corporations has made social responsibility the business of businesses (Freeman 1984; 2004; Carroll 1999). In other words, the interrelation of business and social responsibility is growing stronger. However, and the entanglement of the two concepts is becoming increasingly difficult for organizations to deal with.

Our point of departure will be that the link between social responsibility and business targets is not achieved as easily as sometimes perceived. Theoretically we argue that:

> Social Responsibility or Corporate Social Responsibility (CSR) is a dynamic and contextual concept.

The dynamic and contextual aspect of CSR is a big challenge to companies. They must for example, be able to manage the mutual expectations between itself and its stakeholders. Empirically, we argue that:

> CSR is a participative process. Companies need to invite both employees and public actors (in Denmark) to participate in defining CSR. Only in this way is it possible for companies to explore the expectations or the concerns of their stakeholders, a crucial factor in achieving a link between social responsibility and business targets (Freeman 1984).

We use two cases to support our theoretical and empirical statements. The cases describe the complexity of managing and communicating social responsibility – internally and externally. The first case outlines some of the internal difficulties of achieving a balance between the practice of social responsibility and the achievement of business advantages. The second case outlines some of the external difficulties of achieving the same balance. The main challenge is seen as the 'competition' between two discourses, the business discourse on strategy, and the public discourse on social responsibility. Inviting the employees on the one hand and public actors on the other to participate in defining CSR is seen as the most effective way to obtain a balance between the two competing discourses. Finally, in the concluding remarks we will discuss benefits and difficulties in relation to managing an organization in the battlefield of the competing discourses of social responsibility and business competition. This discussion opens up for a debate of the contextual character of the concept of CSR.

Managing the business of social responsibility

We have argued above that social responsibility is fundamentally a question of the relations between the company and its environment. The concept becomes operational when it engages with the specific stakeholders and their expectations. This encounter gives way for a potential conflict, as the concept of social responsibility is about ethics and values and contains an implicit demand for a solution (Thyssen 2004: 127). The conflict manifests itself in two competing discourses, the public discourse on social responsibility and the business discourse on strategy and profit.

In this regard, the literature on CSR typically distinguishes between three different approaches to the question of what companies are responsible for. The first approach is the classical view that: 'The Social Responsibility of Business is to Increase its Profits' (Friedman 1970). Here, the owners of the company, who are supposed to be interested in profit maximization, are the turning point of the decisions made by the company. Social responsibility is considered primarily to be the responsibility of the government. This approach also covers companies, which consider social responsibility primarily as something that contributes to attaining the goals of the company, often in the form of long-term value creation for the owners of the company.

A second approach could be labelled the stakeholder perspective. According to this approach companies are not only accountable to the owners of the company, but also to the other stakeholders. R. Edward Freeman defines a 'stakeholder' as: 'Any group or individual who can affect or is affected by the achievement of the firm's objectives' (Freeman 1984: 25). According to Freeman the primary stakeholders are those who have a legitimate interest in the company, these are the owners, investors, employees and customers. Competitors, distributors, local society, interest groups, media, and society are secondary stakeholders. The argument is that stakeholders influence the activities of the company and/or are influenced by the activities of the company (Freeman 1984). Companies are, for example, accountable to politicians who can curb the activities of the company by proposing legislation on CSR.

The third and broadest approach to social responsibility is the societal approach in which companies are considered to have a responsibility to society in general. The view is that companies are part of society. Since they require a 'licence to operate' from society (Committee for Economic Development, CED, 1971). Today companies representing this approach are characterized as 'good corporate citizens' (see for example Waddock 2004). Carroll boils down the essentials of the three approaches. He considers the role of companies today as a role which includes four dimensions, i.e. an economic, a legal, an ethical and a philantropic aspect: *'The CSR firm should strive to make a profit, obey the law, be ethical, and be a good corporate citizen'* (Carroll 1991: 43).

This early definition does not say anything about the emphasis that should be put on the different dimensions. In his article from 1999 Carroll mentions different contributions to the debate on CSR, especially Thomas M. Jones (1980) and Peter F. Drucker (1984). Jones' contribution is to consider CSR as a process. According to Carroll, however, Jones does not contribute to the necessary debate on the expectations with regard to the content and the limits of CSR (Carroll 1999: 285). Drucker is more explicit stating that the proper social responsibility of business is to *'turn a social problem into economic opportunity and economic benefit, into productive capacity, into human competence, into well-paid jobs, and into wealth'* (Drucker 1984: 62). According to Carroll, Drucker is a good example of the increasing focus on the economic dimension and on the demands of measuring CSR. When establishing a link between CSR and the stakeholders of the company Carroll is influenced by Jones and Drucker:

> Arguing that the term "social" in CSR has been seen by some as vague and lacking in specificity as to whom the corporation is responsible, I suggested that the stakeholder concept, popularized by R. Edward Freeman (1984), personalizes social or societal responsibilities by delineating the specific groups or persons business should consider in its CSR orientation and activities. Thus, the stakeholder nomenclature puts "names and faces" on the societal members or groups who are most important to business and to whom it must be responsive (Carroll 1999: 290).

Frederick (1994) highlights the implications of the above outlined shift from the philosophical-ethical approach to CSR to a more profit-oriented managerial approach to CSR:

> The implications of this shift include a reduction in business defensiveness, an increased emphasis on techniques for managing social responsiveness, more empirical research on business and society relationships and constraints on corporate responsiveness, a continued need to clarify business responsibilities, and a need to work toward more dynamic theories of values and social change (Frederick 1994: 150).

In this chapter we argue in line with Freeman, Carroll and Frederick, that the stakeholder concept personalizes social responsibilities by delineating the specific groups or persons a business should consider in its CSR orientation and activities. In order to manage the business of social responsibility, companies need to reduce the defensiveness of business by building long-lasting relationships and engaging in genuine CSR dialogues with their internal and external stakeholders.

CSR dialogues

In organizational settings dialogue is often considered a strategic tool that can lead to organizational gains such as motivation, learning, development, collaboration and so forth. (Bohm 1996; Ellinor & Gerard 1998; Isaacs 1999).

Companies can, for example, engage in dialogue with their stakeholders in connection with the development and implementation of a CSR initiative. According to Freeman (1984: 52) the concept of Stakeholder Management can be used to understand and manage internal and external changes. Freeman distinguishes between three perspectives or levels: the rational level, the procedural level and the transactional level. In this article, we are primarily interested in the transactional level, that is the stakeholder dialogue. Among others, the questions raised by Freeman, are: 'How do the organisation and its managers interact with stakeholders? What resources are allocated to interact with which groups' (Freeman 1984: 69). Freeman stresses the importance of behaviour and mutuality:

> Suffice it to say that the nature of the behavior of organizational members and the nature of the goods and services being exchanged are key

ingredients in successful organizational transactions with stakeholders (Freeman 1984: 70–73).

Stakeholder Management is a voluntary concept. However, according to Freeman organizations with an expressed Stakeholder Management Capability develop and implement communication processes with many different stakeholder groups, communicate with stakeholders about critical issues, and aim to sign voluntary agreements with their stakeholders. Furthermore, they attempt to understand the needs of their stakeholders, involve the different functions or departments in the development of the strategy, act proactively and allocate resources in a way which takes into consideration the expectations of the stakeholders. In general, such organizations think in 'stakeholder-serving' terms. In this relation, Freeman (1984) provides several examples to illustrate how the lack of coherence between the goals, strategies, and processes and the lack of consistency in the internal and external messages sent out by the organization, creates problems in the interaction and communication with the stakeholders. The importance of linking the three levels is stressed:

> Clearly, there must be some "fit" among the elements of an organization's Stakeholder Management Capability – defined as its understanding or conceptual map of its stakeholders, the processes for dealing with these stakeholders, and the transactions which it uses to carry out the achievement of organization purpose with stakeholders (Freeman 1984: 70–73).

With regard to partnerships with public actors (e.g. municipalities) on social purposes, for example, it is affirmed that the cross-sector element or 'spirit' facilitates the link between the three levels and that this will lead to business opportunities in the form of innovative thinking and reduced expenses in connection with recruitment and sickness leave. The business argument for social partnerships is expressed in the definition provided by Sandra Waddock:

> A partnership is a commitment by a corporation or group of corporations to work with an organisation from a different economic sector (public or nonprofit). It involves a commitment of resources – time and effort – by individuals from all partner organisations. These individuals work coop-

eratively to solve a problem that affects them all. The problem can be defined at least in part as a social issue; its solution will benefit all partners (Waddock 1988: 18).

With this definition Waddock distinguishes social partnerships from other activities that may fulfil the social responsibilities of a corporation. Social partnerships are described as cooperative, interactive entities that require a good deal of commitment on all sides (Waddock 1988).

To sum up, the aim of the dialogue is for companies to be able to tackle the internal and external expectations. For example, the employees 'on the shop floor' will expect the company to ensure that they will not lose their jobs because of another (cheaper) labour force entering the company in connection with job integration. Managers who are measured by their results will expect the company to set up accounting principles, which take into consideration that parts of the labour force have been recruited as part of the company's policy on social responsibility. The company can manage the mutual expectations by adopting specific rules for the dialogue with the stakeholders. These rules may concern the purpose and the use of the dialogue, the meeting structure, the rules for anonymity, etc. The form and content of the dialogue depend upon the context, i.e. the size of the company, the specific stakeholder groups, the complexity of the issue, the ambition level, and the nature of the engagement specified by the company.

Another challenge consists in motivating CSR initiatives, which in practice means that the company must be able to explain to internal and external stakeholders why it is logical for the company to be socially responsible. Being socially responsible is not evident to companies that operate on ordinary market terms. This explanation is important in order to be credible. If, for example, CSR initiatives cost money, the company must be able to explain to the stakeholders – owners/investors, in particular - why these initiatives are necessary and in which way they will lead to business opportunities.

Our cases show that dialogue is a strategic tool, which can lead to organizational learning and ensures consistency between business and social responsibility and between ideals and practices. Our cases also show that the results of the dialogue depend upon the dialogue partners' approach to the dialogue.

A qualitative approach to social responsibility

Researching the ideals and practices of social responsibility in organizational life is a complex task. The concept of social responsibility is ambiguous, contested and surrounded by a range of differing implicit notions. Hence, to investigate the dynamics of such a concept put into practice, researchers need a rather sensitive data-collection tool. For the cases, we have therefore applied ethnographic fieldwork techniques and data collection with heavy emphasis on observation, participation and interview (Bernard 1995). This approach departs from an ideal of generating questions as well as answers in close relation to the research field. This qualitative approach to a great extent also utilizes interviews to discuss and document the findings gathered in the daily observation.

The context of the studies in this qualitative approach can be said to be controlled more by the informants than by the researchers. While quantitative surveys focus on individuals as units of analysis, one of the strengths of the qualitative approach is the possibility of also including the interaction and communication between individuals, groups and organizations (Spradley 1980). Hence, the qualitative methodology is particularly suited to investigate issues connected to the notions, practice, and communication of social responsibility in organizations, since the business arguments draw on positive feedback and synergies between groups and individuals.

Through the application of ethnographic observations and interviews the researcher can gain an understanding of issues that the informants may take for granted, issues that are not mentioned, but can be observed in action – such as the relation between ideals and practices of social responsibility (see also Bourdieu 1977). Further, this methodology is well suited to investigate issues that could be regarded as personal, critical or of another sensitive nature because the researcher is situated close to the field (Wadel 1991).

In the first case, the company Novo Nordisk is selected because, where formal strategy and targets is concerned, it is a leading actor within the field of social responsibility in Denmark. The Novo Nordisk Corporation is one of Denmark's largest companies and has a reputation of being highly concerned with CSR dating back 50 years. A central statement is that 'Social responsibility is more than a virtue – it is a business imperative'. In the general management guidelines it is mentioned that close relations between social responsibility and economy is the aim of the organization. The international marketing department, from which the data material was collected is a knowledge intensive business unit focusing considerably more on business issues and useful individual resources than on ethics and the representation of minority affinities such as race, ethnicity, and gender. Still, the case represents an interesting example of some of the dilemmas between business arguments and social responsibility and ideals and practices, which can be observed in many Western organizations at present. All in all, 30 interviews with different employees and managers were combined with extensive observation throughout a one-month period in the department.

The second case is developed in the Danish rescue company Falck A/s, Region Nord. This company is selected because of its tradition for social responsibility and cross-sector collaboration. The personnel policy of the company is a good example of the focus on CSR. However, at the time of the data collection the management of Falck A/s realized that 'a page was missing' in the personnel policy, and they decided to prepare this page together with a public partner, namely Jobcentre Aarhus Nord (county of Aarhus). Thus, the case is a good example of how a company with a long-term tradition for social responsibility collaborates with a public partner and other stakeholders on a CSR related issue (job retention and job integration), and succeeds in establishing a link between social responsibility and business opportunities. A in the first case, this case also illustrates some of the dilemmas between business arguments and social responsibility, which can be observed in many Western organizations at present, for example the distribution of the roles between the private company and the public partner. Extensive observation throughout a two-year period in the social partnership (4 seminars, 25 steering group meetings, 11 background meetings, 6 sparring group meetings, 6 evaluation meetings and 3–4 meetings in the different working groups from 2000 until 2002) was combined with interviews (from 2000 until 2005) two of which were in-depth interviews with the partnership management (Falck A/s and Jobcentre Aarhus Nord).

Applying the public discourse as desired image: an internal perspective

At the time of the data collection Novo Nordisk was one of the Danish organizations that had worked hardest to uphold an image as an ethical corporation. The company defined its guidelines with reference to both social responsibility and competitiveness and the two concepts were claimed to complement each other.

Some of the most important efforts at social responsibility were the removal of discriminatory organizational structures and the introduction of 'equal opportunity' strategies and diversity management. These initiatives were linked to business strategy in such a way that social responsibility was supposed to attract and retain skilled employees. Social responsibility could thus be applied to recruitment and retention on the one hand, and to promoting the image of the company on the other hand. Another strategy was focusing more on the employment of resources arising from human differences; an initiative that was supposed to lead to knowledge synergies, international understanding and market intelligence. Thereby, the removal of discriminatory structures managing the diversity was seen as leading to innovation and creativity, linking business opportunities to social responsibility. As it was written:

> Social responsibility is more than a virtue – it is a necessity to run a business. It is an investment in our future.
> (Sustainability Report 2002)

The international marketing department, which was the focus area of the research project was the most ethnically and culturally diverse department in the corporation. Here, a genuine need for human diversity was expressed in strategies of international product promotion, pricing, sales and market analysis, and planning of international conferences. This meant that apart from the dedication to social responsibility, there were powerful business motives for recruitment of what was termed as ethnic or cultural minorities. The problem was that the organization through its recruitment strategy aimed to get 'the best of the best', and this strategy could be seen as a barrier toward the practice of social responsibility. As mentioned by managers in the department, special treatment of weaker minorities in the labour market should not determine the combination of different employees, and quotas for recruitment were looked upon with scepticism. Rejection of quotas for recruitment did not mean that non-Danish people were in a more difficult position for a job than Danes – on the contrary. In accordance with the profit arguments for CSR, non-Danes as a minority held competencies making them especially qualified for the job: e.g. knowledge of foreign markets and international communication skills. Still, access barriers or indirect discrimination could be identified. High demands regarding education, professional qualifications and language skills made it difficult for particular groups to enter the department in spite of the hard work to keep up the percentage of non-Danish employees.

Most people in the international marketing department had noticed that very few employees really stood out from the crowd. Hardly anyone was dark-skinned or wore different clothing. With the exception of a small group of Chinese, non-Danes generally came from OECD countries. Unofficially, it was mentioned that efficiency-wise the most beneficial combination of staff seemed to be a 'collection of Western backgrounds' (informant). This had made some managers consider the possibility that recruitment policies had been developed to 'mirror ourselves' (informant). 'We claim that we are open, but, anyway, there are some countries and some colours we are not entirely open towards' (informant). Managers in the department were not unaware of the problems, but the heavy emphasis on professionalism in the organization led to market forces determining the recruitment criteria.

Only a highly educated group of international experts could match the required individual competencies and qualifications. Minority groups such as immigrants and refugees were not to be found in the organization despite the fact that non-Danish employees were highly needed.

It is a shame we don't have any immigrants or refugees, but they do not have the language skills that make them good enough to join. Also, the fact that if they are doctors their education is usually from one single country and they are not raised internationally and so on, because the ones educated at Harvard don't go to Denmark, they go to England or USA. So the leftover pool can be all right, but we have to say that they need to be Danish doctors first and then probably they can also improve their English language skills as well. (Top Manager, Denmark)

Thereby, the recruited human differences was based more on a business-oriented focus on international and professional experience, than on affiliation with minority groups based on age, gender, race or handicap. In this case, the business strategy discourse was too strong for the public discourse of responsibility to be related to anything else than the desired image or PR.

In the Novo example, it becomes clear that the relation between social responsibility and competitive advantages is a complex one. Even though the practice of social responsibility toward disadvantaged minorities in the labour market might add competitive advantages to organizations, this outcome cannot be taken for granted. Furthermore, there is a great probability that social responsibility will not be a direct financial asset in corporate life. When understanding the dynamics of social responsibility it is therefore crucial to include the context within which the responsibility is actualized. The above case has shown the danger of neglecting ethic considerations in the promotion of a balanced or synergetic relationship between business arguments and social responsibility, thus actually leaving the disadvantaged minorities in an increasingly difficult position. When rhetoric and desired image of a corporation promote social responsibility and practice does not follow the ideals, the superficial ideology can act as a barrier preventing minorities from gaining access to the organization. Therefore, many organizations should dedicate more attention to ensuring consistency between the internal practice and the externally expressed ideals. The process of actualizing this through communication and dialogue will be described in the following case.

Applying the public discourse as business: an external perspective

Between 2000 and 2002 when the main data were collected, the parties involved in the social partnership between the private rescue company Falck A/s, the municipality of Aarhus and the vocational rehabilitation centre, Jobcentre Aarhus Nord, worked hard to develop and implement a model for social responsibility for Falck A/S. Some of the most important efforts at social responsibility were: a) job creation/job development for Falck A/S employees with a fragile/reduced working capability; b) development of vocational rehabilitation activities in the form of job testing, job maturing or clarifying activities, etc.; c) implementation of a partnership with the municipality of Aarhus on the follow-up aimed at employees who suffered from long-term illness. These initiatives were linked to business strategy in such a way that social responsibility and the tools developed were supposed to save time and money and lead to better and quicker results, and ultimately, a better image.

The public partner, Jobcentre Aarhus Nord, initiated the collaboration and assumed the role of project coordinator. From the beginning, however, the partners agreed upon a cross-sector project organization. In this way the partnership gave high priority to relationship building and mutuality. The public discourse on social responsibility and social partnerships was dominant (Nelson & Zadek 2000:14), which made it possible for the company to express the ideals on social responsibility externally, not only to the public partner but also to other stakeholders. However, there was a mutual understanding in the partnership that in order to succeed it was necessary to consider the business discourse on strategy and to develop the strategy. Thus, the public partner and the employees of the company were invited to participate in the development of the strategy. The ambition expressed was that CSR in practice should come to follow company ideals. The case study shows how the strategy was developed in a participative/dialogical process, which was open to adjustments to accommodate the mutual expectations. The model used for the change process (Table 1) is characterized as a dialogue-change model (Thomsen 2007).

The process and the dialogue between the partners on the content and form of the agreement were of vital importance to the outcomes and the results obtained. It was necessary to establish a 'platform for dialogue' and to ensure that the conditions for the change process were ideal. The aim was to build mutual understanding and good relations between the private company and the public partner and between the partners and different groups that had a stake in the partnership, for example, trade unions and NGOs.

Table 1: Dialogue-change model	
DIALOGUE STRUCTURE (EXCHANGE CONSISTING OF THREE TURN-TAKINGS) (ROULET ET AL. 1986)	CHANGE PROCESS Step no 1: establishing a sense of urgency (Kotter 1997)
A: Initiative (opening seminar)	The partnership with the public partner in front: presentation of the context for social responsibility.
B: Reaction	The employees in the private company and other stakeholders: identification and discussion of crises, potential crises and essential possibilities.
A: Evaluation/closing	The partnership: thank you very much for your contribution – and the future work.

The platform was established in three phases:

1. Negotiation of what was called the "platform for dialogue":

    a. Agreement upon the common goals.

    b. Elaboration of a communication model. The model was based upon the needs of the persons involved. There was, for example, a need for interorganizational and intercultural learning, and there was a need for explaining to the employees in the private company and other stakeholders why the social partnership with the public sector was necessary or beneficial.

    c. Adoption of a cross-sector project organization chart.

2. Opening seminar. The project was initiated at an opening seminar that was later followed by two working seminars. These three seminars represented the development phase of the project and can be seen as part of a basic dialogue structure consisting of three exchanges; an initiative, a response and an evaluation. They paved the way for the implementation of the project.

3. Start-up seminar. The implementation of the project was initiated at a start-up seminar that was followed by a testing of the model in the workplace and by the evaluation of the project. The dialogue in connection with implementing the strategy was more closed than the dialogue that took place in connection with developing the strategy. The communication was two-way but asymmetrical compared to the two-way and symmetrical communication in the development phase. This is

not unexpected in the communication of decisions. According to James E. Grunig the situation and the purpose determine which form of communication is best (Grunig 2001).

It was characteristic for the change process that the employees in the private company and other stakeholders were invited to participate. Their active participation was required particularly in the first part of the process (bottom-up approach) and less so in the second part of the process (top-down approach). It was also characteristic that the public partner was actively involved. A close investigation into the role distribution between the private company and the public partner showed that the public partner played a well-defined and somewhat alternative role. The role of the public partner can be characterized as a role of legitimization, change agent and professional sparring partner (for example social legislation and political 'winds'). The public partner helped the company to establish a sense of urgency by explaining to the employees why social responsibility is a 'common' issue. Furthermore, the public partner helped the company to communicate the new CSR strategy, providing in this way a third party legitimization, and a valuable contribution to corporate image (Schultz, Morsing & Ulf Nielsen 2004).

The results of the process were both quantitative and qualitative. The main quantitative result was that the company retained a number of people in their jobs and that a number of people were integrated into the company. According to the partners the main qualitative results were related to the partnership or the relationship and to the new tools and models developed. The company stresses the establishment of good relations to the public partner and other stakeholders as a main result of the partnership. One interesting aspect here is that the public partner is also a customer. The company also mentions that the new models and tools developed help them save time and money. Furthermore, the company mentions that cross-sector collaboration often leads to innovative thinking, and they give several examples of new business opportunities created as a result of a cross-sector collaboration (for example, Survival Centre Esbjerg).

> In the beginning you see it (the pressure from the public sector to take a social responsibility or engage in a partnership) as a problem because it is detrimental to competitiveness. However, new methods and new

technologies often follow that become business activities in themselves.
(Rescue Manager, Falck a/s)

The public partner stresses the establishment of good relations to
the private company as one of the main results of the partnership.
They mention that it is important to have a private ambassador
who can communicate the results to others, for example, the central administration. The public partner also stresses that it is of
vital importance to be in dialogue with a private company who can
help them train rehabilitees in a more business-like context.

> The collaboration with Falck in 2000 was an important factor in our
> development of company rehabilitation as an internal tool and in our
> development of partnerships. It was also the starting point for our par-
> ticipation in the project on "Company Rehabilitation" launched by the
> (Danish) Ministry for Social Affairs and for a development project under
> the auspices of the EU-Commission. Today the collaboration is primarily
> important because of the agreement on the delivery of services to Falck
> and the agreement on permanent job training places in 5 departments in
> Falck. Altogether, having a private ambassador who can communicate the
> results of our collaboration makes a difference. (Economy and Planning
> Manage, Vocational Rehabilitation Centre)

Today both partners organize their work in new ways. The partnership can be seen as an example of organizational learning, as
the structure, the culture and the processes have changed in both
organizations (Argyris & Schön, 1978). The dialogue-forum created by the partners has made possible cross-sector learning. The
main condition for creating this forum was that the partners in the
very beginning made a strong effort to create a 'we'-identity (joint
purpose, joint value creation, mutual benefits, clear role distribution, etc.). In this case, the business discourse on strategy and the
public discourse on social responsibility complemented each other,
and social responsibility did not remain a desired image only.

Concluding remarks

It is often argued that business logic and social responsibility issues
are at conflict with each other. By outlining the context depend-

ency of the concepts, we have argued that the relationship between CSR and business is a complex one. In other words, the concept of social responsibility is an ambiguous term closely related to the situation, and often manipulated with regard to political, social, or economical incentives. Our case studies show that the solutions to a balance between CSR and business can be sought from different approaches and through different means, some of which are more apt than others.

We have used a thorough qualitative approach to elaborate and investigate the link between social responsibility and business, resulting in a different kind of information compared to the results of data collections that are initiated at greater distance from the setting for actually practicing CSR initiatives.

The two case studies have highlighted the understanding of how corporations attempt to and actually sometimes succeed in achieving a balance between social responsibility and business results. This can be approached in a number of different ways, and both a good image and increased productivity could be the results. As such, the two cases outline some of the benefits and difficulties managing an organization in the battlefield of the competing discourses of social responsibility and business competition.

In the first case, the main difficulties were linked to the fact that the recruitment strategy of the marketing department had been defined in a closed system – 'out of context'. The second case described a situation in which an organization strategically used the concept of social responsibility, creating business opportunities in the negotiation of the public discourse. Here, the balance was managed through elements such as cross-sector partnership, bottom-up approach and a change management perspective.

As illustrated through the case studies, several dilemmas surround the practice of CSR. We have focused on two: the relationship between business/profits and responsibility on the one hand, and the relation between ideals and practice on the other hand.

We have shown that the balance between business/profits and responsibility can be disturbed in different ways. Our case studies show, for example, that the balance is disturbed if the company strategy is ambiguous and open to divergent interpretations. This might be the case if the company has just been sending out (written) guidelines instead of launching a process or inviting stakeholders to participate in the development of the CSR strategy. In that case CSR remains merely rhetoric and desired image. In order to achieve a balance, companies should focus more on the definition of CSR at the strategic management level. The coherence between the goals, strategy and processes and the consistency in the messages sent out by the top management are crucial elements in obtaining this balance (Freeman 1984: 70–73). Our case studies show, that the elements of a successful implementation of CSR are a process-oriented or dialogical approach focusing on inviting internal and external stakeholders to participate in the dialogue. In doing so, the study is in line with Porter and Kramer (2007), who argue that many efforts to improve the social consequences of companies' activities fail. The explanation they give is that such efforts turn business against society, where the two are interdependent, and that they pressure companies to think of CSR in generic ways instead of in the way most suitable to each firm's strategy.

We have also shown, that a lack of efficient strategic communication makes it difficult for companies to 'practice what they preach' or in other words to secure a relation between ideals and practice. Our case studies show, for example, that the relationship can be disturbed if the company fails to involve the closest leaders in the company strategy using them as some form of change agents (Larkin & Larkin). The result of this is that the leaders will do what seems most evident or logical in an organizational context, that is focus on profitability. In order to link ideals and practice, companies need to focus more on developing and implementing communication processes with their internal and external stakeholders, and on communicating with them about critical issues, on signing voluntary agreements, trying to understand their needs, involving the different functions or departments in the development of the strategy, acting proactively, allocating resources in a way which takes into consideration the expectations of the stakeholders and in general, thinking in 'stakeholder-serving' terms (Freeman 1984: 70–73). This means that companies should be less defensive and more responsive (Frederick 1994: 150) – the best way to do this being to engage in genuine CSR dialogues with their internal and external stakeholders. This also means that companies need to change if this is necessary which is very often the case in today's globalized world.

In order to achieve the best results in managing social responsibility, it is necessary to learn from the second case stating that CSR is a participative process. Companies need to invite employees and other stakeholders – public actors in Denmark – to participate in defining CSR. In this way, it is possible for companies to manage internal integration and external adaptation at the same time (Schein 1994). The dialogue with primary stakeholders facilitates the establishment of a link between ideals and practice or between social responsibility and business targets. In this dialogue, it is possible to explore the expectations or the concerns of the stakeholders vis-à-vis the company, while simultaneously accepting changes when they are necessary (Morsing & Schultz 2006) – a crucial factor in obtaining economic results, stability, and growth (Freeman 1984).

We have argued that the limits to CSR depend upon the company strategy and the expectations of the specific stakeholders. Thus, contextual cues such as for example the purpose, the participants, and the setting are of vital importance for the definition of CSR. Adopting a corporate strategy as a formulated ideal is an important step but it is not, by itself, necessarily a solution and may introduce other problems, as the first examples presented in this chapter demonstrate. Much depends upon how successful organizations are, not only in developing a CSR-oriented strategy but also in developing CSR-oriented leadership, that is leaders and managers who are successful in conducting a genuine dialogue with internal and external stakeholders. In this way it is possible to manage the mutual expectations and communicate consistently on CSR, which is crucial for the corporate image and reputation.

In conclusion, managers in the modern world are to recognize and respond to the critical position the practice of social responsibility has assumed in the global arena. Given the issues we outlined above, it is obvious that managers need to take the practice and communication of CSR issue more seriously, not only focusing on formulating ideals.

10. Something good for everyone? Investigation of three corporate responsibility approaches[1]

MINNA HALME

Introduction

During the past decade, the negative side-effects of globalized market economy and the ever increasing power of multi-national corporations have become more evident (Stiglitz 2002, Korten 1995). The ability of nation states to tackle disparities of wealth distribution and other inequalities with traditional legal and regulatory means has turned out inadequate. As the international regulatory bodies have not been able to form a sufficiently strong counterforce to corporate power either, high hopes are being placed on a complementary mechanism: self-regulation of companies in the form of voluntary corporate (social) responsibility (Jenkins 2005, Zadek 2004). Governments expect this trend to advance social justice and decelerate environmental degradation, while companies usually aspire the same trend to retain their licence-to-operate and minimize mandatory intervention of external parties.

At the first look corporate responsibility appears like a motherhood and apple pie-concept. It holds the inherent promise that companies voluntarily take on to themselves societal tasks, which are beyond the legislation or other mandatory requirements, and which may involve no apparent economic gains for the shareholders. At the second look we may notice that by asking companies to take voluntary responsibilities beyond their business, we actually

---

1   The content in this essay is similar to the one Minna Halme published in *Feelings & Business*, (2009) Lindahl, M. & Rehn, A. (Ed.) and Halme, M. & J. Laurila (2009) 'Philanthropy, integration or innovation? Exploring the financial and societal outcomes of different types of corporate responsibility', *Journal of Business Ethics*. 84: 325–339.

legitimize their increased power to decide about societal matters. In certain societal contexts it is righteous to ask, whether corporate responsibility trend poses a threat for democracy. For example, let us think of a large corporation that successfully lobbies for tax reductions, but at the same donates funds for information technology purchases for libraries or sets up art museums. Both of the latter deeds can be easily be perceived as implementation of corporate responsibility, but in essence the corporation has transferred decision-making power over usage funds to itself. The tax funds for public spending have reduced while spending decided upon by the corporation has increased. This is problematic from at least two perspectives. Firstly, some causes will always be more attractive targets of donations than others. Art, ICT and sick children for example, are attractive targets for donations, but who is interested for instance in the elderly? Another concern with regard to increased societal involvement of corporations, is the question of skills and expertise of corporate managers in societal work. Moreover, we need to scrutinize what kind of long-term societal development perspective there will be if societies are headed by corporations .

This concern is particularly relevant.

The above concern about democracy and its long-term development is relevant mainly for such societal contexts where democratically chosen government is functional, where the governance mechanism works through effective legislation and regulation and public sector. But even in the context of corrupt states or developing countries with weaker governance structures we must be prepared to ask whether corporations have long-term interest in developing these societies. While at present corporations may be the only engine for development in weak societies, we must ask if CR offers the most meaningful long-term solution for societal development in the long-term. Perhaps even more importantly, we should ask whether certain kind of CR is more beneficial than others. In other words, what kind of CR produces the desired outcomes?

There is very little analysis of the above (McWilliams & Siegel 2000). The research on the outcome side that there is, focuses mainly on the influence of CR on 'the bottom line', i.e. financial performance (FP) of the firm. Even in this stream of research there is much to improve. As I find that the financial and societal outcome questions of CR should understood as parts of the one and same whole, let me next discuss the CR-FP research briefly, and then link this to the discussion about societal outcomes of CR. Despite a couple of recent meta-analyses that provide evidence of a positive relationship between corporate responsibility and financial performance (Margolis & Walsh 2003, Orlitzky, Schmidt & Rynes 2003), the evidence from the abundant studies on the 'business case', however, remains mixed (Barnett & Salomon 2006, Porter & van der Linde 1995; Aragón-Correa & Sharma 2003; Orlitzky *et al.* 2003; Schaltegger & Figge 2000; Wagner *et al.* 2001; Salzmann *et al.* 2005;).

One of the likely reasons for inconclusive evidence is that previous research on the influences of CR on financial performance (FP) frames CR as a monolith (Salomon 2006). I expect that further progress in the study of the outcomes of corporate responsibility (CR) would require research designs and conceptualizations to be more fine-grained. They tend to disregard that corporate behaviour varies depending on the firm-specific and industry-related factors (Lankoski 2000, Reinhardt 1999, Fox 2004). The monolithic view of CR is misleading also because it ignores the fact that corporate responsibility can be implemented in different ways – irrespective of the industry or other contextual factors. In other words, the question is not only whether companies practice corporate responsibility or not, but also what kind of responsibility is practiced.

It is likely that the mode of implementing CR influences its outcomes, including the financial ones (Porter & Kramer 2006). Even though several conceptualizations of distinctive CR types have been presented, empirical study of the link between the type of CR practiced and its performance outcomes has been rare. This means that the conceptual development in the entire field of CR has not been incorporated into research on financial performance. This also means that those who have recognized different types of CR in their conceptualizations, have not problematized the societal and financial outcomes of these types. An exception is the study by Hillman and Keim (2001), which demonstrates with quantitative empirical evidence that the content of CR makes a difference in corporate financial performance. Similarly, evidence from mutual funds that practice socially responsible investing indicates that the financial returns from these investments differ depending on the operationalization of social responsibility used by the fund

(Barnett & Salomon 2006). Consequently, rather than repeating the question of whether CR improves financial performance, we ought to refine the question and ask

> what kind of CR improves financial performance and under what conditions?

Second, further progress in this domain requires that the research on the performance outcomes of CR should be extended to cover also the societal realm. At present, most research in this domain concentrates on describing or analyzing CR policies, programmes, initiatives and the like, but it seldom scrutinizes their societal effects. The amount of attention dedicated to the study of financial implications of corporate responsibility would almost lead us to assume, that either the primary reason-to-be of CR is to increase the profits of business enterprises or that any other than financial outcomes of CR do not deserve to be evaluated systematically. Nevertheless, even if the business community and business academics appear to be most keen on the financial outcomes of CR, few would dispute that a major rationale behind CR lies in its societal outcomes. These include the quest of environmental protection and social decency and the need to even out some of sharpest inequalities brought about by the globalizing market economy. Yet, business scholars hardly question whether the whole CR trend is beneficial for its recipient, the society or its parts. It appears to be taken for granted that corporate responsibility is good for society – as long as corporations not only use CR as a sole public relations gimmick, but truly engage in it. At the same time, however, questions such as the effects corporate responsibility actions on society remain largely unexplored (Margolis & Walsh 2003). If, however, we take seriously the recommendation that business scholars should not loose the grip of broader societal issues (Ghoshal 2005, Rocha & Ghoshal 2006, Pfeffer 2005), our task becomes to understand the societal outcomes of CR better.

The aim of this chapter is to start exploring the financial and societal outcomes of different CR types The chapter proceeds as follows. At first, existing CR typologies will be examined and elaborated. Using these as a baseline, I will outline three broad pragmatic CR action-orientation types that are especially intended to clarify how different ways of implementing CR deviate from each other. From this the chapter moves to discuss the financial and societal outcomes of these different CR action-orientation types.

Alternative corporate responsibility approaches

It is widely agreed that regardless of the specific label, corporate responsibility is a concept that not only defines the duties of business enterprises towards societal stakeholders and natural environment, but also describes how managers should handle these duties (*cf.* Windsor 2006)[2]. It assumes that companies have responsibilities that sometimes go beyond legal compliance and that they have responsibility for others with whom they do business with (Blowfield & Frynas 2005). Beyond this general level, interpretations of CR vastly differ. In this article, CR is treated as policies and activities that go beyond mandatory obligations such as the economic responsibility (being profitable) and legal responsibility (obeying the legislation and adhering to regulation). This is because in a market economy these two issues are considered to form a baseline for business activity. Unprofitable business usually ceases to exist and an enterprise that breaks laws or regulations will be dealt with by the legislative mechanism (Carroll 1996). This is although it is recognized that there are local contexts where the formal written law is not enforced. In such contexts, despite that legislation exists, situations arise in which corporate actions enter the area of 'voluntary responsibility' rather than being codified by law (Fox 2004).

The fact that corporate responsibility has a number sister concepts such as corporate sustainability, 'business in society', corporate citizenship, social issues in management, corporate accountability and the like (Garriga & Melé 2004, Meehan, Meehan &

---

2   Corporate responsibility (CR) is a nebulous concept. Today, it is often used interchangeably with the previously dominant term corporate social responsibility (CSR). This article prefers applying the term corporate responsibility in order to stress the equal importance of social, environmental and economic responsibilities of corporate actors. In fact, for some the term corporate social responsibility may indicate denial of environmental responsibility of business (DesJardins 1998), which is a confusion that we want to avoid.

Richards 2006, Waddock 2004), adds confusion surrounding the responsibilities of corporations. However, expectations toward and interpretations about responsibilities of business enterprises vary not only because of this conceptual obscurity, but also because CR is inherently a concept that relates business to society. Since societies are different, conceptions about CR are bound to differ, too. Different national, cultural and social contexts call for different sort of responsibility from companies (Midttun *et al.* 2006). For instance, in countries where social necessities are not taken care of by the government or by non-governmental organizations, more requirements and expectations tend to become directed toward the corporate sector.

Previous corporate responsibility typologies

Attempts to understand the complex corporate responsibility phenomenon have lead not only to proliferation of sister concepts, but also to multiple typologies used to describe it. Most often these typologies seem to serve research purposes rather than business practice. This is because a majority of them remains at conceptual level and thus does not easily translate to practitioners interested or involved in the CR efforts of companies. In any case, we recognize three main types of typologies that will be briefly elaborated next.

Firstly, it is possible to distinguish CR typologies based on the firm's motivation to undertake CR efforts. Here the term motivation refers to 'the reason why a firm engages in CR'. For instance, Husted and Salazar (2006) distinguish three CSR types based on the motivation of the firm. They differentiate between altruism, enforced egoism and strategic intent. Windsor (2006), on the other hand, makes a distinction between economic and ethical CSR, and corporate citizenship conception. In Windsor's terms, in economic CSR, the firm's rationale would be utilitarian, i.e. it is motivated by the competitive and market gains. In contrast, ethical CSR corresponds to altruistic motives. Finally, corporate citizenship refers to the strategic use of philanthropy as a motivational lever. Like many other motivation-based CR typologies, the ones mentioned here are conceptually deduced categories. Motivation for CR has also been studied in the form of qualitative empirical analysis but the results from these studies are mainly case descriptions that are not easily converted into typologies. Quantitative empirical studies on the motivation of corporations for responsibility, on the other hand, are difficult to conduct because such motivation tends to be a complex bundle of principles and attitudes that are, furthermore, conditioned by various contingencies.

Secondly, some authors approach corporate responsibility by scrutinising responsibilities that a firm is expected to accomplish. These can be called normative responsibility typologies. Among the most well-known of such typologies is Carroll's (1991 and 1996) four-part pyramid classification. The first two parts of responsibilities include the economic responsibility of being profitable and the responsibility to conform to the legislation and regulation. Failure to fulfil these responsibilities usually leads to some form of a sanction – either a legislative one or extinction from operation because of economic failure. Beyond necessary economic and legislative responsibilities are ethical responsibilities. These refer to those activities that are expected or prohibited by societal members even if they are not codified in the law. These responsibilities are reflected by norms, standards and expectations of society. Finally, the fourth part in Carroll's model is philanthropic responsibilities, comprising of responsibilities, which are purely voluntary from the business' point of view. Contribution to humanitarian programmes or purposes would represent such responsibilities. The difference between ethical and philanthropic responsibility is that the latter is not expected, but rather desired by societal stakeholders. According to Carroll's (1996) typology, a company is usually not considered unethical if it does not engage in philanthropy, whereas if it breaks against an ethical norm, accusations for immoral behaviour tend to arise.

Thirdly, the stage typologies are based on the idea that companies can be at different levels or stages of their CR development or awareness of CR. These models tend to begin with a stage labelled as 'defensive' or 'reactive/compliance'. These refer to behaviour patterns where firms defend against demands for CR by external constituents or react to them reluctantly. The models then move towards the other stages characterized by strategic and transformative orientation to CR, referring to going beyond legislation or other requirements, and aligning responsibility in their business strategy (Hunt & Auster 1992, Post & Altman 1992; Zadek 2004, Mirvis & Googins 2006). Some of these models explicitly adhere to a dynamic view, presenting firms as agents that move from one stage to another (for instance from lower level of CR awareness to a higher one), whereas others at least implicitly see 'defensive', 'reactive' or 'proactive' CR-orientation as static states characterizing different organizations (see e.g. Carroll 1979).

We have already argued that previous literature has downplayed the fact that different types of CR may accrue different outcomes. The other side of the coin is that typologies most often encountered in corporate responsibility literature do not easily lend themselves for empirically observable linkages with financial performance or societal outcomes. Motivation-based CR categorizations are difficult to utilize, because there tend to be so many intervening factors between motivation and financial and societal outcomes, that an empirical research on these factors would be overly complex. Husted and Salazar (2006), for instance, have proposed a micro-economic model, which seeks to link altruistic versus egoistic CR motivations with profitability and social performance. Despite its theoretical merit, the model would be difficult to apply in an empirical study because studying links between motivations and outcomes is problematic, particularly if we speak of research designs that involve more than a single case. On the other hand, responsibilities assigned for firms are categories based on legal and moral obligations and as such somewhat difficult to link to performance-level outcomes. On the contrary, stage typologies comparing the outcomes of reactive versus strategic CR would appear a promising starting point for outcome comparisons, but such a starting point has rarely been applied. Presumably this is because empirical operationalization of each category would require multiple determinants and classification of many firms into multi-determinant categories is overly cumbersome.

Consequently, if we aspire to compare the financial and societal outcomes of different types of corporate responsibility, the existing typologies do not provide a healthy basis for such research. Instead, we need a CR typology that is formed from a more pragmatic perspective. In order to assess the impact of different corporate responsibility types on the firm's financial performance and societal outcomes, the content of categories should be empirically observable. To that end we suggest an action-oriented CR typology in the following section.

Suggestion for an action-oriented corporate responsibility typology

This article extends the existing CR typologies by suggesting another typology that is based on the dominant mode of CR activities practiced by the firm. This is especially because it may be the most feasible solution is to scrutinize the outcomes of CR. Moreover, examining the mode of CR action is informative from the managerial perspective. When the mode of implementing CR is the target of analysis, our question is: 'What type of responsibility actions should the firm primarily apply in order to generate the targeted financial and societal outcomes?' With this approach we would obtain the previously missing means to pragmatically assess the relationship between CR actions and their outcomes.

The seminal work of Wood (1991) urged researchers to assess corporate responsibility in a comprehensive fashion. To that end she introduced the corporate social performance (CSP) model which captures 'principles of CSR, processes of corporate social responsiveness and outcomes of corporate behaviour' (pp. 692-693). Thus, a part of her model tackles the responsibility actions[3] and their outcomes. This often cited model, however, has not been applied as guidance for empirical studies on the relationship between CR action and outcomes. In the attempt to understand the CR action-orientation of companies, we can draw on some of questions asked by Wood (1991), such as: 'What action orientation does a company bring to its relations with the external environment?' and 'what methods does a company use to respond to environmental conditions and social demands?' (pp. 706-707). There are also other issues touched upon in CR literature, such as what is the relationship of CR action to core business of the company (Porter & Kramer 2006) and what the are expected benefits of CR action (Zadek 2004). However, despite that these issues have been discussed in the literature, they have not been systematically put into one framework. In contrast, we here employ these issues in the pursuit to develop an action-oriented corporate responsibility

3   Responsiveness in Wood's (1991) model.

model. This is done by combining three dimensions on which CR activities practiced by the firm may differ: CR's relationship to core business; target of responsibility actions and benefits expected from CR activities. It is possible to distinguish at least the following three CR types that differentiate from each other with regard to the above listed dimensions:

(1)   Philanthropy (emphasis on charity, sponsorships, employee voluntarism etc.)

(2)   CR Integration (emphasis on conducting existing business operations more responsibly)

(3)   CR Innovation (emphasis on developing new business models for solving social and environmental problems)

One of the observable differences between firms engaging in CR is usually whether a firm conducts selected philanthropic activities or whether it concentrates on integrating responsibility considerations in its own business activities. The latter includes issues such as the environmental soundness of products and production, treatment of workforce in the company and suppliers facilities and so on. This distinction resembles the CR categorization applied by Hillman and Keim (2001), who divided firms into two broad categories based on how they practice CR. In their division, firms that focus on responsibility of their own business are contrasted to those that engage in charitable activities and use corporate resources for social issues[4]. The latter bears similarity with philanthropy CR type.

However, during the last few years, a trend has arisen, that may eventually broaden our understanding of CR beyond the previously dominated dichotomy. This trend entails seeing CR as a source of business innovations The key manifestation of this trend is the base-of-the-pyramid (BOP) approach that especially seeks to solve problems of socially disadvantaged groups within a society while simultaneously creating new businesses or at least

4   The difference between the suggested typology is that Hillman and Keim (2001) take stakeholder orientation as the basis for categorizing the actions of the analysed firms. CR Integration in their terminology would resemble the category of firms that act responsibly toward their primary stakeholders such as customers, employees and suppliers.

a lucrative business opportunities for companies (Prahalad 2006; Prahalad & Hart 2002; Prahalad & Hammond 2002 Fox 2004, Bendell & Visser 2005; WBCSD 2004). It is interchangeably called bottom-of-the-pyramid approach. Another parallel indication of the same trend are the new service business models based on energy or material efficiency opportunities and sustainable energy technologies (Lovins, Lovins & Hawken 1999). Furthermore, United Nations Environmental Programme's Human Development through Market-initiative is an example of promoting business that explicitly tackles both social and environmental sides of CR (UNEP 2006, *cf.* Hart 2005). This trend of a firm taking selected social and/ or environmental problems as a source of innovating new business has strong implications to the CR action perspective. When evaluated against the above defined dimensions, it clearly differs from the two previous CR types. We call this type CR Innovation (see Table 1 below).

Table 1. Comparison of CR action types

		CR action type		
		Philanthropy	CR Integration	CR Innovation
Dimension of action	Relationship to core business	Outside of firm's core business	Close to existing core business	Enlarging core business or developing new business
	Target of responsibility	Extra activities	Environmental and social performance of existing business operations	New product or service development
	Expected benefit	Image improvement and other reputation impacts	Improvements of environmental and social aspects of core business	Alleviation of social or environmental problem

We may present the three CR action types in a condensed form as follows. The primary CR orientation of the firms that conform to philanthropy is on charitable actions and using corporate resources for 'doing good' (i.e. donations, other charitable activities, or encouraging personnel to engage in voluntary work)[5]. In essence, the charitable activities take place outside of the firm's immediate own business and no direct business benefits are sought from them. They are extra activities, not a part of the core business. Indirectly, a company can seek to minimize intrusive public policy or improve corporate reputation and market opportunities with philanthropic activity (Godfrey 2005).

On the contrary, firms characterized by CR Integration attempt to combine responsibility aspects into their *core business* operations. In terms of stakeholder management, they are primarily concerned about responsibility toward their primary stakeholders such as customers, employees and suppliers. This type of responsibility is characterized by actions like ensuring high product quality and investments to R&D (responsibility toward customers), paying just wages and avoiding overcompensation to top managers at the cost of other employees, taking diversity-oriented measures (responsibility toward employees), paying in time to suppliers[6], supplier training programs, supporting responsibility measures of the supply chain (e.g. no child labour; responsibility toward suppliers) and applying environmentally benign practices and policies (responsibility toward the local community). In other words, in CR Integration the responsibility considerations are integrated into the business operations of the company in question. As to the expected benefits, the company may simultaneously seek benefits related to corporate reputation, cost-savings, risk reduction, or anticipation of legislation.

The third CR action type, CR Innovation, is different from the two previous ones in several respects. Most important, a business enterprise takes an environmental or social problem as a source of business innovation and seeks to develop new products or services, which provide a solution to the problem. Contrary to philanthropy, however, this kind of CR should fulfil the win-win condition. While

---

5   Hillman and Keim (2001) termed this approach to CR as 'Social issue participation', which comprises issues such as charity, giving programs, donations and avoidance of 'sin industries', that is nuclear, tobacco, alcohol or gambling.

6   Payment delays are a common problem in supplier relationships in which large client has consirable power over a supplier. These situations occur when there are few large industrial buyers and multiple small or medium sized suppliers who mainly depend on one or two clients (Zadek 2004).

the company tries to develop new business that would alleviate an environmental problem or benefit a chosen poor market segment, it aims to simultaneously also create revenue for the enterprise. Inherent in CR Innovation is a strong win-win idea: corporations are not expected to provide products or services to low-income markets or to protect the environment because of the willingness to do good or to help. Instead, the underlying idea is to cater an underserved market or to benefit the environment so that it also makes business sense.

While the aim for the win-win condition distinguishes CR Innovation from philanthropy, this difference is no longer as obvious with respect to the CR Integration type because the latter can also increase corporate profitability. For instance, eco-efficiency improvements cut costs while simultaneously reducing the environmental burden. Or good working conditions are likely to further employee loyalty and lessen employee turnover. The key difference between CR Innovation and Integration, however, is that the former is about creating *new* business aiming at reducing a social or environmental ill, while the CR Integration is concerned about conducting *existing* business responsibly. In this case the added value brought about by the responsibility aim means that the business is conducted with the aim of reducing harm (necessary condition) or doing good to the involved stakeholders, if possible (additional condition). In the CR Innovation, solutions to social or environmental problems are a *starting point* for planning *new* business, products or services (Table 1). Hence, forming of such solutions cannot be delegated to CR professionals. Instead, to be materialised, these activities must be an elementary part of corporate R&D, business development and most likely also strategic management work. In some cases CR Innovation may require even deeper integration of the idea of responsibility into business than is the case when the already existing operations are being made more responsible. As a result, it may also be asked whether CR Innovation is eventually nothing but good business. This question may especially be raised by those for whom corporate responsibility equals to sacrifices of corporate funds. For this apparently dominant view in the U.S., philanthropy would qualify as the truest form of CR (Godfrey 2005, Carroll 1996, Mirvis & Googins 2006, Global Market Insite 2005). We maintain, however, that if business delivers new solutions to social or environmental ills, it is justified to call it responsible.

We recognize that the identification of the three CR types alone is not a major contribution to extant literature in this domain. While developing yet another CR typology has its merits, our aim is to go a step further and examine the influence of the CR mode to the outcomes that result. With the help of the above outlined typology of CR action types this should be possible. We will next discuss how and the extent to which this typology makes it possible to scrutinize the links between CR actions and their outcomes.

Financial and societal outcomes of different CR types

We can analytically differentiate between financial and societal outcomes of CR. On the one hand, CR influences the financial performance of the firm and on the other hand it has societal consequences. We have already mentioned that the study of the outcomes of CR is deficient in two respects. First, the studies of financial outcomes of CR predominantly neglect the fact that different ways of implementing CR are likely to generate different outcomes. Second, business academics have been strikingly disinterested in the societal outcomes of corporate responsibility (Margolis & Walsh 2003; Blowfield & Frynas 2005). In this section we tackle both of these deficiencies by utilizing the CR action typology developed above. We will first address the financial performance question, and then focus on the social outcomes of corporate responsibility.

The influence of action type to financial outcomes of CR?

The traditional perception in previous CR research has been that corporate responsibility and financial performance are a zero-sum game: a responsible company would have to compromise on the financial side. Over the past few decades, however, many researchers have tried to show that CR pays off, if not in the short-term, at least in the longer run in the form of social legitimacy, employee motivation, eco-efficiency or other benefits. For one, there is plenty of case study evidence indicating that responsibility brings along economic benefits based on increased employee loyalty, longer-term relationships with customers, better risk management and efficiency improvements (Dunphy *et al.* 2003; Reinhardt 1999; Orsato 2006). Secondly, a number of quantitative studies indicate that proactive CR – particularly environmental responsibility – is profitable for the firm (Porter & van der Linde 1995; Guimaraes & Liska 1995; Hart & Ahuja 1996). A couple of recent meta-analysis indicate a positive link between corporate social and financial performance (Orlitzky *et al.* 2003; Margolis & Walsh 2003).

Nonetheless, in aggregate the results on the financial outcomes of CR remain inconclusive (Margolis & Walsh 2003, McWilliams & Siegel 2000, Godfrey 2005; Aragón-Correa & Sharma 2003; Schaltegger & Figge 2000; Wagner *et al.* 2001; Barnett & Salomon 2006). Usually imperfect methodologies are blamed for the contradictory findings (McWilliams & Siegel 2000, Orlitzky *et al.* 2003). It has also been pointed out that framing CR as monolith causes problems (Salomon 2006). To yield feasible results the research designs and conceptualizations should be more fine-grained. For example, the majority of current CR-FP studies take into account neither the influence of industry nor the geographical nor societal setting to their findings (Salzmann *et al.* 2005). Yet the financial performance outcomes of responsible corporate behaviour vary depending on the firm-specific and industry-related factors (Lankoski 2000, Reinhardt 1999, Fox 2004).

We maintain, however, that the mixed evidence implies also that the repeated question, 'is CR profitable or not', is formulated incorrectly. Most studies fail to take into account that there are different ways of practicing corporate responsibility, and that these ways may yield different outcomes (Barnett & Salomon 2006; Hillman & Keim 2001). A more correct formulation could, therefore, be 'What kind of CSR is profitable?'

The analysis of Hillman and Keim (2001) is one of the few studies investigating the influence of the type of CR to financial performance from an empirical vantage point. Testing the financial performance of over three hundred Standard & Poor's 500 companies, they found that responsible management of primary stakeholder relationships accrues improved shareholder value, whereas charity-type of CR (i.e. philanthropy), which is not related to primary stakeholders is negatively associated with shareholder value. Integrating responsibility in core business means investing in key stakeholder relations, which in turn may lead to improved customer loyalty, lesser employee turnover and the like. These tacit assets appear to be a source of competitive advantage which is difficult for competitors to copy. This is not the case in charity–based CR activities (Hillman & Keim 2001).

Hence, there is already some empirical evidence to support our claim that the type of CR action makes a difference for CR financial outcomes. In the same vein, the microeconomic analysis of Husted and Salazar (2006) indicates that strategic rather than altruistic CR approach is more profitable for the firm. In our view, CR can be judged as 'strategic' when it supports core business activities and thereby contributes to the firm's effectiveness in accomplishing its mission. Philanthropy can also be strategic, but in practice it seldom is (Porter & Kramer 2002 and 2006, Burke & Logsdon 1996).

On the basis of the above, we can argue that the action-type CR Integration is more prominent in terms of financial outcomes than Philanthropy. But how about CR Innovation and its influence on financial performance? At the time of writing this only few quantitative comparative studies based on large samples are available. There is more quantitative data regarding eco-efficiency than BOP initiatives. Many eco-efficiency innovation cases show that eco-efficiency improvements of companies create cost savings or new business (WBCSD 2000). A recent quantitative comparison of 65 European countries indicates that eco-efficiency has clear monetary value to companies (Advance 2006, Figge & Hahn 2006). Base-of-the-pyramid research is a recent trend, but there are documented BOP-business examples that can be assessed. Multiple economically successful examples are described for instance in Prahalad (2006), Hart (2005), Hart and Christensen (2002) and Hart and Milstein (2003). This evidence implies that CR Innovation is in many cases financially profitable, but due to the research settings where the evidence comes from, it is best considered as indicative.

Like CR Integration, CR Innovation is also usually close to core business. Its strategic role can, however, be different from that of CR Integration. Namely, CR Innovation involves creating new products, services or business models that may be particularly important for the future of the company. Occasionally CR

Innovation also means conquering major new markets – particularly in the case of BOP approach.

As activities conforming to CR Integration and CR Innovation types are usually related closely to the core operations of the companies, they are more often strategic to the organization than activities representing philanthropy. CR which is close to core business, allows the firm to collect particular benefits of CR programmes and activities, rather than simply creating collective goods which can be shared by others in the industry, community or the society at large (Porter & Kramer 2006, Burke & Logsdon 1996). In sum, the above suggests that CR Integration and CR Innovation types carry more financial performance potential than philanthropy (Burke & Logsdon 1996).[7]

The influence of action type to societal outcomes of CR

It is important to note that, to date, little effort has been dedicated to investigate what is the contribution of CR to various societal stakeholders (Margolis & Walsh 2003). Only a few studies ask whether CR benefits society, be it society at large or the specific target groups that should reap the benefits of CR efforts. It can be argued that particularly among business scholars it is taken for granted that CR is automatically advantageous to society (Blowfield & Frynas 2005). There is, however, substantial evidence on the contrary.

A case in point here is the work conducted among developing countries. Decades of failed governmental efforts have turned expectations to corporations as the agents that could deliver better solutions to pressing development problems (Easterly 2006). CR has been widely accepted as an approach or a tool in this task. However, it appears that when interests of business are not aligned with those of the poor and marginalized in the developing countries, the business case tends to override the development case (Blowfield & Frynas 2005; Frynas 2005). Voluntary standards and

7　It should, however, be noted that Hillman and Keim focus on practical activities whereas Husted and Salazar use motivation of CR as basis of categorization. The support is valid only if we interpret the altruistic approach in Husted and Salazar's model to corresponds to what Hillman and Keim call charity approach.

codes of corporate conduct have become popular in the North, but they may not be transferable to development country conditions with major power disparities. In those strikingly different conditions these approaches may not deliver the expected societal benefits. When pressure from donor, NGOs or government is absent, there is little incentive for companies to act if the financial outcomes of CR activities are not immediately observable (Nevell 2005). Moreover, there is indication that even major charitable corporate spending does not deliver expected results due to corruption, the problems of short-termism, and the fact that company staff tends to focus on technical and managerial solutions and is unable to involve beneficiaries of CR work. For instance the effectiveness of the estimated $500 million CR spending of oil, gas and mining companies in community development in different countries has been increasingly questioned (Frynas 2005).

The above, however, does not imply that all kinds of CR endeavours are doomed to fail. The negative evidence presented above comes mainly from philanthropic type of CR. CR Integration and CR Innovation types are based on a different logic. CR Integration would mean high standards in environmental management of production[8], paying fair compensation to workers in own facilities and applying similar responsibility policies for suppliers' operations[9]. As to CR Innovation, its very starting point is a social problem, which the company seeks to solve or alleviate with its own products or services. But unlike in the case of philanthropy, the very essence of CR Innovation is that the solution should be lucrative for the company, instead of aiding the underserved customers at the cost of the company. This is exemplified by a number of practical BOP business cases documented for instance by Prahalad (2006) and

8   For instance oil drilling in development countries causes clearance of land leading to long-lasting or permanent loss of vegetation, release of drilling fluids to the ecosystem, damages from leaking pipelines or atmospheric emissions from the flaring of gas (Frynas 2005: 594–595). CR Integration would require minimising the harmful impacts of these operations. For paper companies this approach would entail that wood comes from sustainably managed forests, that paper-making processes are eco-efficient and do not pollute waterways and air.

9   At a macro-economic level, one of the first steps for companies that are large players in national development country context, publicising the amount of revenues and taxes paid to the host government is one part of bearing responsibility.

Hart (2005)[10]. However, due to its very starting point of solving a social or an environmental problem, it can be argued that CR Innovation type of corporate responsibility may have the greatest potential also in terms of societal outcomes. This is especially if the practicing firm does not take short-cuts and make compromise when crafting business models that benefit both ends.

In the previous sub-section we reviewed evidence to suggest that Integration and Innovation types of CR action are economically more beneficial to a company than philanthropy. Somewhat more surprisingly, there is indication that such strategically oriented approaches to CR also yield more substantial societal outcomes charity and philanthropy (Porter & Kramer 2006, *cf.* Husted & Salazar 2006, Burke & Logsdon 1996). There are multiple reasons to this observation. Philanthropic activities tend to remain disconnected and isolated from the corporate operating units. This is not to say that philanthropy could not be well-targeted and long-term – it can (Godfrey 2005) – but much of corporate philanthropy consists of incidental initiatives toward generic social issues. The social impacts of these initiatives are often sporadic (Porter & Kramer 2002; 2006). Business benefits, on the other hand, do not usually exceed short-term reputation improvements or sometimes hypothesized assurance against reputation risks (Godfrey 2005). On the contrary, when a company addresses its own existing business from the responsibility perspective the efforts tend to be aligned with business operations. Thus, they have also a greater potential to accrue business benefits that are more specific than, for instance, reputation enhancement. Moreover, when the social benefits and business incentives are aligned, more managers, also the less socially attuned ones, are more likely to engage in responsible activities. It should also be taken into account, that in times of economic hardship, philanthropic activities are at risk. On the contrary, in the strategic case there is less likelihood that CR activities are abandoned.

10 Yet it should be noted that there are also voices that are critical against BOP approach (Karnani 2007). They maintain that the business benefits as well as advantages to the poor or other underserved are often exaggerated. In general, BOP-criticism is seldom substantiated with empirical evidence, but it is evident that some BOP business models may fail to advance the position of the underserved customers.

Figure 1 summarizes the main observations made above. It suggests that of the three types of CR outlined in this chapter, philanthropic CR tends to be least integrated with the core business of the company, whereas CR Integration and CR Innovation approaches are more tightly interwoven with core business. For reasons outlined above, it is proposed that the CR Innovation type of responsibility may accrue highest potential benefit – both for the practicing firm as well as society (Figure 1). However, CR

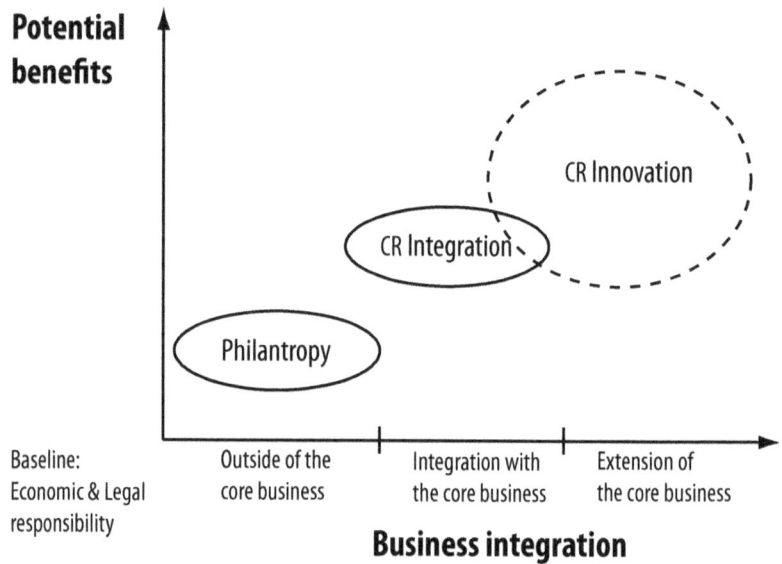

Figure 1. Level of business integration of CR types and the potential for expected financial and social benefits.

Innovation is circled by a dotter line. This indicates that there is only case-based and anecdotal evidence regarding the financial and societal outcomes of CR Innovation.

When interpreting the figure above, it should be kept in mind that it is intended to depict the dominant CR approach of a company. On most occasions, companies have a CR portfolio which is likely to include activities conforming to different types. For instance, companies that primarily follow CR Integration approach may also conduct some philanthropic activities especially in such cultural settings where it is expected from them for 'licence to operate' reasons. On the other hand, firms that engage in CR Innovation most likely also conduct activities that fall in the category of CR Integration. Small or medium-sized companies (e.g. Vertergaard-Frandsen 2006) which predominantly offer products that solve problems of the poor populations are a minority. In larger companies, such as Philips, more ordinary and established CR activities that conform to philanthropy or CR Integration types usually precede BOP initiatives (cf. Philips 2004). Moreover, when a multinational or large national company adopts a BOP strategy, its former CR Integration activities are likely to remain and co-exist aside of BOP activities. Despite this co-existence, it is usually possible to distinguish firms from one another with respect to the dominant CR action type. This is especially if we accept the above presented three CR types as a convenient short hand notation rather than strict mutually exclusive categories.[11]

Conclusions

The starting point of this chapter was that corporate responsibility trend is expected to deliver 'something good for everyone'. Not only business managers but also many other constituencies outside of the business community, such as politicians and global aid institutions, put trust on corporations as agents that will provide solutions to social and environmental problems. Similarly, the research community at business schools is keen to report on CR policies and programmes of companies. So positive are the expectations, that we do not scrutinize what outcomes actually result from CR trend at many different levels from single companies and single beneficiaries to change of political ideologies of global governance.

Following from this point, the chapter argues for the importance of careful study of the outcomes of CR – not only for the financial performance of the firm but also for the societal stakeholders and the society at large. Furthermore, I maintain that in

---

11 A couple of final limitations of Figure 1 should be taken into account. Firstly, it is a visualisation of the general argument. It is not claimed to apply to all single cases. Secondly, it is possible that some single CR measures and undertakings have negative social impacts, which is a situation excluded from the above graphical illustration.

the studies about the outcomes of corporate responsibility we ought to give up seeing CR in a monolithic fashion and rather distinguish between different CR approaches. This is because corporate responsibility is practiced in various ways in different business companies. In other words, rather than asking what the financial and societal outcomes of CR are, the financial and societal outcomes of different CR action types call for attention. In its entirety, the present study should be taken as an indication of a need to pay attention to the different ways in which corporate responsibility is practiced in contemporary business companies. This is especially because these different ways lead to different financial and societal outcomes.

In order to address this knowledge gap three distinct corporate responsibility action types, termed as Philanthropy, CR Integration and CR Innovation were outlined, and their financial and societal outcomes were explored. The material reviewed and discussed suggests substantial differences in the financial performance of companies with respect to the type of CR action conducted. It appears that, philanthropy is least profitable from the financial performance perspective, and somewhat counter-intuitively, it also seems to accrue the most modest societal benefits. CR Integration and CR Innovation appear to have more potential with regard to both financial and societal outcomes. When making this observation it should be emphasized that hardly any contemporary company conducts only one type of CR actions, but that usually a predominant action-type for a company can be distinguished.

The typology suggested here is only one of the first steps toward an improved understanding about corporate responsibility actions and their financial and societal outcomes. With respect to future studies we have two points to make. First, although there are previous studies about the ways through which companies may benefit from corporate (social) responsibility, the benefits (or disadvantages) are hardly ever connected to CR practices, but the analyses remain at a general level. Future studies about the financial and societal outcomes of CR ought to be more fine-grained. Future research needs to investigate the kinds of outcomes are produced by each type of CR. The CR types presented here offer one possible springboard for that study.

Finally, this article has named a few societal outcomes from CR activities for illustrative purposes. Future studies need to address these outcomes in a more detailed fashion. These outcomes need to be both classified and measured. For the time being, there are some promising – mainly single-case studies – on the societal outcomes of CR. Systematic review and analysis of these studies offers one avenue toward a more comprehensive understanding of societal outcomes of CR.

11. Middle-Managers Work/ Non-Work Boundaries[1]

JEAN-CHARLES LANGUILAIRE

Introduction

The relationships between work and personal life have been a growing research interest for more than 35 years (See Near, Rice, & Hunt, 1980, for one of the first reviews in the field). During this period, organizations have modified their attitudes toward work/ non-work relationships. Indeed, up till the massive entrance of women into the labour market in the 1990s, practitioners considered work and personal life (mainly family in the earlier research) as two distinct domains. They totally ignored their interrelations and their reciprocal influences on work and personal life attitudes and behaviours and created and perpetuated the 'myth of separate spheres' (Kanter, 1977 in Hall & Richter, 1988, p. 213). Nowadays, organizations recognize the fact that they influence each other and that their interaction may be both negative and positive for individuals and organizations (and even society). Organizations implement work-life programmes helping their employees to manage their work and non-work activities and responsibilities. One of the strong arguments of these programmes is that both domains need to be more integrated. This integration should reduce conflict and favour enrichment in order to increase individual's well-being and, in turn, organizational performance. In practice, integration is based on higher flexibility. Flexibility may be formal referring to different types of working arrangements (flexitime, part-time,

---

1   The author would like to thank the two anonymous reviewers for comments on an earlier version as well as Ethel Brundin and Leona Achtenhagen for their comments and support.

compressed hours, telecommuting, parental leaves etc.). In France, the 35-hour act[2] reducing the legal working time from 39 to 35 hours per week may be seen as a formal flexibility. It may be informal via flatter organizations, team works, quality circles and project work (See Cartwright, 2003; Packendorff, 2002; Pettigrew & Massini, 2003). Since the implementation of the 35-hour act, 30% to 50% of French employees reported more multi-tasking and team-working (Bué, Hamon-Cholet, & Puech, 2003). Flexibility is also supported by information technology (IT) making work 'portable' i.e. available anywhere at anytime (Kossek, Lautsch, & Eaton, 2005; Valcour & Hunter, 2005). 51% of French managers report that the use of IT has intensified due to the reduction of working time (Bué, Hamon-Cholet, & Puech, 2003). However, the results of flexibility on individuals' perception of their working situation still need to be discussed. In Europe, employees denounce rather unsatisfying working conditions, with higher pressures and higher workloads – an intensification of work affecting their well-being, i.e. their physical, mental and social health[3] at work as well as outside work (Paoli & Merllié, 2001).

The fact that working place, work conditions and working atmosphere may affect individuals' well-being is agreed upon in diverse fields of research like organizational behaviour, stress management, work psychology, among others (Burke & Cooper, 2006; Cooper, 1994; Jones, Burke, & Westman, 2006; Karasek, 1979; Karasek & Theorell, 1990; Mißler & Theuringer, 2003; Pratt, 2000; Robbins, 2003). Hence, when organizations are 'healthy' i.e. work enables meaning, structure, identity, self-respect of employees as well as material rewards (Watson, 1995) the working situation and the workplace are 'spices of life' rather than 'kisses of death' for individuals and organizations turning them also into 'financially healthy' institutions (See Lennart, 2002; McHugh & Brotherton, 2000; Randell, 1998). The metaphor 'healthy organi-

2   'Loi d'orientation et d'incitation à la réduction du temps de travail (Law of orientation and incentive toward the reduction of the working time or 35-hour act) regulating working time to 35 hours per week promulgated in 1998 by Martine Aubry, Minister of Work and Solidarity (1997–2001). Law Revised in 2000.

3   The notion of well-being may be largely defined as including physical, mental and social health (McDowell & Newell, 1996)

zation' relates to the individual, the organizational and the societal level. The challenge is for managers and leaders to recognize and act such relations to develop healthy employees and create sustainable healthy organizations and society.

This chapter focuses on the first level. Considering that a 'healthy organization' is an organization with healthy employees, the metaphor 'healthy organization' emphasises the social responsibility of the organization towards one of its main stakeholders: employees. It relates thus to the field of Corporate Social Responsibility (CSR) as it highlights the well-being of employees. In order to act as socially responsible, management teams should therefore understand how employees view, perceive and manage their relationships between work and non-work. This chapter explores French middle-managers' work/non-work experiences and discusses how organizations could act socially responsible. It presents and investigates the individuals' stories of four French middle-managers. It comprises 5 parts. The first part introduces a framework to understand work/non-work relationships i.e. a boundary perspective. The second part presents briefly the method. The third narrates the work/non-work experiences of the four French middle-managers. The fourth offers a discussion of these stories. Finally, going back to CSR, the offers reflections on how organizations could act socially responsible when dealing with work/non-work issues.

By presenting individual stories, this chapter shows that exploring and trying to understand each individual story is part of acting socially responsible. Such stories contribute to how the work/non-work discourse is genuinely connected to CSR and not uniquely a means to enhance competitive advantage. Indeed, this chapter highlights that acting socially responsible should not only mean having work-life policies but rather paying attention to work/non-work issues at all organizational levels and processes. It illustrates that different practices, beyond special work-life programmes, may impact the work/non-work experiences. This relates to two central conclusions: 1-life is composed of variety of different domains more than work and family; 2- tensions between the individuals valuing segmentation on daily basis and their organizational context based on an integrative paradigm may occur and be detrimental to individuals' well-being and the creation of healthy organizations and society.

Work/Non-Work Relationships From a Boundary Perspective

The work-life field adopts 'a focus on the relationship between work and personal life' (Lambert & Kossek, 2005, p. 515). This field emerges from the recognition and agreement among researchers as well as practitioners that life is not only a matter of work and family demands, but a question of activities and responsibilities at work and outside work (work vs. non-work) and that work and non-work are interrelated (Kossek & Lambert, 2005). Within this work-life field, the work/non-work relationships are conceptualised via diverse notions such as conflict, balance, interface or interference. It also offers diverse theoretical frames to understand how work and non-work domains intermingle such as the traditional segmentation, spillover and compensation theories (see Geurts & Demerouti, 2003). These theories are based on role theory for which work and non-work roles are, at some point in time and space, incompatible creating a work/non-work conflict (see for example Geurts & Demerouti, 2003; Zedeck, 1992). Among recent theoretical frameworks, the 'boundary perspective' looks at the work/non-work relationships in the contemporary context of higher flexibility. It recognizes that work and non-work are more or less integrated and overlapping. Such integration is largely supported with today's flexibility and today's IT system. Overall the boundary perspective is based on a continuum between 'segmentation' and 'integration' as shown in figure 1 below:

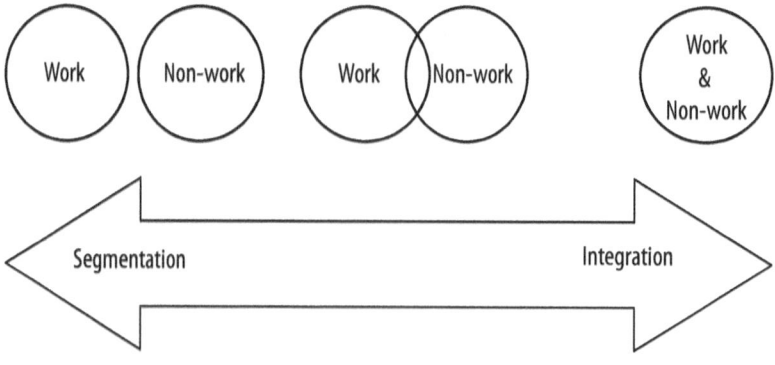

Figure 1: The segmentation-integration continuum

This continuum reflects the extent to which work/non-work boundaries overlap one another leading to non overlap (segmentation), some overlap or a complete overlap (integration) of the work and non-work domains. The boundary perspective via its two theoretical pillars 'boundary theory and boundary management' addresses 'the construction of work-family boundaries [or work/non-work boundaries][4] as a complex interplay between employees' strategies and preferences, the social context in which they are embedded, and both the idiosyncratic and cultural meanings attached to work and family' (Desrochers & Sargent, 2003, p. 6). As it will be explained below, boundary theory answers why do (or do not) people draw boundaries and what are these boundaries whereas boundary management focuses on how individuals draw them or shun them.

Boundary theory

One of the basic tenets for boundary theory is that people are constructing, maintaining, and negotiating boundaries between different life domains in order to simplify and order their environment in the ultimate aim to make sense of their experiences (Ashforth, Kreiner, & Fugate, 2000). A boundary is defined as 'something that indicates bounds or limits' (*Webster encyclopaedic unabridged dictionary of the English language*, 1994). One specific boundary delimits where one domain ends and one domain starts. One domain is identified by three components: 1) *people* participating in the domain, 2) *objects and ambiances of surroundings* belonging to the domains and 3) *thoughts, activities associated* with how one presents him(her)self in a specific domain (Nippert-Eng, 1996, p. 8). Three types of boundaries are primarily discussed namely the *spatial, temporal and psychological* boundaries. The first two types respectively refer to where and when the activities of work and non-work are done. The third one refers to the rules created mentally by individuals stating which and when behavioural, emotional, strain, thinking patterns for one domain are appropriate for one but not the other (Clark, 2000). More broadly, Nippert-Eng

4   Most of the literature in this field has been first defined in terms of work-family but can be applied in a larger sense to work/non-work.

(1996) views psychological boundaries as the meaning one associated with a certain category, for example the meaning associated with 'work' or the meaning associated with 'non-work'. These psychological boundaries influence and are influenced by the temporal and spatial boundaries as well as by the environment in which one individual lives.

Boundaries are said to be flexible and permeable (Ashforth, Kreiner, & Fugate, 2000; Clark, 2000; Hall & Richter, 1988; Nippert-Eng, 1996). Flexibility is defined as the extent to which a border may contract or expand, depending on the demands of other domains (Clark, 2000). Hall and Richter (1988, p. 125) define flexibility as 'the extent to which the physical time and location markers, such as working hours and workplace, may be changed.' Flexibility is associated with spatial and temporal boundaries because the assumption is that time and space are scarce resources which are not extensible. Clark (2000) also considers flexibility for psychological boundaries, e.g. when I increasing my thinking about work, I decrease my thinking about family. The flexibility of psychological boundaries represents also the extent to which the idea of one domain mentally expands or contracts, e.g. what one considers mentally as non-work may increase due to the arrival of a 4th child.

Permeability refers to the degree to which elements from one domain may enter the other domains (Clark, 2000). Permeability is defined as 'the degree to which a person physically located in one domain may be psychologically concerned with the other' (Hall & Richter, 1988, p. 215). Psychological boundaries may also be seen as permeable when the meaning of work and the meaning of non-work are not entirely distinct when some elements give sense to both domains. Spatial and temporal boundaries are permeable when individuals from one domain enter other domains, e.g. kids coming to the office during working time or when objects from one domain are placed in other domains. Permeability is directional i.e. 'work-to-family' or 'family-to-work' permeability. These two types of permeability are recognized as distinct and not correlated constructs (Frone, Yardley, & Markel, 1997) Hall and Richter (1988) conclude that family boundaries are more permeable than work boundaries. In that sense, work and family boundaries are said to be asymmetrically permeable (Frone, Russell, & Cooper,

1992). This asymmetry may explain how individuals prioritize one domain (or sub-domains) over others.

Overall, the degree of flexibility and permeability refers to the strength of the boundaries (Clark, 2000). When boundaries are completely flexible and permeable, they are qualified to be weak. This corresponds to an integration situation. When boundaries are entirely inflexible and impermeable, they are thick or strong. This is consistent with a segmentation situation (Ashforth, Kreiner, & Fugate, 2000; Clark, 2000; Nippert-Eng, 1996). Flexibility and permeability are two dimensions influencing the degree to which domains blend and thus partly define the 'segmentation-integration' continuum (see figure 1, p. 242).

Boundary management and boundary work

Kossek, Noe, and DeMarr (1999, p. 166) describe boundary management as 'the strategies, principles and practices one uses to organize and separate role demands and expectations into specific realms.' Boundary management is seen as the visible part of boundary work defined foremost by Nippert-Eng (1996) as a mental process enabling to create and maintain boundaries. Both take place at a macro level, e.g. how one creates and maintains new boundaries when going to retirement, and at a micro level, e.g. how one commutes between the office and home everyday (See Ashforth, Kreiner, & Fugate, 2000). Nippert-Eng (1996) defines boundary work through two essential and dependant mechanisms: placement and transcendence taking place for each domain's components. Via placement one defines a line between the domains, e.g. defining *who* may belong to one domain or more. By means of transcendence one keeps the boundaries fixed so that one can cross them back and forth, e.g. not letting people from another domain enter the domain in focus. Both processes of placement and transcendence relate to the strength of the boundaries. If a boundary is more permeable, boundary work will aim at drawing the border more clearly (placement) and if a boundary is less permeable, boundary work will aim at keeping the borders in places (transcendence) (See Nippert-Eng, 1996).

Boundary work and the 'segmentation-integration' continuum

Boundary work defines a process where individuals as social agents are central in segmenting and integrating life domains. At first, the 'segmentation-integration' continuum does not assume that any specific situation is better than another. Nonetheless, it relies on the fact that one specific individual has a certain preference for one or the other (Edwards & Rothbard, 1999; Kossek, Noe, & DeMarr, 1999). Then, taking into account his or her environment one individual will place and fix boundaries according to his or her preference. A fit between the individuals' preferences and the boundaries allowed in their environment eases the boundary management and results in higher degree of satisfaction and well-being. For Edwards and Rothbard (1999), Kossek *et al.* (1999), and Desrochers and Sargent (2003) a misfit implies that the individual should start a new boundary work. Hence, boundary work is seen as a proactive process (See: Ashforth, Kreiner, & Fugate, 2000; Kossek, Noe, & DeMarr, 1999), but may also be viewed as an active, a reactive and even a passive process. First, as a proactive process, individuals are able to foresee changes in their situation and mentally change in advance the boundaries concerned to fit their preference and their environment. Boundary work can then take place according to these new mentally defined boundaries (See: Ashforth, Kreiner, & Fugate, 2000; Kossek, Noe, & DeMarr, 1999; Lambert & Kossek, 2005). Second, it could be an active process. In that case, individuals adapt their conceptions of each domain, mentally, as an immediate reaction to actual visible change. Third, one might also argue that boundary wok is a reactive process because individuals mentally reconstruct boundaries in order to legitimate and rationalise their choices previously done. In all three types of process, the individual shows a capacity to see or even foresee changes in different domains and intentionally act, react or pro-act according to these changes. This implies that an individual's preference is in these cases explicit. Finally, one may have no explicit strategy, no clear view on what the various domains are, on where the mental and tangible (time and space) boundaries are or how these domains relate one another. Nonetheless, this person still may feel to belong to different domains which are natural and legitimate. In that case, boundary work may be considered as a passive and unintentional process where the preferences are implicit.

One must bear in mind that boundary work is a personal process highly dependent on individuals' professional and personal goals, their expectations in regards to their well-being and their perception as well as their interpretation of their situation and context (See Kossek, Noe, & DeMarr, 1999). Individuals', socio-cultural but also organizational contexts may constrain and facilitate their boundary work. The forces behind boundary work may be the individuals themselves (self-management) but also their relatives (spouses, children...) or even the organization through the work content as well as work context via colleagues, organizational policies, practices and culture.

Method overview

This chapter is based on the four middle-managers' 'life stories'[5] focusing on how middle-managers create, maintain and change boundaries. Following Pettigrew (1990) the four cases have been selected among thirteen because they represent more extreme situations, critical incidents and social dramas that are interesting by themselves and from which one can benefit from a better understanding of the phenomena (Pettigrew, 1990). This section offers an overview of the selection of the middle-manager in the entire research and then briefly presents the four cases. It also reviews how stories have been written.

The main criterion of selection was that participants should be currently active in a middle-manager position. Indeed, research points out that taking up a middle-management position reinforces negative impacts on external activities achievement especially family activities (Thomas & Dunkerley, 1999). Middle-managers have been identified according to their roles, i.e. having responsibilities both towards their higher managers, subordinates and peers or even being project manager. Middle-managers have been selected at different hierarchical levels, in different industries, in both SME

5   The term 'life story' is used in its simple sense of story of life and represents the empirical material of this research. In narrative research, such terms may be used in a more profound sense. In this chapter, it still keeps its meanings that a narrated story is constructed by narrators, here both the middle-managers and the researcher, as knowledge is constructed in interaction during the interview.

and large companies and in national or international organizations. The choice of France is twofold. First, the overall working context which has been illustrated in the introduction. Second, the researcher being French, the access to life story was facilitated by sharing language and cultural background with the individuals. No criteria related to the individuals' context such as demographics and non-work situations were set. Table 1 and 2 present the four individuals in focus in this chapter.

The focus of this research is to access individuals' work/non-work experiences. The stories narrated in the next part are based on qualitative interviews. Their aim was to get an overview of middle-managers' life i.e. how they define their life domains and experience their relationships. Therefore they offer for each middle-manager a broad view of their life domains and their relationships. The interviews took place in September and October 2005 and lasted between 1 and 2 hours. They have been transcribed and analysed by the researcher in French. The transcripts have been coded in the light of the theoretical framework. The main codes correspond to the bolded terms in the theoretical framework: *domains, types of boundaries, flexibility, permeability, integration, segmentation, boundary work, placement, transcendence, proactive process, active process, reactive process and passive process.* The coding was made using the data management programme NVivo4 enabling while scrutinising the transcripts to add codes like *outcomes of the boundary work, personal reflection on equilibrium, professional and personal context.* After coding, the transcripts were reviewed on an individual basis in order to write 'life stories'. Each story was, in a second time, coded using the main codes. This was done to assure the trustworthiness of the data reduction from the interview to the stories.

The interviews were analysed to show: 1) How do middle-managers view their life (definition of life domains)? 2) How do middle-managers experience their work/non-work relationships (management of boundaries) and 3) How do organizations influence individual's experiences? It is important to note that the 'organizational life' discussed in these stories reflects individuals' perception. This, on the one hand, limits the scope of any generalization. Therefore, generalization is not the aim of this chapter. On the other hand, this may also be seen as a point of strength for the following discussion on CSR Indeed, it draws attention to how

Table 1: Personal Situation

NAME*	GENDER	AGE**	MARITAL STATUS	FAMILY SITUATION	TOWN	COMMENTS
Thibault	M	32	Co-habiting	His partner has 1 boy (12) and 1 girl (9)	Stras-bourg***	
Paul	M	44	Separated	1 daughter (7) living with her mother	Dijon	In a relationship
Marine	F	27	Has a boyfriend		Dijon	
Del-phine	F	51	Married	1 son (20) and 1 daughter (16)	Dijon	

*Names have been changed; ** at the date of interview (September/October 2005); ***Lived in Dijon but moved to Strasbourg for professional reason*

Table 2: Professional Situation

NAME	MAIN POSITION	TEAM MEM-BERS	SIZE AND SCOPE	TYPE OF ORGA-NIZATION*	COMMENTS
Thibault	Project Manager		Large - National	Construction	In charge of quality security and environment
Paul	Responsible of Communication (Regional level)		Large – National	Electricity, gas and water supply	works as a project manager
Marine	Head of International Relationships	1 pers.		Public administration	First employment
Del-phine	Head of International Development	8 pers.		Education	

Based on NACE – Classification of Economic Activities in the European Community ('NACE – Classification of Economic Activities in the European Community', 2002) people are making sense of their organization. It offers a reflection on the organization and its practices from the individuals' points of view. It emphasises boundary work not only as a mental process but also as a social process in and out of the organization. In turn, it is valuable for understanding how individuals build boundaries and how they enact and manage them in their environment and how organizations play a role in such process.

Work/non-work stories of four French middle-managers

In this part, four stories are narrated. Each story highlights how one views life domains and the relationships between them. It also highlights the contexts for the boundary work especially the organizational context.

Thibault

After different positions in various departments in Dijon and showing interest in organizational quality, Thibault was asked to be in charge of harmonizing the quality systems of the entire North-East office. He therefore works as a project manager for quality, but in Strasbourg! Nowadays, Thibault weekly commutes between the European and Burgundy capital cities to join what he consider his 'almost' family. Thara and Thibault met more than 3 years ago in the company. Before that Thibault was single. Thara has two children from her previous relationship. As a step father, even if he does not like this expression, he feels that he may have a role to play towards the children, especially the boy who has difficulties at school. These two domains are completed by personal activities like golfing that Thibault was introduced to by one of his friends/colleagues which now he practices as often as possible. For him, golfing is a sport to calm down and concentrate without thinking about anything else than a small-white ball.

From a general point of view, Thibault aims at separating his private and professional lives. For him, this is how he can get some kind of balance.

> I try to have a certain balance between both; that is to say when I am at the office I am at work and if something goes wrong in my life I do not; at least I try; but only the others could confirm this; not to make the others feel it and vice-versa.

This is true despite the fact that he and Thara work in the same company. When they worked at the same location they did not act as a couple and were not close to each other even during breaks.

> The fact not to make our relationship official is that I consider that my private life is my private life and since it does not influence my work; people do not need to know with whom I am living; I am not going to ask them with whom they sleep ...

In addition, Thibault does not like to talk about work at home or even to talk about personal life at work. Today, this segmentation is somehow eased by his new location in Strasbourg. Overall, Thibault wishes to concentrate on his role and enjoys each moment in each domain. Today, he does not want to leave after 6 p.m. so he can go and golf. But beyond that he does not want the others to become used to work long hours. Similarly, he enjoys and wants to protect the time he spends with Thara during the weekends.

> 'It is weekends when we watch a DVD, it is not the DVD but the entire evening, we eat together, we watch TV or read a book together; these are sort of moments when we do not ask ourselves questions'

Nonetheless, Thibault admits that such segmenting is not easy and sometimes it feels also natural to talk of work at home. Nonetheless, this does not mean he is 'thinking' work at home. As they both work in the company, Thibault appreciates Thara's opinion about his work and feels it is easier to share problems and ideas as she knows the context.

> So, when I discuss together with Thara, there are obviously times when we are talking about what she is doing at work, what I am doing at work ... I like to ask her opinion. Effectively I take the advantage that she is working in the same company. I do not have to explain the context so I have a vision that is complementary to mine.

It is also easier to communicate during the week via e-mails, unless it disturbs work as Thibault says. It is also easy to bring the laptop home and work a while. Being in the same company is not always positive. Knowing how much he does not fully enjoy to implement projects, in comparison to developing them, also feeling how the company may change, Thara had reservations when Thibault accepted the position. For Thibault, this was important in his decision and then he realised he was no longer single.

In addition, Thibault describes a sort of social life with friends and colleagues. First, Thibault enjoys talking with colleagues, especially during the cigarette and lunch breaks. It happens that they have been out together for a drink. This, nonetheless, does not imply they for him are on the same level of other people that he views as real friends. With those, Thara and he may go out and have a dinner at home to share more about their private lives. These colleagues are, nonetheless, not hierarchically related to him and are even stationed in other regional office. Finally, Thibault has friends from his childhood. Even if they do not meet as often as they want, he feels he is emotionally connected to them. He recognizes that technology helps to keep contacts such as Internet games where he might meet Tristan.

Today, the challenge for Thibault is to know under what conditions he will make it possible for Thara and the kids to move to Strasbourg. For now, they exchange SMS and he is carrying her picture, in his night book.

Paul

Paul describes his life as composed of three main domains. First, his 'family' includes Paola, his daughter, his parents, and his brother's family. In 2001, Paul separated from his wife since he moved to Dijon for his work. Now he is a new relationship but at distance[6] he still sees himself as single. Second, his 'personal interests' include reading (books and newpapers), going to theatre or cinema and practicing sports, e.g. jogging, tennis, cycling, attending games or looking the evening sport news. Finally, his 'work'. When graduating, Paul had a strong desire to work for a large national company.

6   They live 200 km apart

Consequently, Paul has been working for the same company for 20 years at different positions (including internal consultancy work) in various parts of France. Nowadays, he works at the communication department. He is coordinating corporate communication in Burgundy and its outlying regions by deploying a group of local people and by working with local media.

Overall, Paul sees his domains as just different parts of one entity: his life

> For me, they (private and professional lives) are one. It is like if I had two children, sometimes I am with one, other times I am with the other, but, I would say, I love to hug them both because I love them both a lot.

This indicates that Paul values both work and non-work but does not mean that there are no distinction. Indeed, Paul daily sets limits between them. First, he tries not to bring negative aspects of work home and does not appreciate talking about 'work' at home especially with regard to problems. He may sometimes talk about positive experiences with his new partner over the phone. But, more generally he does not like to talk about his work outside the work context because he defines himself not only by his position.

For him, work related troubles 'stop at the office door', especially when he sees the few trees out of the office building. On weekends, he also concentrates on personal activities.

> Generally on Friday nights I shut all. I am in weekends ... I will describe them [work and non-work] as one. But this does not mean I think about work on weekends.

In addition, he does not take work home. But if he does, it has to be interesting material to read. Then, he will sit on his terrace reading it. He does not have a computer at home. He does not have lunch with his colleagues but enjoys going home to get one. He actually prefers walking and feeling alone for a few minutes; this time for him is work-related. In the evening, he plans for part-time activities, alone or with friends, to have a contrast to work. Paul has developed friendship with some of his current and former colleagues. However, they rarely talk about private matters when they meet at work. He would rather invite them home for that even there talking about work take no more than few minutes.

Such will to segment is, nonetheless, largely moderated by some of his practices. He would not mind to meet work acquaintances during his weekend and exchange a few words with them.

> Last Saturday or Sunday, I went to the theatre where I met some journalists, the person in charge of the communication of xxx, other regional personalities ... etc. I was pleased to see them. We talked a bit of work, we talked about other stuffs; it is part – one can say – of my daily life.

Paul talks to some journalists during private time, but on the condition that it does not affect the time he has allocated to spend with his daughter. He will also not mind leaving the office a little bit early to meet a friend for 'recharging his batteries'. He will not mind when on trip staying one additional night on to get good sleep, not stress but also meet an acquaintance or discover the town.

For Paul, the most important factors linking work and non-work are 'pleasure' and 'enrichment'. When one domain creates pleasure or enriches the other, then Paul will naturally blend both.

> I would first consider it [an invitation getting by work to attend a handball game on a Saturday] as leisure time, but I will obviously meet people I work with. It will enable me to tie up the relationship with them, to place the relationship; I will say; on more a personal basis rather than a professional basis. So it is at the border. No! It is not actually, it is how work and non-work overlap and this is not at all a problem, on the contrary! I would say working and having fun or having fun and simultaneously meeting professional contacts; it is fine.

Integration would not take place if he would be invited to a sport game he does not appreciate. Integration takes place by reading news both for pleasure and work. Indeed, he admits that listening to company and market news when getting up eases his daily working routines and provides him pleasure.

Such attitude towards the work/non-work relationships is due to Paul's former work/non-work experiences. In his previous working tasks, Paul had a negative relation to work so the experience taught him to draw a line between work and non-work activities.

> This is astonishing because during my first job when I did not manage well as my work was 'eating' my personal life, i.e. I could not sleep well, I was stressed, my entire energy was used for work, the weekends I had to sleep early because I was working the day after. My life was not as agreeable as it should be. Today, when I am at work, I am at work. When I say 'I work' I could say 'now I need a break' so I go and see a friend during lunch time and come back later. Weekly I switch on Fridays, same for holidays ...

When he was, for a short while, an internal consultant he discovered that work could provide satisfaction via a higher level of autonomy. When four years ago [in such company it is normal for people to change location every 4-5 years] he looked for a job, getting a balance was of importance so that he turned down job openings that could have enhanced his career.

> After my education [French Engineering School], you dream to be CEO after 10 years. I did not know myself, I did not know who I was and year after year I learned my strengths and weaknesses, my ways of functioning and I now know that there were positions that I refused I could have managed but it would have been against my well-being; so I climb the hierarchical ladder more slowly than younger colleagues.

Nowadays, Paul's challenge is to keep this balance between integration and segmentation and confront the forthcoming organizational changes.

Marine

Marine moved to Dijon for her first job, leaving her gang of friends but taking with her Mathieu her new boyfriend. Marine portrays fours life domains: her 'life with Mathieu', her 'life with her friends' every weekend in Paris, her 'family' especially her privileged relation with her younger brother and, last, her 'position as head of the international relationships' in a local administration. Marine accepted the post because she felt, somehow, under social and familial pressures to get a job being jobless for two years. This decision was made easier for her by Mathieu who was ready to follow her as he was unemployed. Nowadays or two years later, Marine still feels that she is still in an adaptation phase.

I switch from a student world to a world which is different professionally, socially, schedule-wise, so I try to adapt myself and I think I am still in this phase.

In addition, Mathieu is still not working and she still does not feel that Dijon is 'home'. In her overall context, Marine recognizes, as if it was required, that it is difficult to blend work and personal life.

Emm, I have difficulties to blend my private and professional lives ...

In fact, she draws barriers between her work and her personal and private life on a daily basis. First, Marine does not talk about private matters at work. She may talk a bit about non-professional issues like overall plans for a future career or holidays but not about 'too private' matters. Second, she does not feel comfortable with having family pictures in her office.

It is funny but when I see someone with responsibilities having a picture of his wife or his baby, I tell myself 'he is not so strict after all'. But I really do not see myself doing that. I do not imagine having this [a picture] here [her office] because this is my private life. I do not want everyone knowing what my boyfriend or my parents look like.

Third, she does not feel comfortable with the idea that friends and colleagues are of the same category when it comes to social relations. Consequently, she often turns down invitations from colleagues.

It is someone [a colleague] I could have a drink with. But once he brought his girlfriend who is also working in the same administration, so I told Mathieu not come because we were going to talk about work. I really do not manage to mix, *a priori* I do not want to mix.

Thus, she rarely has lunch with colleagues and prefers going home to eat with Mathieu and get a break.

Most of the time I go and have lunch home, especially when Mathieu is here and cooks [smile]. Then I take a small rest, I read my mail etc. I really try to take a break. I do not think over and over the problems at work.

For her, this is due to her atmosphere and her specific work situation. First, her relationships with her boss she reports to, an elected representative, is not simple. She feels that she and her boss do not have always the same objectives so it takes time to argue for projects. Second, her position is rather new and still unclear to the other units. Finally, her office, on the ground floor, seems isolated from other departments. All in all, she does not feel comfortable to meet people from work because she is afraid of talking about work issues that are too specific to her situation. When it comes to draw the line, Marine feels that she has hard time to be the same person both at work and outside work. She does not, for example, wear the same clothes at work and outside work. For her, this is due to her age. She is actually one of the youngest managers in the organization.

> I cannot wear at work what I wear at home, because I have clothes with flashy colours, crested t-shirts ... old jeans and large trousers, I do not see myself coming at work like that ...

Nonetheless, gradually the gap tends to reduce. Today (on the day of interview) she is wearing a pair of jeans; a 'working jeans' as she underlines with a smile. Finally, she does not take office work home and does not perform personal activities at work. If the phone rings for personal reasons at work it has to be an emergency.

But beyond this desire to segment work and non-work, Marine thinks and even ruminates about work. She feels that her level of responsibilities is somehow too high and that her job does not fulfil her expectations. This creates a high level of stress and less restful sleep. This also leads to anxiety when taking the train back to Dijon. For Marine these are the factors which make work creep into her personal life:

> Work is creeping because of the fatigue and the stress it causes me, because of the nights in which I do not sleep well, because of the anxiety on Monday mornings. Indeed my work does not creep into my life because of business travels on weekends, or longer working hours on interesting projects but not after 10 p.m.; this is positive stress. But it is rather the impact of work which is sort of invading my life.

Such anxiety is reinforced by concerns about Mathieu's situation of not finding a suitable job and her projections in the case of him finding a job but in Paris. This makes her think about 'non-work' at work. This overall anxiety affects her behaviour as she feels more emotionally sensible and is prompted to talk to Mathieu about her work, even if she does not want to and feels guilty about it. This also limits her energy after work when she feels that she lacks the energy to exercise and practice her favourite past-time, photography. To alleviate stress, Marine spends sometime shopping on her way back home between 6.30 and 7 p.m. On arrival she takes a long shower.

> I come home, I take a shower. It is really important the shower ... I change skin. I relax.

Nowadays, Marine's main challenge is to find a new job. She spends time at home looking for new job opportunities. Since the leas t year, she actually thinks she has a double working day when private phones calls become some sort of 'working tasks' written down on Post-it® notes; like she is doing for tasks at the office. In her quest, she would accept a work with a lower hierarchical position if it would enable her to be closer to her friends and would not creep into her private and personal life.

Delphine

Delphine moved from Paris to Dijon in 1988 one year after her husband, Denis. For that, she given had to give up an interesting job in Paris but start her own consultancy agency only one month after her arrival. This shows how work is important for Delphine who says that her work is part of her life.

> work is not separated from my life, sure, work is part of my life

This attitude towards work/non-work relationships is due to Delphine's perception of her mother's life after her divorce as meaningless just because her mother was only a 'housewife'. In one sense, she would like to follow her father's path by creating an enriching working life, but is also keen not to enrich bot aspects.

Today, Delphine portrays her life as composed of a 'couple life', a 'family life' with her two children, a 'social life' with 'friends' living in Rome or Brussels and her 'work' as head of international development and lecturer (though she had not been teaching for almost a year). Delphine has somehow no friends in Dijon, a town she still feels that she is not belonging to. At work, she is in charge of the overall international development and leads a team of eight women. She enjoys the autonomous nature of her task especially when starting new contacts and new projects with international partners.

Viewing work and non-work as integrated she is not hesitant to talk about work at home, the thing in her family seen as normal and she easily brings work home.

> As I will think of a personal matter when I am in the office, I will think of work when I am home. There is no clear separation. I cannot say when I close the door of my office: 'it is finished, I will not think of at home'... For sure we will talk about it.

In addition, she tends to view her foreign contacts as her friends though she may rarely come across them. When they are in Dijon, she would gladly invite them to her place and let them interact freely with her life outside the office because it may enrich it.

> This Saturday, Délia [her daughter] went to the cinema with an American girl. In fact, there is a group of American students this semester and they came with two teachers. And these teachers are here with their family. So I discovered last week that they had a 15 year-old daughter; I presented her to Délia who is 16 ... and they went to cinema together, and then Délia introduced her to her friends.

Delphine considers being the same person whether in the office or at home. In both arenas she strives to create an environment characterized with respect and friendship. She is as affective in both domains. She has devised her own way of dealing with problems by listening, trying to be consensual and if necessary imposing her choice.

However, Delphine daily sets some temporal boundaries between work and non-work. She tries not to check her e-mails in the eve-

nings as she considers to have been working somehow from 7 a.m.
to 8 p.m. During weekends, she may nonetheless work on her laptop to finalise some issues. Then the only discernible home artefact
in her office is a picture of her children but though:

> It is a picture taken by my husband when the children were still kids. But,
> in fact, it is here because I like this picture. It is here more for its artistic
> value. I like the way they look at each other, the connection between
> them. Secondary, they are my kids.

Delphine has not formed any close friendships through work. She
feels somehow an affective connection with some colleagues and
shares some personal or familial issues with them especially when
they are children-related. But she seldom meet them outside of
work and would not describe them as friends. At lunch time, she
prefers to remain in her office to do administrative tasks. Indeed
with almost everyone out having lunch she can be certain not to
be disturbed. She may go home if her husband is there. Delphine
sets some boundaries around her 'couple life' by reserving time to
spend with her husband chatting in the evenings and planning for
example at the present time some renovations in the house.

The work/non-work interaction has not always been easy and
she has been using her accumulative experience to find her path.
As a consultant, Delphine thought at first that her freedom would
help her to preserve a work-life balance. However, she needed to
be where the market demand was so that she had to be away entire
weeks. She felt her mother's role in danger. Currently, even if she
is away around three months a year, she makes sure that, wherever
she could be, her children can stay in touch with her. Overall, her
well-being depends on to what extent she can please her children
and to what extent she can share experiences with others even if
sometimes small conflicts can arise. Nowadays, one of Delphine's
challenges is to negotiate her new contract as sole international
director in a manner that will make her available for her family and
her elderly mother.

How do French middle-managers define and manage boundaries of their life domains?

The following discussion investigates individual stories by answering two main questions, i.e. 1) what are middle-managers' life domains? 2) how do they manage their life domains' boundaries?

Life as a multi-domain arena

From the individuals' stories, we can see that work is somehow discussed as a whole whereas non-work is seen through diverse sub-domains. Four large non-work sub-domains can be identified across the four middle managers: 1) Family, 2) Social life, 3) Personal time and 4) Joint activities. Table 3 offers an overview of the experience of work and non-work.

Table 3: Experience of work and non-work

NAME	WORK	NON-WORK
Thibault	• Office, papers/documents, colleagues	• Relationship with Thara and her two kids • Friends from childhood • Acquaintance maybe from work • Extended family • Golfing
Paul	• Office, the department, contacts with communication professionals, reading (newspaper)	• Family (daughter Paola, nephew, parents, and brother's family) • Personal interest : cultural activities, theatres and readings
Marine	• Her office, the organization	• Life with Mathieu, her flat in Dijon and Mathieu's in Paris • Life with her friends in Paris • Her parents • Her privileged relation with her brother, • Searching for a new work
Delphine	• Office, travels, documents, team	• Her family with a distinction between couple and with kids, and her mother, the house. • Friends • Extended Family – Mother

The meaning and the scope of these domains vary across individuals as well over time for each one of them. In the frame of boundary theory this indicates that the elements of the domains, the nature of the boundaries and boundaries' permeability and flexibility are personal constructions that may evolve over time. Family as a mental representation is seen as flexible over time, e.g. Thibault talks of his 'almost family' like if it will be his 'family' soon. Work as psychologically defined is also flexible as its importance may reduce over time as in the case of Paul. Therefore, how one structures and experiences his/her life domains is personal and dynamic in time.

Above all, the distinction between different life domains takes form when considering the three components of a domain. In that sense, work but also the non-work sub-domains are defined based on *people*, e.g. depicting family as family members; social life via friends or work via colleagues, or management. In addition, 'family' for some includes the closest members of the nuclear family (spouse and children) whereas for others parents or relatives. Domains are based on the *objects* representing them. On the one hand, you find working documents or even the desk, office, laptop representing work. On the other hand, non-work is described through family portraits but also the house or the town. Domains are based on *activities,* e.g. viewing friends as people we meet regularly to do specific activities in comparison to acquaintances who we only meet sporadically. This is a central issue when discussing 'personal time' via cultural or personal development activities or the 'couple' via activities such as having a glass of wine with one's spouse. Finally, these domains are based on the *attitudes and thoughts* associated with them, e.g. how one presents him/herself (clothing at work and at home) or how one sees work and non-work as a mental activity. The association of these components leads to the emergence or non-emergence of a domain. Indeed, the differentiation between peers or management is not enough for individuals to distinguish sub-domains. Both types of actors are still seen as part of the work domain as a whole. This differs from what is available in the current middle-management literature where different people in the work domain are associated with different roles (See Engel, 1997). In parallel, the definition of the domains relates also to the types of boundaries (spatial, temporal, and psychological). To illustrate this process, we can consider 'people' as the element of one domain. First, people may be considered in relation to a physical domain; colleagues as people sharing the office or the same building; family members as people sharing the same flat. Then, people may be considered in relation to a temporal domain; colleagues as people coming together during working hours, partners as people met during working hours and business trips or friends as people meeting outside the working hours. Third, people may be considered in relation to psychological domain; e.g. work partners as people one work with (mental conception) as in the case of Paul and the journalists who may meet outside working hours, in the street or, e.g. friends as people one can count to get support when having problems or spend good leisure time with.

Conclusions

First, life is a 'multi-domain' (elements of the domain) and 'multi-layer' (types of boundaries) arena. Then it seems to be a shared meaning of work as a domain, but the meaning of non-work is broad and may include four large dimensions; 'family'; 'social life'; 'personal time' and 'joint activities' This is thus more than the traditional 'work' and 'family' domains and provides a finer view than having two just broad 'work' and 'non-work' domains. Second, the definition of each of these life domains is based on individuals' perceptions and believes about the combination of elements that makes up a domain, spatially, physically and mentally. It relates thus to how permeable a domain is. Third, the conception of one domain of life seems to evolve over time which refers to the extent to what a domain is flexible.

Middle-managers' boundary work process

As just concluded, identifying domains and sub-domains depends on the combination of the domains' elements one relates to a domain spatially, temporally and psychologically. This combination depends first on how the domains (spatially, temporally and psychologically defined) are *a priori* segmented or integrated (environment). Then, it depends on the extent to which one wishes the domains (spatially, temporally and psychologically defined) to be segmented or integrated (preference). Finally, it relates to how the domains (spatially, temporally and psychologically defined) are *de facto* integrated or integrated (experience).

It is thus central to consider, on the one hand, individuals' overall preferences (how work and non-work should interact together from one's point of view) and, on the other hand, individuals' experiences (how work and non-work are *a priori* and *de facto* interacting together). Looking at the gaps between both dimensions reveals the process of boundary work. Indeed, experience is first the result of the boundary work (placement and transcendence) enabling to enact boundaries where a 'fit' between the environment and the preference is central. Second, experience shapes the environment one lives in. Finally, until an individual is not experiencing what he or she wishes for, boundary work takes place. Both dimensions – experiences and preferences – are represented in the matrix below where gaps revealing the process of boundary work can be observed.

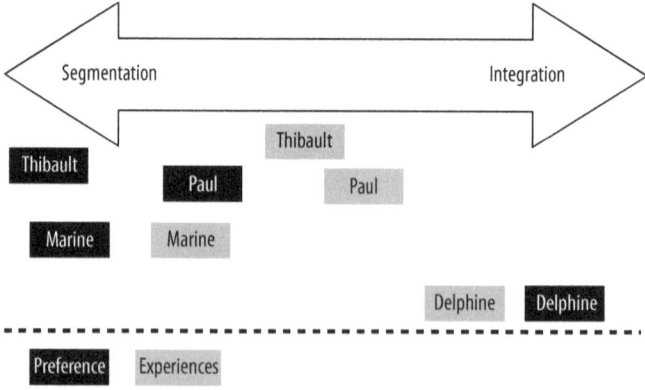

Figure 2: The dynamics of boundary work: experience versus preferences

Integration and segmentation as individual preferences

In line with the boundary management view, each individual has a preference for 'integration' or 'segmentation'. The four middle-managers are well aware of their preferences so that figure 2 relies on their explicit preferences.

Thibault is explicitly looking for a high degree of segmentation. Marine expresses also a preference for segmentation but in a vaguer way. Delphine is the only one who explicitly seeks for a high degree of integration by seeing work and non-work as one because she does not want to reproduce the familial scheme. Paul has a more balanced preference. Hence, he sees work and non-work as one but he daily and intentionally separates them without excluding the possibilities to integrate them when 'pleasure' and 'enrichment' is at stake.

Overall, by looking at segmentation and integration as preferences in the stories, one can conclude and, bear in mind, that segmentation is valued at the individual level. First, it is mostly perceived as a proactive choice, and, then, all of them, including Delphine, are daily segmenting their work and non-work domains. Segmentation represents thus a daily preference especially and precisely between work and family defined from a temporal, spatial and mental point of view.

Conclusion

'Segmentation' is valued at the individual level as an overall strategy between some large domains and as a daily strategy mainly between work and family.

Integration and segmentation as experiences

The work/non work experience is revealed by the individual boundary management process (placement and transcendence) through which individuals create, maintain and change boundaries fitting their preferences in their bounded environment. Overall, individual stories show that each middle-manager has placed some sort of boundaries when boundary work activities aiming at segmenting are mainly seen more as a proactive. For example, having no computer at home or refusing to get one from work are proactive choices to segment. The choice not to have friends among people who are hierarchically related to oneself is also a proactive way to segment. Deciding to stay longer at work so you do not take work documents home is discussed as a proactive choice. More precisely, the stories reveal that segmentation is, to different extent, individually required to 'feel well' especially on a daily basis between work and family. Segmentation is also strong when it relates to what middle managers refer as 'too private', as in the case of Marine and the look of her boyfriend, or Thibault's relationship with Thara.

However, boundary work activities aiming at integrating are mainly described as active or reactive processes. Indeed integration is especially put in place when positive interferences between work and other domains may occur, for example Paul feels it is natural and nice to meet work partners outside work or stop working a bit earlier to have lunch (permeability of working time). This is as well the case with Delphine who has a picture of the children in her office for its artistic rather than familial value. Thibault feels, after second thoughts, that it is natural to talk about work with Thara as it enables him to reflect about how to perform better.

In practice, segmentation and integration are put in place via diverse activities aiming first at fixing and placing boundaries then at crossing them. Table 4 presents an overview of some activities with regard to the domains' components expressed by the four middle-managers.

Conclusions

For these middle-managers the objective of segmentation is to protect beforehand one domain from the negative influences of another whereas segmentation naturally or retroactively happens when positive interferences occur. This is in line with most of the coping strategies for stress where segmentation enables restoration (See Sonnentag & Bayer, 2005; Sonnentag & Kruel, 2006) and with the enrichment theory between work and non-work (Greenhaus & Powell, 2006). Nonetheless, this goes still against part of one of the main assumptions of the work-life programmes which defines integration more as a proactive strategy that one should seek in order to reduce stress and increase well-being.

Table 4: Placing and crossing boundaries*

COMPONENTS OF THE DOMAINS	PLACEMENT ACTIVITIES	TRANSCENDENCE ACTIVITIES
People	• Distinction between colleagues and friends • Choices not to have friends among colleagues hierarchically connected to oneself	• Talks and subjects of conversation adapted in regards to the spatial boundaries, work talks at work and private chat outside • Having specific activities with specific people • Do not invite people from work at home or people from the non-work domain at the office.
Objects	• Do not have pictures from the work domain in the non-work domain • Not having family pictures, personal objects at the office • Do not have an office space where I could perform work at home	• Computers and documents from work are not leaving the office. Personal documents are not taken at the office • Emails from one domain are not read at another • Do not have laptops and any mobile devices given by work
Thoughts Action Presentation	• Do not let thoughts cross domains (not thinking of work with family around)…especially negative thoughts. • Be directive in one domain and non-directive in another	• Using a 'third' place to think of work, like the car or the street between work and non-work space • Getting distance between work and non-work • Having fixed working hours may help to control mental switching

*The activities above are expressed as segmentation activities.

So it reinforces the argument of Kossek *et al.* (1999) for whom segmentation is nowadays a result of a desire or an intention. A further explanation could be that the contemporary society is 'organized' so that integration is facilitated whereas segmentation is hindered. This is expressed by Marine for whom integration and blending are perceived as a norm. The contemporary environment is somehow in opposition to the 1980s when the work-life debate started. Indeed, in the 1980's researchers and practitioners created the 'myth of separate worlds' (Kanter in Hall & Richter, 1988, p. 213) so that working part time (80% or 70%) to 'combine' work and family was not the an easy and realistic strategy for 'working mums'. Is it vice-versa nowadays? In other words, this indicates that the implementation of work-life programmes associated with formal and informal flexibility may have reshaped our environment and the organizational mind set so that 'segmentation' demands an effort from the individual. As a result, people who do not want to integrate their domains of life will mostly be proactively to keep these domains separated. This leads to a new conclusion for this chapter. Indeed, there may be a gap between individuals' desires and their context that may engender tensions when trying to place and keep boundaries. Such tensions may be perceived as a new demand and may require new efforts and energy to be overcome. As a result, the integrative paradigm may create counter effects, compared to the expected ones, for individuals' well-being. From another point of view, one could argue that 'segmentation' is a counter strategy to the societal and organizational perceived values of an integrative paradigm, a strategy that makes people still feel to act as free agents. Finally, it is central to recognize that in each story, segmentation and integration are not pure strategies so that individuals are using both in different micro situations.

Back to Corporate Social Responsibility or how organizations can act socially responsible

In this last section I elaborate from a corporate social responsibility point of view on some of the conclusions drawn on the previous section. I reflect on the role of organizations in the work/non-work relationship and how they can act in a socially responsible manner.

The first question asked in this chapter is *what are the life domains?* First, this chapter reveals that life is a 'multi-domain' arena where work is seen as a whole but non-work as multiple sub-domains. To act in a socially responsible way, this suggests that work-life pro-grammes should be extended so that they cover more sub-domains than the traditional 'work' and 'family'. Work-life programmes should not be designed to balance solely work and family but really work and life especially 'personal time' that is often the domain which is the most flexible and more permeable. The complexity of the sub-domains should be taken into account especially social life via different types of friends, family and different levels - spouse, children and relatives. Second, this chapter shows that the distinc-tion between domains is personal and may differ according to the types of boundaries. Indeed one middle-manager may consider one domain as physically impermeable but at the same time as mentally permeable. To act socially responsible, work/non-work policies and practices should take into account individuals with their diverse 'personal situations'. This is in line with criticism towards the restrictions on the availability and access to work-life options (See Kodz, Harper, & Dench, 2002).

The second issue raised is *how do they manage their life domains?* The individual stories show that nowadays at the individual level 'segmentation' is valued, whereas at the organizational level 'integration' seems to be esteemed. To act socially responsible, companies should respect the extent to which middle-managers desire to integrate or/and segment their different domains (See Geurts & Demerouti, 2003; Kirchmeyer, 1995). Work-life programmes should also be carefully implemented so that integration is not seen as a norm and segmentation as a deviance. This is in accordance with research showing that the organizational climate/culture especially the reactions of the colleagues and managers may be a barrier to the effectiveness of work-life arrangements (See Kodz, Harper, & Dench, 2002). In addition, as integration and segmentation are not extreme strategies but specific strategies applicable in specific situations (work/non-work segmentation as short term and daily versus work/non-work integration as life time, when enrichment is at stake), work-life solutions should be as personalised as possible to fit specific individual situations. Work-life programmes should integrate solutions covering both aspects or, at least, offer a certain degree of adaptation in a way so that one do not feel forced to either segment or integrate.

An overall question in this chapter is *how do organizations influence individual's experiences?* Table 4 listed diverse work/non-work activities where most of them are based on self-management and individuals' initiatives. Nonetheless, looking closer at the stories, such work/non-work initiatives are influenced by the organization. Overall, beyond specific work-life policies, the organization and its policies, routines and culture shape the individuals' environment by essentially making work/non-work boundaries more or less permeable. To illustrate this, one of the aspects emerging in most stories is the organizational culture or atmosphere. Marine's working atmosphere is a factor making work to creep into her social and couple life so that it is important for her to place psychological boundaries. Such placement is supported by also placing physical boundaries: Nonetheless this makes the transcendence harder (train between Dijon and Paris, when she feels anxious). Thibault's feeling that the organizational culture may not to share the existence of his relationship with Thara somehow supports his segmentation preference. To develop socially responsible organizations, decision makers could scrutinize organizational policies and process taking into account how they will influence the individual environment i.e. the 'a priori' boundaries. Two main aspects should be taken care of when performing such review. First, management teams should explore the two questions above i.e. employees' work/non-work experiences. Second, management teams should bear in mind that one same policy may affect people boundary work both by supporting or hindering their choices i.e. taking into consideration once and again individual work/non-work experiences. Without both aspects, tensions between the individuals' work/non-work desires and their organizational context may occur so that it may be detrimental to individuals' well-being and the development of sustainable healthy organizations.

Above all this chapter reveals that the 'work/non-work stories' themselves are already part of how organizations can act more socially responsible and develop healthy organizations. Indeed, listening to and trying to understand individual work/non-work stories is an important step for acting in a socially responsible way as it places individuals, their work/non-work situations and preferences in the centre of the organization. This chapter demonstrates clearly how 'managing the work/non-work relationships' becomes part of the Corporate Social Responsibility agenda.

12. Matching Ethical Demands – or not: That is the Question

Introduction

Businesses must have a license to operate, not only legally, but also morally. Any firm must care for their legitimacy of operations, meaning to make sure that the surrounding society approves of their business idea and ways to achieve the business goals. Network researchers (the so-called IMP-school) call this the social embeddedness of firms (for instance Mainela 2002, Törnroos 1997). However, there seems to be a real problem in this outset: my initial claim in this chapter is that firms will never reach a full approval from society. I argue that firms are bound to be in imbalance with society, as they constantly aim for balance with the same. This paradox constitutes the problem setting, which gives rise to a number of subsequent questions. How can we understand the concept of corporate citizenship, having this paradox in mind? Is there a real possibility for firms to act as a member of society, i.e. by the same norms as other citizens? And if such a possibility would exist, what would be the implications of this? Let us briefly explore the thought that firms really behaved ethically in every way, meaning that there would be no conflicts between the surrounding environment (including people, local institutions, government etc.) and the business market. What kind of society would this create? Kristensson Uggla (2002:368) draws upon this thought, arguing that society would be absurd. Where does this leave us? It seems that we have a setting in which the firm is stuck: the quest for legitimacy implies that firms must aim for harmony with society – yet, the true vision of such a goal is ridiculous.

By exploring this problem setting, the research question of the chapter reads: *Can one expect business and society to be in balance, what do corporate citizenship and corporate social responsibility imply?* The chapter starts by focusing on a conceptual discussion on different ways to approach the morally loaded tension between business and society. A model on the interrelatedness of corporate social responsibility and corporate citizenship is proposed. This more abstract theoretizising is brought to a more concrete level in discussing Normann's (2001) concept of prime movers and analysing the role of a networking firm aiming for a business ethics profile. A synthesizing discussion then deals with issues of power, shift of responsibility and integration of diverse interests in the ethical strategy of a firm. The chapter constitutes a typical theoretical discussion, with interpretation and analysis leading to the proposition of conceptual clarifications and managerial implications.

The main contribution lies in a conceptual discussion of ethics as a means of identity construction in a glocal firm, and is consequently theoretical. Managerially, the chapter contributes with a clarification business ethics concepts, especially the terms corporate social responsibility and corporate citizenship. It is argued that managers needs to reflect over the identity of the company when engaging in activities linked to the business ethics profile of the company. The main issue is accordingly to address the unavoidable question of how to legitimize the firm in a situation where one accepts that it will never be accomplished in fully. Integrated diversity is finally suggested as a theoretical and managerial term which could be used to transfer abstract ethical thoughts to real business life.

Key Definitions

Studies on the morally loaded relationship between business and society have brought a plethora of terms (e.g. Arrow 1973/1979, Bowie 1978/1979, Dienhart & Curnutt 1998, Fleckstein & Huebsch 1999, Gordon & Miyake 2001, Sen 1995, Nijhof & Rietdijk 1999, Chonko 1995, Laczniak & Murphy 1993). Johnson and Smith (1999) write that over 300 different definitions on *business ethics* have been found in the literature. Brytting and Egels (2004) make a definition of business ethics as either moral philosophy or a form of applied research of the ethical management or sustainability artefacts in a company. This chapter defines business ethics according to the latter definition: discussing and understanding of ethics for strategic purposes in the market. Here, also other terms could be used. *Corporate citizenship* (cc) is a concept which seems to be one of the newest additions to the smorgasbord of terms dealing with ethical consciousness in business (Juholin 2004, also Jeurissen 2004, Waddock 2004). Garriga and Melé (2004) propose cc to be a political theory, while *sustainable development* (sd) is a value-based concept that belongs to ethical theories. Other terms that will be addressed are *corporate social responsibility* (csr), *corporate responsibility* (cr) and *sustainability.*

The European Commission has made csr the official term for a sustainable interaction between business and society. In the Green Paper*: Promoting a European framework for corporate social responsibility* (2001:10) csr is defined as: 'a concept whereby companies integrate social and environmental concerns in their business operations and in their interaction with their stakeholders on a voluntary basis.' Being socially responsible means going beyond compliance and not merely fulfilling legal expectations. Investing 'more' into human capital, the environment and the relations with stakeholders, implies that the company's competitiveness increases. Brytting and Egels (2004:19) discuss the implications of why the Commission chose csr as the European official concept. They see that csr refers to a more theoretical and normative discussion with an external perspective on business. The company is, accordingly, perceived to be an outside actor, an opposing part to society. Such a perception of the firm can also be noted in the academic discussion on globalization. Opposed to this, cc as a concept rather integrates the company into society. Brytting and Egels define cc in a more descriptive manner, finding that it is used mainly in empirical studies that focus on social projects or other types of charity by businesses. cc then rather determines the effect of business operations from a management perspective. In addition, it seems that cc is more common in the usa and csr more common in Europe. Sustainability, in turn, has become frequently used by firms themselves when referring to actions taken towards a sd. Stora Enso, for instance, developed its ethical framework by starting out with CSR in 2001. Then, it decided to leave out the word 'social' and apply the more general term CR. In 2004 Stora Enso adopted the overall framework 'Code of Ethics', which included a model of sustainability, which was identical to the former CR (Lindfelt 2006). The current model has been used since then and is visualized in Figure 1.

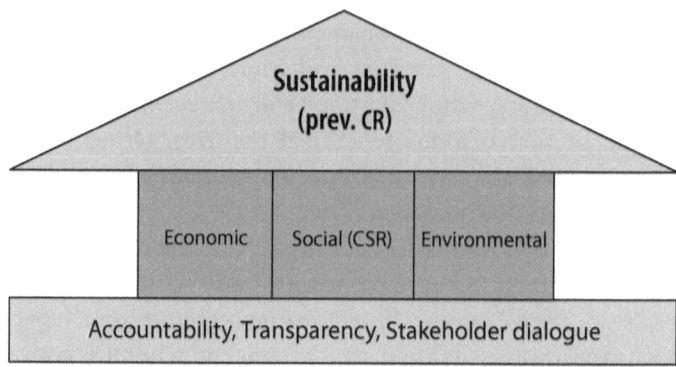

Figure 1: Stora Enso's definition of sustainability and related terms. Source: Stora Enso Sustainability (2004:7).

Sustainability is closely related to the concept of SD, which was first mentioned in the so-called Brundtland Report (*Our Common Future* 1987). Accordingly, development is sustainable when it meets the needs of the present without compromising future generations' ability to meet their own needs. This definition has been used in broad scope, both in natural and social sciences. In business literature, it seems that sustainability includes a wider aim, leaving CSR to deal with the business-oriented efficiency perspective. So is the case also in a is a study by the Finnish Ministry of Commerce, which examines how SMEs in Finland made CSR a competitive advantage. The study finishes by stating the aim of CSR: 'The all-pervading principle is the competitiveness of enterprises in relation to sustainable development' (Taipalinen & Toivio 2004: 68). What we see is that CSR not only functions as a strategy for competitive advantage, but also contributes to SD. In line with this lies also the definition by Dow Jones upon sustainability: 'Corporate Sustainability is a business approach that creates long-term share-holder value by embracing opportunities and managing risks deriving from economic, environmental and social developments' (*Dow Jones Sustainability Indexes* 2003). Here should be noted that CSR extensively is defined to include the same three issues, i.e. economic, environmental and social dimensions. A brief reference back to Figure 1, shows how Stora Enso avoided the plethora of definitions by simply naming their ethical framework 'Sustainability'. The last concept I want to discuss is the first one mentioned in the chapter, CC. Juholin (2004) wrote a book with the Finnish title *Cosmopolis – Yhteiskuntavastuusta yrityskansalaisuuteen*, which translates into: Cosmopolis - From CSR to CC. She claims that social responsibility as a term entered the everyday (Finnish) language of business and politics at the turn of the millennium.[1] Environmental issues had been on the agenda for a decade, when social issues turned up as additional responsibilities, argues Juholin, and this forms the *raîson d'être* for CC. She represents an exception to the Finnish mainstream research, which likes to use the concept CSR (for instance Donner-Amnell 2004, Takala 2000, Rytteri 2002, Vehkaperä 2003). Juholin defends her choice of terminology by stating that CC is a natural consequence when businesses accept their role in society and fulfil responsibility in all functions, on all levels of the company (Juholin 2004: 13). Juholin thus takes a standpoint that seems to oppose Kristensson Ugglas (2002: 368) view: that reality becomes absurd if there is no opposing tension between a firm and surrounding society. On one hand here, it seems that Juholin takes an utopistic stance, which leads one to question whether also the term CC is utopistic. Or does CC benevolently serve (only) as an ideal goal? On the other hand, one may also argue that Kristensson Uggla's example is not so absurd at all, but in fact even constitutes a valuable aim. Before going into these opposing views in more detail, I will return to how I understand business ethics. Here, *business ethics* fathoms the whole issue discussed above, meaning that it becomes inclusive of CSR, CC, CR, SD and sustainability. Business ethics is a phenomenon which occurs when the firm strives for something good and desirable from a moral point of view. This is, in consequence, a broad conceptual definition of business ethics. Gaumnitz

---

1   Donner-Amnell (2004: 233), in turn, suggests that 2003 is the year when 'yhteiskuntavastuu' (Finnish for CSR) entered the everyday language in Finland, as a result of major lay-offs in business.

and Lere (2002:35), rather similarly, sees business ethics as the part of ethics that is applicable on business. Yet other researchers have used additional concepts for approximately the same purpose, like Pearson's (1995) *business integrity*. However, this chapter is limited to the concepts introduced and defined above. The only addition is *integrated diversity*, which will be proposed as an alternative to business ethics as the chapter reaches its conclusions.

The Business-Society Tension: A Conceptual Proposition

So far, it has been argued that CSR often stands for a view on business ethics, where competitive advantage is emphasized. We saw this in the EU official approach and the study by the Finnish Ministry of Commerce. CSR thus becomes a strategic instrument for addressing issues of business ethics. In other words, CSR enables firms to be ethical in a business context. This approach accepts the moral agency of firms, but takes into account that the firm strategically operates in a business market. An deviant view would be to say that business is amoral, and need not take any responsibility whatsoever for ethical or moral matters. Thus, we see that this CSR-perspective opens up the possibility of strategic business ethics. In its ontology, this concept also deviates from how CC is used and defined. CC is not only more idealistic, but actually takes its foundation in an assumption that the firm strives to fulfil all its responsibilities - on all levels, in relation to all of society(Juholin 2004: 13). This resembles a theoretical standpoint, where one sees the firm as embracing the same set of morality as do all individuals, or citizens (*cf.* Steiner & Steiner 1997). CC thus ontologically assumes that the firm shares a moral unity with the rest of society. Such a perspective comes close to an institutional theory of the firm and its ethics approach (see e.g. Halme 1997). It seems that these two terms – CC and CSR – actually incorporate the paradox which formed the problem setting of this chapter (see above). Figure 2 models how CSR and CC are incompatible, because of ontological differences. Theoretically, these concepts stand apart. Managerially this implies that a firm should not make use of both concepts at a time, since this will include conflicting aims and set-outs for business ethics activities. The theoretical and managerial contribution at this stage is, accordingly, that concepts must be chosen with care as these are implemented in the ethical profiling of a firm. This means that both perspectives on business ethics cannot be taken at the same time. As one concept takes the winning position – the other goes in the opposite direction, according to the physical laws of scales. Juholin's (2004) idea that we are moving from CSR to CC is one way of understanding the business ethics development. However, it may be argued that this is rather unrealistic in a world, where post (post)industrialist values rather develops towards larger entities and quarter capitalism (Kristensson Uggla 2002). Such a development clearly favours the use of CSR as a strategic instrument for businesses in efficient ethics profiling of a competitive advantage in a tough market context. Hand-in-hand with this development, we see ethical indexing, sustainable investing and the moral argument of Milton Friedman's stockholder approach. Friedman actually proposed, but has often been misunderstood, that by doing business as well as possible, also society will benefit in the most favourable way (Friedman 1982/1962). In favour of Juholin's (2004) view and the concept of CC, however, we concurrently also experience strong winds of vivid anti-capitalist and anti-globalist movements.

Business Ethics

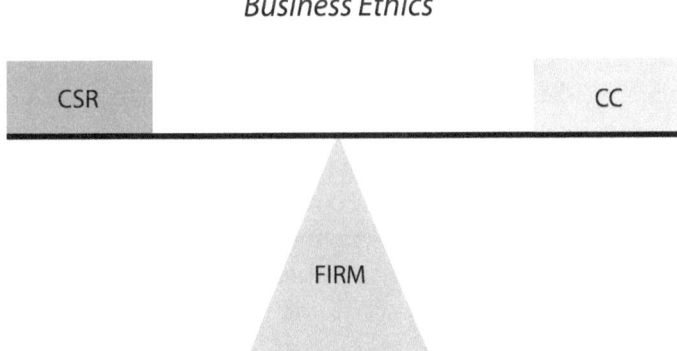

Figure 2: CSR and CC as opposing perspectives of business ethics.

Ethics Codes – A Way to Deal With the Tension Between Business and Society

Ethics codes have been used extensively by firms to balance on the paradox outlined above. Quite like the term of business ethics, an ethical code of conduct does not necessarily need to be named *code of ethics*. Gaumnitz and Lere (2002), for instance, include all official statements that contain comprehensive behavioural guidance in their study of ethics codes. Dienhart and Curnutt (1998) use a similarly wide approach in taking Johnson & Johnson's *credo* as an example of an ethics code. Gasparski (2000) also include differently named codes in his study. He writes about of *codes of values, codes of practice, codes of conduct* and *codes of compliance*. Brytting (1998:196) suggests that an ethics code should be embraced both locally and centrally, express good practice and ideals and that it needs relevance in practical issues and has general applicability. One way to identify an ethics code is to quite straightforwardly ask the firm in question of their perception of their own statement. This procedure is weak in comparative studies, but if one wants to study a particular case firm, essential is indeed what the firm *itself* perceives as its ethics code. Studies show that the ethical consciousness increases in firms that have codified ethical values, values that may have existed also prior to the construction of the formal code (Berenbeim 2000). Table 1 shows a brief overview of various studies on ethics codes in business firms.

Other than the appearance of ethics codes, there are studies investigating the influence of codes of ethics, the role such codes play, comparison of professional codes of ethics vs. corporate codes of ethics, and various other comparative studies on ethics codes (Gaumnitz & Lere 2002, Somers 2001). Tucker *et al.* (1999) categorize the research in the area of ethics codes into two groups: the more external approach of institutionalization of ethics codes and the more internal approach of the nature and composition of ethics codes (Gordon & Miyake 2001, Stevens 1999). The external approach has been primarily descriptive and lacks conceptual development (Tucker *et al.* 1999:290). Furthermore, studies show that ethics codes are used with different motives. Fleckstein and Huebsch (1999) for instance, characterize three types; codes of *regulatory types* with specific guidelines on behaviour and conduct,

Table 1: An overview of the research of ethics codes in business firms.

AUTHOR(S)	PURPOSE OF STUDY
Arrow (1973/1979)	To discuss the economic efficiency of having an ethics code in business. Argues that it is efficient to have a code only in areas of imperfect knowledge or misunderstanding.
Berenbeim (2000)	To discuss why ethics codes have limited success, despite the growing seriousness of such codes.
Bowie (1978/1979)	To discuss if codes of ethics are a good alternative to government regulation or if it is only for public relations related reasons that codes are used.
Breshanan (1999)	To explore how ethical codes give competitive advantage in attracting customers, employers and investors in a few case studies.
Brytting (1998)	To explain the function of the ethics code in the business firm. Subordinates the ethics code to a function of moral support in the firm.
Dienhart and Curnutt (1998)	To explain the reasons behind ethical codes. Explanation of what characterizes detailed codes and general codes of ethical conduct.
Fleckstein and Huebsch (1999)	To ask whether also firms in the service sector, with the example of tourism, find it relevant to develop codes of ethics.
Gasparski (2000)	To report on the design, implementation and adoption of codes of ethics in Poland.
Gaumnitz and Lere (2002)	To identify common ethical dilemmas among business professionals. Researching ethics codes of professional business organizations in the USA.
Gordon and Miyake (2001)	To analyze corporate approaches to anti-bribery commitment and compliance management by a large quantitative study.
Huang (2001)	To argue for the necessity of ethical codes in business.
Nijhof and Rietdijk (1999)	To analyze whether an ethical code raises the ethical behaviour in organizations.
Schwartz (2000)	To argue against the use of ethical codes in business firm. Codes are a way of the management's control system, Schwartz argues.
Sen (1995)	To argue for the need for morality in business and the problematic area of ethics codes, written and unwritten.
Somers (2001)	To study the connection between corporate and professional codes of ethics and employee attitudes and behaviours.
Stevens (1999)	To learn how employees understand what ethical behaviour means in an organization. Ethics codes do not suffice alone for this understanding, Stevens argue.
Tucker et al. (1999)	To compare ethical codes of professional associations.
Wilson (2000)	To report on how ethics codes elevate the ethics performance in business firms. To explain the codification of ethics
Wotruba et al. (2001)	To propose that the focus should shift from ethics codes themselves to the persons who are expected to behave accordingly to the code.

short broad codes with statements of value or mission and finally *elaborate codes* with carefully defined social responsibilities to different stakeholders. Brytting (1998), in turn, also define three types of codes, which, in fact, overlap the ones by Fleckstein and Huebsch on two categories. (See Table 2) Brytting sees the following main types of codes; the *commission type*, which proposes the function of the good firm in society, the *stakeholder type*, which aims at pointing out responsibilities to stakeholders and finally the *professional type*, which focuses on different divisions and professionals in the firm. When combining the two contributions in the field (Brytting's 1998 and Fleckstein & Huebsch's 1999), four types of ethics codes appear. I suggest these may be referred to as 1) mission and vision focused, 2) responsibility focused, 3) profession focused and 4) rule focused. This categorization is relevant for our understanding of the proposed model of CSR and CC by suggesting that ethics codes may be used in both approaches, but then these are with different focus. The profession focused pertain to a specific working group and is not relevant in this context. Mission and vision focused codes link closest to the identity formation of a firm and is the type which most closely links to the CC-concept. Responsibility focused codes are likely to appear in CSR-statements, where various responsibilities to the stakeholders are listed. Rule focused codes are similar to these, but may also be used for controlling purposes in internal management. With this theoretical background of CSR and CC on one hand, and research of ethics codes on the other, I will discuss the existence of prime movers and ethics codes in managing on the business market.

Table 2: A typology of ethics codes.

	MISSION AND VISION FOCUSED	RESPONSIBILITY FOCUSED	PROFESSION FOCUSED	RULE FOCUSED
Brytting (1998)	Commission type	Stakeholder type	Professional type	–
Fleckstein & Huebsch (1999)	Short broad codes	Elaborate codes	–	Regulatory type
Relation to CC/CSR	CC	CSR	–	(CSR)

Kristensson Uggla's position emphasizes a view, where failure lies close to success. The ideal is all at once the absurdity. He argues (2002: 96) that there is a fundamental duality that cannot be avoided; society is bound to balance on a sharp edge. This is further characterized by the opposition between business and society. Although seemingly dejected, this state is in fact what drives also ethics development forward. He gives environmental damage as example (p. 368), contending that the damage, in turn, gives rise to moral development in society. In a study on Stora Enso (Lindfelt 2006) similar processes can be observed. Labor accidents, child labor in suppliers' operations and environmental scandals are in fact important drivers in the process of developing the Stora Enso ethics framework. As the large business actors, including Stora Enso, launch ethics principles and implement corporate values, the ethics practice spreads along the supply chain, to competitors, to customers etc. (cf. Berembeim 2000). Lindfelt (2006) also found that the first years of the new millennium has seen Finnish business practice rapidly developing in a direction where more and more firms feel pressure to launch sets of ethics principles. Not only is this because of scandals, but also American business practice bears influence, as do anti-globalization movements and an increasing ethical consciousness among citizens and NGO movements. In this rapid development lies a risk. A high pace does not give time for contemplation. Without contemplation, I argue there is no time for maturation and implementation of values. And without implementation of values, the scandal of not matching words to deeds unequivocally lies around the corner. In consequence, the ethics code may become a simple ritual without real effects, other than being a high-risk document. Thus, a necessary question for the firm in this process may be whether to make use of CSR or CC in ethical profiling or strategy.

Several researchers are in fact critical to use of ethics codes, claiming these are problematic from various points of view. Granovetter's notes that generalized morality or institutional arrangements not necessarily creates trustworthiness (1985: 491). Others critics are e.g. Stevens (1999), Sinclair (1993), Schwartz (2000) and Huang (2001). Husted and Allen (2000) even asks if it is ethical to use ethics as strategy (cf. Gustafsson 1990). Thus, it is clear that the tension between business and society is complex and includes several aspects that can be problematized. Below, three issues are discussed. Common for these is that all depart from the same source, i.e. Normann (2001), being the father of the concept of prime movers. First follows an exemplification of how ethics become a way of managing a 'glocal' business network. Second follows thoughts on power and responsibilities. Third, integrated diversity poses to be an alternative solution for the paradox of business ethics as balancing between business and society.

Ethically Driven Prime Movers

Normann (2001), quite like many recent researchers, discusses how value creation all the more takes place in networks.[2] Networks are characterized by horizontal structures and boundless existence, why these largely move freely over physical territories. As local and global perspectives gain strength over national perspectives, we see a *glocal* dimension (Normann 2001: 68–69, *cf.* Kristensson Uggla 2002). In this new glocal space, there is a group of actors who benefit from globalization by overriding the juridical (national) boundaries that traditionally limited organizational entities. This is possible by managing a network of actors, all of which are connected to a focal firm in various links. Through network management, value is co-created within the set of actors in the network (*cf.* Ulaga 2001, Walter, Ritter & Gemünden 2001, Ramírez 1999). The network thus functions in another way than in traditional horizontal logic. Networks provide an interesting perspective when aiming to understand ethics code use. A business network takes into consideration not only society, but also other business partner's interaction and their role in relation to a focal firm. Normann (2001) proposes that the focal managing firm is in fact a first mover, why he calls such firms *Prime Movers*. Researchers (for example Jarillo 1988, Håkansson & Ford 2002, Möller & Svahn 2003) argue over whether networks can be managed or not. However, if accepting the existence of prime movers, I propose that

2   The last decades have also brought an extensive focus on business network research, such as in eco-industrial networking (Hasler, Sterr & Jacobson 2005), the industrial network approach (Håkansson & Ford 2002), actor-network theory (Nylén 1996) etc.

there are *ethical* prime movers, who first influence and manage the ethical level of the network - for instance by demanding that their partners follow the same set of social and environmental responsibilities. This exact procedure is found in Stora Enso and also in Metso, the latter even aimed to have supplier firms legally state in a document that the responsibilities were in line with Metso's (Lindfelt 2006). I suggest these are ethically driven prime movers. Accordingly, a business network's ethical prime mover pro-actively shapes the ethical dimension. This actor believes that ethics creates value. Therefore, I see that ethics codes form part of the financial co-creation of value among actors in the business network. Ethics management also becomes part of strategically managing the network. Even if the initiative originates with the prime mover, such as for instance with Stora Enso or Metso, the prime mover is dependant on reciprocity over values implementation. This meaning that only by knowing that ethical values are expressed in return, is it possible to maintain a certain ethical level in networking production with suppliers and sub-suppliers.

On the basis of empirical data in Lindfelt (2006), I pose that ethically driven prime movers exist in the cases of Stora Enso and Metso. This proposition leads further to ask what happens to the locus of responsibility when power shifts from national to glocal. This perspective is omitted in the otherwise rather detailed launch of Normann (2001) on the concept of prime movers. In an important sense, leadership is power – and power always implies responsibility. When gaining glocal power on behalf of national responsibility, who is then to care for national environment, culture, people and traditions? Yet, another dimension of the globalization process is the turbulence which follows the change of locus of responsibility and power. Researchers claim that society is in a more or less static turbulent state (Normann 2001, Hadjikhani 1996, Kristensson Uggla 2002). I propose that with the shift of power, business and society encounter new ethical problems, such as resource exploitation, layoffs and closedowns, larger rift between rich and poor etc. New ethical problems imply an uncertainty within firms; what is the role of the firm in a new glocal situation? Except of taking all the strategic advantage it can – of course. However, power is unmistakenly connected to responsibility, a perspective perhaps overlooked by business. When taken into account, such responsibility may form instrumental CSR-approaches and create competitive advantage. A more defensive approach is to create risk management strategies. Least favourable would be to follow in the line of others, not taking time to consider the ontological differences in different strategies, as discussed above. If however taking time to ponder the *raison d'être* of ethics codes, giving management time for contemplating and maturing into business ethics, what really is at stake is the identity of the firm. This is typically expressed in documents of values, mission statements on or visionary goals. These can even be ethics codes, as of Table 2. According to Normann (2001) mission is contemporary and expresses the firm's value creating role in a larger system. Vision, in turn, is projected on the future and includes issues of efficiency, competence and ways to power. Organizational values need to be meaningful in a larger context, argues Selznick (1957/1984) if the firm is to survive competition. Issues of mission, vision and values are central in the business ethics of any contemporary firms. Lindfelt (2006) concluded that the Stora Enso case showed ethics to form part of the identity process of the firm. Its competitors and partners used risk management for avoiding problems, e.g. Metso and UPM. In order to manage in this turbulence, common understandings of values and ethics are essential. In sum, contemporary society sees ethically driven prime movers managing networks. Ethical maturity influences the identity formation of a firm – and vice versa: the identity formation invokes contemplation on issues of CSR- or CC-approaches. It seems that, as the world becomes more and more turbulent, business managers are forced to aim for cognitive stability (*cf.* Kristensson Uggla 2002).

In the quest for a mature identity of a business, managers need to address society. A glocal business approach consequently also invokes local and global adjustments. This is a challenging task for any corporation with one single identity. How can it adapt to a diversity of cultures, people, business traditions, market structures, national characteristics etc.? The ethics code of a global company, be it in any of the forms above, must be composed in a way of integrating diverse characteristics into a common identity, which can then be implemented into a common operational strategy. The term *integrated diversity* is a term adapted from Normann (2001), and conceptually provides a way of gaining legitimacy across diverse nations and cultures. Diversity, however, necessarily also creates tension, which is useful for innovativeness and the growth in ethical consciousness. However, research prove this not unproblematic. Again, let me take the example of Stora Enso, which is a Finnish-Swedish company and consequently bound by the labour standards of the International Labour Organization (ILO), in which the nation states are members. Although stating in the company's ethics code that it complies with ILO standards, which provide workers the right to come together in labour unions, Stora Enso had to deviate from these principles in China - simply because labour unions are forbidden by Chinese law. However, Stora Enso negotiated with Chinese governing institutions and found a legal form of gathering which is applied in Chinese locations (Lindfelt 2006). This exemplifies how integrated diversity transfers from a theoretical concept to a managerial praxis. Normann claims that this approach creates synergy, which is born out of the integration of diversity. The synergy leads to a principle-lead culture with norms of conduct that are in discourse with the environment and society, he contends, clearly showing how he lines up with the responsibility and rule focused ethics codes and the CSR-ontology. Integrated diversity, nevertheless, becomes a way to deal with the tension between business and society. All the same, sometimes firms tend to go beyond the idea of legitimacy by engaging in activities that clearly fall outside of the firm's operational environment, for instance donating money to research on cancer or digging wells in Africa. Such 'overlegitimacy' can be argued to constitute a form of repressive tolerance, where management aims to control new ways of thinking and keep ethical considerations in tight control: Normann (2001) likes to envision it as management's putting the new thinking in a black box. Integrated diversity can in that case be a way of matching the relation between business and society. In sum, I propose that integrated diversity provides an excellent way of handling ethical issues, and thereby avoiding the choice between CC and CSR – or even CR, SD or other similar concepts in the plethora of business ethics terminology. This possibility may have been much under-evaluated in business ethics approaches.

Concluding Discussion on the Balance Between Business and Society

In summary, the chapter started of asking whether business and society can be in balance. A simple answer would be no. A rather more nuanced is brought forward in the chapter. A conceptual discussion claimed it may be utopistic to embrace the understanding of CC as proposed by Juholin (2004). Rather, the idea behind CSR, which is inclusive of strategic and competitive aspects, seems feasible. In the chapter, however, the overall conceptual term business ethics has been used, which is broadly defined and inclusive of CC, CSR, CR, SD and sustainability. The theoretizising discussion was brought down to a market level by exemplifying Stora Enso as an ethically driven prime mover. The company makes use of an ethics code in the business aim towards a consensus with ethical expectations both in society and in its business market. In this change process where ethical issues all the more appear as part of the business' legitimacy (see def of CC) and competitive advantage (see def of CSR), several things happen. The chapter discussed a few of these:

- The power of the nation state diminishes in favour of local and global interests, referred to as *glocalization*. The glocal operating environment opens up new arenas for ethics issues, instruments, identity issues and management challenges.
- As power shifts, also responsibility shifts. Management presupposes power, power means responsibility, consequently management includes responsibility. Responsibility can be tackled proactively through ethics codes or risk management strategies.
- The glocal business market demands an integration of diverse values into the identity of the firm. Integrated diversity is a way to manage ethics issues around various production plants and facilities around the globe – a proposed alternative to CC or CSR choices for ethics strategy and profiling.

Finally, as a set out for further research issues, I want to use a matrix first launched by Normann (2001), but which here is developed further. The model addresses how internal and external cultures affect business. In both cases various interest groups (stakeholders) influence the firm through intrigues or by principles such as ethics codes. Intrigues are typically leading to conflict, while a responsibility or rule focused ethics code would could be either a formal document or constitute tacit values. See Table 3. The matrix shows the following characteristics:

Table 3: The firm's own culture (internal stakeholders) and society's culture (external stakeholders) influences the ethics process in the firm (cf. Normann 2001: 337).

	Intrigues	Principles / Ethics code	
Intrigues	1 Hopeless case?	2 Internal management looses its trustworthiness. *Principles (e.g. in ethics codes) are not enough, action is needed.*	*Dominating culture of internal stakeholders, e.g. the firm*
Principles/ Ethics code	3 Essential to defend/build legitimacy and organizational structure. *After intrigues from NGOs in mid 1990's, this was the position of Stora Enso.*	4 Co-operation based on loyalty and trust together with solving of conflicts. *The ideal position when the ethics code reflects the actions of the firm and not only functions as an ethical document.*	
	Dominating culture of external stakeholders, e.g. society		

With both internal and external intrigues, the dominant form of societal stakeholder expectations and relations is problematic. This situation proposes a hopeless case and I can only suggest that this situation is impossible, because the business won't live long.

Where external ethics principles are present (such as e.g. ILO-standards, competitor's ethics codes, laws, ethical recommendations etc.), but internal intrigues take place, management looses its trustworthiness. Principles of external stakeholders may not sufficiently help internal management conflicts. In this case, management needs to carefully ponder the identity of the firm. Companies at risk in this group, are the ones that tend to over-legitimize themselves, in a desperate approach to show ethical maturity.

Where external intrigues are disturbing a company, it is of high importance to carefully consider and build the identity of the company. Only by contemplating the vision, mission and values (type of codes) can external legitimacy be achieved. Internal principles (such as an ethics code) need to be built and supported. Again, Stora Enso can exemplify this situation in the late 1990s. The company had been in heavy disputes with Greenpeace in the German market, leading to partner firms' demands for a more ethical production of chapter. The conflict was directly leading to the creation and launch of a mission-vision-value statement at Stora Enso in 1999, a statement which later led the way to the ethical identity formation of the company. Today, Stora Enso is a forerunner in the forest industry on ethical matters. This is a good example of when the firm is in imbalance with society, and how such a tension is a driver for ethics maturity.

The fourth group shows on a situation where principles/ethics codes dominate both internally and externally. Characteristics for this situation are cooperation based on loyalty and solving of conflicts (Normann 2001). I suggest this as an ideal position, where ethics is fully adapted – on all levels of the firm. Accordingly, this represents a position of cc, following Juholin's (2004) definition of the term. Quite like in the first group, I pessimistically predict this fourth group to be impossible, here because it is a utopia.

This matrix and the role of ethics codes in different situations could preferably serve for further research. Empirical data that enrich the model would probably deepen the arguments and bring more understanding to the tension between internal and external pressures in societal relations, where the firm uses an ethics code. Such research could also provide more managerial contribution, which there seem to be need for (Lindfelt 2006).

The aim of the chapter has been to contribute to the discussion on the tension and relationship between business and society, and how firms can manage in this paradoxical context. In addressing this issue, six main theoretical and managerial propositions summarize the key contributions of the chapter:

Businesses can not be expected to meet society's demands in fully. Approaches that expect such a scenario are idealistic and utopistic. However, businesses must meet the demands in some way, in order to gain legitimacy of operations.

The chapter proposes a model for understanding the interrelation of corporate citizenship (cc) and corporate social responsibility (CSR) as opposite ontological concepts of business ethics.

Ethics codes are useful documents, which may be used to reach for this legitimacy in both the CC- and CSR-approaches. The focus of an ethics code based on CC-ontology would be on the identity of the firm and include visions, mission and values. The focus of an ethics code based on CSR-ontology would be on responsibilities and other types of rules.

There are ethical prime movers who function pro-actively to shape the ethical dimension of a business network.

The most stimulating situation for ethical growth in a firm is a situation where the firm is engaged in conflict with society, but when it has contemplated the firm identity and manifested this is some kind of ethics code, which could be based on CSR-ontology (i.e. responsibility or rule focused) or even CC-ontology (mission-vision-values focused).

Integrated diversity is suggested to be an underestimated strategy which could be used to transfer abstract ethical thoughts to real business life.

13. Company Strategies for Corporate Responsibility and Sustainability in an Era of Fragmented-Globalization

NIGEL ROOME

Introduction

Sustainable development and corporate responsibility are concepts of our time. Yet they also provide contested ground among organizational theorists and practitioners. This contest operates at four levels. First, the meaning and understanding of corporate responsibility and sustainable development is imprecise and unstable, as is the case with many newly emerging concepts. Corporate responsibility and sustainable development are no exceptions. Second, the relative novelty of the concepts means that the ways in which they are made operational, and therefore our ability to learn from the experience that comes from their practice, is still relatively limited. Third, some commentators view sustainable development and corporate responsibility as the leading-edge of a fundamental shift in the configuration of the relationship between business, the environment and society. This has potentially far-reaching implications for our understanding of the wider theory and practice of the firm. Indeed, as Kuhn suggests paradigm change of this kind invariably involves contest between the views of those who seek to uphold the old paradigm and those who advocate the new. Finally, sustainable development as an agenda and as a process and, corporate responsibility as a way of thinking and acting are emergent and dynamic phenomena. They interact with context, in particular with the shifting ground of our economic and social systems and specifically with the processes of globalization, such as the internationalization of business and the development of global flows of trade.

With this background the purpose of this chapter is to examine the way companies are developing strategic responses to corporate responsibility and sustainability in the context of the current era of globalization. The chapter is divided into three main sections. The first introduces and defines how the two central concepts - corporate responsibility and sustainable development – are understood in the chapter. It briefly examines the way they connect and then reviews a series of early approaches to corporate responsibility from the first period of industrialization as a way to draw out the main characteristics of corporate responsibility as an agenda and the skills on which it depends as a process involving business. The second section introduces globalization, placing sustainable development as the forerunner of three recent waves of globalization. It also addresses the more recent signals of globalization taking on a more fragmented form. The implications of this form of globalization for our contemporary understanding of corporate responsibility are highlighted. The third and concluding section, then, draws out what the intersection of sustainable development, corporate responsibility and globalization means for company practices, the competencies of managers and the possible implications for management education.

Background and Key Concepts

'If you do not know where you come from you will forever remain a child' (anon)

Corporate responsibility is not a new practice. Forms of corporate responsibility can be found in most capitalist societies since the industrial revolution. However, the growing concern for sustainable development and the advance of globalization has renewed interest in corporate responsibility as a way to understand the management of the firm's economic, social and environmental relationships.

While present-day interest in corporate responsibility is often connected with the call for sustainable development and the broader shifting relationship between business and society that are accompanying globalization, earlier theoretical conceptions of corporate responsibility were framed against different circumstances and contexts. For example, Friedman (1962) argues from the perspective of free-market economics that choice in business is conventionally guided by the market, legal codes and regulations (Friedman, 1962). He then argues that the only social purpose of business is to maximize wealth for shareholders, even going so far as to suggest that managers are not skilled to make any other types of choice. Key points to developing a more critical appreciation of Friedman's ideas follow from the vantage point from which he addressed the issue of corporate responsibility and, the context of business at the time in the USA. In terms of theory Friedman's arguments are wholly consistent with free-market economics and agency theory, which holds that the purpose of the firm is to maximize profit and the role of managers is to act as agents of the owners of capital. It terms of context, corporate responsibility in the USA during the period Friedman was writing principally took the form of corporate philanthropy. Other authors argue that responsible companies and managers should pay attention to social mores and the stakeholders they consider salient to their activities (Carroll, 1989; Freeman, 1984). However, neither of these authors took much note of the calls for sustainable development or the advancing context of globalization. Rather their views were also informed by business in the USA as seen from the viewpoint of social issues in management and business ethics, respectively. A more far-reaching view of corporate responsibility is found the strategic thinking of Igor Ansoff (1979) who held that in the later part of the twentieth century the key strategic issues for companies would be what they stood for and whose interests they aligned with. Ansoff referred to this as 'enterprise' strategy. His views are based on the perspective that firms are embedded in shifting social and economic systems through their relationships with other actors. Enterprise strategy involves assessing and maintaining the relationships that enable a firm to survive and succeed.

The position adopted in this chapter follows Ansoff but recognizes that the notion of sustainable development, as expressed in the Brundland Report (1987) and Agenda 21 (Agenda 21, 1992), gives critical attention to the new relationships between business, society and the environment. Sustainable development is not a business issue according to this view but a social and business issue that takes the form of a 'social and industrial project'. It is maintained that this 'project' will not come about through grand-design but because political, social and economic circumstances provide conditions that support the move to more sustainable forms of development (Roome, 1998). Corporate responsibility, then, can be viewed as the business contribution to this social and industrial project (Roome, 1992). Indeed, this view is now found in policy documents such as those from the European Commission (European Commission, 2006).

In practical terms corporate responsibility involves the recognition and voluntary management of relationships that exist between companies and other actors and interests in society. These relationships provide the potential for mutual learning, and potentially involve significant technological, organizational and intuitional innovation and organizational and social change. It is a dynamic process directed either to protect the value of a firm's existing assets, in which case innovation and change is rather incremental, or, it provides a basis from which to create new value for both business and the societies in which it operates. This second type of innovation has far greater potential to involve change as it implies the development of new business activities as a way to secure different ways to create value, which is held to be the purpose of the firm. In this way corporate responsibility is seen to contribute both to the performance of business while enhancing the potential for society to achieve a greater level of sustainability.

In this view corporate responsibility demands that managers show an awareness of trends and sensitivity to the issues and events that surround their business. It involves anticipation and responsiveness to complex economic, social and environmental forces and the relationships that operate between the firm and other actors, together with an ability to work with some of those actors in ways that provide the potential to deliver new value.

Over the past ten years corporate responsibility, as a managerial practice, has become increasingly strategic and a more regular part of the professional repertoire of managers, in line with Ansoff's prediction. The development of contemporary corporate responsibility has also been accompanied by the advancement of tools and techniques designed to support managers better to understand, prioritize, and contribute to relationships between their company and other actors. This casts a rather different light on Friedman's idea that managers are only skilled to manage the narrow economic dimension of the firm. However, while the relational view of the firm, set out above, holds that managers need skills to participate in innovation and change with others, there is growing realization that this approach to corporate responsibility requires organizational capabilities and managerial competencies that are rare and difficult to find. Yet, the survival and success of business will depend on the availability and deployment of those skills and capabilities.

With this contemporary view of corporate responsibility in mind it is useful to explore some examples of corporate responsibility found in earlier periods of industrialization as these provide some useful insight into the agenda and the skills required for corporate responsibility. The three examples given below are taken from Britain in the period 1800 to 1888 but similar examples are found in many European countries, America and also Japan during this time.

Robert Owen managed the New Lanark woollen mill, in Scotland, from 1800–1825. Owen sought to run a successful and profitable business. However, when he took over the mill he was intent not only to run the business successfully but to abolish the practices of child-labour and corporal punishment, to provide employees and their families with decent homes, and to offer them education through schools and evening classes. Finally, Owen set out to provide free health care and affordable food of reasonable quality to workers through the shops that the mill also owned. To place these ideas in historical context during the same period 1807 to 1833 legislation was being passed in Britain to outlaw the trade in slaves in its colonies, through the Slave Trade Act 1807, and finally to abolish slave ownership throughout the empire through the Abolition of Slavery Act, 1833. While there was a prevailing view of reform, Owen was surely in the vanguard of that movement in relation to his dominion in New Lanark.

In 1853 Sir Titus Salt, a cloth manufacturer and mill owner, began the construction of a new factory and village for his workers in the settlement of Saltaire, near Bradford in Yorkshire. In designing this mill and village Sir Titus set out to ensure decent working conditions for his employees and to provide homes of quality that reflected the status of employees in the mill. A school was built for the children of workers and a mechanics institute for the educational advancement of employees. He built an almshouse to house retired employees after long service and an infirmary to meet the needs for health care. The village of Saltaire had other modern amenities: a park, street lighting, and a sewerage system. Stores provided food that was not contaminated and was available at a fair price. Certainly, Sir Titus expected some duties to be observed by his workers. As a committed Unitarian he provided a church for worship and his employees were obliged to attend.

A notable point is that Sir Titus acted against the common labour and housing standards of the mill owners of his day. In fact the ordinary conditions of mill workers can be understood from a contemporary account of an observer of industrialization: 'As result of the ebbing and flowing of capital and labour, the state of the dwellings of an industrial town may to-day be bearable, to-morrow hideous. Or the ædileship of the town may have pulled itself together for the removal of the most shocking abuses. To-morrow, like a swarm of locusts, come crowding in masses of ragged Irishmen or decayed English agricultural labourers. They are stowed away in cellars and lofts, or the hitherto respectable labourer's dwelling is transformed into a lodging-house, whose personnel changes as quickly as the billets in the 30 years' war. Example: Bradford (Yorkshire)'. Karl Marx, *Capital: A Critique of Political Economy. Volume I: The Process of Capitalist Production* [1867]. 3rd edition.

Thirty-five years later, in 1888, William Hesketh Lever, owner of Lever Brothers had his vision to build a new soap factory and village to house its workers in a way that ensured a content, healthy and efficient workforce engaged in production of the first 'branded' soap. Sunlight soap was known and marketed on the basis of its quality and reliability. Lever Brothers merged with Margarine Unie of Holland to form Unilever in 1929. In 2007, the group chief executive office of Unilever, Patrick Cescau said 'I believe that we have come to the point now where this agenda for corporate responsibility is not only central to business strategy but will increasingly become a critical driver of business growth. I would go further: I believe that how well and how quickly businesses will respond to this agenda will determine which companies succeed and which one fail in the next few decades' (Cescau, 2007).

Before examining the reasons why corporate responsibility has become so strategic and a core part of business success, it is important to take some key points from these three historic cases. The work of Owen, Salt, and Lever can all be seen as the undertakings of relatively isolated individuals, running counter to the practices of many of their contemporary capitalists. There were, however, informed by common ideas. These included the notion that successful business required honest and trustworthy relationship with its shareholders, good working conditions for employees, and quality, reliable products, sold at fair price to customers. All three pioneers, Owen, Salt and Lever, were attentive to the environmental concerns of the day, especially impoverished housing and poor sanitation, and, all had a deep concern for the neighbours and communities close to their factories by providing for the education, health and nutrition of employees and their families.

The skills these pioneers deployed in their practice of corporate responsibility are relevant too. For them corporate responsibility was an integral part of the model for successful business. They were visionaries, committed to innovative ideas about business that were influenced by people outside business. They were courageous in their efforts to develop a different approach to business than prevailed at the time and they mastered, with others the skill to apply knowledge beyond the economic analysis of the firms they owned or managed. They recognized that good relationships with others were important attributes for business. Moreover, while this approach to business was regarded as obvious to those involved it was viewed with scepticism by those who were not involved.

Globalization and Fragmented Globalization

'He who will not innovate is lost for time is the greatest innovator of all.'
Francis Bacon (1561–1626)

Having proposed that contemporary corporate responsibility should be seen as the contribution by business to sustainable development and that corporate responsibility has existed since the early period of industrialization, the intent in this section is to consider the influence of globalization on our recent understanding of corporate responsibility and sustainable development. In this section a broader perspective of globalization is taken that goes beyond the conventional narrow view of the internationalization of business, finance, and economics, with the move toward more global production and markets. These aspects of globalization are important but are seen as representing only one of three main waves of globalization that affect our economies and societies around the world.

The broader view sees globalization as the growing interdependence of human and natural systems around the globe brought about through human agency. This perspective has been developed at greater length elsewhere (Roome, 2000 and 2001) however it is important to set out the main arguments of this analysis. The first wave of globalization followed the advance and adoption of notions of development based on the post-war experience of developed economies. Concerns about the social and environmental implications that would follow if this model were to continue unchecked in developed economies and spread to developing nations gave rise to the calls for sustainable development. Sustainable development was advanced as a new form of governance. This was designed to affect all sectors of society including business. It would reorient patterns of production and consumption so that development opportunities could be maintained within environmental and social limits. This would imply more efficient resource use and lower environmental demands in developed economies, while providing new development pathways for the developing economies to enable development to take place without serious loss of environmental quality or social disruption.

As this governance agenda was being developed the second wave of globalization centring on the internationalization of business, finance and trade was taking hold. The advent of digital and other communications technologies, the ascendancy of advocates of open-trade, the collapse of the centrally-planned economies and the opening up of developing economies to foreign-direct investment were all part of what has become the most widely perceived axis of globalization. However, this wave of globalization was not without problems. Deepening connections between countries through trade required the agreement on new rules of order from the WTO; the potential impact of financial collapse in an interconnected world financial system gave rise to the Basel

Accord 11 of the International Bank for Settlements. Although the credit crisis of 2008 reminds us that these and other controls over the global financial system were wholly inadequate in dealing with the instabilities in the system created by the decisions of bankers themselves. While the opening of trade has brought opportunities for the poor, for example, some 450 million Chinese have moved out of poverty during the past 15 years, economic and financial globalization has provoked even greater pressures on the world's environment than was anticipated by the Brundtland Report and Agenda 21.

The third wave of globalization concerns the globalization of culture and the movement of people. The development of trade, the advance of wealth, the consumption of tourism has contributed to the movement of people around the globe. This movement is conceived as the domain of the elite, it is reproduced by the internationalization of business. On the other side, the portrayal of developed economy life-styles in the global media coupled to economic migration, political refugees and those fleeing conflict and hardship has also promoted the movement of people. For these migrants destinations of choice are in developed economies. The effects of cultural globalization are found in the cultural, religious and ethnic diversity of our major cities, symbolized by exotic foods in the shops and a varied cuisine on the high street. Behind these visible symbols is the confrontation of different people with different identities and origins, living or working or sharing the same place. This has a potential for the harmonious exchange of experiences and cultures as well as providing the ground for clashes of identity. Unlike the first two waves there is, as yet, no concerted response to the governance of the cultural wave of globalization. Where attempts are made to limit migration they have focused mainly on the poor rather than the elite. They are designed to protect national identities and borders and to avoid or limit any clashes and conflict of cultures, ideologies and religions. Governance of migration is bound to ideas such as identity and security.

Critically all three waves of globalization are increasingly woven together creating unpredictable and turbulent conditions. In particular globalization has been accompanied by the commoditization of time and the apparent collapse of space. This process began in the world of Owen, Salt and Lever, as time was standardized to support the movement of goods and people by railway and as clocks were introduced to ensure control of work in factories. However, recent globalization has seen the acceleration of human control over time and space through the application of knowledge and technologies that advance communications and transport and through the adoption of ideas that distort our sense of days and seasons such as 'just in time delivery', 24/7 or year round seasonal fruits and vegetables. The significance of the apparent effects of globalization on time and space arises because of the paradoxes it presents managers who often have to make rapid choices against a background of ever more complex information, from different sources, taken from many contexts.

This for example creates the paradox that managers and companies operating with global span often search for standardized solutions while it is also recognized that locally adapted choices support local complexity and global diversity, which is a basis for resilience. The development of information and communications technologies might seem a way for managers to minimize risks, yet, the same information and communications technologies are available to those disaffected by companies and their projects to portray their messages and concerns around the globe using powerful and graphic images. Finally, the very pace of change and the complexity of information oblige managers to draw on reduced, partial, information in determining choice. At the same time there is a counter pressure for managers to engage in wider consultation with an evermore diverse set of actors; consultation that often generates complex, nuance-rich and culturally-specific narratives that are not readily reduced.

What we observe is that each wave of globalization and the connections between these waves leads to a series of simple dimensions. First, each wave of globalization has created its own institutions and agendas for governance. Second, what has emerged through globalization is ever greater interconnection, turbulence, uncertainty, ambiguity, paradox and contest within each wave and between successive waves of globalization. Third, rather than leading to trust between peoples, and, between people and institutions, including business, globalization is accompanied by greater scepticism, lack of trust, and a loss of a sense of security. Possibly this is because the certainties of the past have become blurred and fuzzy, much like the view from a speeding train. With the dissipation of reference points and certainties so individual and collective identity is lost, which is now followed by a search to recover identity. This is known to affect second generation migrants as they belong neither to the communities their parents left nor the communities their parents brought them to. But it also affects those who stay where they are as their neighbours move and the pace of change reshapes their heritage. As the world becomes ever more connected so we have lost our full sense of time and place both as individuals and collectively.

In conclusion, if we compare corporate responsibility from the nineteenth century with that of today, the arenas for concern are little changed. They include, employees working conditions, environmental issues, the relationship between the managers of companies, employees, customers and the owners of capital. What has changed is that the agenda of corporate responsibility has become far more complex and systemic. It is understood to take different form in different parts of the globe, making corporate global responsibility a mosaic of local concerns, where the task of managers is to decide what if anything is the underlying pattern and what is unique, which interests to take cognizance of, or, ignore and which interests to weigh most highly at local and global level.

Moreover, the individual work of the early pioneers of corporate responsibility have been replaced by modern corporate responsibility as a social and business movement, involving many companies, national and international bodies, codes and standards, signals to companies provided through ethical investment funds and sustainability-driven investors and pressure groups, international and local actors, as well as the those in knowledge institutes, such as consulting companies, business schools and universities.

As corporate responsibility develops as a managerial response to global systemic complexity, so the institutions and standards and definitions that managers might call on to guide their actions are themselves proliferating through globalization. The complex becomes yet more complex and the quest for information and guidance is replaced by the need for experience.

One aspect of this complexity within complexity is that as our understanding of globalization develops and our responses sharpen, so, by its very nature, globalization and corporate responsibility take on new form and new meaning. For example, there are strong signals that globalization has become more fragmented in the past 5 years. And to understand that fragmentation and its implications it is necessary to appreciate the organising and countervailing power of individual and collective identities, especially the search for identity as a consequence of globalization. To illustrate these points: Before 1989 the old dialectic between capitalism and communism was a dominating force in world affairs. The collapse of the Berlin Wall in 1989 represented a tipping-point. Many of the advances in communications and transport technologies developed for military use found their way into business applications. they drove economic and financial globalization. Previously centrally-planned economies opened themselves to the market and foreign-direct investment as did many emerging economies. Market capitalism was the dominant global force and took most before it. But what emerged to replace the dialectic between communism and capitalism?

The characteristics of fragmented globalization are rooted in the emerging dialectic, which has two dominant strands. First, the opening of new parts of the world to the full force of market capitalism has not led to a one-capitalist model based on Anglo-Saxon shareholder model. Instead it has led to an eclectic set of different variants of capitalism. The Anglo-Saxon shareholder model competes with the social-market capitalist model of the enlarged continental European Community, the network capitalism of Japan and South Korea, and the new capitalism of India or the blended capitalism found in communist China or Russia that are in formation. This is still a relatively unclear territory but it seems that questions of national identity and national interest combined with economic interests are found at the root of these variant models. There are already some examples of the strange twists as these different forms of capitalism contest under the dynamic forces of economic competitiveness and the political and economic interests of nation states. The rise of sovereign-capital is one case in point where China and Russia are using the market combined with political power to ensure secure access to scare mineral and energy resources beyond their national boundaries. During the first period of globalization, from the late 1980s to about 2000, the power of companies was seen to develop at the expense of nation states.

But in the current period of fragmented globalization the security interests and search for the maintenance of the power of the state is a matter that is played out in markets.

Along with the dialectic between variants of capitalism there is a further dialect between advocates of markets, on the one side, and those who do not accept the idea of consumerism and markets for ideological or religious reasons, on the other. Curiously the same information, communication and computer technologies that support market capitalism provide the means for those oppose it or who reject the market, preferring their own more traditional or new wave ideologies, to exercise influence. This again takes many forms. Some illustrations include the resistance by the US administration to the proposed takeover of P&O's port operations in the United States by the Arabian-owned DP World, the development and distribution of Mecca-coke as a substitute for coca cola, or, the zones of conflict in the Middle-East, where capitalist enterprise is the target of local hostility. The intersection of cultural, economic and environmental waves of globalization coupled with the question of identity is characterized by what you buy and wear and by what you reject. This has enormous destabilising influence.

While some remedies are to be found in corporate responsibility, as a new form of governance and collaboration, its limits are that it is only appropriate for those that want to engage with business and its managers. More important are the forces that do not want to engage because their interests and identities are shaped in part by their opposition to business and what it stands for. It is curious to observe that at the time of Owen, Salt and Lever nation states exercised their administrative and military might to ensure that the resources were available through their empires and for their economies to draw on. It seems, little has changed, except that nation states are also now using a combination of the markets and diplomacy to help secure their interests.

Company Practices, Managerial Competences and Management Education

> The future is not a result of choices among alternative paths offered by the present, but a place that is created – created first in the mind and will, created next in activity. The future is not some place we are going to, but one we are creating. The paths are not to be found, but made, and the activity of making them, changes both the maker and the destination.
>
> John Schaar, Professor of Political Science, University of California Santa Cruz

During the first period of globalization, large and successful companies increased in relative position and power as against the nation state. They grew by acquisition and strategic alliances. In the main these large companies focused on their core managerial and technological competencies. The acquisition of other companies provided for market growth, organizational synergies and cost savings. Off-shoring led to further opportunities to reduce costs of manufacture. Technological developments opened up new markets. This has created great wealth for a few, a wider distribution of disposable income to many and for others deep resentment. In the main this period of globalization has seen companies following relatively predictable trends in the way they envision their growth and development. They draw on skills of shrewd acquisition, production relocation and technological development combined with sophisticated marketing.

Competition was seen in terms of the competition in final markets and performance required good cost control. Corporate responsibility developed because of the growing value of 'brands' and their vulnerability to poor reputation factors. It embraced environmental concerns, touching companies with high resource and energy intensity, those with a large environmental footprint, or those close to final consumer markets, where brand, reputation and leadership have a significant role. More recently social concerns have accompanied the off-shoring and foreign-direct investment as operations in many different parts of the globe have led to demands for the wide adoption of labour and work practices normally found in developed economies. More recently there has been a shift among leading companies to see corporate responsibility as a basis for innovation to inspire new products, services and business models.

However, the focus of competition is shifting in the period of fragmented globalization. Here the issue is less about competition for consumers. The pace of industrial growth has begun to place significant demands on our resource base. Minerals, energy, water and agricultural land become scarcer and companies, nations and communities are entering a period of hyper-competition to secure those resources and the services they provide for their use. However, once those resources are secured for the benefit of a company how does the market serve to allocate those services between the range of needs. Water is a case in point. As coca cola realizes that secure water supplies are a strategic concern and it, or its agents, secure those resources, how then are water services allocated between – coca cola, the swimming pools of the middle-class living in the watershed, or, the needs of farmers. Previously these services were allocated through state water interests, but now, how will the market respond to need? In these cases are the rights of ownership supreme over the responsibilities of ownership.

Beyond this direct competition for resources is the less direct competition for the services of natural and other systems. After all the water shed not only provides a source of supply for bottled water at the same time it is the base for agricultural production. And within that relationship in the watershed, the use of pesticides and chemicals by farmers is a potential source of contamination to the water stored below and then bottled. In this case does the bottling company become involved in agricultural practice, therefore developing its competencies as a 'systems' manager. And if so what are the skills needed for successful systems management?

This resource scarce world is also bringing forward unusual economic competitors. Coca cola and Intel compete for water resources. Unilever and Shell compete for agricultural land as both now see this resource as crucial in their distinctive oil-based businesses. Nestle and Dupont compete for specialists in the new sciences of biotechnology and genetic engineering. Nutrition companies and pharmaceuticals begin to converge, as do communications and transport.

It has already been suggested that the corporate responsibility is becoming more strategic and that the organizational capabilities and managerial competencies that support corporate responsibility are rare and difficult to find. However, these points were made in the context of corporate responsibility as a response to sustainable development and the advance of the first wave of globalization. The competencies included tracking trends and issues, knowing the actors with whom the firm has relationships, identifying who to have relationships with and how to engage with them and for what purpose. They included the ability to generate, develop and test innovative approaches to the development of new products and business models.

However, the organizational capabilities and managerial competencies that support corporate responsibility in the era of fragmented globalization go a step further. They are less easy to describe or label. But the hallmark of fragmented globalization is conflict for scarce resources. It creates situations where there are more interests to serve than resources to serve them. This raises questions of how to allocate resources beyond the market. The convergence of nation state and company interests suggests that the firm might need to begin to deploy the skills of successful nation states. Those skills combine the capacity to defend borders and boundaries, the ability through diplomacy to build relationships with allies, while knowing who is not an ally, and the capacity for good governance that ensures a reasonably cohesive society, when opportunities are not limitless and resources are distributed unevenly.

If these skills and competencies have growing significance for companies over the next 10–20 years the key questions are where will these skills be developed, and which business school or university will build them into the management curricula, and how?

14. Epilogue Corporate Social Responsibility: The Next Agenda?

RICHARD WELFORD

Introduction

Most of the chapters of this book have been written by people living and educated in the West and therefore take a somewhat Western perspective. This is useful stuff but the challenge we all face now is taking these lessons and translating them into a perspective that fits a developing country perspective where there is still much to be achieved. This is perhaps the next big challenge for CSR: How does the private sector begin to engage with the massive challenges in the world where the majority of the population lives?

There are three important themes, amongst others, that are raised in this book and in research more widely in the field of business and sustainable development. They are the context of globalization, the measurement of CSR outcomes and the practice of CSR. My aim in this epilogue is to try to develop some of these themes in a way that is consistent with what is happening and what is needed in developing countries. Since I know Asia better than anywhere else perhaps, some of my examples are from that region, where, depending on where you draw borders, between 55 and 65 percent of the population lives.

The Context of Globalization

Many of the authors in this book have explicitly linked CSR to the context of globalization. Like much of the research being done on

CSR, there is recognition that global players such a multinational corporations have global responsibilities, should adopt global standards and can adopt global practices that transcend national interests. Yet, the vast majority of research being done on CSR still positions it very much as a Western mindset with a Western research focus. Very little extends to considering developing countries and very little research deals with that part of the world where most people live: Asia, where most of the world's supply chain now resides.

In the excellent chapter in this book by Egels-Zandén and Kallifatides, their four paradigms used to analyse ABB's initiatives linked to a Global Compact type of approach could well be applied more generally to globalization. Their conclusions implicitly highlight an important issue connected to where CSR ends and where the role of legitimate government begins. But the fact that corrupt inefficient government exists makes the CSR agenda for multinational companies more difficult. I am not one who advocates companies building schools and thereby replacing a central role of government to provide education. But if a rural school or a school for disadvantaged groups is never going to exist anyway, is there a role here for CSR?

One of the challenges for CSR and the multinational corporations that push the agenda is therefore to deal with a world where many governments do not govern. Governments often serve an elite of some sort and the interests of the majority are less important than those of the few. What is good CSR is a sea of corruption? Is it appropriate to link promises to protect human rights with inward investment? Should a multinational corporation invest and create jobs in a country controlled by a military dictatorship or allow its citizens to wallow in isolated poverty? Is it ethical to do business in a country with a corrupt justice system? These are the types of questions that multinational corporations are now asking themselves and their stakeholders.

Answers to these sorts of questions are not easy and are compounded by the fact that globalization impacts on different countries in very different ways. That implies that CSR will need to differ from location to location, industry to industry and company to company as a result of different economic and social circumstances existing in different places. Effective CSR will therefore involve stakeholders in identifying priorities that fit with both the aspirations of companies and the needs of local populations and the local environment. Indeed, a company cannot undertake effective CSR unless it does engage in meaningful and ongoing stakeholder engagement.

Some of the differences that we see around the world are well typified by examining some of the ongoing trends in Asia. Here we have important supply chains that service the rest of the world. Large brands increasingly source their products from supply chains in Asia and that immediately implies that one key focus of CSR will be a supplier one. The rapid economic growth in the region has also take its toll on the environment and that too needs to be a concern for businesses' CSR programmes.

The drivers for CSR in Asia come from a wide range of stakeholders, but some are more demanding than others (Studer *et al*, 2006). It is often assumed that consumers (particularly in the West) exert a tremendous amount of pressure on companies but in fact CSR managers do not experience that much pressure from consumers in a direct way. Whilst they want to be reassured that companies are not abusing workers, using child labour and the like, consumers rarely come directly to companies for that information. They tend to rely on second hand information mainly through the media, which is in turn strongly influenced by NGOs and trade unions (and sometimes, although not always, a coalition of the two).

Companies are clearly now experiencing a great deal of pressure from some of their shareholders, particularly those who are long term investors (e.g. pension funds and investment trusts) rather than short term speculators. Unit trust managers, pension fund managers, venture capital companies, the investment banking sector and others are all asking for more information about CSR practices and more assurances about how potential risks in Asia (and elsewhere) are being handled. Many of them realize that protecting reputation and brands are central to protecting their investments. It is also one of the reasons why some companies are expanding the number of brands in their portfolio rather than relying on one overarching brand name in the future.

However, Welford (2007) points out that such shareholder pressure is completely absent from many smaller companies that make up the bulk of suppliers in Asia because they are often family owned or in the hands of a small group of partners (who often have more than one small company). In some circumstances, the family business is naturally benevolent and wants to see staff treated as an extended family, but this is not always the case and poor employment practices, environmental damage and safety failures (and even deaths) are common and often relatively easy to conceal in companies in developing countries.

When discussing CSR in an Asian context most of the best practices come from the activities of companies from the leading Western brands and those of a few locally based companies that have a brand and image to protect. The three key areas for CSR in Asia tend to boil down to the environment, labour and supply chain issues.

The Environment

Pollution in Asia is amongst the worst in the world. Air pollution continues to damage health, at least a third of all water resources are severely polluted, energy use is highly inefficient, desertification continues and biodiversity loss is alarming (Liu and Diamond, 2005). China is building a new coal-fired power station every 12 days. In 2007, alone it added 80,000 megawatts of new power generation.

Leading companies are taking the rapidly degrading environment seriously but there is still much to be achieved. The environmental situation facing Asia is nothing short of a crisis. The degradation of the environment caused by economic growth and a shortage of many basic resources are constraining further growth as well as creating huge hidden costs associated with health, an inability to do business (e.g. at times of water shortages) and trans-boundary impacts.

Good environmental performance and associated disclosure is now becoming both more common and more important. Sustainable development is an important national strategy in most countries. Yet the continued growth that we see in the region is far from sustainable and a common strategy seems to be to grow first and to clean up the crisis later. Such a strategy might have worked in the West but the sheer scale and magnitude of what is happening in Asia goes beyond comparison. Over the next couple of decades we have some tough choices to make over what is a sustainable economic model but unless the West takes the lead, Asia is unlikely to follow, preferring poverty alleviation over environmental due diligence.

There is little doubt that Asia's growth will soon be constrained by a lack of resources (including water). But again this leads to huge opportunities for those companies with the knowledge and know-how relating to resource efficiency. And with such inefficient industry across the whole region, the potential efficiency improvements are both achievable and relatively easy given experiences and lessons learned from more developed countries. The environmental challenges facing Asia might not be that different to elsewhere but they are more acute therefore.

Compounded by the impacts of climate change over the next two decades, the environment has re-emerged as a major issue for the private sector to engage with. There is a need for more research into effective environmental strategies that are not only capable of reversing current trends, but that are also compatible with notions of social sustainability and poverty alleviation.

Labour Rights

According to the International Labour Organization labour rights should be at the heart of any debate on CSR in Asia because so many migrant workers in the region are denied their rights and are at significant risk of exploitation. The Chinese government, for example, agrees and has also made labour rights a key issue in recent years and is expecting companies to abide by comprehensive labour laws. In the view of many CSR experts in China, labour issues are as important as price, quality and delivery therefore (Welford & Frost, 2006).

But ensuring workers in factories work to legal limits and are paid correctly is proving near impossible. The downward pressure on prices in many sectors, along with shorter lead times and the increasingly shorter periods between the release of new models (or fashions) has increased pressure along the supply chain to the factory floor. Rising wages in the most developed parts of Asia have been welcomed by most labour activists but not by some investors who have already moved to cheaper countries (most notably Vietnam).

Freedom of association is a fundamental human right as stated in the United Nations Universal Declaration on Human Rights and ILO Conventions 87 and 98. Increasingly, collective action is on the rise. We have seen an increase in the number of labour disputes in a number of different parts of Asia, particularly China. CSR managers may not want to see more workers going on strike but it is true that they want to see workers being empowered to recognize their own rights and insist that they are respected.

The majority of workers in countries such as China are migrants from rural areas and pose particular challenges for companies committed to CSR. Migrants face specific problems due to lack of family and community networks. Often housed in dormitories, they face a unique set of issues including finances (remittances home), relationships (a lack of partners or places for intimacy), and boredom (often confined to the factory compound or quarters for long periods).

Working practices in many factories have improved over the last few years, in part, due to a shortage of migrant workers (in some places) and the need for companies to retain workers, making sure they return to work after holiday periods. Here, increased levels of trust between workers and the factories and improvements in the way the workforce is treated have led to win-win outcomes. Many factory owners are for the first time being forced to consider how they might attract and retain a workforce. In an attempt to retain workers, some companies are now paying long service bonuses to staff returning to the factory for another year, for example. Labour shortages may have helped to combat the existence of sweatshops in China more than factory inspections ever did. Many factory owners are realising that CSR is good for business!

Supply Chains

Of course many of the labour issues discussed above are related to the extensive supply chains to be found in Asia resulting from globalization trends. China alone produces 80 per cent of the world's toys, 70 per cent of kitchen appliances, 75 per cent of all shoes and 50 per cent of all garments. One of the main focuses of CSR in Asia is therefore on the supply chains that make products for the leading brands as well as more generic goods to be found on the shelves of the world's budget supermarkets. In many cases the real prices of these products have been falling over the last decade as competition amongst retailers increases and people seem ever more desirous of cheap bargain products.

Asia has long been associated with the accusation that many products are being made in sweatshop conditions that exploit people and damage the environment (Chan, 1998). It is true that factories can be found in Asia where this is the case but those factories are normally producing low-priced generic goods, often for domestic consumption. They disregard the law, cheat their staff, bribe officials and pay little regard to their impacts on local communities.

But for the world's leading brands compliance with local laws, regulations and norms is not an option (Schmitz & Knorringa, 2000). Asian companies supplying to foreign clients understand that unless they can act in accordance with comprehensive codes of conduct, they are unlikely to get orders. However, full compliance in the supply chain remains elusive and we have seen many cases where systems have failed leading to scandals over child labour, poor health and safety records and the need for product recalls.

Codes of conduct have to be enforced and this has been the reason that we have seen a massive growth in the auditing and inspection industry in Asia. Social and environmental audits may have been an optional extra a decade ago but now they are standard practice and any factory supplying well known brands. Many suppliers run highly efficient, responsible factories where workers are paid well and where health and safety is seen as a priority. But others struggle to pass audits and here we often see a good degree of cheating going on. Factory owners and managers often keep duplicate books in order to comply with stipulations over working hours in codes of conduct. Protective equipment is often issued when auditors are in the factory and taken back subsequently. Environmentally damaging processes may be turned off. Workers are often coached to give auditors the answers that they want to hear.

Although factory audits and inspections are now mandatory for any company seeking to protect brand, reputation and market position, their quality is variable leading to accusations that auditors are sometimes complicit in the cheating. Moreover, market forces have driven audit prices and quality down leading to uneven results across the industry. The increasingly sophisticated cheating by manufacturers and some poor quality auditing has led to growing distrust of audit results that has further diminished their effectiveness. Clients sourcing from factories require reliable information on workplace practices, environmental performance and product safety, but in the absence of such reliable data new approaches are needed.

It is no surprise, therefore, that many companies are now working towards building trusting relationships with fewer rather than more factories. Where factories cannot do as they are asked then the termination of contracts becomes inevitable. There is also a desire to move to factories where shared values, skills development, adequate training and capacity building ultimately means there is no need for an audit and inspection process. Many companies talk about building a 'world class supply chain' rather than policing it; a fundamental shift from auditing to consulting.

Whilst auditing and inspections in the supply chain will remain the backbone of any compliance program, there is now a widespread realization that these alone will not ensure better workplace practices or increased product safety. Building skills in supply chains (for employees and managers) and capacity in civil society are now seen as key ingredients in the compliance mix. Capacity building is now very much at the cutting edge of good CSR practices. That capacity building is about building skills and knowledge through training that facilitates compliance through hands-on techniques that make business sense.

Measuring CSR Impacts

As Minna Halme points out in her chapter, there is a fixation with dealing with the links between CSR and financial performance which (in my view) often turns out to be a spurious correlation, to say the least. There is less of a focus on measuring societal impacts of CSR and here we ought to be looking at links between CSR and poverty reduction and the attainment of the other Millennium Development Goals (MDGs). Whilst much is being achieved in this respect by many multinational corporations, it often goes unrecognized by academics. But perhaps even more importantly, there is actually very little work on measuring outcomes and impacts. It is no longer enough for companies to report on how much they gave to good causes – we need to know what was actually achieved in terms of outcomes. How this is measured is an area where we need much more work. Indeed, those providing the funding are eager to find better and more effective ways of measuring their impacts (positive and negative) on societies in which they operate.

At the core of many of the MDGs is the fact that many problems we face are linked to poverty and a lack of access to resources, including education and health care. Poverty breeds poverty when people do not have rights to these sorts of resources and lack the empowerment to move outside economic and cultural settings that maintain disadvantage. Governments and their international arms including the agencies grouped under the umbrella of the United Nations, have largely failed in their attempts to rid the planet of under-development and poverty. And whether they like it or not, corporations are involved in development and should be seen as agents of development. Large corporations, with their power and economic strength, have taken a dominant position in society and need now to recognize their obligations.

Addressing global poverty is now on the agenda of the world's leading CEOs. Whilst the contribution of corporations to periodic crises is clear, there is also now debate about how companies can eradicate poverty and promote the MDGs through their normal course of business. Top business leaders are now increasingly seeing the poorer regions of the world as places they can do business and thereby help local populations. A particular area of interest has been the idea that rather than being a cause for old-style philanthropy, serving the needs of the world's poor is actually a vast untapped and profitable market for business.

Concepts such as the bottom of the pyramid (BOP) are now well rehearsed. This approach to development argues that there are opportunities for corporations to source from or sell to disadvantaged people in ways that generate wealth, improve their quality of life while being simultaneously profitable. The argument goes on to purport that there is an undeveloped and untapped market waiting at the bottom of the world's economic pyramid – a market of over three billion people who earn less than US$2 a day. Transnational companies such as Unilever, Philips, HP, and Johnson & Johnson have all looked at new business models and strategies aimed at low income markets.

The development potential arising from new corporate strategies to serve low income markets makes this an area of interest for the CSR community. The private sector has been one of the biggest alleviators of poverty over the last two decades and it can do even more by entering new untapped, low income, mass markets. The argument is therefore that business is key to solving the problems of poverty and that this idea should also be recognized by a (sometimes) doubtful NGO, inter-governmental and donor community. Indeed, donors need to begin to look at more ways in which they can use their funds as leverage for involving corporations in development projects.

At the micro level, large corporations are doing more and more to assist in development and there is a lot more practical support that they can provide. However, at the macro, policy level, corporations are reluctant to act and this is missing an opportunity to raise the issue of poverty alleviation and the other MDGs with the world's rich. At this macro-level businesses need to begin to partner with others (including UN agencies) if we are really going to tackle the scale of poverty and the broader challenges of the other MDGs. It necessarily involves businesses becoming political and some may resist that. But running a large business is a highly politicized activity, in actual fact, and CEO's, in particular, do have an obligation to provide leadership at this macro-level.

To some extent therefore, the CSR approach taken by many companies in supporting particular projects and initiatives needs to be extended to a consideration of how the major global problems outlined by the MDGs can be resolved. The expanding CSR movement has shown companies that their responsibilities do not lie simply in making profits, what is important is *how* profits are made. Moreover, there needs to be a renewed debate as to how the benefits of business are subsequently distributed. Some of the most talented people in the world run businesses and it would be useful to channel some of that talent into solving some of the biggest problems facing us today.

Only time will tell how vigorously corporations can and will want to take on this new aspect of CSR. But they can be pressured and persuaded to take on the wider challenge of development. As global players, large companies should recognize their global obligations. It is clear that large private corporations are heavily involved in development and in many places in Asia (particularly China) have been largely responsible for poverty alleviation through massive job-creating investments, new supply chain relationships and sourcing strategies.

The new CSR agenda in developing countries is certainly about how CSR can contribute to societal development through poverty alleviation, micro-enterprise development, the empowerment of women and putting in place pro-poor development strategies. Partnerships are the only feasible way forward in achieving a more sustainable development. But what is clear is that the private sector has a key role to play in this process and measuring outcomes and impacts ought to be linked to measure of human wellbeing.

The Practice of CSR and the Need for Capacity Building Strategies

The actual practice of CSR has been discussed in this book through a number of global initiatives, standards, case studies and challenges. What is important is that we fully learn the lessons of those. In many parts of the world (particularly in developing countries and deep into supply chains) companies are not recognizing their societal obligations either by choice or because they lack the capacity so to do. Getting larger parts of the private sector engaged in good CSR practices and upholding labour standards, protecting human rights, acting responsibly towards the environment and even simply obeying the law is still a major challenge that we ought to be more interested in. There is a need for much more work on how we move CSR from a Western agenda to a truly global one and this involves work on capacity building of companies, NGOS and consumers.

An interesting addition to some of the initiatives discussed in this book is China's home-grown social responsibly standard for the apparel sector launched in May 2005. Similar to SA8000 (i.e.

a management systems approach), CSC9000T was developed and administered by the China National Textile and Apparel Council (CNTAC), a national non-profit organization of all textile-related industries set up to help modernize China's textile industry. It is based on the relevant Chinese laws and international standards, but does not call for freedom of association and collective bargaining.

It is clear that China is reluctant to adopt and international standards that are in conflict with the government's other agendas. But what we are seeing is the development of new standards that can accommodate Chinese idiosyncrasies. At the local level many local and regional governments are also progressing from the environmental initiatives outlined above and into the development of their own CSR instructions, guidelines and standards. Stock exchanges have been examining various policy measures to encourage reporting and other aspects of CSR in listed companies as well (Chan & Welford, 2005)

But the problem with many CSR practices in developing countries is that there is not the capacity to fully implement them that we might take for granted in the West. It is very difficult to put systems in place when no one has been trained to use them. It is impossible to have good health and safety practices if no one understands the law. Good employment practices do not arise when managers think that making workers work longer hours increases productivity.

Further training is the key to improving CSR in developing countries. There is a need to both raise the awareness of managers about CSR issues and to develop the capacity to begin to implement CSR practices within companies. This must involve managers in identifying priorities for their country, sector and company as well as developing effective skills in putting ideas into practice. One starting point here is to develop training programmes that are accessible to managers.

Such programmes need to be developed in areas where there is already little capacity and will therefore need to have the support of organizations and agencies that are able to bring expertise to the table. Local government officials with particular responsibilities for specific factory issues, the small but growing NGO community, academics, consultants and experienced CSR managers need to be brought together in a programme of information sharing and skills development.

However, a serious problem exists within China and that revolves around a lack of people to lead such training events with sufficient expertise and experience to provide a meaningful introduction to CSR. In such circumstances there needs to be 'training the trainers' programmes put in place in advance of launching training programmes.

But training programmes, should, in time be extended beyond just factory managers. There is a need to build capacity within workforces and within national and local government, NGOs and local communities. Training programmes can also be targeted at particular issues (e.g. health and safety, employment law, environmental protection, wages) or at particular groups (e.g. women workers, migrant workers, NGOs, the media, etc.). It may well be that business associations can be a focal point for training initiatives in many locations.

Many developing country companies barely understand the relevant laws or importance of CSR standards that exist. Moreover, their employment practices, manufacturing processes and management systems are inconsistent with a move towards CSR. The challenge lies in the need for capacity building. But as noted previously, the capacity to build capacity is also lacking. One solution lies in developing coalitions and partnerships to train trainers and in turn to convince factories along supply chains that CSR can be good for business.

Conclusions

Most CSR activities globally are still led by the large Western brands keen to protect their image and reputation and avoid accusations of making products in sweatshops. Amongst the majority of developing country companies there is much less happening although it should be noted that the pace of change on these issues is very rapid indeed. The next big challenge for CSR is to take the lessons to be learned from publications such as this one and begin to apply them to tackling some of the world's remaining challenges associated with climate change, environmental degradation, species loss, poverty alleviation, the empowerment of women, human rights and corruption.

In developing countries some governments have been increasingly intervening in order to promote policies associated with sustainable development. We have seen CSR laws passed in Indonesia, major initiatives undertaken by stock exchanges in Malaysia and Thailand and in China the promotion of the concept of 'harmonious society' that has an explicit role for CSR. But implementation of the law and other initiatives to promote CSR are often highly dependent on the actions and activities of local officials. Some of the developments outlined here provide opportunities for the corrupt activities rather then progress toward better CSR practices.

The picture is very mixed but there is evidence to suggest that CSR will grow in importance over the coming years in developing countries. As well as government encouragement, pressure from the brands, growing community protests and an increasingly vocal workforce we are seeing a new breed of Asia workplace where owners and managers have experienced the benefits of CSR programmes through improvements in productivity and a reduction in staff turnover.

The picture may be mixed but there are some important conclusions. Firstly, unlike in the West, CSR in developing countries is often seen as getting companies to obey local laws rather than necessarily exceed them. There is a need to move the agenda forward. Secondly, although international standards influence supply chains it is more likely to be internal issues such as shortages of skilled labour that will drive CSR in developing countries. In some cases international standards may actually be resisted. Thirdly, picking up CSR models from the West and dropping them into developing countries is unlikely to work well. There is a need for CSR to engage all stakeholders at a local level. Finally, there is a need for much more work on linking the CSR agenda to other global challenges including the achievement of the MDGS and action to combat climate change in developing countries that did not cause it but will suffer disproportionately from it.

References

Abrahamsen, R. (2004) 'The World Bank's Good Governance Agenda'. In: *Ethnographies of Aid. Exploring development texts and encounters,* J. Gould & H. Secher Marcussen (Eds.), pp. 15–44, Roskilde: International Development Studies, Roskilde University.

Abrahamsson, E. (1996) 'Management Fashion'. *Academy of Management Review,* 21(1): 254–285.

Adams, C. A. & Zutshi A. (2005) 'Corporate disclosure and auditing,' In: *The Ethical Consumer,* R. Harrison, T. Newholm & D. Shaw, (Eds.) London: Sage.

Adams, J. S., Tashchian A. & Shore, T. H. (2001) 'Codes of Ethics as Signals for Ethical Behavior', *Journal of Business Ethics* 29: 199–211.

Adolfsson, P., Dobers, P. & Jonasson, M. (Eds.) (2009): *Guiding and Guided Tours.* Göteborg: BAS Publishers.

Agenda 21. 1992 Earth Summit '92: The United Nations Conference on Environment and Development. The Regency Press Corp: London.

Åhlström, J. & Egels-Zandén, N. (2006) 'The processes of defining corporate responsibility: a study of Swedish garment retailers' responsibility'. *Business Strategy and the Environment,* Vol. 17, Issue 4, May 2008, p. 230–244.

Allison, G. T. & Zelikow P. D. (1971/1999) *Essence of decision: explaining the Cuban missile crisis* (2. ed.). New York: Longman.

Altman, B. W. & Vidaver-Cohen, D. (2000) 'A Framework for Understanding Corporate Citizenship Introduction to the Special Edition of Business and Society Review "Corporate Citizenship for the New Millennium"', *Business and Society Review,* 105 (1): 1–7.

Alvesson, M. (1983) *Organisationsteori och teknokratiskt medvetande: en kritisk studie om rationalitet, ideologi och förutsättningarna för arbetslivets humanisering.* Stockholm: Natur och Kultur.

— (1987) *Consensus, control, and critique.* Avebury: Brookfield, VT.

Alvesson, M. & Willmott, H. (Eds.)
(1992) *Critical Management
Studies*. London: Sage, AMA:
Chicago.

Ansoff I. (1979). *Strategic
Management*. London:
MacMillan Press.

Antil, J. & Bennett, P. (1979),
'Construction and Validation
of a Scale to Measure Socially
Responsible Consumption
Behavior,' In: *The Conserver
Society*, K. Henion & T. Kinnear
(Eds.), Chicago: American
Marketing Association. 51–68.

Aragon-Correa, J. A. and Sharma,
D. (2003) 'A Contingent
Resource-Based View
of Proactive Corporate
Environmental Strategy'.
Academy of Management Review
28(1): 71–88.

Argyris, C. & Schön, D. (1978)
Organizational Learning.
London: Addison-Wesley.

Arrow K. J. (1973/1979). 'Business
Codes and Economic
Efficiency'. In: *Ethical Theory
and Business*, Beauchamp, T. L.
& Bowie, N. (Eds.) Englewood
Cliffs: Prentice-Hall.

Ashforth, B. E., Kreiner, G. E. &
Fugate, M. (2000). 'All in a
day's work: boundaries and
micro role transitions'. *Academy
of Management Review*, 25(3):
472–491.

Auger, P., Burke, P., Devinney,
T. M. & Louviere, J. J. (2003)
'What will consumers pay
for social product features?'
Journal of Business Ethics, 42 (3):
281–304.

Autio, M. (2004), 'Finnish Young
People's Narrative Construction

of Consumer Identity'.
*International Journal of Consumer
Studies*, Vol. 28 Issue 4, pp.
388–398

Bakan, J. (2004), *The corporation:
the pathological pursuit of profit
and power*. London: Constable
& Robinson.

Barnett, M. & Salomon, R.
(2006) 'Beyond Dichotomy:
The Curvilinear Relationship
Between Social Responsibility
and Financial Performance'.
Strategic Management Journal 27:
1101–1122.

Baudrillard, J. (1994) *Simulacra
and Simulation*. Michigan: The
University of Michigan Press.

Bauman, Z. (1989) *Modernity and
the Holocaust*. Cambridge: Polity
Press.

— (1993) *Postmodern Ethics*. Malden,
MA: Blackwell Publishing.

— (1995) *Life in Fragments. Essays in
Postmodern Morality*. Cambridge,
MA: Basil Blackwell.

— (2002) *Society under Siege*.
Cambridge, MA: Basil
Blackwell.

Bé, D. (2004) Paper presented at
the International conference
on CSR Humboldt University,
Berlin.

Beise, M. & Rennings, K. (2005)
'Lead markets and regulation:
A framework for analyzing
the international diffusion of
environmental innovations.'
Ecological Economics, 52(1): 5-17.

Bentley, M. *Sustainable consump-
tion. Ethics, national indices and
international relations*. Paris:
American Graduate School of
International Relations and
Diplomacy, 2003.

Berg, P-O., Linde-Laursen, O. & Löfgren, O. (2002) 'På Plats'. In: *Öresundsbron på uppmärksamhetens marknad: regionalbygge i evenemangsbranschen*. P.-O. Berg, O. Linde-Laursen & O. Löfgren (Eds.), Lund: Studentlitteratur.

Berry, Hannah & Morven McEachern (2005), 'Informing ethical consumers,' In: *The Ethical Consumer*, R. Harrison, T. Newholm & D. Shaw, (Eds.) London: Sage.

Bil Sweden (2006) 'Vem köper miljöbilar? Unik undersökning slår hål på fördomar!' (Who buys environmentally friendly cars? Unique research crushes preconceptions!). Press release, Bil Sweden (Car Sweden), 2006-02-09.

Bohm, D. (1996) *On Dialogue*. London & New York: Routledge.

Bonfiglioli, E. (2003) Paper presented at the CSR Europe Conference Warszawa, Warszawa.

Bonifant, B.C. (1995) 'Gaining Competitive Advantage through Environmental Investments.' *Business Horizons* 38, 37–48.

Boström, M. (2001) *Voluntary Rule-Making in the Environmental Field – New Alliances Between the State, Enterprises and Environmental Organizations*. Score Report Series 2001:10, Stockholm University.

Bowie N.E. (1978/1979), 'Business Codes of Ethics: Window Dressing or Legitimate Alternative to Government Regulation?' In: *Ethical Theory and Business,* Beauchamp T.L. & Bowie N. Englewood Cliffs: Prentice-Hall.

Bresnahan J (1999). 'For goodness sake'. *CIO*, 12(17): 54–62.

Brundtland G H. (1987). *Our Common Future: The Report of the World Commission on Environment and Development.* Oxford University Press: Oxford.

Brytting T. (1998). *Företagsetik*. Malmö: Liber Ekonomi.

Brytting T. & Egels N. (2004). Svensk *Företagsetisk Forskning 1995–2001*. Gothenburg: BAS.

Bué, J., Hamon-Cholet, S., & Puech, I. (2003). *Organization du travail: comment les salariés vivent le changement* (No. 24.1). Paris: Ministère des affaires sociales, du travail et de la solidarité.

Burchell, J. (Ed.) *The corporate social responsibility reader*. London: Routledge, 2008.

Burke, R. J., & Cooper, C. L. (Eds.) (2006). *The human resources revolution; why putting people first matters*. Oxford: Elsevier.

Callon, M. (1986) 'Some Elements of Sociology of Translation: Domestication of the Scallops and the Fisherman of St Brieuc Bay', In: *Power, Action and Belief: A New Sociology of Knowledge?* J. Law (Ed.) , pp. 196–223. London: Routledge.

— (1991) 'Techno-Economic Networks and Irreversibility', In: *A Sociology of Monsters: Essays on Power, Technology and Domination*. J. Law (Ed.) , pp. 132–161. London: Routledge & Keegan Paul.

— (1998) 'The Embeddedness of Economic Markets in Economics', In: *The Laws of the Markets*. M. Callon (Ed.), pp. 1–57. Oxford: Blackwell Publishers.

— (1999) 'Actor-Network Theory: The Market Test' In: *Actor Network Theory and After*. J. Law and J. Hassard (Eds.) pp. 181–195. Oxford: Blackwell Publishers.

Callon, M. & Latour, B. (1981) 'Unscrewing the Big Leviathan: How actors macro-Structure reality and how sociologist help them to do so', In: *Advances in Social Theory and Methodology: Towards an Integration of Micro- and Macro Sociologies*. K. Knorr-Cetina and A.V. Cicourel (Eds.) pp. 277–303. Boston MA: Routledge.

Callon, M. & Law, J. (1997) 'After the Individual in Society: Lessons on Collectivity from Science, Technology and Society', *Canadian Journal of Sociology*, 22(2): 165–182.

Campbell, J. L. (2004) *Institutional change and globalization*. Princeton, NJ: Princeton University Press.

— (2007). 'Why Would Corporations Behave in Socially Responsible Ways?: An Institutional Theory of Corporate Social Responsibility', *Academy of Management Review*, 32(3): 946–967.

Carroll A. (1979) 'A Three-Dimensional Conceptual Model of Corporate Social Performance.' *Academy of Management Review*, 4(4): 497–505.

— (1989). *Business and Society: Ethics and Stakeholder Management*. South Western Publishing Company: Cincinnati.

— (1991) 'The Pyramid of Corporate Social Responsibility. Toward the Moral Management of Organizational Stakeholders'. *Business Horizons* (July–August): 39–48.

— (1996) *Business and society: Ethics and Stakeholder Management*. (International Thomson Publishing, Cincinnati).

— (1998) 'The Four Faces of Corporate Citizenship,' *Business & Society Review* (100/101): 1–7.

— (1999) 'Corporate Social responsibility. Evolution of a Definitional Construct.' *Business and Society*, 38(3): 268–295.

Carroll, A. and Buchholtz, A.K. (2000) *Business & society: ethics and stakeholder management* (4. ed.). Cincinnati, Ohio: South-Western College Publ.

Cartwright, S. (2003) 'News forms of work organization: issues and challenges'. *Leadership & Organization Development Journal*, 24(3): 121–122.

Cassell, C., Johnson, P. & Smith, K. (1997) 'Opening the Black Box: Corporate Codes of Ethics in Their Organizational Context', *Journal of Business Ethics* 16(10): 1077–1093.

Castells, M. (1996) *The Information Age: Economy, Society and Culture. Volume I. The Rise of the Network Society*. Oxford: Blackwell.

Cescau P. (2007) *Beyond Corporate responsibility; Social Innovation and Sustainable development as drivers fro Business Growth*. INSEAD INDEVOR Alumni Forum, Fontainebleau, France, May 25.

Chan, A. (1998) 'Labor Standards and Human Rights: The Case of Chinese Workers Under Market Socialism', *Human Rights Quarterly* 20(4): 886–904

Chan, J. C. and Welford, R. J. (2005) 'Assessing Corporate Environmental Risk in China: An Evaluation of Reporting Activities of Hong Kong Listed Enterprises', *Corporate Social Responsibility and Environmental Management*, 12, 88–104

Chonko L B (1995) *Ethical Decision-Making in Marketing.* New York: Sage.

Clark, S. C. (2000) 'Work/family border theory: a new theory of work/family balance'. *Human Relations*, 53(6): 747–770.

Clegg, S.R. (1975) *Power, Rule and Domination. A Critical and Empirical Understanding of Power in Sociological Theory and Organizational Life.* London & Boston: Routledge.

Clouder, S. & Harrison, R. (2005) 'The effectiveness of ethical consumer behaviour,' In: *The Ethical Consumer*, R. Harrison, T. Newholm & D. Shaw, (Eds.) London: Sage.

Code of Ethics (2004) Stora Enso: Helsinki.

Conolly, J. & Prothero, A. (2003) 'Sustainable Consumption: Consumption, Consumers, and the Commodity Discourse', *Consumption, Markets, and Culture*, 6(4): 275–291.

Cooperative Bank (2004) Ethical Purchasing Index.

Cooper, C. L. (1994). 'The costs of healthy work organiza-tions'. In: *Creating healthy work organizations.* C. L. Cooper & S. Williams (Eds.) (pp. 1–15). Chichester: John Wiley.

Cowe, R. and Williams, S. (2001) *Who are the Ethical Consumers?* Co-operative bank/Mori survey, Report.

Cox, T.H. & Blake, S. (1991) 'Managing cultural diversity: Implications for organizational competitiveness.' *The Executive* 5(3): 45–58.

Crane, A. (2000) 'Facing the back-lash: green marketing and stra-tegic reorientation in the 1990s,' *Journal of Strategic Marketing*, 8 (3): 277–96.

Crane, A. & Matten, D. (2004) *Business ethics: a European perspec-tive: managing corporate citizen-ship and sustainability in the age of globalization.* Oxford: Oxford University Press.

Crane, A. and Matten, D. (eds.), (2007a) *Corporate social reson-sibility. Volume 1: Theories and concepts of corporate social respon-sibility.* Thousands Oaks: Sage Publications.

— (2007b) *Corporate social responsi-bility. Volume 2: Managing and implementing corporate social responsibility.* Thousands Oaks: Sage Publications.

— (2007c) *Corporate social respon-sibility. Volume 3: Corporate social responsibility in global context.* Thousands Oaks: Sage Publications.

Crane, A., Matten, D. & Moon, J. (2004) 'Stakeholders as Citizens? Rethinking Rights, Participation, and Democracy,' *Journal of Business Ethics*, 53 (1/2): 107–22.

Creyer, E. H. & Ross Jr, W. T. (1997) 'The influence of firm behavior on purchase intention: do consumers really care about business ethics?' *Journal of Consumer Marketing*, 14 (6): 421–32.

CSR Europe. (2003a) Goals of the Conference. Paper presented at the Responsible Business – a New Strategy for Development, Warsaw.

— (2003b) It Simply Works Better! Campaign Report on European CSR Excellence 2002–2003: The Copenhagen Centre,.

— (2003c) It simply works better! Campaign Report on European CSR Excellence, 2003–2004, : CSR Europe.

— (2006a) About Us. Retrieved 25 August, 2006 http://www.csreurope.org/

— (2006b) A European Roadmap for Businesses: Towards a Sustainable and Competitive Enterprise: CSR Europe.

— Corporate Social Responsibility – The European Business Campaign.

CSR Sweden. (2005) Om CSR Sweden. Retrieved 27 December, 2005, from http://www.csrsweden.se/se/omcsr-sweden/

— (2006) Invitation The Nordic Marketplace on CSR: CSR Sweden.

Cutler, I. (2005) *Cynicism from Diogenes to Dilbert*. Jefferson, North Carolina: McFarland & Company.

Czarniawska, B. (2004) 'On Time, Space, and Action Nets'. *Organization* 11(6): 773–791.

— (2004) 'Turning to Discourse', In: *The SAGE Handbook of Organizational Discourse*, D. Grant, C. Hardy, C. Oswick & L. Putnam (Eds.), pp. 399–404. London: Sage Publications.

— (2005) 'The Styles and Stylists of Organization Theory'. In: *The Oxford Handbook of Organization Theory Meta-Theoretical Perspectives*, H. Tsoukas & C. Knudsen (Eds.), pp. 237–261. London: Harvester Wheatsheaf.

Czarniawska, B. and Joerges, B. (1996) 'Travel of Ideas'. In: *Translating Organizational Change*, Czarniwaska, B. and Sevón, G. (Eds.). pp. 1–17. Berlin: de Gruyter,

Czarniwaska, B. and Sevón, G. (2005) 'Translation Is a Vehicle, Imitation its Motor, and Fashion Sits at the Wheel'. In: *Global Ideas: How Ideas, Objects and Practices Travel in the Global Economy*, Czarniwaska, B. and Sevón, G. (Eds.) . Malmö: Liber, pp. 7–12.

Czarniawska B., Sevón G. (Eds.) (1996) *Translating Organizational Change*. Walter de Gruyter: Berlin.

Dagens Nyheter – One of the Swedish Daily Newspapers, February 2006.

Daly, H. E. Cobb, J. B. (1994), *For the Common Good – redirecting the economy toward community, the environment, and a sustainable future*, 2nd ed, Boston: Beacon Press.

Das, T. K. (1993). 'A multiple paradigm approach to organizational control'. *The International Journal of Organizational Analysis* 4(1): 385–403.

Deborah, A. (2004) Paper presented at the International conference on CSR, Humboldt University, Berlin.

Deetz, S. (1995). *Transforming communication, Transforming Business. Building Responsive and Responsible Workplaces*. New Jersey: Hampton Press.

DesJardins, J. (1998). 'Corporate Environmental Responsibility'. *Journal of Business Ethics* 17, 825–838.

Desrochers, S., & Sargent, L. D. (2003, 9/09/03). Boundary/border theory and work-family integration. http://wfnetwork. bc.edu/encyclopedia_entry. php?id=220&area=academics. Retrieved 22/02, 2006

Dettmar, D., Morris, P., (2004) Paper presented at the International CSR Conference, Berlin.

Diamantopoulou, A. (2003) Paper presented at the CSR Europe Conference Warszawa, Warszawa.

Dickinson, R. A. & Carsky, M. L. (2005) 'The consumer as economic voter,' In: *The Ethical Consumer*, R. Harrison, T. Newholm & D. Shaw (Eds.) London: Sage.

Dienhart J W & Curnutt J (1998). *Business Ethics: a reference handbook*. Santa Barbara (CA): ABC-CLIO.

Dillard, J.F. & Yuthas, K. (2002) 'Ethical Audit Decisions', *Journal of Business Ethics* 36: 49–64.

DiMaggio, P.J. & Powell, W.W. (1983) 'The iron cage revisited: Institutional isomorphism and collective rationality in organizational fields', *American Sociological Review*, 48(x): 147–160.

— (1991) 'Introduction'. In: *The New Institutionalism in Organization Analysis*, Powell, W.W. & DiMaggio, P.J. (Eds.) Chicago: The University of Chicago Press.

Doane, D. (2005) 'The Myth of CSR', *Stanford Social Innovation Review*, Fall, 23–29.

— (2005) 'Beyond corporate social responsibility: minnows, mammoths and markets', *Futures*, Vol. 37, Issues 2–3, pp. 215–229.

Dobers, P. (2004) 'Stockholm as a Mobile Valley. Empty spaces or illusionary images?' *Journal of Urban Technology*, 11, (3): 87–108.

Dobers, P. and Strannegård, L. (2004) 'The Cocoon. A travelling space.' *Organization*, 11, (6): 829–852.

— (2005), 'Design, lifestyles and sustainability. Aesthetic consumption in a world of abundance,' *Business Strategy and the Environment*, 14 (5): 324–36.

Dobers P., Strannegård L., Wolff, R. (2001). 'Knowledge interests in corporate environmental management'. *Business Strategy and the Environment* 10(6): 335–343.

Donaldson, T. & Preston, L.E. (1995). 'The Stakeholder Theory of the Corporation: Concepts,

Evidence, and Implications.' *Academy of Management Review*, 20(1): 65–91.

Donner-Amnell J (2004). 'Vastuullisuus kansainvälistyvän metsäteollisuuden haasteena'. In: *Leipäpuusta arvopaperia. Vastuun ja oikeudenmukaisuuden haasteet metsäpolitiikassa*, A. Lehtinen & P. Rannikko (Eds.), pp. 223–244. Hämeenlinna: Metsälehti.

Dow Jones Sustainability Indexes (2003). www.sustainability-indexes.com. 17.12.2004.

Drucker, P. F. (1984) 'The new meaning of corporate social responsibility.' *California Management Review* 26, pp. 53–63.

Dunphy, D., Griffiths, A. & Benn, S. (2003) *Organizational Change for Corporate Sustainability*. London: Routledge.

Easterly, W. (2006) *The White Man's Burden: Why the West's Efforts to Aid the Rest Have Done So Much Ill and So Little Good*. New York: Penguin Press.

Edwards, J. R., & Rothbard, N. P. (1999) 'Work and family stress and well-being: an examination of person-environment fit in the work and family domains'. *Organizational Behavior and Human Decision Processes*, 77(2): 85–129.

Egels, N. (2005) 'CSR in Electrification of Rural Africa: The Case of ABB in Tanzania', *Journal of Corporate Citizenship* 18: 75–85.

Egels–Zandén, N. (2007) 'Suppliers' Compliance with MNCs' Codes of Conduct: Behind the Scenes at Chinese Toy Suppliers', *Journal of Business Ethics* 75(1): 45–62.

Egels-Zandén N., Hyllman, P. (2006) Exploring the effects of union-NGO relationships on corporate responsibility: the case of the Swedish Clean Clothes Campaign. *Journal of Business Ethics*, 64(3): 303–316.

Egels-Zandén N., Kallifatides M. (2006) 'The corporate social performance dilemma: organizing for goal duality in low-income African markets', In: *Corporate Citizenship in Africa: Lessons from the Past, Paths to the Future*, Vissner W, McIntosh M, Middleton C (Eds.) Sheffield: Greenleaf Publishing.

Ekstrand, L. (2006) 'Miljön betalar högt pris för billigt flyg.' 2007, March 21. Place Published. http://www.gp.se

Ekström, K. and Forsberg, H. (1999) *Den flerdimensionella konsumenten*, Gothenburg: Tre Böcker.

Ellinor, L. and Gerard, G. (1998) *Dialogue: Rediscover the Transforming Power of Conversation*. New York: John Wiley & Sons, Inc.

Engel, M. V. (1997). 'The New Non-Managers'. *Management Quarterly*, 38(2): 22–29.

Ethical Corporation Magazine (2004) Levi Strauss and participatory approaches to social auditing challenges, 9th of March, 2004, www.EthicalCorp.com

Etienne, V. (2003) Paper presented at the CSR Europe Conference Warszawa, Warszawa.

— (2006) Paper presented at the Nordic Marketplace on social responsibility, Stockholm.

EU Commission. (2001) *Greenpaper on Corporate Social Responsibility.* Brussels: EU Commission.

European Commission (2006) *Implementing the Partnership for Growth and Jobs: Making Europe a Pole of Excellence on* CSR, COM 136-final, European Commission: Brussels.

European Commission, Internet, EMAS, http://ec.europa.eu/environment/emas/about/participate/sites_en.htm, 2007-06-30.

Europeiska kommissionen (2000) Riktlinjer för utformning och bedömning av miljömärkning. Generaldirektoratet för hälsa och konsumentskydd. Kontraktsnummer B5-1000/99/000051, Rapportnummer 67/94/22/1/00281.

Fair Trade Center, Interview with Kristina Bjurling and Henrik Lindholm, Stockholm, 2005-06-24.

Falk, R. (2002) 'Liberalism at the Global Level'. In: *The Globalization of Liberalism,* E. Hovden & E. Keene (Eds.), pp. 75–98. Basingstoke & New York: Palgrave.

Faulks, K. (2000) *Citizenship.* London: Routledge.

Fergus A. H. T. & Rowney J. I. A. (2005a) 'Sustainable development: epistemological frameworks and an ethic of choice'. *Journal of Business Ethics* 57(2): 197–207.

— (2005b) 'Sustainable development: lost meaning and opportunity?' *Journal of Business Ethics* 60(1): 17–27.

Ferguson, J. (1997) 'Anthropology and its evil twin: development in the constitution of a discipline'. In: *International development and the social sciences: essays in the history and politics of knowledge,* F. Cooper & R. Packard (Eds.) Berkeley: University of California Press.

Ferraro, F., Pfeffer, J. and Sutton, R. (2005) 'Economics Language and Assumptions: How Theories Can Become Self-Fulfilling'. *Academy of Management Review* 30(1): 8–24.

Fleckenstein M P & Huebsch P (1999). 'Ethics in tourism – reality or hallucination'. *Journal of Business Ethics,* 19(1): 137–142.

Fligstein, N. (1990) *The transformation of corporate control.* Cambridge, MA: Harvard University Press.

Flink, L. (2004) Paper presented at the ISO SR Conference, Stockholm.

Foucault, M. (1975/1977) *Discipline and Punish. The Birth of the Prison.* New York: Vintage. (Transl. Alan Sheridan)

— (1979) *Governmentality. Ideology and Consciousness,* Vol. 6, pp. 5–21

Fox, T. (2004) 'Corporate Social Responsibility and Development'. *Development* 47(3): 29–36.

Frederick, W. C. (1994) 'From CSR1 to CSR2. The Maturing of Business-and-Society Thought.' *Business & Society,* Vol. 33. No. 2: 150–164.

Freeman R. E. (1984). *Strategic Management: A Stakeholder Approach.* Pitman: New York.

Freeman, R. E. and Velamuri, S. R. (2006) 'A New Approach to CSR: Company Stakeholder Responsibility.' In: *Corporate Social Responsibility: Reconciling Aspiration with Application,* Kakabadse, A. & Morsing, M. (Eds.), pp. 9–23. Palgrave MacMillan.

Frenkel, S. & Kim, S. (2004) 'Corporate Codes of Labour Practice and Employment Relations in Sports Shoe Contractor Factories in South Korea', *Asia Pacific Journal of Human Resources* 42(1): 6–31.

Friedman M (1982/1962) *Capitalism and Freedom. Reissue.* Chicago: The University of Chicago Press.

— (1962) 'The responsibility of business is to increase profits'. *New York Times Magazine,* 13 September.

— (1970) 'The Social Responsibility of Business is to Increase its Profits. *The New York Times Magazine.* September 13.

Frone, M. R., Russell, M. & Cooper, M. L. (1992) 'Prevalence of work-family conflict: are work and family boundaries asymmetrically permeable?' *Journal of Organizational Behavior,* 13(7): 723–729.

Frone, M. R., Yardley, J. K., & Markel, K. S. (1997) 'Developing and testing an integrative model of the work-family interface'. *Journal of Vocational Behavior,* 50: 145–167.

Frynas J. (2005) 'The False Developmental Promise of Corporate Social Responsibility: Evidence from Multinational Companies'. *International Affairs* 81(3): 581–598.

Fuchs, D. and Lorek, S. 'Sustainable consumption governance. A history of promises and failures.' *Journal of Consumer Policy,* 28, (2005): 261–288.

Furusten, S. (1995) *The Managerial Discourse – A Study of the Creation and diffusion of Popular Management Knowledge,* Uppsala: Department of Business Studies, Uppsala University.

Gardner, G., Assadourian, E. and Sarin, R. (2004) 'The state of consumption today.' In: *State of the world 2004. Special focus: The consumer society,* Worldwatch Institute (Eds.) New York: w w Norton & Company, pp. 3–21.

Gardyn, R. (2003) 'Eco-Friend Or Foe?' *American Demographics,* 25 (8): 12–13.

Garriga E & Melé D (2004) 'Corporate Social Responsibility Theories: Mapping the Territory'. *Journal of Business Ethics* 53(1–2): 51–71.

Gasparski W W (2000) Codes of Ethics, Their Design, Introduction and Implementation: A Polish Case. Second World Congress of Business, Economics and Ethics, July 19–23 2000, São Paulo.

Gaumnitz B R & Lere J C (2002) 'Contents of Codes of Ethics of Professional Business Organizations in the United States'. *Journal of Business Ethics,* 35: 35–49.

Geertz, C. (1973) *The Interpretation of Cultures.* New York: Basic Books.

Generaldirektoratet för hälsa och konsumentskydd. Kontraktsnummer B5-1000/99/000051.

Gergen, K.J. (1991) *The saturated self*. New York: Basic Books.

— (1994) *Realities and relationships*. Cambridge, MA: Harvard University Press.

Geurts, S.A.E. & Demerouti, E. (2003) 'Work/non-work interface: a review of theories and findings'. In: *The handbook of work and health psychology*, M.J. Schabracq, J.A.M. Winnubst & C.L. Cooper (Eds.), pp. 279–312. Chichester, West Sussex, England: John Wiley & Sons. Ltd.

Ghoshal, S. (2005) 'Bad Management Theories Are Destroying Good Management Practices'. *Academy of Management Learning and Education* 4(1): 75–91.

Giddens, A. (1984) *The Constitution of Society*. Cambridge: Polity press.

— (1990) *The consequences of modernity*. Cambridge: Polity in association with Blackwell.

— (1991) *Modernity and self-identity: self and society in the late modern age*. Cambridge: Polity press.

— (2002) *Runaway world: how globalization is reshaping our lives*. London: Profile Books.

Gill, S. (2002) 'Globalization, Market Civilization and Disciplinary Neoliberalism'. In: *The Globalization of Liberalism*, E. Hovden & E. Keene (Eds.) pp. 123–151. Basingstoke & New York: Palgrave.

Gilmore, J.H. & Pine, J.B. (1997) 'The four faces of mass customization', *Harvard Business Review*, January 1: 91–101.

Gioia, D.A., Donnellon A. & Sims, H. (1989) 'Communication and cognition in appraisal'. *Organization Studies* 10(4): 503–529.

Gioia, D.A. & Pitre, E. (1990) 'Multiparadigm perspectives on theory building'. *Academy of Management Review* 15(4): 584–602.

Gioia, D.A. & Thomas J.B. (1996) 'Identity, image, and issue interpretation: sensemaking during strategic change in academia'. *Administrative Science Quarterly* 41(3): 370–403.

Global Market Insite: (2005) 'Consumer Survey Finds Doing Good is Good for Business'. www.sustainablemarketing.com/content/view/150/. Accessed on Dec. 1, 2005.

Godfrey, P. (2005) 'The Relationship Between Corporate Philanthropy and Shareholder Wealth: a Risk Management Perspective'. *Academy of Management Review* 30(4): 777–798. Gothenburg University.

Gordon K & Miyake M (2001) Business Approaches to Combating Bribery: A Study of Codes of Conduct. *Journal of Business Ethics*, 34, 161–173.

Grankvist, G. (2002) *Determinants of Choice of Eco-Labeled Products*. Dissertation. Gothenburg: Gothenburg University

Grankvist, G. and Biel, A. (2001) 'The Importance of Beliefs and Purchase Criteria in the Choice of Eco-Labelled Food Products', *Journal of Environmental Psychology*, 21(4): 405–510.

Granovetter, M. (1985) 'Economic Action and Social Structure: The Problem of Embeddedness'. *American Journal of Sociology*, 91(3): 481–510.

Graves, W. B. (1924) 'Codes of Ethics for Business and Commercial Organization', *International Journal of Ethics* 35(1): 41–59.

Greener, I. (2006) 'Nick Leeson and the Collapse of Barings Bank: Socio-Technical Networks and the "Rogue Trader"', *Organization* 13 (3): 421–441.

Greenhaus, J. H. & Powell, G. N. (2006) 'When work and family are allies: a theory of work-family enrichment'. *Academy of Management Review*, 31(1): 72–92.

Griffin, J. J. & Mahon, J. F. (1997) 'The corporate social performance and corporate financial performance debate'. *Business & Society* 36(1): 5–31.

Grint, K. (1991) *The sociology of work: an introduction*. Polity Press: London.

Grunig, J. (2001) 'Two-Way Symmetrical Public Relations: Past, Present, and Future.' In: *Handbook of Public Relations*, R. L. Heath (Ed.) pp. 11–30. Thousand Oaks: Sage Publications.

Guimarães, T. & Liska, K. (1995) 'Exploring the Business Benefits of Environmental Stewardship'. *Business Strategy and the Environment* 4, 9–22.

Gustafsson, C. (1990) *New Values, Morality and Strategic Ethics*. Memo-Stencil 148. Dept. of Organization and management. Turku: Åbo Akademi Univ.

Habermas, J. (1981/1984) *The theory of communicative action* (T. McCarthy, Trans.) Boston: Beacon Press.

Hadjikhani A (1996) *International Business and Political Crisis. Swedish MNCs in a Turbulent Market*. Diss. Acta Universitatis Upsaliensis, 40. Stockholm: Almqvist & Wiksell.

Håkansson, H. & Ford, D. (2002) 'How should companies interact in business networks?' *Journal of Business Research*, 55(2): 133–139.

Hall, D. T. & Richter, J. (1988). 'Balancing work life and home life: what can organizations do to help?' *The Academy of Management Executive*, 2(3): 213–223.

Halme, M. (1995) 'Environmental issues in product development processes: paradigm shift in a Finnish packaging company'. *Business Ethics Quarterly* 5(4): 713–733.

— (1997) *Environmental Management Paradigm Shifts in Business Enterprises. Organizational Learning Relating to Recycling and Forest Management Issues in Two Finnish Paper Companies*. Diss. University of Tampere.

Halme, M., Anttonen, M., Kuisma, M., Kontoniemi, N. & Heino, E. (2006) 'Business Models for Material Efficiency Services: Conceptualization and Application'. *Ecological Economics* 63: 126–137.

Halme, M. & J. Laurila (2009) 'Philanthropy, integration or

innovation? Exploring the financial and societal outcomes of different types of corporate responsibility', *Journal of Business Ethics*. 84: 325–339.

Halme, M. & Niskanen, J. (2001) 'Does Corporate Environmental Protection Increase or Decrease Shareholder Value? The Case of Environmental Investments'. *Business Strategy and the Environment*. 10(4): 200–214.

Hamadan, Fouad (2004) Paper presented at the CSR Conference Humboldt University, Berlin.

Harrison, R. (2005) 'Pressure groups, campaigns and consumers,' In: *The Ethical Consumer*, R. Harrison, T. Newholm & D. Shaw, (Eds.) London: Sage.

Harrison, Rob, Newholm, Terry & Shaw, Deirdre (Eds.) (2005a) *The Ethical Consumer*, London: Sage.

Harrison, R., T. Newholm & D. Shaw (2005b), 'Introduction,' In: *The Ethical Consumer*, R. Harrison, T. Newholm & D. Shaw, (Eds.) London: Sage.

Hart, S. (2006) *Capitalism at the Crossroads: the Unlimited Business Opportunities in Solving the World's Most Difficult Problems*, Upper Saddle River, NJ: Wharton School Publishing.

Hart, S. & Ahuja, G. (1996) 'Does It Pay to Be Green? An Empirical Examination of the Relationship Between Emission Reduction and Firm Performance'. *Business Strategy and the Environment* 5: 30–37.

Hart, S. & Christensen, C. (2002) 'The Great Leap: Innovation From the Base of the Pyramid.'

MIT Sloan Management Review (Fall), 51–56.

Hasler, A, Sterr, T. & Jacobson, N. B. (2005) 'Confidence as a Key Factor for Sustainable Eco-Industrial Networking'. In: *Proceedings for the 11th Annual International Sustainable Development Research Conference*, 6–8.6.2005. Helsinki.

Hassard, J. (1991) 'Multiple para-digms and organizational analy-sis: a case study'. *Organization Studies* 12(2): 275–299.

— (1993) *Sociology and Organization Theory: Positivism, Paradigms and Postmodernity*. Cambridge, MA: Cambridge University Press.

Helin, S. & Sandström, J. (2008) 'Codes, ethics and cross-cultural differences: stories from the implementation of a corporate code of ethics in a MNC sub-sidiary'. *Journal of Business Ethics* 82(2): 281–291.

Henderson, D. (2003) Paper presented at the Förtroendekonferensen, Stockholm.

Hertz, N. (2003) *The silent takeover: global capitalism and the death of democracy*. New York: Harper Business.

Hillman, A. & Keim, G. (2001) 'Shareholder Value, Stakeholder Management, and Social Issues. What's the Bottom Line?' *Strategic Management Journal* 22: 125–139.

Hockerts, K. & Moir, L. (2004) 'Communicating corporate responsibility to investors: the changing role of the investor relations function,' *Journal of Business Ethics*, 52(1): 85–98.

Holbrook, M. B. (1999) *Consumer Value: A framework for analysis and research*, London: Routledge.

Horkheimer, M. & Adorno, T. W. (1944/1997) *Upplysningens dialektik: filosofiska fragment* (New, rev. Swedish ed.). Gothenburg: Daidalos.

Hovden, E. & Keene, E. (Eds.) (2002) *The Globalization of Liberalism*. Basingstoke & New York: Palgrave.

Huang, Y-H (2001) 'Should a public relations code of ethics be enforced?' *Journal of Business Ethics*, 31(3): 259–270.

Hummels, H. & Timmer, D. (2004) 'Investors in need of social ethical, and environmental information,' *Journal of Business Ethics*, 52(1): 73–84.

Husted B. W. & Allen D. B. (2004) 'Is It Ethical to Use Ethics as Strategy?' *Journal of Business Ethics* 27(1–2): 21–31.

Husted, B. & De Jesus Salazar, J. (2006) 'Taking Friedman Seriously: Maximizing Profits and Social Performance'. *Journal of Management Studies* 43(1): 75–91.

Insight Investment Management Ltd and Acona Ltd, (2004) Buying your way into trouble? The challenge of responsible supply chain management, www.insightinvestment.com/documents/responsibility/ir_bulletin_winter2004.pdf

Institute of Management Humboldt University, (2004) Call for Papers International Conference on Corporate Social Responsibility (Vol. 2005):

Institute of Management Humboldt University.

Interview Catherine Rubbens. (2004, 18 June). CSR Europe. Personal Interview.

Interview with Maria Palm, Svenska Naturskyddsföreningen, February 2006.

IPCC (1999), 'Aviation and the Global Atmosphere,' IPCC, Intergovernmental Panel on Climate Change, Report.

Isaacs, W. (1999) *Dialogue and the Art of Thinking Together: A Pioneering Approach to Communicating in Business and in Life*. New York: Doubleday.

ISO (2007) Internet, ISO 9000/ISO 14000, 2007-07-03;

ISO World (2007) Internet, http://www.ecology.or.jp/isoworld/english/analy14k.htm, 2007-06-30.

ISO, http://www.iso.org/iso/en/iso9000-14000/understand/basics/general/basics_3.html, 2005-05-19.

ISO (2004) Draft Seminar Program, The Development Dimension of Social responsibility: ISO.

Jackall, R. (1988) *Moral Mazes. The World of Corporate Managers*. New York: Oxford University Press.

Jackson, N. & Carter, P. (1991) 'In defence of paradigm incommensurability'. *Organization Studies* 12(1): 109–127.

— (1993) '"Paradigm wars": a response to Hugh Willmott'. *Organization Studies* 14(5): 721–725.

Jansson, J., Marell, A. & Nordlund, A. (2009) 'Elucidating green consumers: A cluster analytic approach on proenvironmental purchase and curtailment behaviors.' *Journal of Euromarketing*, 18(4): 245-267

Jarillo, J. C. (1988) 'On strategic networks'. *Strategic Management Journal*, 9(1): 31–41.

Jenkins, R. (2005) 'Globalization, Corporate Social Responsibility and Poverty'. *International Affairs* 81(3): 525–540.

Jensen, T. (2004) *Översättningar av konkurrens i ekonomiska laboratorier: Om ekonomiska teoriers förenkling, komplexitet och fördunkling i hälso- och sjukvården* (Translations of competition in economic laboratories: How economic theories are simplified, complex and blurred within health care). Diss. Umeå: Umeå University.

Jensen, T. (2006) 'Fördunklad Organisering i en Heterogent Materiell Värld', In: *Den Oavsedda Organizationen*, D. Ericsson (Ed.) pp. 46–66. Lund: Academia Adacta.

Jensen, T., Sandström, J. & Helin, S. (2009) 'Corporate codes of ethics and the bending of moral space'. *Organization* 16(4): 529–545.

Jeurissen, R. (2004) 'Institutional Conditions of Corporate Citizenship'. *Journal of Business Ethics* 53(1–2): 87–96.

Johansson, R. (2002) *Nyinstitutionalismen inom organisationsanalysen*. Lund: Studentlitteratur

Johnson, P. & Smith, K. (1999) 'Contextualizing business ethics: Anomie and social life'. *Human Relations*, 52(11): 1351–1375.

Johnson, L. (2003) Paper presented at the CSR Europe Conference Warszawa, Warszawa.

Jonas, H. (1984) *The Imperative of Responsibility: In Search of an Ethics for the Technological Age.* Chicago: The University of Chicago Press.

Jones, C. (2003) 'As if Business Ethics Were Possible, "Within Such Limits"', *Organization* 10 (2): 267–285.

Jones, F., Burke, R. J. & Westman, M. (Eds.) (2006) *Work-life balance: a psychological perspective.* Hove, East Sussex: Psychology Press.

Jones, T. M. (1980) 'Corporate social responsibility revisited, redefined.' *California Management Review*, Spring: 59–67.

Jonsson, P. (2004) 'Capturing the Elusive Simplifier – Consumers Choosing Simpler Alternatives in Consumer Society', Mellanseminarierapport (Mid-seminar report) Gothenburg Research Institute (GRI), School of Business, Economics and Law, University of Gothenburg.

Jordan, A., Rüdiger K. W., Anthony, R. Z., Brückner, L. (2004) 'Consumer responsibility-taking and eco-labeling schemes in Europe,' In: *Politics, Products, and Markets: Exploring political consumerism past and present*, M. Micheletti, A. Follesdal & D. Stolle (Eds.) New Brunswick, New Jersey: Transaction Publishers.

Juholin E (2004) *Cosmopolis. Yhteiskuntavastuusta yrityskansalaisuuteen.* Keuruu: Otava.

Kandachar, P. & Halme, M. (Eds.) (2008) *Sustainability challenges and solutions at the base of the pyramid*. Sheffield: Greenleaf.

Kaptein, M. (2004) 'Business Codes of Multinational Firms: What Do They Say?', *Journal of Business Ethics* 50(1): 13–31.

Kaptein, M. & Wempe, J. (1998) 'Twelve Gordian Knots When Developing an Organizational Code of Ethics', *Journal of Business Ethics* 17: 853–869.

Karasek, R. A. (1979) 'Job demands, job decision latitude, and mental strain: implications for job redesign'. *Administrative Science Quarterly*, 24(2): 285–308.

Karasek, R. A. & Theorell, T. (1990) *Healthy work: stress, productivity, and the reconstruction of working life*. New York: BasicBooks.

Kardash, W. J. (1974) 'Corporate Responsibility and the Quality of Life: Developing the ecologically concerned consumer', In: *Ecological Marketing*, Henion, K. E. & Kinnear, T. C. (Eds.) American Marketing Association: Chicago, IL,

Karnani, A. (2007) 'Misfortune at the Bottom of the Pyramid'. *Greener Management International*. Issue June 1.

Kirchmeyer, C. (1995). 'Managing the work-nonwork boundary: an assessment of organizational responses'. *Human Relations*, 48(5): 515–536.

Kodz, J., Harper, H., & Dench, S. (2002). *Work-life balance, beyond the rhetoric* (No. Report 384). Brighton, England: The Institute for Employment Studies.

Konsumentombudsmännen (2005) 'De nordiska konsumentombudsmännens vägledning kring användning av etiska och miljörelaterade påståenden i marknadsföring'.

Konsumentverket (2002) 'Omsättning av miljömärkta dagligvaror. Utveckling 2001–2002.' 2007, March 30. Place Published. http://www.svanen.nu/pdf/marknadsandelar.ppt

Koolhaas, R., Chung, C.J., Inaba, J. & Leong, S. T. (Eds.), *Great leap forward*. Project on the city 1. Harvard Design School. Cologne: Benedikt Taschen Verlag, 2001a.

— *Guide to shopping*. Project on the city 2. Harvard Design School. Cologne: Benedikt Taschen Verlag, 2001b.

Koolhaas, R., Hommert, J. & Kubo, M. (Eds.), *Projects for Prada*, part 1. New York: OMA-Office of Metropolitan Architecture, 2001.

Korten, D. C. (1995) *When corporations rule the world*. London: Earthscan.

Kossek, E. E. & Lambert, S. J. (Eds.). (2005). *Work and life integration: organizational, cultural and individual perspectives*. Mahwah, New Jersey: Lawrence Erlaubaum.

Kossek, E. E., Lautsch, B. A. & Eaton, S. C. (2005). 'Flexibility enactment theory: implications of flexibility type, control, and boundary management for work and family effectiveness'. In: *Work and life integration: Organizational, cultural and individual perspectives*, E. E. Kossek & S. J. Lambert (Eds.), pp. 243–261. Mahwah, New Jersey: Lawrence Erlbaum Press.

Kossek, E. E., Noe, R. A. & DeMarr, B. J. (1999). 'Work-family role synthesis: individual and organizational determinants'. *The International Journal of Conflict Management*, 10(2): 102–129.

Kotter, J. P. (1996) *Leading Change*. Boston: Harvard Business School Press.

KRAV (2006) www.krav.se, 2007-04-06.

Kristensson Uggla, B. (2002). *Slaget om verkligheten: Filosofi – omvärldsanalys – tolkning*. Eslöv: Symposion.

Kuhn T. (1970) *The structure of scientific revolutions*. Chicago, IL: University of Chicago Press.

Labuda, B. (2003) Paper presented at the CSR Europe Conference Warszawa, Warszawa.

Laclau, E. & Mouffe, C. (1985) *Hegemony & socialist strategy*. London: Verso.

Laczniak E. R. & Murphy P. E. (1993) *Ethical Marketing Decisions: the higher road*. Boston: Allyn and Bacon.

Lambert, S. J. & Kossek, E. E. (2005) 'Future frontiers: enduring challenges and established assumptions in the work-life field'. In: E. E. Kossek & S. J. Lambert (Eds.) *Work and life integration: Organizational, cultural and individual perspectives*, pp. 513–532. Mahwah, New Jersey: Lawrence Erlbaum Press.

Lampe, M. & Gazda, G. M. (1995), 'Green marketing in Europe and the United States: an evolving business and society interface,' *International Business Review*, 4 (3): 295–312.

Lankoski, L. (2000) *Determinants of Environmental Profit: an Analysis of Firm-Level Environmental Performance and Economic Performance*. Diss. 2000/1, Helsinki: Helsinki University of Technology.

Larkin, T. J. & Larkin, T. (1994) *Communicating Change: Winning Employee Support for New Business Goals*. New York: McGraw-Hill.

Latour, B. (1986) 'The Powers of Association'. In: J. Law (Ed.) *Power, Action and Belief: A New Sociology of Knowledge?* pp. 264–280. London: Routledge.

– (1987) *Science in Action: How to follow Scientists and Engineers through Society*. Cambridge, MA: Harvard University Press.

– (1988) *The Pasteurization of France*. Cambridge, MA: Harvard University Press.

– (1999a) 'On Recalling ANT'. In: *Actor Network Theory and After*, J. Law and J. Hassard (Eds.) pp. 15–25. Oxford: Blackwell.

– (1999b) *Pandora's Hope: Essays on the Reality of Science Studies*. Cambridge MA: Harvard University Press.

– (2002) 'Morality and Technology: The End of Means', *Theory, Culture and Society* 19(5/6): 247–260.

Law, J. (1994) 'Organization, narrative and strategy'. In: *Towards a New Theory of Organizations*, J. Hassard & M. Parker (Eds.) pp. 248–268 London: Routledge.

– (1994) *Organizing Modernity*. Oxford: Blackwell.

— (1999) 'After ANT. Complexity, naming and topology.' In: *Actor network theory and after.* J. Law & J. Hassard (Eds.) pp. 1–14, Oxford: Blackwell.

— (2002) 'Economics as Interference'. In: *Cultural Economy: Cultural Analysis and Commercial Life,* P. du Gay & M. Pryke (Eds.) pp. 21–38. London: Sage.

— (2004) *After Method: Mess in Social Science Research.* London: Routledge.

Law, J. & Hassard, J. (Eds.) (1999) *Actor network theory and after.* Oxford: Blackwell.

Law, J. & Mol, A. (2002) 'Complexities: An Introduction'. In: *Complexities: Social studies of Knowledge Practices,* J. Law & A. Mol (Eds.) pp. 1–22. Durkham & London: Duke University Press.

Law, J. & Singleton, V. (2005) 'Object Lessons', *Organization* 12(3): 331–355.

Lecture with Alice Bah, Fair Trade, Spring 2005.

Lee, A. S. (1991) 'Integrating positivist and interpretivist approaches to organizational research'. *Organization Science* 2(4): 342–365.

Lee, N. & Hassard, J. (1999) 'Organization Unbound: Actor-Network Theory, Research Strategy and Institutional Flexibility', *Organization* 6(3): 391–404.

Lennart, L. (2002) 'Spice of life or kiss of death?' *Magazine of the European Agency for Safety and Health at Work,* 5.

Levinas, E. (1969) *Totality and Infinity.* Pittsburgh: Duquesne University Press.

Lewis, M. W. & Grimes, A. J. (1999) 'Metatriangulation: building theory from multiple paradigms'. *Academy of Management Review* 24(4): 672–690.

Lewis, M. W. & Kelemen, M. L. (2002) 'Multiparadigm inquiry: exploring organizational pluralism and paradox'. *Human Relations* 55(2): 251–275.

Lindfelt, L-L (2006) *Etik – den saknade länken.* Diss. Turku: Åbo Akademi University.

Lindgren, A. (1946/1992) *Pippi Långstrump går ombord,* Stockholm: Rabén och Sjögren.

Liu, J. & Diamond, J. (2005) 'China's environment in a globalizing world', *Nature,* 435: 1179–1186.

Lovins, A., Lovins, L. & Hawken, P. (1999) 'A Road Map to Natural Capitalism'. *Harvard Business Review* 77(3): 145–158.

Lustig, T. (2004) *Jakten på den fullkomliga bananen,* Stockholm: Svenska Naturskyddsföreningen.

Macnaughten, P. & Urry, J. (1998) *Contested Natures.* London: SAGE.

Magnusson, M. K., Arvola, A., Koivisto Hursti, U-K., Åsberg, L. & Sjödén, P-O (2001), 'Attitudes Towards Organic Foods among Swedish Consumers', *British Food Journal,* 103: 209–226.

Maguire, S., Hardy, C. & Lawrence, T. (2004) 'Institutional entrepreneurship in emerging fields: Hiv/Aids treatment advocacy in Canada', *Academy of Management Journal,* 47(5): 657–679.

Maignan, I. & Ferrell, O. C. (2001) 'Corporate citizenship as a marketing instrument – Concepts, evidence and research directions,' *European Journal of Marketing*, 35 (3/4): 457–81.

Mainela T (2002) *Networks and Social Relationships in Organizing International Joint Ventures. Analysis of the Network Dynamics of a Nordic-Polish Joint Venture*. Diss. Acta Wasaensia, 103. Vasa: Universitas Wasaensis.

Mannheim, K. (1936) *Ideology and utopia: an introduction to the sociology of knowledge*. London: Routledge and Kegan Paul.

Margolis, J. & Walsh, J. (2003) 'Misery Loves Companies: Rethinking Social Initiatives by Business'. *Administrative Science Quarterly* 48: 268–305.

Marquis, C., Glynn, M. A. & G. F. Davis (2007) 'Community Isomorphism and Corporate Social Action', *Academy of Management Review*, 32(3): 925–945.

Marshall, T. H. (1964) *Class, citizenship, and social development: essays*. Garden City, N.Y.

Martin J. (1992) *Cultures in organizations: three perspectives*. New York: Oxford University Press.

Marx, K. (1867) *Capital: A Critique of Political Economy. Volume I: The Process of Capitalist Production*. 3rd ed.

Matten, D. & Crane, A. (2005) 'Corporate citizenship: toward an extended theoretical conception'. *Academy of Management Review* 30(1): 166–179.

Matten, D., Crane, A. & Chapple, W. (2003) 'Behind the Mask: Revealing the True Face of Corporate Citizenship,' *Journal of Business Ethics*, 45 (1/2): 109–20.

Mau, B. (Ed.) (2000) *Life Style*. New York: Phaidon Press.

McCracken, G. (1988) *Culture & consumption*. Bloomington, IN: Indiana University Press.

McDowell, I. & Newell, C. (1996) *Measuring health: a guide to rating scales and questionnaires*. New York: Oxford University Press.

McHugh, M. & Brotherton, C. (2000) 'Heath is wealth – organizational utopia or myopia?' *Journal of Managerial Psychology*, 15(8): 744–770.

McKendall, M., DeMarr, B. & Jones-Rikkers, C. (2002) 'Ethical Compliance Programs and Corporate Illegality: Testing the Assumptions of the Corporate Sentencing Guidelines', *Journal of Business Ethics* 37(4): 367–383.

McKinely, K. (2004) Paper presented at the ISO SR Conference, Stockholm.

McMahon, C. (1995) 'The Ontological and Moral Status of Organizations'. *Business Ethics Quarterly* 5(3): 541–554.

McWilliams, A. & Siegel D. (2000) 'Corporate Social Responsibility and Financial Performance: Correlation or Misspecification'. *Strategic Management Journal* 21: 603–609.

Meadows, D. H., Meadows, D. L., Randers, J. & Behrens, W. W. *The limits to growth*. New York: Universe Books, 1972.

Meehan, J., Meehan, K. & Richards, A. (2006) 'Corporate Social

Responsibility: the 3C-SR Model'. *International Journal of Social Economics* 33(5/6): 386-398.

Mendleson, N. & Polonsky, M. J. (1995) 'Using strategic alliances to develop credible green marketing,' *Journal of Consumer Marketing*, 12 (2): 4-19.

Merck, (2005) A roof over one's head. www.merck.de/servlet/PB/menu/1454810/index.html. Accessed on March 16.

Meyer J. W. & Rowan, B. (1977) 'Institutional Organizations: Formal Structures as Myth and Ceremony'. *American Journal of Sociology* 80(2): 340-363.

Meyer, A. D., Gaba, V., & Colwell, K. A. (2005) 'Organizing Far for Equilibrium: Nonlinear Change in Organizational Fields'. *Organization Science*, 16(5): 456-473.

Meyer, J. W. (1996) 'Otherhood: The Promulgation and Transmission of Ideas in the Modern Organizational Environment'. In: *Translating Organizational Change*, B. Czarniawska & G. Sevón (Eds.) pp. 241-252. Berlin: Walter de Gruyter.

Micheletti, M. (2002) 'Shopping som den lilla människans stora ansvar,' In: *Svenska värderingar? att se och ompröva det invanda*, Peter Hallberg & Claes Lernestedt, (Eds.) Stockholm: Carlsson.

— (2003) *Political Virtue and Shopping: Individuals, Consumerism, and Collective Action*. Basingstoke: Palgrave MacMillan.

— (2004) 'Introduction'. In: *Politics, products, and markets: exploring political consumerism past and present*, M. Micheletti, A. Follesdal & D. Stolle, (Eds.) New Brunswick, NJ: Transaction.

Micheletti, M., A. Follesdal & D. Stolle (2003), *Politics, Products, and Markets: Exploring Political Consumerism Past and Present*, New Brunswick, NJ: Transaction.

Midttun, A., Gautesen K. & Gjolberg, M. (2006) 'The Political Economy of CSR in Western Europe'. *Corporate Governance* 6(4): 369-385.

Mirvis, P. & Googins, B. (2006) 'Stages of Corporate Citizenship'. *California Management Review* 48(2): 104-126.

Mißler, M. & Theuringer, T. (2003). Brave new working world? Europe needs investment in the workplace health promotion – more than ever before. European Network for Workplace Health Promotion Retrieved June 15, 2005, from http://www.enwhp.org/download/ENWHP_BRAVE%20new%20world%20of%20work.pdf

Mol, A. (1999) 'Ontological Politics. A Word and Some Questions'. In: *Actor Network Theory and After*, J. Law & J. Hassard (Eds.) pp. 74-89. Oxford: Blackwell.

Möller, K. & Svahn, S. (2003) 'Managing strategic nets: A capability perspective'. *Marketing Theory*, 3(2): 201-226.

Mombiot, G. (2006) in the documentary *The Planet*, Charon Film AB.

Montoya, I. D. & Richard, A. J. (1994) 'A Comparative Study of Codes of Ethics in Health Care Facilities and Energy Companies', *Journal of Business Ethics* 13(9): 713–717.

Moon, J., Crane, A. & Matten, D. (2005) 'Can corporations be citizens? Corporate citizenship as a metaphor for business participation in society.,' *Business Ethics Quarterly*, 15 (3): 429–53.

Morgan G. (1986) *Images of Organization*, Beverly Hills, CA: Sage.

Morsing, M. & Schultz, M. (2006) 'Corporate social responsibility communication: stakeholder information, response and involvement strategies.' *Business Ethics: A European Review*. Vol. 15. No. 4, pp. 323–338.

Mosse D. (2005) *Cultivating Development: An Ethnography of Aid Policy and Practice*. London: Pluto Press.

Mueller, F., Sillince, J., Harvey, C. & Howorth, C. (2003) 'A Rounded Picture Is What We Need: Rhetorical Strategies, Arguments, and the Negotiation of Change in a UK Hospital Trust'. *Organization Studies*, 25(1): 75–93.

NACE – Classification of Economic Activities in the European Community. (2002). Retrieved 04-09-2007, 2007, from http://www.fifoost.org/database/nace/nace-en_2002AB.php

Nakao, Y., Amano, A., Matsamura, K., Kenba K. & Nakano, M. (2007) 'Relationship Between Environmental Performance and Financial Performance: an Empirical Analysis of Japanese Corporations. *Business Strategy and the Environment* 16(2): 106–119.

Near, J. P., Rice, R. W. & Hunt, R. G. (1980) 'The relationship between work and nonwork domains: a review of empirical research'. *The Academy of Management Review*, 5(3): 415–429.

Nelson, J. & Zadek, S. (2000) *Partnership Alchemy. New Social Partnerships in Europe*. Copenhagen, The Copenhagen Centre.

Nevell, P. (2005) 'Citizenship, Accountability and Community: the Limits of CSR Agenda.' *International Affairs* 81(3): 541–557.

Newton, T. (2005) 'Practical Idealism: An Oxymoron?' *Journal of Management Studies*, 42:4, June, pp. 869–884

Nicholson, N. (1994) 'Ethics in Organizations: A Framework for Theory and Research', *Journal of Business Ethics* 13(8): 581–596.

Nijhof AHJ & Rietdijk MM (1999) 'An ABC-analysis of ethical organizational behavior'. *Journal of Business Ethics*, 20(1): 39–50.

Nippert-Eng, C. E. (1996) *Home and work: negotiating boundaries trough everyday life*. Chicago & London: The University Chicago Press.

Nordfält, J. (2005) *Is Consumer Decision-Making out of Control?: Non-conscious Influences on Consumer Decision-Making for*

Fast Moving Consumer Goods,
Diss, Stockholm: Stockholm
School of Economics.

Norman, Wayne & McDonald,
C. (2004) 'Getting to the bottom of "Triple Bottom Line"',
Business Ethics Quarterly, 14(2):
243–262.

Normann, R. (2001) *När kartan för-
ändrar affärslandskapet.* Malmö:
Liber Ekonomi.

Novo Nordisk. Sustainability
Report 2002.

Nylén, U. (1996) *Gott och ont inom
affärslivet – Utveckling av ett etiskt
perspektiv på företags relationer
mellan aktörer.* Diss. Umeå:
Umeå University.

Obermiller, C. & Spangenberg, E.
(1998) 'Development of a Scale
to Measure Skepticism toward
Advertising', *Journal of Consumer
Psychology,* 7(2): 159–186.

Orlitzky, M., Schmidt, F. & Rynes,
S (2003) 'Corporate Social and
Financial Performance: a Meta-
Analysis'. *Organization Studies*
24(3): 403–441.

Orsato, R. (2006) 'Competitive
Environmental Strategies'.
California Management Review
48(2): 127–143.

Our Common Future (1987). World
Commission on Environment
and Development. Oxford:
Oxford University Press.

Packendorff, J. (2002) 'The temporary society and its enemies:
projects from an individual
perspective'. In: *Beyond project
management: New perspectives
on the temporary-permanent
dilemma,* K. Sahlin-Andersson &
A. Söderholm (Eds.) pp. 39–58.
Malmö: Liber.

Paoli, P. & Merllié, D. (2001)
*Third European survey on work-
ing conditions 2000.* Dublin:
European Foundation for the
Improvement of living and
working Conditions.

Pearson, G. (1995). *Integrity in
Organizations. An Alternative
Business Ethic.* London:
McGraw-Hill.

Peattie, K. (1992) *Green Marketing,*
London: Pitman.

— (1995), *Environmental marketing
management: meeting the green
challenge.* London: Pitman.

— (2001), 'Towards Sustainability:
The Third Age of Green
Marketing', *The Marketing
Review,* 2: 129–146.

Perlas, N. & Center for Alternative
Development Initiatives
(Philippines). (1999) *Shaping
globalization: civil society, cul-
tural power, and threefolding* (1st
ed.) Quezon City, Philippines:
Center for Alternative
Development Initiatives.

Pettigrew, A. M. (1990)
'Longitudinal field of research
of change: theory and practice'. *Organization Sciences,* 1:
267–292.

Pettigrew, A. M. & Massini, S.
(2003) 'Innovative forms of
organizing: trends in Europe,
Japan and the USA in the
1990s'. In: *Innovative forms of
organizing,* A. M. Pettigrew,
R. Whittington, L. Melin, C.
Sánchez-Runde, F. A. J. van
de Bosh, W. Ruigrok & T.
Numagami (Eds.) pp. 1–32.
London: Sage.

Petty, R., Cacioppo, E. & John,
T. (1986) *Communication and*

persuasion: central and peripheral routes to attitude change, New York: Springer.

Philips (2004) Sustainability Report. Available at www.philips.com.

Pondy, L. R. & Boje, D. M. (1980) 'Bringing mind back in'. In: *Frontiers in Organization and Management*, Evan W. M. (Ed). pp. 83–101. New York: Praeger.

Power, M. (1997) *The Audit Society, Rituals of Verification*, Oxford/ New York. Oxford University Press.

Porter, M. & Kramer, M. (2002) 'The competitive advantage of corporate philanthropy'. *Harvard Business Review* 80(12): 57–68.

— (2006) 'Strategy and Society: the Link Between Competitive Advantage and Corporate Social Responsibility'. *Harvard Business Review* 84(12): 78–92.

Porter, M. & van der Linde, C. (1995) 'Green and Competitive: Ending the Stalemate. *Harvard Business Review* 73(5): 120–134.

Post, J. & Altman, B. (1992) 'Models of Corporate Greening: How Corporate Social Policy and Organizational Learning Inform Leading Edge Environmental Management'. *Research in Corporate Social Performance and Policy* 13: 3–29.

Prahalad, C. K. (2006) *The Fortune at the Bottom of the Pyramid: Eradicating Poverty Through Profits*, Upper Saddle River, NJ: Wharton School Publishing.

Prahalad, C. K. & Hammond, A. (2002) 'Serving the world's poor, profitably.' *Harvard Business Review*, 80(9): 48–57.

Prahalad, C. K. & Hart, S. (2002) 'The Fortune at the Bottom of the Pyramid'. *Strategy+Business* 26: 1–15.

Prasad, P. & Elmes, M. (2005) In the Name of the Practical: Unearthing the Hegemony of Pragmatics in the Discourse of Environmental Management. *Journal of Management Studies*, 42:4 June, pp. 845–867

Pratt, D. (2000) 'Creating healthy organizations'. *CMA Management*, 74, 10.

Preston, L. E. & Post, J. E. (1975) 'Measuring corporate responsibility'. *Journal of General Management* 2(3): 45–52.

Princen, T., Maniates, M. & Conca, K. (2002) *Confronting consumption*. Cambridge, MA: MIT Press.

Promoting a European framework for corporate social responsibility. Green Paper 8.7.2001. COM (2001) 366 final. Brussels: European Commission.

Quarles van Ufford, P. & Giri, A. K. (2003) 'A Moral Critique of Development'. In: *Search of Global Responsibilities*. London & New York: Eidos/Routledge.

Rahbek P., Esben & Neergaard, P. (2006) 'Caveat Emptor – Let the Buyer Be Ware! – Environmental Labelling and the Limitations of Green Consumerism', *Business Strategy and the Environment*, 15(1): 15–29.

Rainforest Alliance, www.rainforestalliance.com

Ramírez, R. (1999) 'Value co-production: Intellectual origins and implications for practice and research'. *Strategic Management Journal*, 20: 49–65.

Randell, G. (1998) 'Organizational sicknesses and their treatment'. *Management Decision,* 36(1): 14–18.

Rao, H., Monin, P. & Durand, R. (2003) 'Institutional Change in Toque Ville: Nouvelle Cuisine as an Identity Movement in French Gastronomy', *American Journal of Sociology,* Vol. 108, pp. 795–843. Chicago: University of Chicago Press.

Reed, M. (1985) *Redirections in organizational analysis.* London: Tavistock.

— (1996) 'Organizational theorizing: a historical contested terrain'. In: *Handbook of Organization Studies,* Clegg S. R., Hardy, C., Nord W. R. (Eds.) Thousand Oaks, CA: Sage, pp. 409–423.

Reinhardt, F. (1999) 'Bringing Environment Down to Earth'. *Harvard Business Review* 77(4): 149–157.

Reisch, L. (1998) 'Sustainable Consumption: Three Questions about a Fuzzy Concept'. Working paper.

Rhodes C. (2000) 'Reading and writing organizational lives'. *Organization* 7(1): 7–29.

Robbins, S. P. (2003). *Organizational behavior* (10th ed.) Upper Saddle River, NJ: Pearson Education International.

Roberts, J. (2003) 'The Manufacture of Corporate Social Responsibility: Constructing Corporate Sensibility', *Organization* 10(2): 249–265.

Roberts, J. A. (1995) 'Profiling levels of socially responsible consumer behavior: A cluster analytic approach and its implications for marketing,' *Journal of Marketing – Theory and Practice,* 3(4): 97–117.

Roberts, P. (2005) *The end of oil: the decline of the petroleum economy and the rise of a new energy order.* London: Bloomsbury.

Roberts, S. (2003) 'Supply Chain Specific? Understanding the Patchy Success of Ethical Sourcing Initiatives', *Journal of Business Ethics* 44(2/3): 159–170.

Rocha, H. & Ghoshal, S. (2006) 'Beyond Self-Interest Revisited'. *Journal of Management Studies* 43(3): 585–619.

Roome, N. (1992) 'Developing environmental management strategies'. *Business Strategy and the Environment.* 1 (1): 11 24.

— (1998) 'Introduction'. In: *Sustainability Strategies for Industry: The Future of Corporate Practice.* Roome N. (Ed.) Washington, DC: Island Press.

— (2000) 'Globalization and Sustainable Development: Toward a Transatlantic Agenda'. In: *Security, Trade, and Environmental Policy: A US/European Union Transatlantic Agenda,* Bonsar, C. (Ed.) Dordrecht: Kluwer, pp. 161–186.

— (2001) 'Metatextual Organizations – Innovation and Adaptation for Global Change'. Inaugural address Erasmus Center for Sustainable Development and Management, Rotterdam: Erasmus University Rotterdam.

Roper A. S. W. (2002) Green Gauge Report.

Rosling, H., Lindstrand, A., Bergström, S., Rubenson, B., & Stenson, B. (2006) *Global Health: An Introductory Textbook.* Lund: Studentlitteratur.

Ross, R. & Schneider, R. (1992) *From Equality to Diversity: a Business Case for Equal Opportunities.* London: Pitman.

Rossiter, J. R. & Percy, L. (1987) *Advertising and Promotion Management,* New York: McGraw-Hill.

Roulet, E. (1986) *L'articulation du discours en français contemporain.* 3rd ed. Bern: Peter Lang.

Rövik, K. A. (1996) 'Deinstiuttionalization and the Logic of Fashion'. In: *Translating organizational change,* B. Czarniawska & G. Sevón (Eds.) Berlin: Walter de Gruyter.

— (2002) 'Management ideas that flow'. In: *The Expansion of Management Knowledge. Carriers, Flows, and Sources,* Sahlin-Andersson, K. & Engwall, L. (Eds.) Stanford, CA: Stanford University Press.

Rowley T. & Berman, S. (2000) 'A brand new brand of corporate social performance'. *Business & Society* 39(4): 397–418.

Rytteri, T. (2002). *Metsäteollisuusyrityksen luonto. Tutkimus Enso-Gutzeitin ympäristö ja yhteiskuntavastuun muotoutumisesta. Diss. Joensuu: Joensuu* University.

Sahlin-Andersson, K. (1996) 'Imitating by Editing Success: The Construction of Organizational Fields'. In: *Translating organizational change,* B. Czarniawska & G. Sevón (Eds.) Berlin: Walter de Gruyter.

Sahlin-Andersson, K. & Engwall, L. (2002a) 'Carriers, Flows, and Resources of Management'. In: *The Expansion of Management Knowledge. Carriers, Flows, and Sources,* Sahlin-Andersson, K. & Engwall, L. (Eds.) pp. 3–32. Stanford, CA: Stanford University Press.

— (2002b) 'The Dynamics of Management Knowledge Expansion'. In: *The Expansion of Management Knowledge. Carriers, Flows, and Sources,* Sahlin-Andersson, K. & Engwall, L. (Eds.) Stanford, CA: Stanford University Press.

Sahlin-Andersson, K. & Engwall, L. (Eds.) (2002c). *The Expansion of Management Knowledge. Carriers, Flows, and Sources,* Stanford: Stanford University Press.

Salzmann, O., Ionescu-Sommers, A. & Steger, U. (2005) 'The Business Case for Corporate Social Responsibility: Literature Review and Research Options'. *European Management Journal* 23(1): 27–36.

Schaltegger, S. & Figge, F. (2000) 'Environmental Shareholder Value: Economic Success with Corporate Environmental Management'. *Eco-Management and Auditing* 7: 29–42.

Schein, E. H. (1994) *Organizational culture and leadership.* (2nd Ed.) San Francisco, CA.: Jossey Bass.

Schmitz, H. & Knorringa, P. (2000) 'Learning from Global

Buyers', *Journal of Development Studies*, 37(2): 177–205.

Schultz M. & Hatch M. J. (1996) 'Living with multiple paradigms: the case of paradigm interplay'. *Organizational Culture Studies* 21(2): 529–557.

Schultz, M. & Morsing, M. & Nielsen, K. U. (2004): 'Kommunikationsstrategi for Social ansvarlighed'. Reputation Institute: http:// www.reputationinstitute. com/international/articles/ Kom_27ED13.pdf

Schwartz, B. (1997) *Det miljöanpassade företaget: strategiska uppträdanden på den institutionella scenen*. Stockholm: Nerenius & Santérus.

— (2006) 'Environmental strategies as automorphic patterns of behaviour.' *Business Strategy and the Environment*, 18(3): 192–206.

Schwartz, B. & Tilling, K. (2009a) '"ISO-lating" Corporate Social Responsibility in the Organizational Context: A Dissenting Interpretation of ISO 26000.' *Corporate Social Responsibility and Environmental Management*, (16)5: 289–299.

Schwartz, M. S. (2001) 'The Nature of the Relationship between Corporate Codes of Ethics and Behaviour', *Journal of Business Ethics* 32(3): 247–262.

— (2004) 'Effective Corporate Codes of Ethics: Perceptions of Code Users', *Journal of Business Ethics* 55: 323–343.

Scott W. R. (1987) The adolescence of institutional theory. *Administrative Science Quarterly* 32(X): 493–511.

Selznick, P. (1957/1984). *Leadership in Administration. A Sociological Interpretation*. Harper & Row. (New ed. 1984) Berkeley: University of California Press.

Sen, A. (1995) 'Moral codes and economic success'. In: *Market Capitalism and Moral Values*, Brittan, S. & Hamlin, A. P. (Eds.) Aldershot: Edward Elgar.

Sen, S. & Bhattacharya, C. (2001) 'Does doing good always lead to doing better? Consumer reactions to corporate social responsibility,' *Journal of Marketing Research*, 37 (May): 225–43.

Sevón, G. (1996) 'Organizational imitation in identity transformation'. In: *Translating organizational change*. B. Czarniawska & G. Sevón (Eds.) pp 49–67. Berlin: Walter de Gruyter.

Shanahan, S. & Khagram, S. (2006) 'Dynamics of corporate responsibility'. In: *Globalization and Organization: World Society and Organizational Change*, G. S. Drori, J. W. Meyer and H. Hwang (Eds.) New York: Oxford University Press.

Shaw, D., Newholm, T. & Dickinson, R. (2006) 'Consumption as voting: an exploration of consumer empowerment,' *European Journal of Marketing*, 40(9/10): 1049–67.

Shrum, L. J., McCarthy J. A. & Lowry T. M. (1995) 'Buyer Characteristics of the Green Consumer and Their Implications for Advertising Strategy', *Journal of Advertising*, 2(Summer): 71–82

Siemens, R. R. (2004) Paper presented at the International CSR Conference Humboldt University, Berlin. SIS, Internet, http://www.sis.se/DesktopDefault.aspx?tabname =%40Projekt&PROJID=1478, 2005-05-09.

Sloterdijk, P. (1988) *Critique of Cynical Reason*. Minneapolis, MN: University of Minnesota Press.

Smircich, L. (1983) 'Concepts of culture and organizational analysis'. *Administrative Science Quarterly* 28(3): 339–358.

Snell, R. S. & Herndon Jr., N. C. (2004) 'Hong Kong's Code of Ethics Initiative: Some Differences between Theory and Practice', *Journal of Business Ethics* 51(1): 75–89.

Solér, C. (2001) *Att köpa miljövänliga dagligvaror*. Diss, Gothenburg: Gothenburg University.

Solli, R., Demediuk, P. & Sims, R. (2005) 'The Namesake: On Best Value and Other Reformmarks'. In: *Global Ideas – How ideas, Objects and Practices Travels in the Global Economy,* B. Czarniawska & G. Sevón (Eds.) Malmö: Liber.

Somers, M. J, (2001) 'Ethical codes of conduct and organizational context: A study of the relationship between codes of conduct, employee behavior and organizational values'. *Journal of Business Ethics*, 30(2): 185–195.

Sonnentag, S., & Bayer, U.-V. (2005) 'Switching off mentally: predictors and consequences of psychological detachment from work during off-job time'. *Journal of Occupational Health Psychology*, 10(4): 393–414.

Sonnentag, S., & Kruel, U. (2006). 'Psychological detachment from work during off-job time: the role of job stressors, job involvement, and recovery-related self-efficacy'. *European Journal of Work and Organizational Pschychology*, 15(2): 197–217.

Soppe, A. (2004) 'Sustainable corporate finance'. *Journal of Business Ethics,* 53(1/2): 213–224.

Spradley, J. P. (1980) *Participant observation*. New York: Holt Rinehart and Winston.

Stadeus, C., Johansson, J. Anselmsson, J. & Isaksson, Y. (2004) *Etik och socialt ansvarstagande i svensk dagligvaruhandel. En studie av leverantörernas och de egna varumärkenas positionering.* Lund International Food Studies Report.

Starik, M., Rands, G. P. (1995) 'Weaving an integrated web: Multilevel and multisystem perspectives of ecologically sustainable organizations', *The Academy of Management Review*, 20(4): 908–935.

Steiner G. A. & Steiner J. F. (1997) *Business, Government, and Society. A Managerial Perspective*. New York: McGraw-Hill.

Stevens, B. (1994) 'An Analysis of Corporate Ethical Code Studies: 'Where do we go from here?'', *Journal of Business Ethics* 13(1): 63–69.

— (2004) 'The Ethics of the US Business Executive: A Study of Perceptions'. *Journal of Business Ethics* 54: 163–171.

Stiglitz, J. (2002) *Globalization and Its Discontents*. New York: W.W. Norton.

Stohs, J.H. & Brannick, T. (1999) 'Codes and Conduct: Predictors of Irish Managers' Ethical Reasoning', *Journal of Business Ethics* 22(4): 311–326.

Stora Enso Sustainability (2004) Annual Report. Helsinki.

Stormer, F. (2003) Making the shift: moving from 'ethics pays' to an inter-system model of business. *Journal of Business Ethics* 44(4): 279–289.

Strannegård, L. & Salzer-Mörling, M. (2004) 'Leadership in a branded world', In: *Next generation business handbook*, Chowdhury, S. (Ed.) New York: John Wiley.

Straughan, R.D. & Roberts, J.A. (1999) 'Environmental Segmentation Alternatives: A Look at Green Consumer Behavior in the New Millennium', *Journal of Consumer Marketing*, 16(6).

Studer, S., Welford, R.J. & Hills, P.H. (2006) 'Engaging Hong Kong Businesses in Environmental Change: Drivers and Barriers', *Business Strategy and the Environment*, 15: 416–431

Suddaby, R. & Greenwood, R. (2001) 'Colonizing knowledge: Commodification as adynamic of jurisdictional expansion in professional service firms', *Human Relations*, 54(7): 933–953.

Sum M.C. & Hills, P. (1998) 'Interpreting sustainable development'. *Journal of Environmental Sciences* 10(2): 129–143.

Swedish Environmental Protection Agency (SEPA) (Svenska Naturvårdsverket, www.naturvardsverket.se) (2003) *Effektivare miljöledningssystem – en studie om brister, behov och möjligheter till förbättring*, Rapport 5304.

— (2005) *Environmental Management System (EMS) in central government agencies, Sweden's experience*, Report 5358.

Swedish Government, 2001, Government decision, 12 July, 2001, M2001/3171/Kn: Statsförvaltning för hållbar utveckling – uppdrag till myndigheter att införa miljöledningssystem.

Taipalinen J & Toivio T (2004). Vastuullinen yritystoiminta pk-yritysten voimavarana. KTM Julkaisuja 16/2004. Finnish Ministry of Trade and Industry. Helsinki: Edita.

ten Bos, R. (2003) 'Business Ethics, Accounting and the Fear of Melancholy', *Organization* 10 (2): 267–285.

Thomas, R. & Dunkerley, D. (1999) 'Careering Downwards? Middle managers' experiences in the downsized organization'. *British Journal of Management*, 10: 157–169.

Thomas, R.R.J. (1990) 'From Affirmative Action to Affirming Diversity. *Harvard Business Review* 68(2): 107–117.

Thomsen, C. (2007) 'Public Sector CSR Communication: A Dialogical Approach.' *Hermes. Journal of Language and Communication Studies*. 38: 41–64.

Thyssen, O. (2003) 'Values – The Necessary Illusions'.

In: *Corporate Values and Responsibility – The Case of Denmark,* Morsing, M. & C. Thyssen (Eds.) pp. 163–175. Copenhagen: Samfundslitteratur.

— (2004) *Værdiledelse: om organisationer og etik.* Copenhagen: Gyldendal.

Tilling, K. (2006) 'When Environmental Issues meets the Logic of Business and Quality Management – A Study of the Environmental Management System Project in Swedish Government Agencies'. In: *Science for Sustainable Development, Starting Points and critical reflections* Frostell, B. (Ed.) Uppsala: VHU.

— (2008) *Att styra hållbar utveckling. Miljöledning och dess översättningar i statsförvaltningen.* Diss. no. 66, Västerås: Mälardalen University Press.

Tobón, F. (2004) Paper presented at the ISO the Stockholm Conference on SR Stockholm.

Törnroos, J.-Å. (1997) 'Networks, NetWorks, NETWorks, NETWORKS'. In: *Competitive Papers: Interaction, Relationships and Networks in Business Markets,* Mazet, F., Salle, R. & Valla, J.-P. (Eds.) 13th IMP Conference. Lyon: 4–6 September, pp. 615–631.

Tucker, L.R., Stathakopolous, V. & Patti C.H. (1999) 'A multidimensional assessment of ethical codes: The professional business association perspective'. *Journal of Business Ethics,* 19(3): 287–300.

Ulaga, W. (2001) 'Customer value in business markets: An agenda for inquiry', *Industrial Marketing Management,* 30(4): 315–319.

UN (2007) Global Compact, Codes of Conduct. UN, Global Compact, http://www.unglobal-compact.org, 2007-06-29.

UNEP (2006) Background Paper for UNEP 9th High Level Seminar on Sustainable Consumption and Production. Wuppertal Institute Collaborating Centre on Sustainable Consumption and Production and United Nations Environmental Programme.

Valcour, M.P. & Hunter, L.W. (2005) 'Technology, organizations and work-life integration'. In: *Work and life integration: Organizational, cultural and individual perspectives,* E.E. Kossek & S.J. Lambert (Eds.) pp. 61–84. Mahwah, NJ: Lawrence Erlbaum.

van Marrewijk, M. (2003) 'Concepts and definitions of CSR and corporate sustainability: between agency and communion'. *Journal of Business Ethics* 44(2/3): 95–105.

van Tulder, R. & Kolk, A. (2001) 'Multinationality and Corporate Ethics: Codes of Conduct in the Sporting Goods Industry', *Journal of International Business Studies* 32(2): 267–283.

Vehkaperä M (2003) Yrityksen yhteiskuntavastuu – vastuuta voittojen vuoksi? Jyväskylä: Jyväskylä University.

Vestergaard-Frandsen (2006) Vestergaard-Frandsen – Disease Control Textiles. Available at: www.vestergaard-frandsen.com. Accessed on Jan. 20.

Visser, W., Matten, D., Pohl, M. & Tolhourst, N. (Eds.) (2007) *The A to Z of corporate social responsibility. A complete reference guide to concepts, codes and organizations.* Chichester: John Wiley & Sons.

Waddock, S. (2004) 'Parallel Universes: Companies, Academics and the Progress of Corporate Citizenship'. *Business and Society Review* 109(1): 5–42.

Waddock, S. & Smith, N. (2000) 'Relationships: The Real Challenge of Corporate Global Citizenship.' *Business & Society Review* 105(1): 47–62.

Waddock, S., Bodwell, C. & Graves, S. B. (2002) 'Responsibility: The New Business Imperative'. *Academy of Management Executive* 16(2): 132–48.

Waddock, S. A. (1988) 'Building Successful Social Partnerships'. *Sloan Management Review*, 29(4): 17–24.

Wadel, C. (1991) *Feltarbeid i egen kultur: en innføring i kvalitativt orientert samfunnsforskning.* Flekkefjord: Seek.

Walgenbach, P. & Beck, N. (2002) 'The Institutionalization of Management Approach in Germany'. In: *The Expansion of Management Knowledge-Carriers, Flows, and Sources.* K. Sahlin-Andersson & L. Engwall (Eds.) Stanford: Stanford University Press.

Watson, T. J. (1994) *In Search of Management. Culture, Chaos & Control in Managerial Work.* London: Thomson.

— (1995) *Sociology Work and Industry* (3rd ed.). London and New York: Routledge.

WBCSD (2000) *Eco-Efficiency: Creating More Value with Less Impact.* Geneva: World Business Council for Sustainable Development.

WBCSD (2004) *Doing Business with the Poor: A Field Guide.* Geneva: World Business Council for Sustainable Development.

WCED (1987) The World Commission on Environment and Development, *Our common future,* Oxford: Oxford Univ. Press

Weaver, G. R. & Gioia, D. A. (1994) 'Paradigms lost: incommensurability vs structurationist inquiry'. *Organization Studies* 15(4): 565–590.

Web, D. L., Mohr, L. A. (1998) 'A typology of consumer responses to cause-related marketing: from skeptics to socially concerned', *Journal of Public Policy and Marketing,* 17(2): 226–238.

Webb, K (2004) ISO The Stockholm conference on SR.

Webster encyclopaedic unabridged dictionary of the English language. (1994) (Deluxe Edition ed.). New York: Gramercy books.

Welford, R. J. (1998) 'Corporate environmental management, technology and sustainable development: postmodern perspectives and the need for a critical research agenda'. *Business Strategy and the Environment* 7(1): 1–12.

— 'Corporate Governance and Corporate Social Responsibility: Issues for Asia', *Corporate Social Responsibility and Environmental Management,* 14: 42–51

Welford, R. J. & Frost, S. D. (2006) 'Corporate Social Responsibility in Asian Supply Chains', *Corporate Social Responsibility and Environmental Management*, 13: 166–176

Wenneberg, S. B. (2001) *Social-konstruktivism: positioner, problem och perspektiv*, Malmö: Liber Ekonomi.

Wheale, P. & Hinton, D. (2007) 'Ethical Consumers in Search of Markets', *Business Strategy and the Environment*, 16(4): 302–315

Wheeler, D., Fabig, H. & Boele, R. (2002) 'Paradoxes and Dilemmas for Stakeholder Responsive Firms in the Extractive Sector: Lessons from the Case of Shell and the Ogoni'. *Journal of Business Ethics*, 39(3): 297–318.

Willmott, H. (1993) 'Breaking the paradigm mentality'. *Organization Studies*. 14(5): 681–719.

Wilson, I. (2000) *The new rules of corporate conduct. Rewriting the social charter*. Westport, CT: Quorum Books.

Windell, K. (2006) *Corporate social responsibility under construction. Ideas, translation and institutions*. Uppsala: Uppsala University.

Windsor, D. (2006) 'Corporate Social Responsibility: Three Key Approaches'. *Journal of Management Studies* 43(1): 93–114.

Wood, D. (1991) 'Corporate Social Performance Revisited'. *Academy of Management Review* 14(4): 691–718.

Wood, D. J. & Logsdon, J. M. (2001) 'Theorising business citizenship,' In: *Perspectives on corporate citizenship*, J. Andriof

& M. McIntosh (Eds.) Sheffield: Greenleaf.

Wood, G. & Callaghan, M. (2003) 'Communicating the Ethos of Codes of Ethics in Corporate Australia, 1995–2001: Whose Rights, Whose Responsibilities?', *Employee Responsibilities and Rights Journal* 15(4): 209–221

World Economic Forum (2003) 'Global Corporate Citizenship Initiative.' 2007, March, 21. Place Published. www.weforum. org/corporatecitizenship

Worldwatch Institute (Ed.) (2003) State of the World 2004: Special Focus: The Consumer Society (1. ed.). New York: Norton.

Worldwatch Institute (2004) State of the World 2004. Special focus on the consumer society. New York: W. W. Norton.

Young, T. (2002) 'Global Liberalism and a New World Order'. In: *The Globalization of Liberalism*, E. Hovden & E. Keene (Eds.) pp. 173–190. Basingstoke & New York: Palgrave.

Zadek, S. (2001) *The Civil Corporation, The New Economy of Corporate Citizenship*, London: Earthscan.

— (2004) 'The Path to Corporate Responsibility'. *Harvard Business Review* 82(12): 125–132.

Zbaracki, M. J. (1998) 'The Rhetoric and Reality of Total Quality Management'. *Administrative Science Quarterly*, 43: 602–636.

Zedeck, S. (1992). 'Introduction: exploring the domain of work and family concerns'. In: *Work,*

Families and Organizations, S. Zedeck (Ed.) San Francisco: Jossey-Bass Publishers.

Zinkhan, G. M. & Les Carlson (1995) 'Green Advertising and the Reluctant Consumer'. *Journal of Advertising,* June.

Zizek, S. (1989) *The Sublime Object of Ideology.* London/New York: Verso.

Zukin, S. (2004) *Point of purchase. How shopping changed American culture.* New York and London: Routledge.

Zyglidopoulos, S. C. (2002) 'The Social and Environmental Responsibilities of Multinationals: Evidence from the Brent Spar Case,' *Journal of Business Ethics,* 36(1): 141–51.

The Authors

PETER DOBERS has an interest in how ideas of corporate (social) responsibility, broadband, city images or sustainable development travel the world, are enabled or disabled. He holds a chair in management and sustainable development at Mälardalen University and is currently associate dean of the Faculty for Humanities, Social and Caring Sciences. He has also been visiting professor at Umeå School of Business and Economics in the years of 2006–2008. Dobers has published widely in areas such as corporate (social) responsibility, sustainable development, urban studies and modern information and communication technology and is frequently commissioned as guest speaker by industry and municipalities. peter.dobers@mdh.se

NIKLAS EGELS-ZANDÉN is a PhD and researcher at the Center for Business in Society at School of Business, Economics and Law at Göteborg University, Sweden. His areas of research are international business and corporate social responsibility, especially in relation to multinational corporations in developing countries. He has recently published his Doctoral thesis *Managing responsibilities. The formation of Swedish MNC's firm-society policies and practices*. He has previously published in *Journal of Business Ethics*, *Business Strategy and the Environment*, and *Journal of Corporate Citizenship*. niklas.zanden@handels.gu.se

MINNA HALME is professor of corporate responsibility at Helsinki School of Economics (HSE). Her research focuses on corporate responsibility innovations, business models for sustainable services and sustainability implications of the base-of-the-pyramid (BOP) approach. She teaches Corporate Responsibility at doctoral and executive MBA courses and cooperates with the industry in action research projects, management training and consulting. minna.halme@hse.fi

SVEN HELIN is currently Assistant Professor in business studies at the Swedish Business School, Örebro University, Sweden. His teaching and research are mainly focused on accounting and business ethics. sven.helin@oru.se

LISE-LOTTE HELLÖRE is PhD in International Marketing. Her doctoral thesis focused on value creation through ethics in industrial business networks. She is currently studying the implications of globalization on the agenda of sustainable development, especially its cultural dimension. Her research has been awarded international prizes and been widely published. lhellore@abo.fi

HANNA HJALMARSON is assistant professor at the Department of Advertising and Public Relations at the Stockholm University. Her research interests focus on the relations between consumer behavior, marketing communications, and subjective well-being, which may for example be achieved through environmentally friendly and/or socially responsible consumption. hanna.hjalmarson@gi-ihr.su.se

JOHAN JANSSON earned his PhD on a dissertation concerning consumer behaviour and alternative fuel vehicles in 2009 at Umeå School of Business, Umeå University in Sweden. His research has been published in journals such as *Business Strategy and the Environment* and *Journal of Consumer Marketing*. As an appreciated senior lecturer in courses such as Marketing Ethics and Consumer Behaviour, Johan has received several pedagogical nominations and awards. johan.jansson@usbe.umu.se

TOMMY JENSEN is Associate Professor at the Umeå School of Business. His research interests are in the areas of organiza-

tion theory, sociology and moral philosophy with focus on the intersection between 'private' and 'public' spheres and the social and environmental dilemmas that this intersection give rise to. Co-author of *Economy and Morality: Routes to Increased Responsibility* (In Swedish, Liber 2007).
tommy.jensen@usbe.umu.se

MARKUS KALLIFATIDES is an assistant professor at the Stockholm School of Economics. His research interests span the social constructions of management and leadership, corporate governance in the context of modern financial markets, and the role of the corporation in global society. In English, he participated in the edited volume *Invisible Management* (2001, Thomson). Together with Daniel Ericsson, he has edited the Swedish volume on leadership *Samtalet fortsätter* (2005, Academia Adacta).
kallifatides@hhs.se

JEAN-CHARLES LANGUILAIRE has a PhD in Business Administration from Jönköping International Business School, Jönköping, Sweden from 2009. His research interests is primarily within Human Resource Development and Leadership with a focus on why and how individuals are integrating and segmenting their life's domains. His research presents a theory of individuals's work/non-work experiences. He teaches within the fields of Human Resource Management, Leadership, Organisation and Service Management at Jönköping International Business School but also at Halmstad University.
jean-charles.languilaire@ihh.hj.se

JAKOB LAURING is Associate Professor at the Department of Management, Aarhus School of Business, Aarhus University. His research interests are in the area of Diversity Management, CSR and Cross-Cultural Management. He has published a number of articles on the subject in international journals. jala@asb.dk

MONICA MACQUET finished her thesis on partnerships for sustainable development in December 2007 at the Stockholm School of Economics and is currently Assistant Professor at Audencia Nantes – School of Management, Nantes in France.

Her research focus on sustainable development in supply-chains, alternative sustainable business models, and controversies around sustainability and CSR. mmacquet@audencia.com

JONAS NILSSON is a doctoral candidate at Umeå School of Business (USBE) at Umeå University, Sweden having previously obtained an Econ. Licentiate degree from the School of Business, Economics, and Law at Gothenburg University in Gothenburg, Sweden. At the moment his research focuses on consumer behaviour with regards to pro-socially positioned products and services, with a particular focus on socially responsible investment mutual funds. jonas.nilsson@usbe.umu.se

NIGEL ROOME now holds a professorship at Vlerick-Gent School of Management although at the time this essay was written he held the Daniel Janssen Chair of Corporate Social Responsibility at Solvay Business School, Free University Brussels, Belgium and was professor of Corporate Global Responsibility and Governance at TiasNimbas Business School, Tilburg, Netherlands. He is chair of the academic Board of the European Academy of Business in Society. His research interests range from globalization and sustainable development, through the shifting relationship between business and society and the implications for organizational and social change, to management education, skills and competencies. He has published widely and consults companies and governments through his company Capability Dynamics. nroome@tiasnimbas.edu

JOHAN SANDSTRÖM is Associate Professor at the Swedish Business School, Örebro University, Sweden. His research interest are in the areas of ethics and sustainability in relation to business and business studies. He is currently involved in a project on how corporate codes of ethics are translated in a global context (with Sven Helin and Tommy Jensen). johan.sandstrom@oru.se

BIRGITTA SCHWARTZ (Associate Professor) is a senior lecturer at Mälardalen University, Sweden. Her current research interest is in the area of organizational behaviour and strategy in companies, public sector and civil society organizations in relation to environmental and social responsibility issues. In an ongoing research project she is studying societal entrepreneurship in relation to the creation of Fair Trade markets and how different actors construct CSR and Sustainable Development strategies in their interplay with each other. birgitta.schwartz@mdh.se

EMMA SJÖSTRÖM (PhD) is a researcher and teacher at the Stockholm School of Economics. Her research is focused on corporate social responsibility (CSR). In her Doctoral thesis (2009) she explores how shareholders can use their ownership position to influence corporations with regard to CSR. Emma Sjöström is a co-founder of SuRe, Sustainability Research Group [www.suregroup.se]. emma.sjostrom@hhs.se

CHRISTA THOMSEN is associate professor at the Centre for Corporate Communication, Aarhus School of Business, University of Aarhus. Her research has been in the field of Corporate Communication and its relation to Corporate Social Responsibility (CSR). At the moment the focus is on strategic CSR communication and CSR/ethical identities in Small and Mediumsized Enterprises, CSR reporting, public-private partnership communication and conversations in management (e.g. sickness leave conversations). ct@asb.dk

KARINA TILLING, (PhD) is a researcher and project leader at Mälardalen University, Sweden. In 2008 she finished her dissertation on the implementation and effects of a standardised environmental management system model in the Swedish Government Agencies. Her general research interest is in the area of managing sustainable development, in particular the relation between societal and organizational strategies regarding CSR and environmental issues. Karina is today responsible for a four-year research project focusing the role of personal driving forces in business development in Swedish microsize enterprises. karina.tilling@telia.com

RICHARD WELFORD is one of the founders and the chairman of CSR Asia based in Hong Kong. He is also a professor at the University of Hong Kong and a director of ERP Environment, a

UK-based publisher. He has twenty years of experience working in the fields of environmental management and social responsibility. He was one of the early pioneers in developing social audit and reporting methodologies with UK-based organisations such as The Body Shop, IBM and Eastern Electricity in the 1990s. Since then, his work has been increasingly Asian focused as a result of his current position as director of the Corporate Environmental Governance Programme at the University of Hong Kong. rwelford@hkucc.hku.hk

KAROLINA WINDELL holds a PhD in Business Studies from Uppsala University. Her primary research interest concerns the spread and construction of ideas about management, in particular how ideas develop in interconnectedness between corporations and their counterparts such as media, NGOs, governmental organizations, investors, and consultants. Karolina's research specifically focuses on the emergence of the idea CSR (Corporate Social Responsibility). karolina.windell@fek.uu.se

www.ingramcontent.com/pod-product-compliance
Lightning Source LLC
Chambersburg PA
CBHW020639030726
47498CB00002B/287